GUARDIANS
of the
KEYS

Megan J. Wheless

ISBN: 978-1-957723-48-8 (hard cover)
978-1-957723-49-5 (soft cover)

Edited by: Melissa Long

Published by WARREN Publishing
Charlotte, NC
www.warrenpublishing.net
Printed in the United States

*To my parents, who have believed in me from the
very beginning and supported me at every twist and turn.
To my husband, you are the reason this book is out in the world.
Thank you for teaching me how to open to my
creativity and allow myself to dream.*

CHAPTER 1

Elaine tightened the sash of her comfy velour robe, the one with swirling patterns of red and turquoise flowers—a gift from her great-aunts from two Christmases ago—as grief rippled through her chest.

She tore open a package of blueberry scones and bit off a crumbly edge laced with gooey icing while she fumbled through the jam-packed cabinets. She sighed heavily, finally locating the coffee filters in the back wedged between mismatched cups and saucers.

Her beloved great-aunts had been gone for a little over two weeks now, and she still hadn't gotten used to the cold and lonely mornings. She had moved in with her aunts due to a water problem at her old apartment building. Her stay was only temporary, she had promised them, just until she could find a new apartment that was in better shape and closer to her work. Her aunts, charming and clever as they were, always found reasons for her to extend her stay. They first asked her to set up their antique store's profile for a popular online auction site. Then, a few weeks later, they asked her to photograph some of the inventory and upload it to the site. The next thing Elaine knew, three months had passed, and she found herself still living in her childhood home, alone now without the pleasant company of her aunts.

She missed sneaking downstairs to spy on Aunt Daphne dabbing some flour on her hands and cheeks, splattering a little water, and smearing a dab of butter on her apron before peeling off the store packaging. She would plop the scones onto a baking tray and stick them in the oven, finalizing the illusion they were made from scratch. Both Elaine and Aunt Mildred would remark how delicious the sweet dough smelled, never letting on that they spotted the wrapper from the Day-Old Bread Shop—the downtown bakery and bread store—crumpled up on the counter next to the oven. Her aunts were no Betty Crockers. Both fibbed about home-cooked meals from time to time and beamed when Elaine complimented them on their savory yet overly chewy Salisbury steak, or their doughy chicken pot pies with smatterings of frozen vegetables in the center that the microwave hadn't quite radiated.

Once the coffee began to brew, Elaine sat down at the small kitchen table and began to pick through the piles of mail. Two unopened letters—one from the bank and the other from Mr. Sadler, her aunts' financial adviser—sent shock waves up her spine, and she was assailed by the memory of her conversation with Sadler at their funeral dinner. She sat the envelopes on top of the stack of similarly unopened letters she had been amassing for the last two weeks. The thought of opening all the mail left a sinking feeling in the pit of her stomach. Soon, she would have to face what was inside the envelopes, but she didn't feel up to that today. She stood and poured herself a cup of coffee.

For as long as Elaine could remember, her aunts ran The Cooley Sisters' Antiques & Collectibles store in the renovated barn on their property. The shop housed a treasure trove of old furniture, vintage radios and clocks, shelves of dusty first-edition books, a random assortment of knickknacks and dishware, and an array of jewelry covered in rhinestones or encased in Lucite. When she was a young girl, Elaine loved rummaging through their collection of vinyl records and listening to the songs on one of the old record players, its needle scratching and zipping its way across a variety of songs from the Big Band era to the early 1960s.

Elaine took over as the shop's manager after their accident and was only just beginning to realize how much financial trouble her aunts were in. They had kept the store and their lives afloat for many years with estate sales and high-end antiques and collectibles. About a year before the car crash, however, their business started to take a nosedive. They still went to estate sales but didn't buy the big-ticket items that drew customers to their store. Instead, they focused their attention on boxes of junk containing random things like cracked leather belts, containers filled with nails, nuts, and bolts, bicycle pedals, antique toy cars, picture frames with chipped glass and painted wood, and old advertisements from the forties and fifties. Her aunts were nearly obsessed over the most mundane of items, such as antique skeleton keys. They had jars of them in their storage room, which also worked as their office.

Elaine nibbled another bite of scone. She pushed the crumbs together on her plate and smashed them together. She always liked to save the "vittles"—a colloquialism on the word "victuals" her aunts used whenever they referred to a small portion of food— as her last bite. This particular scone was drier than usual. She decided it may taste better warmed, so she walked over and heated it up in the microwave. While she waited, she reminisced about her eccentric aunts.

For the past few months, Elaine had been concerned about their latest obsession with the skeleton keys. One day recently, she had visited their store after working all day at the library and found Daphne and Mildred arguing over a pile of keys they had dumped out of a tattered shoebox.

"That one doesn't have rust on it. It's not real," Daphne argued.

"What do you mean 'it's not real'? It fits the description in this book. Right here," Mildred said as she pointed to the book on the counter.

Elaine set the bag of take-out Thai food from their favorite restaurant on the counter and happened to catch the book's title,

The Key Master's Guide to Unlocking the Secrets, before Mildred flipped to a different page. Elaine had never seen that book before, but she assumed it was from the hefty book collection on one of the store's many shelves.

Elaine giggled as Mildred opened the paper sack and pulled out a container with broth trickling down the side. She placed it on the corner of the book so it would stay open, and some broth transferred onto the open page. Daphne dabbed it up with her finger and licked it while she pulled out another container with a few pad thai noodles hanging out. Her aunts continued their debate as they doled out the food, only stopping to smile at Elaine and thank her. Mildred rummaged in her bra for some dollar bills to give Elaine right as Daphne picked up the disputed key and stirred her noodles and sauce with it.

The microwave beeped, causing Elaine to snap out of her reverie. She punched the lever and took out her scone. She sat back down at the table and used the sleeve of her robe to wipe up the coffee ring her mug had left on the laminated table. She let out a sad sigh. What she wouldn't give for another day of listening to her aunts squabble over skeleton keys or watching them sloppily eat their takeout, never stopping to savor their food.

Elaine picked up her coffee and set the letters back in the wooden letter holder that also acted as a napkin dispenser and silverware tray. It was late morning, and she decided it was time to face reality. Her aunts weren't going to sit down with her at breakfast and tell her one of their clever or funny stories about their childhood back in Chicago post–World War II or about growing up listening to their father playing the fiddle and their uncle playing spoons.

Coffee mug in hand, Elaine shuffled down the hallway and made her way to the storage room/office. The hallway was chilly, and she pulled her robe closer around her. This section of the shop was a late addition that connected her aunts' home to the antique shop. They had contracted Grant Denninger—Elaine's friend since grade school—to construct it. He had surpassed their expectations by adding customized windows on each side and a side door that opened to the backyard. Over the years, the creaky door had warped and allowed in the cold air or the heat, depending on the season. Daphne and Mildred were unperturbed by the small flaw in the design, but Elaine always complained about it. She never got around to asking Grant to fix it, however. She hated inconveniencing anyone, especially her close friends and family.

When Elaine opened the connecting door to the storage room, she looked out at the disarray of paperwork, old collectibles, untidy napkins and tissues, and boxes of old files sitting on her aunts' desks ... and some shelves ... and the floor. There was *so* much stuff. She didn't know where to begin. Without her aunts here talking, laughing, bickering, rushing around, and giving life to this cluttered space, their office looked like the aftermath of a tornado.

Elaine struggled with the possibility that maybe her aunts had become senile before their deaths. Mr. Sadler had added fertilizer to the seed of doubt that was already growing inside Elaine by telling her—at the funeral dinner the church had provided—that they had taken out $4,000 from their retirement fund to pay off the lien the bank had on the shop. He mentioned they had forgotten to pay rent the month before and that the bank came to him for the money.

While she was living with them, Elaine had noticed a decline in their sales and wondered if they would ever close the shop. She tried to get up the courage to ask them numerous times about their plans and the store's future but always sidestepped the conversation, afraid Daphne and Mildred would think she was being meddlesome, or worse, that she was interested in going into the family business in their stead. That was before the police told her about the wreck and her world came tumbling down. She didn't want to think about that too much. It was painful enough to know she now lived in this old house all alone.

She took the last sip of her coffee and walked fully into the room. The blinds were open, and the overcast morning added a soft, matted gray tone to everything.

I really need to go through my aunts' stuff and figure out what can be donated, Elaine thought to herself. She shivered and wished she had brought gloves or at least a scarf. A light rain was falling, and the windows had fogged up a little. She set her mug down on a nearby shelf and walked toward the semicircular window with white trim in a starburst pattern. A small, blue-and-green bird-shaped suncatcher hung in the upper right side. She smiled and remembered the evening when she was eight, and her aunts had bought her a box of do-it-yourself suncatchers. They all laughed and clapped when they opened the box and set out the bags of small glass and copper wire. This suncatcher was the last one that remained. The others must have broken or fallen into oblivion, taking up residence in old boxes or mixed in with chunks of broken terra-cotta pottery and old mosaic supplies—another one of their numerous craft projects throughout the years.

Elaine took in the view of the wheat fields across the street and tracked their rows all the way to the edge of the woods. The same woods she used to explore as a child. The same woods she had adventures in and lived out the wild and silly stories her aunts had told her during bedtime and dinner conversations. Her favorite story was the one about the hidden treasure. Her aunts told her that in the mid-1800s, a man—a widower and shopkeeper—traveled from Prussia with his three daughters and settled on a small farm near the very woods in which Elaine played. He opened up an apothecary store similar to the one he'd owned in his old village and grew herbs and flowers and created elixirs and tonics for the local townspeople. His medicine was coveted by midwives and mothers alike, and soon the rich people in the town became customers as well. His store grew in popularity, but he maintained his modest lifestyle and continued to live in his small cabin in the woods, even when his daughters grew up, married, and moved away.

As his business grew, he accepted all forms of payment, from money to baked goods and anything in between, depending on what his customers could pay. The town filled with gossip once word got out that, supposedly, a beautiful Spanish lady had arrived at his cabin while he was treating the local jeweler's wife and paid him with a very large emerald for a bundle of herbs. Allegedly, a few days later, the apothecary refused to sell or trade the jeweler the emerald and became more of a recluse as more and more people showed up and asked to see the jewel.

He grew old, and one day, with no explanation, he and his cabin just disappeared. There was no trace he had ever lived there except for the weeds and thicket that grew up and over the cabin's foundation.

With each passing generation, children and adults alike would hike the woods in search of the emerald or any item that remained of the old apothecary. No one found a trace except for an occasional rusted mixing tool or mud-encrusted glass medicine bottle.

As a child, Elaine liked to believe she would very well be the one who would solve the mystery. She'd draw out treasure maps and search in hollowed-out trees, stone crevices, and outcroppings in hopes of finding the emerald. She spent many hours alone in the woods with only the trees, the birds, the earthworms, and her imagination as company.

Now, as she gazed across the field and thought about her aunts and their antique store, she realized how deeply this place and her aunts' love had been woven into her psyche. She wiped away a tear. It all felt too surreal that Daphne and Mildred were no longer here.

Elaine never got a chance to tell her aunts how much she loved living with them or how good it felt to be back in this beautiful, old home. She worried that these might be the final days this land and this place would be in her care. She couldn't afford the upkeep on a librarian's salary, that was for sure. She only had distant relatives, and she didn't feel comfortable asking people she barely knew or kept in touch with to help her sustain the fledgling business and maintain the old house and three acres of land.

Her parents had died in a car accident when she was in kindergarten, and her great-aunts, who also raised Elaine's father, became Elaine's guardians soon thereafter. They indulged her curious mind with their creative stories about magical travel and mystical portals. They cultivated her insatiable attention to detail by taking her on trips to junkyards, abandoned barns and houses, and estate sales to look for authentic heirlooms from days gone by. She knew the difference between a cuckoo clock from eighteenth-century Switzerland versus a modern and well-made reproduction by the time she was ten years old.

The onset of puberty brought a sudden change in Elaine, however. Instead of enjoying her aunts' stories or wanting to spend her weekends foraging for collectibles in rundown sections of town, she took more of an interest in her looks and worried more about what others thought of her. She was already labeled a "geek" by the popular crowd at school and worried her association with Grant would keep her from sitting at the "normal" kids' table at lunch. Grant was a neighborhood friend, but his gangly body and odd clothing, not to mention his obsession with stories of the occult, automatically caused kids to label him as the "ultimate nerd" at school. She would have settled for being one of the kids who was liked by everyone at Central Junior High but unrecognizable by Andy Court or Sheila Levin—the most athletic, beautiful, and popular couple at school who every tween admired and tried to emulate. It was a normal concern for most young girls her age, but it was also a trait Elaine didn't fully outgrow as she matured into adulthood.

All of her worries and what-ifs had to wait for now. If she thought too hard about anything, she would unravel and not be able to function. She had to focus on the day-to-day tasks of cleaning up and organizing all this stuff. Sophie, who ran the local thrift shop and charity store, said she would be happy to open the thrift store a few minutes early this week so Elaine could drop off any items she wanted to donate. With that in mind, Elaine forced herself to start on the task right now. Still, she longed for those imaginative tales and to reconnect with the little girl who believed everything her silly aunts told her.

Why did they have to be taken from her so suddenly and in such a violent way?

"Enough," she said aloud as she steeled herself. She did not want to cry. She had to face the fact that they were gone. She focused all her attention on the boxes sprawled before her. Boxes filled with bits and pieces of history and the daily life of people who had gone before her.

It always baffled Elaine why her aunts insisted on making this small room in the back of the store both a storage room and business office. They had struggled this past year to walk over and around the mounds of collected goods, yet Elaine had to give them credit for still being spry and mobile in their late eighties. The main desk, an antique with cubbyholes to store letters in, had become a random filing system of legal papers and bills, with buttons, pens, and other doodads and whatsits littering the last square inch.

Elaine smiled as she surveyed the office. In her mind's eye, she could see Mildred at her desk with her feet propped up on some box, smoking a cigarette and drinking a warm beer—two vices she took pleasure in, and two of the things Daphne found repulsive, according to Mildred. Mildred and Elaine had an understanding: Elaine was not to tell Daphne about Mildred's occasional guilty pleasures. An understanding Elaine also had with Daphne, who smoked as well and drank beer in the silver-polishing alcove on the opposite side of the antique store.

"Mildred doesn't care for this type of behavior," Daphne once told Elaine, who had walked in unexpectedly one day after school. "She thinks it's 'unladylike.' " Daphne had always labeled Mildred the "glamorous sister" while Mildred had always thought of Daphne as the more "virtuous" one. Both sisters were open and honest with each other to a fault, but smoking and drinking were not part of the narrative of how they were raised to believe a "lady" was to behave in a domesticated setting.

Elaine began clearing a space where she could work. She stacked boxes of books and draped across them some of the vintage clothes that hadn't been tagged yet. She moved an old bicycle to the corner of the room and pushed heavy boxes out of the way with her legs to clear a path. Dusty soda bottles rattled and clanked as she shifted the milk crates they were in. A row of antique frames nearly tumbled like dominoes until she propped them up with a drawer of tarnished trophies, ribbons, and medals. Finally, she had enough space where she could sort through all her aunts' belongings and make a few piles for items to be donated versus ones to be sold.

As Elaine sat down, she noticed she was eye level with the original sign for the store. It was propped up against the wall. "The Cooley Sisters' Antiques & Collectibles" was written in black script. The background was white, now yellowing with age. Some of the paint had chipped off over the years, and Elaine could see the original pine planks in some parts. She ran her fingers over the letters. This sign was connected to a lot of fond memories from Elaine's childhood. Like how she and Grant used to sit on the bench underneath it, waiting for the school bus or sucking on melting popsicles in the summertime and trying to belch the alphabet. These flashes of memory reminded her of why she loved old things in the first place. As a child, whenever Elaine came across any type of family heirloom or old relic her aunts had purchased from another antique dealer or an estate sale, she became sentimental and felt her imagination take flight.

When was the last time I allowed myself to daydream and get lost in my imagination? she wondered as she shifted some papers and cleared some space on the floor. *A while.*

She shifted another box into the giveaway pile and started sorting more trinkets and trash. Her actions became rigid and automatic, and she avoided lingering too long on any one item as a way to distance herself from what was and never would be again. Instead, she turned on her midwestern mindset and set to the task of pushing away the pain through the tediousness of organization.

After an hour or so of placing boxes in neat rows, Elaine realized she hadn't taken a break. She was only thirty-five, but she couldn't help but notice how her back hurt, and her knees crackled and popped when she stood up from squatting over and sorting through yet another full cardboard box. Toward the bottom, wedged between a cast-iron skillet and carnival glass wrapped in newspaper, rested an intricately carved wooden jewelry box. The engraving on the lid was a circle with two small crescent moons on each side. Mesmerizing squiggles and lines in geometric patterns filled up each crescent moon. Carved within the center of the large circle were two triangles overlapping each other, creating a look of a six-pointed star with twelve flower petals around it. Elaine couldn't make out the symbol in the middle of the star. It looked like the letter *u* with a line and dot over it. The handiwork of the box was so masterful, Elaine had a hard time discerning if it was crafted by machine or hand.

"I remember this thing," Elaine murmured as she slid her fingertips underneath the ridge of the lid and tried to pry it open with her hands. Years of disuse plus a rusted lock made it impossible to unlatch. Elaine looked around and noticed a few skeleton keys in a plastic bin on Aunt Mildred's desk. She tried opening the lock with each one of the keys but to no avail. On her last try, she chipped her nail, and the edge of the box scratched her other hand.

"Forget it. I don't know why they ever made a big deal out of this thing anyway," she muttered, then placed the jewelry box in the resell pile and moved on to the next task at hand.

Elaine stood and walked over to the metal bookshelf nearest her. She located the stepladder and strategized she could start at the highest shelf and work her way down. At the top, Elaine encountered cobwebs and years of dust.

"Gross." She coughed, then stepped down one rung and took a handful of books with her. More dust floated in the air. She sneezed, causing her to become unsteady and clasp the shelf, pulling it and its contents toward her. She recovered in the nick of time and pressed the shelf up against the wall as books and items cascaded to the floor. The thuds and clanks of the shelf's contents echoed throughout the room. "Dammit!" she exclaimed, more perturbed by the mess at her feet as opposed to her near fall or the fear of injury.

She climbed down the last two rungs and surveyed the damage. Numerous hard cover books had torn or pulled away from their spines. The glass shards of wine goblets sparkled on the hardwood floor. Various items—buttons, old campaign pins, and a wide variety of skeleton keys—slid and rolled around near an overturned storage container, its lid spinning across the floor. Elaine smiled as she remembered her aunts' fascination with skeleton keys. She gingerly stepped over the glass to survey the pile of upturned junk and jumbled items, picking up a handful of the old skeleton keys.

"What *was* their obsession with these rusty old things?" she muttered as she placed the lot in the bin on the nearby desk. She swirled her fingers in the pile, hoping to discover some answer. Just then, her fingers ran across a cold, brass key with an emerald-colored gemstone in the center of it. The gemstone shimmered even though the only light was from the tall window that faced the field. The head of the key was intricately designed with crafted metalwork that held tiny emerald stones as well.

"Strange. I've never seen anything like this," she said as she took it out of the bin to admire it.

It was heavier than the other skeleton keys. Elaine turned it around twice, examining its design. She was so entranced that she could have sworn she heard a low hum. The shaft was like the barrel of a gun—hollow and round with two teeth at the end that would unlock some cabinet, box, or door. She stood up and walked over to the window, holding the key up to see it in the natural light. The hexagon-shaped gemstone was in the center of the key's head. Upon closer inspection, Elaine noticed that the design on the key was an outline of a heart with etchings of flowers and vines looping up, over, and through each other.

Where did my aunts find this? she wondered.

The key appeared more decorative than functional, and she was about to set it down on Mildred's desk and get back to cleaning, when she glimpsed some tiny etchings in the key shaft that caught her attention. She could barely read them, let alone understand what they meant. She took out her cell phone from her robe's pocket and took a picture of the words. She then enlarged the photo to take a closer look.

Dein Herz est mein Herz.

Puzzled, she said the words twice out loud, and they felt like marbles in her mouth. She put away her phone, picked up the key again, and hugged it to her chest. She stared out the window as tears flooded her eyes.

"My dear, sweet aunts. If only I would have paid more attention to you both," she said. A little sob escaped her. She told herself not to cry—not here, not now. She read out loud the words on the key for a third time to help snap her out of her sadness.

Just then, the gemstone began to glow a pale green, and the key warmed in Elaine's hand. The room and the scenery outside the window blurred in front of her. She wiped her tears away with her sleeve, but still her view was distorted. She caught a glimpse of her reflection in the window and felt a rustling breeze toss her hair. There was a subtle ringing inside her ears, and a wave of nausea overcame her. She felt as if she were being pulled forward and floating at the same time. The key became hot to the touch, and Elaine felt a searing pain in the palm of her hand. Startled, she dropped the key, and it clanged on the wooden floor. Instantly, the buzzing noise stopped, and she didn't feel dizzy anymore. She pressed her hand on the cool glass of the window. She rested her forehead on the window, steadying herself and trying to catch her breath that was coming out in short spurts.

Once she gained her composure and her hand felt better, Elaine turned and took inventory of the room. Nothing seemed to have changed. Her aunts' office walls still held up the piles and bins of antiques and collectibles. Solid oak floors were beneath her feet. She bent over and rested her hands on her thighs and took a deep breath. Her hands shook, and she looked at the spot where the key had landed. It looked like a normal key except a faint greenish glow radiated from the key's gemstone. Tiny embers flickered around some of the letters and had burned the words from the strange written phrase deeper into the metal. Small puffs of smoke coiled and snaked around the metallic key.

She circled the key, afraid to pick it up again. A burning itch began to pulsate on her palm where she had been holding the key moments ago. Elaine hesitated, then turned her hand over to look at what she intuitively knew was there: a red mark forming in the center of her palm. She placed her forefinger on the spot and slowly traced the slight but definite burned imprint of the mysterious key.

Chapter 2

Elaine stepped away from the window and sat down in one of the desk chairs.

"That wasn't real," she said aloud. "I must be really stressed, or I'm just super tired. Probably both. That would explain it." She gently rubbed the palm of her hand, still warm from the imprint. Oddly enough, she didn't feel much pain.

"Maybe I'm having one of those weird daydreams I used to have as a child," she rationalized. She had always been a peculiar girl given to flights of fancy. Her teachers told her aunts that she needed to stop fantasizing and to focus on her schoolwork and duties instead of doodling and telling tall tales of ghosts and historical events that never took place. Her aunts usually disregarded her teachers' complaints and allowed Elaine to wander about in her daydreams. It wasn't until she hit high school that she stopped indulging her creativity. Instead, she let her analytical mind consume and drive her in hopes of high academic achievements that would land her college scholarships and help alleviate any financial burdens she may have put on her aunts.

"Maybe I need to take a break," she reassured herself and looked out the window. The same familiar wheatfields stood in straight rows underneath the gray sky.

Elaine focused again on the office, which still had so many more boxes to sort through. Why hadn't she noticed all the storage boxes on the shelves until today? She had been in this room many times over the years, especially the last few months of living here, and never paid any attention to what was inside them. Before she left, she picked up the fallen container and scooped up the keys and dropped them inside. She warily reached for the large, brass key. It was still warm to the touch, and the gem in the center had a luminescent glow to it. A bit nervous, Elaine tucked it inside her robe pocket and backed out of the room. She walked through the attached corridor into the main house, making her way upstairs.

In the bathroom, Elaine ran her hand under cold water, then placed a clean towel gently over her burn. It would fade in a couple of days, but she rubbed aloe vera gel on the red spot anyway and searched for a small bandage to cover it.

She had just finished applying the small adhesive strip to her hand when her cell phone rang. Startled, her shoulders jerked and her breath shortened. She fumbled around a bit until she finally found the phone in her other robe pocket.

"Hello?" she answered.

"Elaine, it's Grant. Why aren't you here?" the voice on the other line asked. Grant volunteered his time at the library, building new shelves, tables, and chairs for the media center that Elaine had advocated for over a year now.

"Oh wow. Yeah, I guess I forgot. How long are you going to be there?" she asked, trying to suppress the shakiness in her voice.

"Maybe another hour or so. I'm waiting for Mrs. Armested to get off the phone with the hardware store. She insisted I use half-inch drywall screws instead of the screws I have. She's calling to see if they have any, and if so, she is going to place an order for delivery. You need anything? I can come over instead. I just overheard her lecturing the young sales clerk about phone etiquette and how he should speak up, which is funny since I can hear him yelling at her through the phone. Their conversation may take a while."

Elaine could almost see Grant rolling his eyes and shaking his head like he always did when talking about their beloved Mrs. Armested, the eighty-five-year-old, semideaf librarian. "No, I'm good. Just stay there, and I'll be over in a few," she replied. She liked the idea of having the distraction.

Elaine and Grant had known each other since the fifth grade. He was the only one in her class who gladly listened to her wild and imaginative stories and daydreams; he himself had a penchant for dark tales of wizardry and the mythical realm of the Celtic world.

In their youth, Grant was a bit of an awkward boy. He wore secondhand clothes that were a little too small on his gangly arms and legs. His hair was always slightly greasy, and his face was covered in pimples. His plaid, button-up shirts and acid-washed jeans highlighted the women's Reebok tennis shoes his mother had bought him because she thought they were boys' high-tops. His big, soulful brown eyes with long black lashes hid behind plastic frames that were too large for his slender face. And kids always made fun of him for wearing a purple crystal pendant tied to a leather strap around his neck.

Once they were in high school, his acne had decreased, as did his body odor, but he was still the odd man out in most social situations. Elaine still felt ashamed that she had distanced herself throughout their high school years, even though she would walk with him to the bus stop and later, when they were upperclassmen, drive him to school. She also would occasionally share a milkshake with him on their break at their job at the local farm and feed store. Still, Grant seemed to understand her need to hang on to her fringe status of being "in" with a more popular crowd. He never complained when Elaine would run past him to join up with her group of track and band friends, and he never sought her attention at after-school events or pressured her to sit with him at lunch. In fact, he seemed content with this arrangement and didn't show any signs of holding a grudge when they reconnected a few years ago when she returned home.

Elaine had been living abroad and working as an English language teacher in a small town in southern Spain. Broke and weary from travel, she had accepted the position in town as head librarian. Grant was the only person from high school who associated with her, and so they fell back into a rhythm of easy friendship like their junior high school days.

Now, as a thirty-five-year-old man, Grant was still slender but with a strong, athletic build. His pimples were gone, replaced with graying stubble and silver specks of hair alongside his temples. His dark, thick hair was slicked back, and a small bald spot was beginning at the top of his head. He wore fashionable wire-framed glasses that fit his face, and his soulful eyes were more readily visible. The only remnant of his awkward stages as a youth was the purple crystal pendant he still wore around his neck.

Grant was the town's jack-of-all-trades. Everyone called on him to fix their appliances, do carpentry work, repair their leaky toilets, and perform other odd jobs. This past month, he had spent most of his days in his workshop designing all the furniture for the library's media center. Once a week, he would drive over to the library in his rusty red Ford truck and bring over a new piece. Elaine was always happy to spend time with him and looked forward to their weekly lunches at the local diner, The Greasy Spoon, that was within walking distance of the library. Grant would insist on treating her to some random dessert after she ate the healthiest thing she could find on the menu.

Mrs. Armested and the handful of volunteers at the library always teased Elaine and insisted she was dating Grant. No one ever believed her whenever she reminded them they were simply good friends. They even scoffed and told her she was a fool when she started dating Eric, an investment banker with the prestigious firm Havener-Simms Inc.

Elaine really cared for Eric. He was assertive, intelligent, and worldly. After a few dates, she stopped listening to everyone's gossip about him. Supposedly, he had moved back from Chicago only after he realized he wasn't going to get the recognition he thought he deserved in the big city. He refused to be a small fish in a big pond and decided their hometown of Brightonville offered more opportunities for others to appreciate his success.

Elaine remembered seeing him at town events and random parties when they were teenagers, but he had gone to the only private high school in the county. Their first real conversation occurred after Eric had moved back to town and stopped by the library to pick up a few books on finance. Elaine helped him locate them in the overpacked aisles of the nonfiction section. Following their brief conversation in which Eric flirted with her, she struck up the nerve to ask him to join her for coffee downtown during her lunch break. She was surprised when he agreed, but he told her afterward that it was nice to talk with someone who didn't know much about his high school days. After an hour of listening to him regale her with wild stories of his youth and college days, Elaine was smitten.

For the past year, their dates tended to be centered around his work—business lunches at the country club, meet-and-greet social hours at the trendy wine bar downtown, weekly dinners with his parents or business associates at posh restaurants, or weekend trips to St. Louis or Chicago, where he would spend each day and part of the evening at a conference in the hotel while she toured the city's sites alone. He always made up for the weekend trips by taking her shopping and buying her an expensive outfit or jewelry at one of the swanky department stores, yet she was getting tired of seeing him on occasional weekends and wished they could spend quiet evenings together. Sometimes, she wondered if he was indulging her with all these material goods in order to keep her from getting too close to him, but then he would whisk her away to a posh night out on the town, and she figured this was how those popular girls in high school felt when they won homecoming queen or dated the star quarterback. She ignored people's comments about how he was grooming her into a socialite rather than appreciating the nerdy, outspoken intellect that she was.

Honestly, Elaine secretly enjoyed escaping town now and again or going to places she couldn't afford on a librarian's salary, so she often looked past Eric's unromantic gestures. Just because people like her aunts and Mrs. Armested warned her that he treated her more like a business partner than a girlfriend didn't make their opinions fact. Besides, she was in no hurry to rush their relationship. Everything was status quo, just as she liked it.

Thinking of Eric, she realized she hadn't spoken to him in a few days. She picked up her phone and shot him a text.

Let's meet up tonight for drinks. Same time, place as usual?

She dropped her phone into her bag and reached again into her robe pocket to pull out the key. She wasn't sure what to do with it, so she placed it into the small pocket in her bag next to her phone.

She saw a faint green glow from inside the dark bag. She hoped it was just the phone's touch screen or that her phone had started an automatic update, but she knew as she picked it up that there would be a blank screen.

"So strange," she murmured right as she saw the glow a second time. "The key?"

She opened the pocket and peered in. A luminous green light radiated from the jewel in the key's center.

"What the ...?" she stammered as she quickly zipped the pocket closed and tossed her purse on the chair. "I've got to get it together," she said as she shook her head and wiped her eyes, as if trying to wake from a bizarre dream.

She wasted no time and pulled her hair into a sloppy bun. The long, hot bath she dreamed of would have to wait. Truthfully, she hadn't indulged in anything so luxurious since her aunts' car wreck. It seemed like she had simply been doing all the necessary chores one must do when such things occur. Since her aunts never married or had children, Elaine had been the one in charge of filling out all the paperwork, meeting with the estate lawyer, paying the bills, and making the arrangements. Before her distant cousins and their small families went back to their homes and their lives, Elaine was the one consoling them and listening to their long-ago stories about Daphne and Mildred. She felt compelled to be a gracious host and avoided any type of mourning for herself, minus her initial crying jag upon learning the news of their tragic deaths.

Going to the library and seeing her friend was the bit of normalcy Elaine could use today. With that thought in mind, she quickly dressed, remembering to grab her green, waist-length jacket and purse before reversing course and running back to her aunts' office.

Always pragmatic and simultaneously trying to persuade herself that she was indeed making headway with her long to-do list, Elaine decided to drop off some items prior to meeting Grant. Sophie's Secondhand Store was only a block or two away from the library, so Elaine gathered up some articles of clothing and placed them in cardboard boxes. When she got to the wooden jewelry box that wouldn't open, Elaine ran her fingers across the carving of the crescent moons. A brief bout of nostalgia welled up inside her, and she wondered if she should hold on to the childhood memento. She tried one more time to open it, but it simply wouldn't budge. Deciding it wasn't worth the frustration or the effort to discover what might be inside, she tossed it on top of the pile and loaded it into her car. She glanced at the antique box one last time as she shut the trunk, fighting the urge to take it back. *It won't do me any good to hold on to something I never paid too much attention to when I was a child.* She opened the driver's side door. "One less thing to remind me of what I've lost," she whispered as she reversed out of the driveway and headed into town.

***

Elaine arrived at the store just as one of the young workers opened the loading dock garage door for the morning's collections. He helped her set the two big boxes on his cart before writing her a receipt. Five minutes later, Elaine pulled open the heavy wooden door at the old library on Main Street. The musty smell of books and the warm air on her flushed skin soothed her. She walked past two old men, Tom and Syd, who were sitting in worn leather chairs facing each other, waiting for the other to make a wrong move in their ongoing chess game. Neither of them looked up as they lifted a hand in a do-not-disturb motion that also acted as a greeting. Mrs. Armested sat in her wheelchair behind the circulation desk, stamping the inside covers of a pile of books, an unnecessary chore ever since Elaine arranged for the books to be put into the online catalog. Elaine greeted her with a loud hello followed by a slow waving gesture of her hand.

Mrs. Armested peered over her thick owl glasses. "Oh hello, dear," she croaked as she stamped the front cover of a new paperback book the library had recently acquired.

Elaine had learned the hard way not to try and change Mrs. Armested or her ancient ways. It would take ten long and loud minutes to explain why she shouldn't stamp the front of the book and another ten minutes to get her to stop stamping the same pile of books she had just finished. Instead, Elaine set her purse behind the counter and went to the media room to look for Grant.

Grant, who was facing a wall with a level in one hand and a pencil in the other, had donated his time and materials to make custom-built shelves for the media room. His plan was to fill the shelves with the rental DVDs and also put in hooks below the shelves so the headphones could be more accessible than having to dig around in the blue bin in the corner of the room. He set his level on the closest desk and smiled. His lips curled up higher on one side, a charming grin that accentuated his square jawline.

"Hey, you," he said as he marked two small lines on the wall. "I'll be ready to go to lunch here in a minute. I just want to get these plumb lines down before we head out."

Elaine glanced around the room as he worked. In the past month, Grant had painted the walls, fixed the wobbly desks, and arranged the electronic cords so they were no longer a jumbled mess.

"I really wish you would let us pay you for all this, Grant," Elaine said. She felt bad that he had taken on this big project pro bono. He made ends meet with the other miscellaneous jobs he did around town, but Elaine knew he wasn't flush with cash. He always wanted to travel overseas, but the farthest he'd ever been was two states over to attend his estranged father's funeral.

"Really, Elaine," he said, "you worry too much. I like helping out. This library has been one of my favorite places ever since I was a kid. It's a landmark in this town." He smiled at her and stuck his pencil behind his ear. "Let me put my tools away, and we'll walk over to The Greasy Spoon. My treat." He put his toolbox in the coat closet at the back of the room and then walked past her, leading the way out.

She smirked at the back of his head. "You only like it here because you get to flirt with Mrs. Armested and the other little old ladies who come here for their knitting circle."

"You got me there." He chuckled. He waited for Elaine to get her purse and looked over at Mrs. Armested, who was in a daze, probably wondering what to do with the pile of books next to her. He winked at her, and she blushed. "Hold down the fort, will ya, Mrs. A? We're going out for a bite to eat."

She waved at both of them and then quickly called Grant back. "Bring me back a milkshake and some fries, will ya, cutes? I haven't had my midafternoon snack today."

Grant rapped the desk with his knuckles and nodded at Mrs. Armested. Elaine smiled and waited for him to catch up with her. They were both almost out the door when they heard Mrs. Armested call after them again. "And grab a cheeseburger with the works and some of Jilly's homemade apple pie too. On second thought, hold the mayo and ketchup on that cheeseburger. I'm diabetic, you know?"

Once they finally made it outside, the brisk autumn air invigorated them. Elaine zipped her jacket all the way up and threw on her hood. She shoved her hands into her pockets and waited for Grant to wrap his scarf around his neck and tuck it into the dark-brown leather bomber jacket he had purchased a few years ago from her aunts' store.

"Last one there is a rotten egg!" He laughed, and they began to walk quickly down Main Street.

They made their way past the hardware store and dry cleaners, but Elaine stopped abruptly in front of the specialty candy shop. She peered in, then grimaced at her reflection until she saw Grant awkwardly dancing in place simply for her amusement. She was embarrassed he had caught her checking herself out in the store window, but she couldn't help but laugh.

"You're so silly," she remarked and picked up her pace again.

"Anything to help you get out of your head and all those deep thoughts that swim around in there," he said.

He grinned at her, his upper lip curling, and winked as they continued to hurry down the sidewalk. The smell of chargrilled burgers and salty fries wafted toward them as they rounded the corner. Grant reached the diner's glass door first and opened it for Elaine. A few of the locals at the counter said hello to them both as they slid into a booth near the large, street-facing window.

While Grant was unwinding his scarf and taking off his jacket, Elaine noticed the bags under his eyes and the scruffy whiskers on his face. He wasn't getting a lot of sleep lately. He recently put his mother into a nursing home. Elaine knew it was a sore subject for him. He and his mother, Gladys, had always been so close.

Elaine had gone with Grant the other week to bring Gladys some antique knickknacks for her new room. Elaine kissed her on the cheek and got a blank stare in return. It was clear to Elaine that Gladys didn't recognize her. Gladys barely spoke, and when she did, she didn't remember Elaine's name.

"Do you think Mrs. A will be too upset if we don't get her a scoop of vanilla ice cream on the side of her apple pie?" Grant asked as he handed Elaine a laminated menu.

Elaine chuckled and perused the list of items, a pointless task because she knew she would wind up ordering either a veggie burger and fries or a chef's salad. "I don't think she'll mind. She's probably snuck into her not-so-secret snack drawer at the circulation desk and eaten one of her candy bars already."

They shared the latest stories of Mrs. Armested and her junk-food extravaganzas before Jilly, their usual waitress and pie maker extraordinaire, came over to their table. After they ordered drinks, Jilly leaned in closer to Grant and asked, "So how's your mother, darling? Us girls in her knitting circle have been praying for her. Terrible shame how she just went catatonic like that."

"She's okay," Grant murmured.

Elaine could sense his uneasiness with the topic. She understood too well the pain and loss of a loved one.

"Trudy said it was because something made her so nervous about a month ago that she was frightened to the point she couldn't function no more," Jilly continued, oblivious to Grant's discomfort. "Trudy's husband said he saw a big red glow in the field behind your mom's house the other night when he was driving home from work. Still can't figure out what it was. Maybe it was a transformer that blew? Wonder if that's what scared her into the state she's been in? Your mom's always had a touch of them nerves ever since I've known her. You know what I mean?"

Grant just stared at his menu. Elaine shifted in her seat, thinking of what she could say to switch the subject. She cleared her throat twice to indicate to Jilly they needed more time to look over the menu, but Jilly was still theorizing about Grant's mother.

"What's this new item on the menu, Jilly? Vegetable tempura? That sounds good," Elaine interjected.

"Oh, honey, you don't want that. It's fried vegetables. We thaw out packages of frozen broccoli and cauliflower in the morning and dip 'em in the same batter we use for the onion rings. Ed is trying to make the menu more 'international.' Problem is, the veggies are too watery from sitting out all morning. Bless his heart. Fried okra's better. Stick with that."

Elaine nodded and looked back down at her menu.

Jilly blathered on. "Still and all, she coulda had a stroke and just not known it. My Aunt Jeanie stroked out and keeled over in her mashed potatoes at Christmas dinner one year. You just never know and all."

Grant just stared ahead and sighed. Once Jilly got on a subject, it was hard to get her off it.

"I'll have the veggie burger, please, Jilly," Elaine said as she passed her menu across the table. "And I bet Grant is going to order the Philly cheesesteak. Am I right, friend?" Her direct tone finally brought both Jilly and Grant out of what could have turned into an embarrassing pity party.

Grant nodded his head and passed both menus to Jilly. He smiled at Elaine and mouthed a thank-you as Jilly walked over to gossip with another customer before placing their order with the fry cook. Elaine lifted her water glass and tipped her chin in a gesture of welcoming return.

"She wasn't trying to gossip. She really has a good heart," Elaine said to Grant as he squeezed the lemon slice into his water glass.

"Yeah, I know." Grant propped his elbows on the table. His fingers and attention were fixated on the paper straw wrapper.

Elaine knew any mention of his mother and her current condition was painful to Grant. If Jilly had kept going on about the topic any longer, Grant would have become sulky and withdrawn. Elaine wondered if maybe some funny videos or silly memes she saw recently on one of her social media feeds would cheer him up. When she reached into her purse to grab her phone, her fingers brushed up against the strange key. She pulled that out instead.

"What's that?" Grant asked.

Elaine twirled the key between her two fingers. She noticed a slight ringing in her ears as she did so. "This? It's just some old key I found today when I was cleaning out the office."

"No, I meant the bandage. What happened to you?"

"Oh. That. Yeah, I reheated the coffee in the microwave this morning and grabbed the mug without thinking. I didn't drop the mug, but I paid for it with a little burn. It's no big deal. It'll go away in a day or so." Elaine hated lying to Grant, but she wasn't sure how she could explain this morning's experience without sounding like she was having a nervous breakdown. "It's a pretty key, isn't it?" she added. "My aunts collected a lot of different things, but they sure did have an eye for unique pieces."

She set the key down on the table in front of Grant and waited to see if he noticed anything out of the ordinary. The burn was real—Elaine was certain of that. What she was uncertain of, however, was what else from this morning was grounded in reality. Elaine had a history of handling her stress by retreating into her imagination. Therefore, she thought it best to wait and see if Grant noticed anything out of the ordinary too.

Grant picked up the key and brought it closer to his face to examine it. The gemstone caught a bit of the natural light that filtered through the window, but it did not have the aural glow like it had earlier. Grant handed it back to Elaine. "That's a really pretty key. Looks more decorative than functional, though. They were always finding such interesting things on their 'treasure hunts,' as they called them," he said. "Man, I miss them. They were the most eccentric, interesting people I've ever known."

"You can say that again." Elaine smiled as she tucked the key back into the pocket of her purse. "I didn't always understand their fascination with junk, but they sure did love going to old, abandoned barns and estate sales to scour for little things like this. I don't know how their business lasted so long."

"True, but people did love them, and your aunts could sell anything as long as they created a story around it," Grant replied. "Remember how they once told our old principal, Mr. Kramer, and his wife that all those porcelain poodle figurines were from seventeenth-century France? They really had them going."

"I think Mr. Kramer bought twenty of them before he realized they were imitation knockoffs made in China in the early 1980s."

Reminiscing had lightened both of their moods, and they laughed as they told more stories about Daphne and Mildred until Jilly brought their meals. Grant placed Mrs. Armested's to-go order and, luckily, before Jilly could ask him any other questions about his mom, another customer beckoned Jilly over. Grant dramatically wiped his brow and whistled. "Phew. Close call." He laughed and unfolded his napkin, placing it on his lap.

Elaine nodded her head in agreement and pulled out a napkin from the dispenser as well. They devoured their food in silence for the next few minutes. At one point, Elaine smiled and looked across at Grant, whose head was bent over his plate as he wrestled a big bite of his sandwich.

As they each savored their last fry dipped in tart ketchup, a tall and slender gentleman who had been sitting at a booth across from them approached. He looked to be sixty to seventy years old, and he was wearing khaki pants and a white button-up shirt with a green ascot tied around his neck. Suspenders and a tweed cap finished off his distinguished look.

Elaine looked up at the elderly gentleman and blushed. She felt as if she had been caught passing a note in class while the teacher was talking. She glanced over at Grant, who had a similar look. Neither of them had done anything more than laugh a little louder than most customers, but this man had a discerning air about him, as if no detail passed by without him first scrutinizing it to determine if it met his approval. Elaine felt like they may have interrupted his meal with their loud chatter and were about to receive a lecture about restaurant etiquette.

The man slid his hands into his pockets and scrunched up one side of his face in a knowing smile. His blue eyes loomed from behind his wire-rimmed glasses and held a twinge of gray steeliness that commanded respect.

"Sorry, my friends," he said, "I don't mean to disturb you. My name is Edmund Wallace. I'm a professor of history over at Lincoln College and also the director of the local history museum on campus. I couldn't help but overhear some of your discussion earlier ... and I, uh, just couldn't leave without asking you about the skeleton key you were looking at. I'm a bit of a collector myself, you see. My specialty is antiquities. I just *have* to know where you found something so unique." He said all this in a pleasant-enough voice with a hint of gravitas in his tone.

Elaine and Grant caught each other's eyes and silently asked each other, "What's with this guy?" He was a complete stranger, after all, barging in on their private conversation. After a short pause, though, Grant decided the dignified gentleman meant no harm and asked Elaine if she wouldn't mind retrieving the key. She hesitated, but then realized it would be strange not to, especially since she had casually shown it to Grant earlier.

Grant nodded at the key in Elaine's hand and picked it up. "Would you like a closer look?"

Elaine felt a wave of anxiety wash over her. This morning's strange encounter aside, she wasn't sure if she wanted a random man nosing around in her business let alone in a private discussion with her friend. Grant, however, was less guarded and reluctant. He motioned for the professor to sit down next to them.

Professor Wallace nodded, took his hands out of his pocket, and straightened his ascot before sliding in the booth next to Grant. He held out his hand and asked, "May I?"

Grant handed the key over to Professor Wallace, who eyed it carefully as he turned it around between his fingers. Grant shared the small details Elaine had previously mentioned while Elaine rubbed her temples in nervous anticipation. She really hoped the key was a simple skeleton key and nothing strange would happen. However, a very faint green glow radiated from the center of the gem as the professor twirled the key with his middle finger and thumb.

Grant hadn't seemed to notice, but the professor looked her square in the eye and said, "This key is special and rare, but I believe you already know that, don't you, my dear?" He handed the key back to Elaine, who immediately shoved it into her purse.

Elaine shrugged. "I just found it this morning," she said, trying to keep her voice casual, but it was evident she was rattled. An intuitive pull in her stomach warned her not to reveal too much to either man. She recalled one afternoon when her aunts had looked through that big book ... *What was it called again? The Key Master's Guide to Unlocking the Secrets* if she remembered correctly. They were comparing a skeleton key to one of the book's illustrations. If the keys had been so important to her aunts, and if this was one they had been studying or researching, maybe she should keep it a secret until she could understand why it had behaved so strangely this morning. On the other hand, it was possible she just didn't want Grant or Professor Wallace to think she was a lunatic talking about strange keys that glowed in broad daylight. She took a sip of her water before continuing. "It was in a container of junk I was clearing out. I don't think it's anything special, really. I just thought it was pretty, that's all."

She picked up her straw wrapper and began folding it between her fingers. She hated to fib so much and was ashamed lying came so easily to her, just like when she was a child and gave creative explanations to her bemused teachers whenever she was caught daydreaming and couldn't remember the answers to their simple questions.

"What makes you think this key is so special, Professor?" Grant asked. His youthful spirit that loved mystery and adventure was evident in his excited voice and wide eyes. He tapped the top of the table with his thumbs, a sign Elaine recognized. Grant was hoping the professor would reveal that the key was connected to an eccentric aristocrat who kept an antique safe in his parlor or to a spiritualist from the Gilded Age who used it as an intermediary to talk to the dead.

"Well, my good man, I would need to inspect it more closely, but it appears to possibly be from the late 1700s or early 1800s and associated with an apothecary guild in the Alsace-Lorraine region of France or the Rhineland area of Germany. Very rare find, if I'm right about what it is, and just the type of thing I love putting on display. A little artifact of yesteryear, one that holds more stories that surpass its functionality if we just dig deep enough."

"Elaine!" Grant exclaimed. "Let Professor Wallace take a better look at the key. If it's what he thinks it is, it could generate some good money and publicity for the antique store."

Elaine took a deep breath and filled her lungs with the scent of french-fry grease and sizzling cheeseburgers. She felt trapped between Grant's enthusiasm and the professor's curiosity and confidence. She was such a guarded person and never liked involving strangers in her business, personally or professionally, without a reasonable amount of caution and mistrust. Besides, she wasn't ready to face the full extent of what she needed to do to keep the antique store afloat. No one, not even Grant, knew the financial woes her aunts had recently experienced.

It was true that local businesses were feeling the effects of customers shopping online, but how could she ever admit to herself or anyone else that her aunts had been heading toward financial ruin and didn't seem all that concerned about it? Mr. Sadler's letters brought up so much worry that she literally had been stuffing them away unopened, hoping the issue would resolve itself in some magical way. She slowed her exhalation just enough to allow her mind to formulate her next move.

At that moment, the professor reached into his pocket, as if to hand her something. He fixed his gaze upon Elaine. His eyes had a piercing look that unnerved her. She felt a moment of dread in her stomach, as if she was being pulled into some sort of vortex. In her peripheral vision, it seemed as if the tables, booths, white walls, and checkered tile floor around her were dissolving. Wallace's eyes looked darker, more mysterious. Then, the professor blinked, and the room returned to normal. He took out a tiny pill from its container and popped it into his mouth.

Professor Wallace grinned sheepishly. "Excuse me. It's my daily heart medicine. I forgot to take it before I ate lunch." He began to chuckle and search his other pockets as well. "I seem to have misplaced my wallet," he commented. "I'm afraid I sometimes live up to the absentminded professor stereotype. Ah, here it is." He produced a worn, brown leather wallet and patted the top of it with his other hand.

Elaine's palms and underarms were sweaty. She looked at Grant, who seemed unfazed. "Elaine," he said. "I think you should let the professor look at the key and give his expert advice on what to do with it."

She slid her purse closer to her thigh and held on to the handles. "I-I'm not sure," she stammered. "I don't think my aunts would have kept something of value sitting around buried in an old bin." She desperately wanted to get out of the restaurant and out of this conversation.

"Professor, what do you advise us to do with the key?" Grant asked.

Elaine noticed how he added the "us," as if he was now a part of this decision. She knew Grant well enough, however, to realize he was stepping in as her friend to help her navigate this new development as opposed to harboring any ulterior motive.

"Well, the key is rightfully your friend's," the professor proceeded with caution. "I would advise her to get it appraised, at least."

He opened his wallet and pulled out a business card. He slid the card across the table, within Elaine's reach. She picked it up and noticed the design of the campus's clock tower was embossed in the center of the card. To the right of the tower was what appeared to be a watermark of a circle surrounded by two crescent moons … just like the one on the jewelry box from earlier that morning. She shook her head and angled the card toward the light for a closer look. The watermark was definitely in the shape of the moons and, though very tiny, appeared to be an addition due to the faint smudge a home printer may make when printing heavy cardstock. *Why would he use this image?* Elaine thought to herself. *Must be a weird coincidence.*

"I'm afraid I've taken up too much of your time," the professor said. "It's quite possible that my quick assessment of the key is incorrect, and I have gotten your hopes up on its value. However, should you change your mind, I would love for you to stop by the museum so I could take a closer look at it." He pointed to his card at Elaine's fingertips. "You will notice my hours of availability and how to contact me, my dear."

He stood up, got out of the booth, and shook Grant's hand. "Thank you for indulging an old man and his love of antiques." He turned to Elaine and touched the rim of his hat. "It's been a pleasure." He pulled out a few dollars and placed the tip on his table before walking out of the diner.

"Elaine, you gotta let him take a look at that key. Think of how many doors it could open for you," Grant pleaded.

She relaxed a little and laughed at his obvious play on words. "You're such a nerd."

He smiled, too, and nodded his head. "That I am. But I really think you should consider it. What could it hurt?"

"You're right," she replied. "I know, you're right. It's just that so much has happened over the past few weeks that I just don't want to get all worked up over what is probably nothing. You know my aunts collected mostly junk these past few years. Little odds and ends that people bought to add charm to their homes. I bet it's not worth anything. Look, let's just settle our bill and go. I need to get back to work before Mrs. Armested stamps the books for a third or fourth time and blocks out the title pages."

"Just promise me you'll consider it," Grant said.

"I will," she said as she picked up the card and put it in her pocket. Part of her wanted to be as curious as Grant and discover more about the key, yet she was still hesitant. Professor Wallace was a stranger, and she wasn't sure she wanted to know any more about the peculiar item that had suddenly come into her life. She desperately needed things to be stable and organized right now. Whatever this key was, she was afraid it may add more to her grief and worries. Having one more thing to figure out and settle might just break her.

Grant smiled in reassurance and then walked up to the counter to pay their bill.

Elaine reached into her purse again to grab her wallet so she could leave the tip. Curiosity got the best of her, and she opened up the side pouch. Inside, the key glowed even brighter than before. She reached in to pick it up. As soon as she touched it, she felt a burning sensation on her fingertips. The key had become hot to the touch again. She let go of it and looked up to see if Grant or anyone else had noticed. No one seemed aware, and Grant's back was still to her. She glanced one more time at the key, and a feeling of vertigo overtook her. She placed her hand on the back of the booth to balance herself. A sense of panic rose inside her as a noise buzzed in her ears.

What's going on? she wondered.

She wiped her sweaty palms on her pants and looped her purse over her shoulder, hugging it with her arm like a football. She slipped out of the booth and made her way up to the counter to Grant. "Quick," she whispered, "I think I better show you something."

He placed his credit card into his wallet before putting the wallet in his back pocket. "What is it?" he asked with concern in his voice.

"Let's get out of here, and I'll show you. C'mon." She took his elbow and all but dragged him out.

Once outside, she walked them toward the roof overhang so they could be in the shadow, out of the midday sun. A buzzing noise lingered inside her ears, but the vertigo seemed to have passed. She handed him her purse and unzipped the side pocket. They both peered inside. The key now had a green glow enveloping it. The gem was an even brighter green, and tiny gold speckles began to swirl inside it until they became golden streaks orbiting around a black center the size of a pinhead.

CHAPTER 3

"What the hell?" Grant exclaimed as he reached into the pocket to take out the key.

Elaine closed the pocket and pulled her purse tight to her chest. "Don't!" she warned him. "It could be dangerous. Maybe it's radioactive?"

Grant stared at her, bewildered. "What did I just see?" He scratched his head and moved toward her. "Let me take another look. I promise I won't touch it." As a gesture of good faith, he put his hands behind his back.

Elaine turned around and saw a covered trash can next to her. She took out a few napkins from inside her purse, unfolded them, and draped them over the square lid before placing her purse delicately on top.

"Swear not to touch it!" she demanded. Her voice held the same reprimanding tone she used with Grant when they were preteens and he would try to gross her out with random findings of organic material and insects when they were on the playground.

"Scout's honor," he said and held up his three fingers in the traditional salute.

Elaine rolled her eyes and half smiled before opening the pocket. When he peered in, the green glow had nearly faded. The swirling streaks of gold were gone, and the gemstone appeared once again like a cloudy green marble.

"You know what we should do, Laney?" he asked. "We should take this thing over to Adele's. She might know something about it."

Elaine smiled and rolled her eyes at the use of her childhood nickname. Both her aunts and Grant used it whenever they wanted to sweeten her up and get her to bend her rules or stubborn ways. "No, Grant. I don't want to drag her into this. She'll make us drink some concoction of chicory root and weird herbs from her garden. Besides, her shop freaks me out with all her energy crystals and moon catchers."

"They're called 'dream catchers,' and her store is awesome. Besides, she was your aunts' closest friend. If anyone knows why they had this weird key hidden away, she would." He held up the white to-go bag. "Let's run this food back over to Mrs. Armested and then go see Adele."

Elaine huffed and reluctantly followed. Adele had been her aunts' best friend, despite the fact that Adele was twenty years younger than Mildred and Daphne. Adele had moved to town when Elaine was a freshman in high school. Soon after, she was a regular at her aunts' antique store and purchased quite a few furniture pieces to decorate her apothecary shop, which she opened the following year. Adele and Elaine didn't always get along as well as her aunts would have liked them to. Elaine felt Adele was too blunt in her commentaries and too hippie-dippie in mannerisms. Likewise, Adele thought Elaine was too uptight and rigid in the treatment of herself and others. The one point they could always agree on was how much they had loved and cared for Daphne and Mildred.

Elaine and Grant made a beeline to a grateful, and hungry, Mrs. Armested. They plopped down her food and walked right out the door again, missing Mrs. A's request for more ketchup packets for her salty fries.

Adele's homeopathic store was just a few blocks from the library. As they walked down the street, Elaine admired the outdoor lights that were strung across Main Street and wrapped around the telephone poles. They were the newest additions to the downtown revitalization project, which also included a small meditation park where an abandoned building used to be. Even though it was daytime, she loved the image of her hometown lit up in the evening so as to enhance the brick veneer buildings that housed the coffee shop, hardware store, local brewery, clothing boutiques, and a used bookstore to name a few.

When they arrived at Adele's store, Elaine cringed. Last year, Adele refused the city council's offer to revamp her 1970s storefront, which many believed to be an eyesore with its mint-green wood paneling decorated with childlike rainbows, orange and yellow flowers, and a misshapen yin-yang symbol. Grant paused to admire Adele's latest display in the store's large window. Crystals of various geometric shapes hung from fishing wire and caught the sunlight. Purple-and-white geodes lined the window seat, and tinctures of Adele's flower essences from her gardens sat atop clear plastic shelves, causing the dark-blue bottles with medicine droppers as caps to appear suspended in midair. The sign on the glass door read Maiden, Mother, Crone. It was painted bright yellow with a white trim. Elaine groaned and rolled her eyes as she peered inside. A bulletin board filled with advertisements for healing circles, tarot card readings, and holistic tinctures and other metaphysical offerings dominated the lobby area.

"Play nice," Grant told her as he opened the door for her.

They passed through another set of glass doors and stepped inside. A little bell chimed as each of them entered. The interior of the shop conflicted with the childish and hippie exterior. The golden, well-polished, hardwood floors paired well with the colonial blue walls lined with buttercream-colored bookshelves filled with books about herbs, flowers, and the natural world. A cozy sitting area with two worn leather chairs, a tattered rug, and a wicker table welcomed shoppers to sit and browse the spiritual self-help books Adele loved to quote so much. The afternoon sun warmed up the leather and provided nourishment for the succulent potted plants that were gathered in front of the large storefront window. Behind the main counter, an antique hutch, painted a muted turquoise, housed glass apothecary jars of dried herbs such as lavender, rosemary, sage, ginseng, echinacea, and various herbal tea mixtures. Samples of herbal soaps and lotions sat on top of a rickety washstand. Customers could also help themselves to a taste of the tea of the week and dispose of the tiny paper cups in the rusted bucket Adele used as a recycling bin.

Elaine walked up to Grant, who was leaning on the counter and peering down at the various gemstones of rose quartz, citrine, moonstone, and others in the display case. He looked up and smiled. "I've always liked looking at these gemstones. They have healing properties, you know."

"Not that again." Elaine sighed, exasperated. "They're just pretty rocks, that's all."

He pulled out the purple amethyst on the leather strap around his neck. "I don't care what you say," he said as he rubbed the smooth crystal between his thumb and forefinger. "This protected me from those bullies in junior high. And it brings me more clarity in my morning meditations. Adele has shown me how this can help open my intuition and my mind to other realms of possibilities."

"Let's not get into this again, okay?"

They looked at each other, waiting for the other to crack.

Grant smiled first. "Deep down inside, you know there is more to this world than the answers that reside in your books and that analytical brain of yours."

"Possibly," Elaine conceded. "Right now, my brain is telling me that we're wasting our time here. Adele is an intuitive woman and has strange ways, but I don't think she'll be able to keep this key business a secret. We're better off forgetting this whole thing."

She turned to leave, but then she happened to see a familiar-looking card next to the cash register. "Wait a minute. What's this?" She scooped up the card. "Oh my god. Grant? You're not going to believe this. Look," she said as she held it up to him. The elegant business card script spelled out the name of Professor Wallace of Lincoln College. The same embossed outline of the college's clock tower framed the top of the card. She lifted it up to the light, which revealed the same watermark of the crescent moons, just like the card the professor had given Elaine earlier. Below his contact information, someone had scribbled the words "Call ASAP" in black ink.

Grant took the card from her and set it back on the counter. "This is none of our business, Elaine."

"Why would she have his card? How long has he been in town? Have you ever heard of this man before today? And why was he asking us about the key, and now *we're* here doing the same? What's going on?" Each question tumbled out of her mouth in this one-sided conversation. In a matter of seconds, she knew she had overwhelmed Grant with her worries, but she couldn't stop freaking out.

Finally, unable to contain his frustration, Grant raised his voice. "Elaine, enough already!" The tenor in his voice brought her to her senses.

"I know. It's just that ...." She took a shallow inhale.

"Just stop for a minute," Grant said in a soothing tone. "Let's not mention him unless she does. We're here about the key, remember? This strange key that you found in your aunts' office? The one that was glowing in your purse about ten minutes ago?"

"Okay, but I have so many questions for her," Elaine said, sliding the business card back where she found it. "And let's not forget, she's not one for holding back her tongue either."

A rustle of macramé beads caused them to stop talking and turn their heads. The beads hanging from the back-room entrance rippled and parted as Adele emerged into the store. The dusting of white and silver hair cut close to her head highlighted her caramel-colored skin. A petite woman, Adele wore a deep purple shawl that hung down to her knees. Her flowy linen pants and long-sleeve blouse were wrinkled yet billowed as she walked. Various silver rings covered each finger, and bangled bracelets clanked up and down on her arms. Her large earrings, featuring dried agave fibers wrapped around thin copper wire, dangled close to her shoulders. A tiny golden hoop earring pierced her right nostril and glimmered in the sun as she took a deep breath. With an air of theatrics, Adele lifted her hands above her head and glided into the center of the room like a prima ballerina ready to take center stage.

"Dah-lings! Welcome!" She grabbed Grant's forearms as he reached out for an embrace. She kissed him on each cheek and then pressed her head into his chest. Her bracelets rattled together as she turned toward Elaine. "Hello, Elaine. Good to see you," she said curtly as she stood up properly, jutting out her chin in a slight act of defiance.

"Adele." Elaine nodded.

Adele took a deep breath through her nose. "Still have a plug up your butt about our last conversation at the funeral home?" Adele arched her eyebrow at the younger woman and placed her hand on her hip, challenging Elaine to new heights of aggravation.

The two rarely saw eye to eye on any topic, but it irked Elaine that Adele believed she could communicate with her aunts' spirits on an intuitive and otherworldly plane. When the hippie guru tried to share with Elaine that her aunts wanted her to connect more deeply to her imagination and let adventure back into her life, it struck a nerve.

Elaine rubbed her temple and set her purse on the counter. "Don't start with me, Adele. I am in *no* mood to hear your supposed intuitive readings or entertain the idea that you can speak with the dead. Enough. My aunts are gone. Let me grieve in peace, even if you won't let them rest in it!"

Grant stepped between the women. "Elaine, why don't you let me do the talking?"

She looked at him and then at Adele, who was now rearranging some items on a nearby shelf and keeping her back to Elaine. Her white hair reminded Elaine of her Aunt Mildred's. A sense of longing and nostalgia overcame her, flooding her heart with emotions that would soon spill out as tears if she didn't turn and walk away.

Grant gave her a nudge. The key was the reason they were here. Elaine would stay if Grant could pull the conversation back to that topic as opposed to listening again to Adele's persistent chatter of attending next month's women's circle or how Elaine should focus more of her attention on her aunts' legacy and the store. She walked toward the seating area, pulled out a magazine, and sat down in the plush leather chair, pretending to ignore the fact that Adele was her last link to her aunts.

Adele, relentless in her belief that she must give her timely message to Elaine, stopped what she was doing and looked up before she quietly remarked, "You need to heed their advice, Laney. It's not good for you to stifle your feelings and pretend you can go it alone." Adele being Adele just had to bring in the dramatics. "You are a light-worker, Elaine. Just like me ... and your aunts. Don't deny that you need to learn how to let love in so you can shine it in the darkest of shadows."

Elaine stood up and faced both Adele and Grant. She squared her shoulders before speaking. "Stop being so ... metaphysical, Adele." She closed the magazine dangling from her hand and walked over to the turquoise hutch.

"So," Adele said, "why are you here? Have you decided you want to sign up for the women's circle next week? Well, I regret to inform you that all the spots are taken. You will have to wait until next month. Serves you right for waiting too long and not listening to me when I and your aunts told you at the funeral that you must come. Although, I could make an exception if you really are ready to open to your powers."

Elaine looked at Grant and sighed. "Make her stop, please, or I'm leaving."

Adele huffed and went back to her task of clearing off another shelf to make way for her latest inventory.

Grant reached across the counter and gently placed a hand on Adele's arm. "Sorry, Delly, that's not why we're here. You're still not making any exceptions for men to attend these meetings, are you?" He smiled at her and winked. "You know I like a good old witchy gathering filled with incantations as you stir an eye of newt and a tongue of toad in your black cauldron."

"Oh, you!" Adele slapped his arm and gave him a stern look before winking back. "What brings you here then? Is your friend here wanting to give me some of her aunts' personal belongings like I requested? I would like *something* to remember them by."

Elaine crossed her arms and shifted her weight to one hip. She rolled her eyes and looked at Grant, who gave her a pleading look.

"There are a few things, yes," Elaine admitted. She uncrossed her arms and placed her hands on her low back. She blinked back tears of guilt and sorrow and searched for a focal point so she could gain her composure. Elaine knew she should look harder to find the brooch her aunts used to take turns wearing on special occasions, but honestly, their office and their bedrooms were a cluttered mess. Adele always admired that brooch, and Daphne had promised they would will it to her should anything ever happen to them. It was one of the things they said should never be sold or given away.

"I'm sure Elaine will be glad to gather some of their belongings and personally deliver them to you, but that's not why we're here." Grant was good at being diplomatic. He knew exactly how to handle awkward situations, so he took the opportunity to broach the subject of the key. "May I borrow a dusting glove, Delly? We have something to show you, and I think you're gonna love it."

Adele walked over to the counter and handed him one of the dusting gloves she used every day. Elaine took that as her cue. She moved to the counter and opened her purse pocket. Grant lifted the key out using the glove. He set it down on the counter for them all to look at it.

Adele jumped back and looked nervously around the shop. "Where did you get this?" she inquired.

Elaine told her the basics, eliminating the scene she had witnessed this morning and the professor's inquiry into the key at lunch. Adele took the other glove and picked the key up off the counter and held it close for further inspection. "This key should not be out in the open like this," she said.

"Why? What's so special about it?" Elaine asked.

Adele glanced at Elaine before looking back at Grant. "This key is one of a handful that came from Europe, from an ancient guild of apothecaries—true healers who had vast knowledge of the medicines of the earth."

"That sounds ... intriguing," Grant said. "Does the guild still exist? Are you part of it?" His fingers absently went to his amulet. "How do you know about this key and the set?" His wide eyes and crooked grin reflected excitement and curiosity.

"From Daphne and Mildred, of course. A few months ago, at one of our full-moon bath rituals, they showed me another key similar to this one. It was so beautiful and had similar markings, but there was a different colored gemstone in the middle. They told me they found it at one of the estate sales outside Nashville. You remember that one, don't you, Elaine? The one you refused to drive them to because you had other plans with that hooty-dooty boyfriend of yours? What's his name again ... Everett?"

"Eric." Elaine sighed. "And yes, I remember. They took a bus and called it their 'old-lady road trip.' " Guilt and a bittersweet memory—watching the two of them searching for their folded bus tickets in their bags—washed over Elaine. Maybe she should have taken that road trip with them. They had been so worried about her and asked her numerous times to join them for a "fun and irreverent jaunt." Elaine stood up straighter and bit the inside of her cheeks to keep the tears from flowing. "I'm allowed a life, Adele." She ended the last quip with a defiant stare and crossed her arms over her chest. She looked to Grant to help her navigate the irritating conversation that always bubbled up between the two women.

"Tell us more about the key, Adele," Grant interjected tactfully. "What caused that green glow and swirling inside the gemstone?"

"I don't know anything about a green glow. Your aunts showed me a key with a red gemstone that had golden streaks of speckled light inside it. They told me the key was one of a set of five, each of which acted as a portal to the land of its origin," Adele remarked. She looked around the store, as if anyone might be eavesdropping. No one but Elaine and Grant were there, but Elaine intuitively scanned the room as well.

"And was it?" Grant asked.

"Was it what?" Adele replied, apparently distracted.

"*Was* the key a portal?" Grant's smile was broad, and the natural light masked his silver-streaked hair, giving him a youthful countenance.

"I wouldn't doubt it, knowing those two," Adele said with a chuckle. "They told me a story about it that evening. Everyone had left the store, and they took the key out of a box and placed it right here on my counter. The gemstone seemed to radiate in the dimly lit store."

"What happened then?" Elaine asked, startled.

Adele turned to her and raised her eyebrows. "Why, nothing happened, Elaine. You know that." She didn't even bother to hide her sarcasm. "Anyway, Mildred told me that when the rightful owner of each key placed it inside the proper place and said some strange incantation repeatedly, that person could unlock powerful magic." Adele giggled and clasped her hands together. "I always loved how good of a storyteller your aunt was."

"Were you able to unlock anything that night?" Grant asked.

Adele was silent for a moment. She leaned up against the counter, closed her eyes, and rubbed her temples with her fingers. Grant and Elaine waited for a response. Adele seemed to be searching inside herself on how to answer. Finally, she said, "Well ... how could we? None of us were that key's owner. Daphne and Mildred told me that key had been missing a guardian for a generation now, and it was passed between the rest of the guild on a monthly basis. I will say, though, we did a lot of guessing on what possible magic that key had witnessed over the centuries. Right about then, we heard clattering and smashing glass in the alleyway behind this store. When we rushed outside, we saw someone running away. We couldn't tell if the person was a man or a woman, but I distinctly remember seeing sparks of light—like the ones you see on sparklers during the Fourth of July—falling from their shoulders and hitting the ground."

Elaine shook her head and scoffed. "Oh, that's rich. It's just like the three of you to behave like imaginative little girls. I have a feeling there was more than just sage that was lit that night." She mimed smoking a joint, and Grant suppressed a laugh.

"Think what you want, Elaine, but I saw everything with my own eyes," Adele snapped. "It was so strange. I was a bit frightened, but Daphne and Mildred were giddy. They said not to call the police. I disagreed, but they insisted they needed to take the key and hide it in a secret, specified location. I tried to get more information out of them, but they grabbed the key, kissed me on the cheek, and left the store before I could. And then, hours later, they were killed instantly in that car crash. Just like that," she said with a snap of her fingers.

Elaine obviously didn't want to believe Adele's far-flung story, yet she couldn't deny her experience with the key this morning or the fact that Grant had witnessed the key glowing as well.

Adele stood up straighter and turned toward Elaine. "Have you found any more keys like this one?" she asked, a hint of nervous energy behind her words.

"No," Elaine responded. "The rest of the box was full of clunky, old skeleton keys that were plain and utilitarian, not fancy and decorative like this one."

As she studied the key, Adele waved her hand. "It doesn't have to be overly decorative; it just has to have special markings and a gemstone like this one does. Your aunts cared less about fancy appearances and more about the details others overlook, you know. Do you have the box the key came in at home?"

Elaine thought for a moment. The key had fallen out of an old plastic container. Her memory lighted on the jewelry box with the lid that wouldn't open. Maybe *that* had been it? Too late to retrieve it from the secondhand store right now, though. She shook her head in response to Adele's question. "I don't, no. I'm curious if the other keys are similar to this ... um ... *unique* one." She reached to grab the key right as Adele swooped it up using her dusting glove.

"Don't touch it with your bare hands, Elaine! This key is too powerful. I'm afraid of what it will do to you."

Elaine put her hands behind her back to hide the small bandage from Adele. She didn't want to give the older woman any reason to say, "I told you so."

Adele motioned with her head for Grant to go behind the counter. He walked over, and she told him to grab one of the small plastic gift boxes she used for her customers. He took a random one and handed it to her, and she dropped the key inside. "Now, let me ask you, darlings, did you see anything else when this key was ... um ... activated earlier?"

Grant's curiosity was piqued even more. "What were we supposed to see?" He licked his lips in anticipation and then bit the bottom one.

Elaine wasn't ready to mention her personal encounter with the key, so she simply repeated what she and Grant had witnessed together. She could tell Adele was suspicious, but thankfully, she didn't push Elaine. Instead, she put the lid on the gift box and warned Elaine not to touch it or read the words on the key until she learned more about its purpose.

"What's inside the portals that these keys unlock, Adele?" Grant asked.

Adele refused to look at Grant's earnest face and again paused before continuing. "I'm not completely sure," she admitted. "They—your aunts—instructed me on some of the ceremonial aspects based on their research, but neither of them gave me a lot of specifics. And now," she paused for dramatic effect, "that other key may be lost along with my dear, sweet friends."

The three of them were quiet for a moment, none of them sure how to move on from the grief that washed over them.

"Wait a minute," Elaine said, breaking the silence. Her voice had an edge of suspicion and annoyance. "Do you think the missing key had something to do with my aunts' deaths? Did that person outside your shop have anything to do with all this? What are you not telling us, Adele?"

Adele began to fidget and stack some flyers that were spread haphazardly on the counter. "I promised your aunts I wouldn't say anything," she began. "They didn't think you were ready. I may have said too much as it is." She fussed with her hair and then spun the bracelets on her right arm before she set her other hand on the counter and tapped her well-manicured fingers on the glass section of the display case. "Well, they're gone now, so I guess it's up to me," she remarked to herself.

"Adele," Elaine started, "you're freaking me out. I swear, if you mention anything about hearing their voices from beyond or any other metaphysical talk, I'm leaving."

"No, no, they haven't talked to me since the day of their funeral," Adele said. "I can't think straight, Elaine. I will need to consult with them. Why don't you come back in a week and a half and join us for the next women's circle? I'll have a clearer answer then."

Anger instantly flashed across Elaine's face. "That's it! Let's go, Grant," she demanded. Her abrupt words cut off any form of bonding that was beginning to arise between the women. She stuck out her hand and stared Adele down with a set jaw and flared nostrils. "May I have the key back, please, Adele?"

For once, Adele complied without a fight. She handed the box to Elaine, who slid it into her purse and zipped the side pocket. Adele lightly grabbed the younger woman's wrist and spoke in a solemn tone. "Elaine, there are more keys out there. Your aunts obviously didn't want a lot of people to know, but I feel someone may be looking for this key and the red key—perhaps the whole set. Be careful, darling. You have something powerful at your disposal."

Elaine rolled her eyes and turned on her heels. "I doubt that," she mumbled as she pushed open the glass door. The chimes above the door frame jingled.

Adele looked visibly upset. She walked over to Grant and put her hand on his arm. "I'm serious, Grant. Look after her. She doesn't realize what she's gotten into. Daphne and Mildred … well, they didn't tell her enough about the business they were in."

Grant gave Adele a kiss on the cheek. "I promise, Delly. I won't let anything bad happen to her. You have my word. I just wish you two could get along like you used to when she and I were kids."

Adele patted Grant on the arm. "Me too." She sighed. "She'll come around one day. Now, go on. Go after our girl." She winked at Grant and gave him a slight nudge out the door.

CHAPTER 4

Grant had to jog across the street to catch up with Elaine. He reached out and touched her arm. She slowed her pace a bit. "Can you believe her?" she asked him. A light breeze had picked up. Elaine hefted her purse onto her shoulder and quickly zipped her jacket before shoving her hands into her pockets.

"That seemed pretty rude, Laney. Are you sure you want to leave it like that with Adele? I mean, she is the only person you have left who was connected to your aunts. I don't think she means any harm."

She snapped her head in his direction. "Don't try to change my mind, Grant! I can tolerate that woman for only so long. She's kooky, and she gives me the chills sometimes."

"I like her for exactly that reason," Grant said. He gave Elaine a charming smile, and they both laughed.

"Well, you never had to sit in on one of those strange women's circles. Tarot cards, incense, crystals, and talk of fairies and magical spirits whose energies resided inside mystical objects. I was sixteen when I went to one, and it was my *only* one. It was supposed to be my official initiation into womanhood. I couldn't believe I was sitting around with grown women who were acting like children and talking about the different energies for each chakra and how to activate their *kundalini* by opening up to their sensuality and sexuality."

Elaine shuddered and then looked at Grant. He was biting his lip and forcing back a smile. "Go ahead and laugh. You didn't have to hear about your great-aunts discussing which Tantric love positions were portals to the divine." At this comment, they both started laughing again. "For my birthday present that night, I got a rose quartz yoni stone, complete with instructions on where and how to use it."

Grant chuckled. "Do I even want to know?"

Elaine linked her arm with his. "Not even a little bit, my friend. Not even a little bit."

By the time they returned once again to the library, Mrs. Armested was asleep at the desk. They smiled at each other, and Grant picked up the food wrappers and crumpled napkins from her lunch and threw them in the trash nearby. Elaine called the nursing home and asked Mrs. A's aide, Teddy, to come and pick her up. She covered Mrs. Armested with the small, crocheted blanket draped around her wheelchair and kissed the top of her head. The rest of the afternoon, Elaine and Grant worked on separate projects in the small library.

Once Elaine had finished cataloging and stocking the pile of books Mrs. A had left unfinished, she opened her desk drawer, reached into the inner pocket of her purse, and took out the key. She made sure Grant wasn't looking before she searched online for the key's inscription, then she slipped it back into her purse. Her fingers were tingling, and that strange buzzing noise echoed in her ears again.

She didn't find anything of relevance on the internet, so she decided to catch up on the rest of her work instead. By this time, Mrs. Armested was awake and snacking on one of the chocolate bars she had pulled from her secret stash while reading one of her "smut novels," as she called them.

A little later, Teddy came in. "How's our Mrs. A today?" he asked as he rolled her away from the desk. Theodore "Teddy"

Clay was a lovable guy. He recently moved to the Midwest with his mother—an African American of Gullah Geechee origin in South Carolina—and attended Lincoln College. He worked part time at the nursing home to help cover tuition. In his early twenties, Teddy oozed coolness and a hip vibe. He styled his black hair in a flattop, complete with a fade and a design shaved on the sides and the back. He sported thick, black-framed glasses that set off his dark eyes, high cheekbones, and strong nose. A hefty man, Teddy always tucked his button-up scrub shirt into his pants, which accentuated his broad chest. Today's footwear: black high-top Converse sneakers. His accessories referenced the 1950s, but today he left some of the buttons on his shirt undone to show off his black-and-red graphic T-shirt underneath, which brought a modern vibe to his professional work uniform.

Teddy adjusted the afghan around Mrs. A's shoulders. "You're such a dear, Theodore," she said as she patted his hand. "So helpful."

Elaine agreed. "It's true, Teddy. I'm always happy to see you come in. I know my aunts appreciated it every week when you helped them bring their Bingo supplies into the nursing home."

"Good ol' Daphne and Mildred. I miss those ladies." He sighed.

"Me too," Elaine admitted.

"Did you know that they always bought the prizes for the Bingo games?" he asked. "They were usually little trinkets or baubles from the antique shop."

"No, I didn't," Elaine said. She still wasn't used to talking about her aunts in the past tense, and it felt even stranger to hear others do the same.

"I won once!" Mrs. A interjected in a loud voice. "It was a silly old skeleton key. Daphne gave it to me after I won three games in a row. Said I had the magic touch."

No way. "A key? What did you do with it, Mrs. A?" Elaine asked. She winced a little when her voice came out a few octaves higher and a tad louder than she intended it to. Their voices echoed and carried into the reading room a few feet away from the circulation desk. A few patrons looked up in annoyance. Elaine decided to break her rules and keep the conversation going, even if it meant she had to talk above a whisper. She was intrigued. The key seemed to be the motif of the day.

"Well, I didn't have it for very long. Daphne slid it in my bag after Bingo and told me to hold on to it for a little while and that she would bring me a better bauble in a few days. I put it in my desk drawer. Had it for about a week. Curious thing, that key. I could've sworn it glowed in the dark. Warm to the touch too. Theodore here told me that couldn't be. Said maybe my doctor had given me the wrong dose of my medication." Mrs. A patted him on the hand again and giggled. "I guess it's possible. Sometimes I do feel loopy."

"Oh yeah. That key. I forgot all about it," Teddy remarked. "If I remember right, you had a bout of dizzy spells that week too. I'm glad your doctor adjusted your dosage. You're doing all right now, though, aren't you, Mrs. A?"

"Oh yes, dear. I'm taking another pill for my heart, and the doctor has me on a pill for my rheumatism now. Anyway, Mildred came by a few days later and told me that the key was very personal, and Daphne shouldn't have given it to me without consulting her. So strange. Mildred was very nervous that day—all fidgety and distracted—so unlike her." Mrs. Armested's loud voice was followed by a small coughing fit and ended with a dramatic nose blow into one of the wadded-up tissues she had stuffed in her pocket.

Elaine ignored the grumbles of Syd and Tom, who were still playing their weekly chess game. "When was this?" she asked.

"What, dear?" Mrs. Armested's hearing seemed to have worsened this past year.

Elaine cleared her throat and spoke louder. "When did Aunt Mildred ask you for the key?"

"Oh, well, you don't have to shout, honey," Mrs. Armested replied as she adjusted her afghan. "It was a week or so before the car crash, if I remember right."

"Did my aunts tell you anything in particular about that key?" Elaine asked. "Did they say something about it in connection to a secret society they were involved in?"

Teddy chuckled nervously. "Secret society? You make it sound like Daphne and Mildred were part of a cloak-and-dagger operation, Elaine."

"I know. I know. I sound like a lunatic. I'll admit that. It's just that I found this key this morning and ... Well, I was wondering ..." Elaine trailed off and walked over to her desk. She took out her purse and brought out the key, disregarding Adele's earlier warning not to touch it with her bare hands. "Was it this key, Mrs. A?" Elaine opened her palm and showed them both the antique key.

Teddy leaned in and pushed up his black-framed glasses. "Where did you get that, Elaine?" he questioned. He looked around the room and then back at her.

"I found it today in my aunts' office," Elaine said as she lowered her hand so Mrs. A could see too. As Elaine stood there in front of them, a buzzing sound started to ring in her ears, and her palm felt warm. A green glow swirled around in the center of the gemstone.

"Do you see that?" Elaine asked. "Do either of you hear a ringing sound as well?" She spoke even louder this time, trying to drown out the buzzing noise, which sounded like a blender.

A few patrons sitting nearby shushed her. A redheaded woman stood up and walked toward the magazine rack closer to Elaine, Teddy, and Mrs. A. Elaine caught a glimpse of her and noticed the woman was wearing a green silk scarf with a gold brooch secured to it. The woman pressed her hand over her brooch and shot Elaine a concerned look before selecting a magazine and returning to her seat. Curious, Elaine took a step toward the woman in the reading room. A dizziness overtook her, and her vision became blurry. She felt unstable on her feet and stumbled a bit. Despite the bandage that covered her hand, the key felt really hot. The key suddenly slipped from her grasp and clanked onto the hardwood floor. She felt faint as she glimpsed Grant running toward her.

"Are you all right, Elaine?" Teddy asked as he took her arm and walked her to one of the cushioned seats along the wall.

Grant was by her side now. "She's fine, Teddy. I think she ate a bad batch of onion rings at the diner this afternoon. My stomach has been a little woozy this afternoon as well."

"Let's let Elaine answer for herself, please, Grant. I wouldn't feel right leaving her here like this if I didn't know she was going to be okay."

They both turned to Elaine, who looked up at them, smiled, and nodded. "I'm okay, Teddy. I think Grant's right. Sometimes those onion rings are a little too greasy and salty for me, but I eat them anyway." She hoped she had come across as casual and unconcerned. Inside, she worried she made a big mistake showing the key to them.

She then realized it wasn't in her hands anymore.

She glanced around, trying not to draw attention to herself. The woman wearing the brooch was no longer in the reading room. Elaine scanned the floor and felt relieved when she saw the key at Grant's foot. She looked at Grant and pointed to the key with her eyes.

He slid his foot over the key. "I'll make sure she gets home all right," Grant said as he bent down and put the key in his pocket. "You two go on back to the nursing home, and we'll see you tomorrow bright and early."

Teddy looked at Elaine. "Are you sure you're all right?" he asked. One of his thick eyebrows peered over the top of his glasses as he bent his head toward her.

"I'm fine, Teddy. Really I am. Grant's right—it's the diner food. I love it, but sometimes it doesn't love me."

He nodded, but he still looked uncertain. "Okay, you two. We'll be back tomorrow." He turned to Mrs. Armested. "Let's get you home, Mrs. A, so you can have the primo dining table. Tonight's dinner features your favorite: homemade mac and cheese."

Grant ushered Teddy and Mrs. A out the door and walked back to Elaine. She was still sitting on the bench and staring at the ceiling. She felt incredibly woozy. She tapped her toes and then her heels repeatedly on the floor, an old trick she used to do as a child whenever she was feeling anxious.

Grant sat down next to her. "Elaine, why did you show them that key? You heard Adele. It's powerful and needs to be protected. Even that stranger, the professor, was interested in it. You need to be smarter with this thing. We don't know too much about it, but we've already seen it has some type of magical properties."

"I honestly don't know what I was thinking! But it's not magical, Grant. I just got light-headed, that's all. Can I have it back, please?" She stretched her hand out to him.

"You're not taking this thing seriously," he said. "I really think you need to investigate this key and why your aunts had it. Maybe you were right back at Adele's? Maybe their deaths weren't an accident after all? Maybe it had something to do with this key?"

"It's just absurd." Elaine huffed. "There's no such thing as magic, and my aunts certainly weren't dangerous liaisons for some secret society. Now, may I have the key back?"

Right at that moment, the redheaded woman walked past them. In addition to the silk neck scarf with the gold brooch, she wore an emerald green satin blouse with ruffles and high-waisted, tight black pants that accentuated her tall stature and lithe frame. To complete the look, she wore sleek black boots. She could have been a runway model, and yet there was a hint of frivolity in the way she carried herself that made one think of a 1920s flapper.

Grant's attention wavered from Elaine as he watched this beautiful stranger glide by. The woman placed her hand on her shoulder and pretended to adjust her scarf and then swung her black leather jacket around her shoulders. Elaine had enough time to steal a glimpse of the intriguing brooch. It was circular and looked like two crescent moons on each side. Her eyes followed the woman to the door. The woman turned and looked back, as if she were checking to make sure no one was following her. Just at that moment, she pushed the door open, and a flash of golden light ricocheted off the glass.

Then, she was gone.

CHAPTER 5

Elaine looked at Grant, who appeared mesmerized. He stood up and walked toward the library entrance. "Where did she go?" he asked quietly. He opened the door and peered out. There must've been no one in sight because he came right back inside, looking distracted. *He is intrigued*, Elaine thought to herself.

She knew Grant's dating life was nearly nonexistent. He mentioned he'd been on a few blind dates in the past year, but those never went past dinner and a movie or a walk around the park. He had been taking on a lot of jobs and side projects lately, and Elaine wondered if that was a way for him to stave off his heartbreak over his sickly mother. Perhaps he was keeping so busy to avoid thinking about himself or his needs. Yet, in the short time it took the mysterious redheaded woman to walk past him and out the door, Elaine noticed some spark had ignited in Grant, and he appeared baffled by it all.

"Grant. Grant? Are you listening to me?" Elaine asked, but her words fell on deaf ears. "Hey! Can I have my key back?"

"What? Oh, sure ...," he said, still in a daze. He had all but forgotten about her fainting spell and seemed to have lost interest in trying to persuade her to take the odd events of the day more seriously. He pulled the key out of his pocket and secured it in his handkerchief before handing it back.

"A little lovestruck, are you? At least you're not going to keep going on about the key," chided Elaine as she took the key from him. Her teasing tone had a bite to it, though she wasn't sure where it had come from.

Her words seemed to have embarrassed him because he quickly pulled back into the moment. He shot her a concerned look. "I was just saying there is more to life than what we can see and make sense of. You know we've seen and heard some strange stuff today that we can't explain. Promise me you'll at least look into the key. Maybe tomorrow we can go visit the professor at the museum?"

"Maybe," she conceded. "I have a lot to do tomorrow, and I still have to clean out my aunts' office." She stood up and walked to her desk to grab her things.

"Elaine, we both know you could do this job with your eyes closed. God knows Mrs. A does. Let's just take off tomorrow and go see what the professor has to say. It may all lead to a dead end, or all of these events may just be coincidental or have some easy, scientific explanation behind them, but at least you'll have more answers and can put everything behind you once and for all."

Elaine knew Grant. He would hound her until she relented. "Fine," she agreed as she put the key away and slid her purse into a drawer. "One meeting, but that's all I am going to do. I want my life back to normal again. I want to move on."

"It won't be a waste of time. I promise," he said. "Besides, it will do both of us good to get out of our routines for a while. I know *I* could use an escape." With that, he turned and walked toward the media room.

Elaine couldn't help but notice his shoulders were slouched and his gait had a slower rhythm than usual. It was quite obvious to her that Grant had been feeling blue lately. She had been too busy worrying about her own life's trajectory to pick up her head and see that someone as strong as Grant was overwhelmed by all this adulting too. In a burst of compassion, she called out after him,

"Pep up, friend! Who knows? Maybe the redhead will be back soon."

He waved his hand in the air and kept on walking.

**

For the next few hours, Elaine focused her attention on shelving books, setting up a new display in the lobby, and vacuuming the reading room area. Grant had left a few minutes before closing time and uttered a moody goodbye to Elaine and a few local patrons sitting in cushioned chairs. Elaine watched him leave and wondered if she should invite him out with her and Eric to help take his mind off things.

Maybe he just needs some time to himself? she thought. They both tended to be introverts, especially when they had a lot on their minds. "He'll come around," she muttered while she walked around the library, locking doors and turning off lights in unoccupied sections.

Once the last patron had left, Elaine closed the library and headed toward her car. She got inside and quickly turned on the heater. As she waited for it to warm up, she picked up the phone to call Eric. He had responded earlier that he couldn't make it for drinks; he rarely could nowadays. After the fourth ring, the call went to voicemail, so she hung up. She always seemed to leave rambling messages anyway. Next, she texted James, the part-time assistant librarian, asking him to cover for her tomorrow, then tossed her phone inside her purse and put the car in gear.

For the majority of the drive to her aunts' home, Elaine worried about her relationship with Eric. She worried he might be on the verge of breaking up with her. He broke their dinner date a few weeks ago and cut their other dates short these past few months. Still, he was busy trying to get his investment firm the type of recognition it deserved. He had a lot on his plate and was really dedicated to making a name for himself through his career as opposed to his family's name, although that didn't hurt. "Ambitious" was the word her aunts used to describe Eric and not always in a good way either. Daphne would complain that he never really listened to their stories while he waited for Elaine to get ready. Mildred said he was always anxious to take Elaine out to big, fancy dinners as his arm candy instead of arranging their dates around activities Elaine enjoyed, like hiking and watching film noir movies from the 1940s.

The classic text message sound chimed from inside her bag as she rounded the corner entrance into the neighborhood. The urge to read the text was strong, but she stayed focused on her driving. She'd always been a careful driver, but ever since her aunts' death, she was taking extra precautions. As she approached the house, she recognized the late 1990s maroon Buick Skylark sedan parked in the driveway. It belonged to Mr. Sadler, her aunts' accountant. She pulled into the driveway and put the car in park. "What does he want now?" she muttered to herself and turned off the ignition.

She remembered the letter from his office that she had tossed aside this morning. He had told her at the funeral home that it was imperative she discuss with him the lien on her aunts' antique shop and the lack of funds they had to buy it back from the bank. Elaine was not one to dismiss such urgent matters, but her aunts' deaths overwhelmed her. Today, the key had consumed her, and she forgot all about Mr. Sadler's three voicemails urging her to contact him.

"Maybe that was him who texted a few minutes ago," she wondered out loud. She fished out her phone, quickly read a text from James and then one from Grant, who reminded her to stay open to the idea of going to see Professor Wallace. He ended with a brief apology for his dismissive behavior earlier.

Elaine shoved the phone into her purse and got out of the car. She could feel the day's stressors mounting on her. Her shoulders were tense, her neck felt stiff, and her breath was shallow. It took all her energy to push back the tears welling up in her eyes. Lately, it felt like she was dealing with too much. She could handle her dating issues, and if she tried hard enough, she could live with the loss of her aunts. But knowing she had some sort of supernatural key on her hands, plus the fact that the antique shop was going under, made her want to slide back in her car, drive out of town, and leave her whole life behind. She could drive until she ran out of gas and then call a taxi and keep going. But where to? St. Louis? Kansas City? Somewhere farther west? It would be nice to leave all her problems behind and start again somewhere else. She knew it was a crazy idea. Then again, her entire life felt pretty crazy right now. If only she could ask Daphne and Mildred what she should do. That would give her some relief. Then the realization of their deaths landed in the pit of her stomach and reminded her once again that they were gone and not coming back.

She wiped away a tear at the corner of her eye. It was no use giving in to her grief. That certainly wouldn't help her. "You can do this," she told herself and stood up straight, willing herself to face this next problem head-on.

Mr. Sadler opened his door and scooted out of the driver's seat. He was a short, robust man with greasy black hair that was swirled on the top of his head to cover his bald spot. Elaine had never seen him in anything other than baggy and wrinkled tan suits that enhanced his girth. Today, he wore baggy khaki pants, a powder-blue dress shirt, and a short brown-and-gold tie held in place by an etched brass tie clip.

"Hello, Elaine." He huffed as he patted his forehead with a handkerchief. The exertion of dragging his briefcase across the passenger seat and out the door with him proved to be too much, so he leaned up against his car and took a breath.

"Mr. Sadler, what a surprise! What brings you here?" Elaine said in her most casual tone possible.

"Don't pretend you haven't been ignoring my communications, Elaine. We both know better than that." He shifted his weight and pushed himself off the car, his briefcase throwing him slightly off balance.

Elaine couldn't help but notice the dark sweat stains under his armpits even though the fall breeze brought a chill to the air. "You're right. I'm sorry," she admonished. "Would you like to come inside? I can fix us some tea."

He nodded and pushed past her, making his way to the front door. He opened the screen door for her while she unlocked the dead bolt, but that was the only common courtesy he was willing to attempt. The sweat had beaded up on his temples, and there was a deep crease on his forehead. This was not going to be an easy or pleasant meeting.

She walked them toward the kitchen and gestured to him to have a seat while she filled the kettle with water. She could hear him rifling through his briefcase while she busied herself setting out the mugs and opening a new package of mint tea.

"Your aunts were nice ladies, Elaine, but I'm afraid they weren't the most astute with business matters," he began. He cleared his throat and spread the documents on the table.

Elaine switched on the burner and turned to face him. "I appreciate your directness, Mr. Sadler, but my aunts managed quite well for as long as I knew them. It seems that their business matters only got more complicated once you talked them into refinancing their loan and mortgage." She sat down across from him and glanced at the paperwork. "What's all this?"

"Well, Elaine, that's what I've come here for," he said, clearing his throat again. He took out his handkerchief and wiped his brow once more before placing the cloth back into his pocket. "I will need your signature on these documents so I can file them with the Internal Revenue Service."

"Wait a minute," she said, standing up and beginning to pace. "You're telling me the IRS is involved in all this now? I thought this ordeal was just with the bank. How is this possible?"

Mr. Sadler pushed his chair back and stood up to meet her glare. "That's what I've been trying to discuss with you, Elaine. You see, your aunts didn't only refinance their first loan, but they took out a second mortgage and failed to pay property taxes on that. I was going through their tax records and noticed the inconsistencies there. They owe some back taxes, and if you don't pay those, plus pay off the debt they owe the bank, then you will have to sell off the store, all its contents, and possibly even this house in order to pay everything off and get the government and the bank off your back."

"Sell the property?" Elaine's voice cracked. This was a nightmare. "There has to be a different way ... They didn't tell me ... This is all too much to take in." Tears welled up in her eyes, and she clasped the back of her chair to steady herself. The kettle began to whistle. It sounded as though it were about to blow along with her head.

Mr. Sadler fumbled for the right words. "I-I-I'm sorry to be the bearer of such bad news. Why don't you take the rest of this evening to look through everything and call me tomorrow so we can begin filing the paperwork. Judy, my secretary, will reach out to me if I'm out of the office."

The kettle whistle drowned out his attempt at sympathy. Elaine turned off the stovetop and moved the kettle to a different burner. "Yes, of course," she stammered, barely able to get the words out of her mouth. "I'll contact you tomorrow." She watched him latch up his briefcase and then followed him to the front door.

"We'll get this resolved, Elaine," he muttered as he pushed the screen door open with his elbow. "It's urgent that you get the completed forms to me by the end of the week so we can put all of this behind us." He nodded his head and stepped onto the front porch and shuffled back to his car without saying goodbye.

Elaine watched Mr. Sadler back out of the driveway. Unable to move, she stared at nothing in particular as he drove away. Wariness drifted over her and settled in her chest. She pulled in deep breaths, and her chest felt tight with each exhale. She clenched her jaw to force back the tears that were on the verge of spilling out. A little sob escaped, and she made herself cough in order to remain in control. A breeze stirred and rustled the maple tree, causing a few orange and gold leaves to fall in front of the house. The early evening was crisp and chilly, a sign that a cold front was coming. She took one last glance at the large, lush front yard, with its mature trees and gravel-lined driveway, and then made her way back inside.

She placed her hand on the doorframe, with its cracking white paint that highlighted the cherry red door her aunts repainted last year. She pressed the heavy door open with her shoulder and hip and stepped inside. Her eyes adjusted to the dim light, and she took inventory of her childhood home. Her aunts had been the ones who nurtured her and helped her adapt after losing her parents. Life was never dull with them. A moment of regret surged through her.

"Oh, Aunt Millie and Aunt Daph, did I ever tell you both how much I loved and appreciated you?" she asked the empty faux-leather recliners that faced the wide-screen TV. Mildred's TV tray with a deck of cards fanned out in a game of solitaire sat near her old recliner. Daphne's lime green and yellow afghan appeared on the back of her recliner like a shedded snakeskin. "No, I didn't," she said out loud. "I've been too caught up in trying to prove I was independent and needing to make my mark on this world."

Elaine passed through the living room, unwilling to linger too much on this revelation, and made her way to the kitchen. She stared down at the manila folder Mr. Sadler had left behind. "What am I going to do?" she said as she sorted through the paperwork.

Eventually, she shoved the papers back into the folder. She paused a moment, then picked up her purse and pulled out her phone and the professor's business card. She flipped the card over once ... twice, then steeled herself and started dialing. He picked up on the third ring.

"Professor Wallace?" Elaine asked. "This is Elaine Colemar. We met today at the diner. I hope I haven't disturbed you this evening?"

"Elaine! What a delightful surprise! What can I do for you, my dear?" The professor barely hid his enthusiasm upon hearing her voice.

"It's about that key I showed you today. I was wondering if you might like to purchase it for your museum?"

There was a brief moment of silence before the professor spoke. "Are you sure that's what you want, Elaine?"

"I'm positive," she replied. She picked up the folder Mr. Sadler had given her and felt the weight of it in her hand. "If it is really as valuable as you think it is, maybe its rightful place is at the museum for others to see." She tried to suppress the anxiety and doubt that bubbled up inside her as she spoke. The antique store and this very home were at stake. Elaine's pragmatism took precedence over her sentimentality, so she pushed forward. "I was going to come see you at the museum tomorrow anyway, so you can take a look at the key and get a better sense of what I have, if you'd like?"

Professor Wallace cleared his voice. "Yes, yes, that would be great. Let's say around eleven o'clock tomorrow morning? I don't teach until three o'clock, which would give us some time to properly meet and discuss your artifact." His words sounded rushed, like he was late for another meeting, so Elaine agreed to the time and they said their goodbyes.

Elaine scrolled through her texts, pulling up the thread in which James had agreed to cover her shift depending on the timing. She let him know what hours she needed him and was relieved when he immediately responded that it wouldn't be a problem. *Phew*, she thought. The idea of leaving Mrs. Armested alone to run the library made her nervous. Sure, Mrs. A would be able to check out books and movies to the patrons, but she definitely wouldn't be able to answer any of the technological questions or run the computer system. Anxiety had Elaine wondering if she should call the professor back and reschedule for a time when the library was closed.

She started dialing her phone, then decided to text Grant instead. "He'll know what to do," she said as she clicked the send button. She paced around the kitchen, waiting for his response. She rummaged through the cabinet and found a box of stale chocolate chip cookies and half a bag of crushed potato chips. She pushed them aside and found the bread and extra-chunky peanut butter. Her stomach growled, so she set about making peanut butter toast, her go-to snack whenever she had a food craving.

Right as the golden toast popped up, Elaine heard the distinct tone of her text notifications.

Everyone will survive without you for a few hours. I'll drive us. See you at the library. 10:30 a.m. work?

Grant signed off with a winking emoji and a thumbs-up. It was just like Grant to assume he was part of the adventure.

Okay. Sounds good.

She picked up her plate with the heavily smeared toast and walked into the living room to watch a little TV and wind down from the day's events. She grabbed the remote and propped her feet up on the coffee table as she leaned back into the overstuffed chair, ready to "zone out," as Daphne and Mildred used to say whenever they watched a beloved Cubs game or soap opera.

As she searched for a lighthearted sitcom or funny romantic comedy, she heard a noise at the front door. She felt a jolt of nerves contract in her low back, and her shoulders tensed. A clatter echoed from outside. Elaine jumped up, grabbed her phone, and ran to the window. She took a breath and opened the curtain ever so slightly. Once her eyes adjusted to the low light of the evening, she saw the metal lid of the trash can rolling around and coming to a stop on the concrete driveway. The trash can itself was turned on its side. She exhaled in relief. "Stupid raccoons."

She was preparing to go outside when out of the corner of her eye, she saw a shadow move behind the maple tree. Seconds later, a bright orange glow radiated from behind the tree trunk. The glowing light faded until there was nothing left but wiry sparks of electricity and flame that fizzled and disappeared as they dropped to the ground.

She rushed to the closet, grabbed her jacket, and threw it on. She shoved her phone into the deep pocket and unlocked the front door. It was jammed again, and she had to push and pull until she had enough momentum to crack it open. She pushed her way outside and jumped off the low porch into the front yard. When she reached the tall maple tree, she saw no signs of the sparks, the glow, or even footprints indicating someone or something had been there a moment before. Elaine rubbed her eyes and did a double take.

Again, nothing was there.

"Could my mind be playing tricks on me?" she asked herself as she leaned up against the tree and rested the back of her head on the gray, ridged bark.

Despite the chilly evening air, she was sweating even though her heart was no longer racing. She pulled her jacket closer to her like a security blanket and decided she was just paranoid after this morning's experience and the crazy ideas Adele had put into her head. She moved away from the tree to make her way inside and suddenly felt a sharp pain on the back of her head.

"Ow!" she exclaimed and put her hand to her scalp. She turned to look at the culprit: a small section of her hair had gotten caught on the rugged bark. As she ran her fingers across the knob, she noticed a faint and rudimentary carving to the right of it.

"What's this?" she asked herself and traced it with her pointer finger.

The design was of two crescent moons on each side of a circle.

It was clear that the carving had been there for some time. A feeling of déjà vu fluttered through her. "I didn't do this ... so who did?" Elaine asked the tree, but it wasn't revealing any secrets.

CHAPTER 6

Late the next morning, Elaine and Grant parked in the visitor's lot at Lincoln College. The morning rain had passed, and the sun peaked out from behind heavy clouds, promising a pleasant afternoon. They walked through the small quad, both of them silent and reserved. Elaine's heels thudded on the concrete pathway, each step a reverberation of determination and resolve.

The history museum, located near the Humanities building, blended in with the other brick buildings in the Georgian architectural style. The portico was supported by four white pillars and offset the glass entrance that had been installed sometime in the mid-1970s. The automatic door swooshed open, and they were met with a burst of cold coming from the air-conditioned vents. The main lobby was empty of visitors. At the reception desk, a young Asian woman with long black hair and white wires cascading down from her earbuds glanced up at them before returning to whatever social media site streamed across her phone screen and reflected in her trendy, large glasses.

"Hi, we're here to see Professor Wallace," Elaine said.

Without raising her head, the woman pulled up a clipboard and set it on the counter while texting with her other hand.

"We have an appointment," Elaine continued. "Could you tell us where his office is?"

"Third floor, to the right when you exit the elevator," the receptionist said as she pulled her phone to eye level and danced her thumbs across the keypad.

"Don't you need to know our names to let him know we're here or at least call his office to tell him we're on our way?" Grant asked, befuddled.

She finally looked at them and smiled. "No, it's all good. Just go ahead and sign in."

With no further explanation, they signed their names and walked toward the elevator. Display cases filled with small relics and information cards lined the wall to the entrance of the first-floor exhibit. Elaine and Grant paid little attention to the items as they approached the elevator and pushed the call button. In a nearby display case hung a yellowed piece of parchment paper with beautiful handwriting dashed across it. Elaine couldn't make out what all the words said, but the title looked as if it was written in Latin. She made out the phrase *Inlustris et luna trabem* in a flourish script. Elaine had minored in Spanish, so she knew *luna* meant "moon."

"What does the rest mean?" she asked herself, walking toward the case.

Just then, the bell pinged, and the elevator door opened. "Elaine, are you coming?" Grant asked as he stepped inside.

"What?" She turned toward Grant, who was holding the door open for her.

He laughed. "We're meeting with the professor, remember? Not touring the museum."

"Right," she said. She took one last glance at the paper. "Strange." She recalled the image of the crescent moons etched on the maple tree. *Wasn't there a marking on Professor Wallace's business cards? And wasn't the mysterious woman at the library yesterday wearing a moon brooch?* She rolled these images over in her mind, trying to make a connection to what seemed like odd coincidences.

"Did you see something?" Grant asked as he pushed the button for the third floor.

"What? No. It was nothing," she lied and leaned up against the back wall and stared at the keypad.

They exited the elevator and turned right like the receptionist had told them. The large windows at both ends of the hallway allowed natural light to stream in, and a few of the overhead fluorescent lights flickered. Their shoes squeaked across the freshly cleaned white-tile floors. They passed old classrooms that now acted as storage units. Elaine peered inside one of the door's small glass windows and saw stacks of chairs, folded tables, rolled banners, and signs. Large white cloths were draped over unknown items of various shapes and sizes.

Grant walked up behind her and peered in as well. "Huh. I guess this is one of the storage rooms for all the museum's fancy fundraising events."

"Yeah, I've hung up some of their flyers in the library over the years. I suppose this is where the 'magic' begins, huh?" She playfully elbowed Grant in the rib cage, then turned and started walking down the hallway.

"You know," she said to Grant as he stepped quickly to catch up, "maybe one day Eric will take me to one of those? He's always saying we should attend more community events. Think of all the potential clients he could add to his investment firm." She glanced over at Grant, whose face held a scowl. "Oh, c'mon. You're not going to start on your diatribe about snobby rich people, are you?"

"I hate those kinds of things," Grant remarked. "Grown-ass men and women getting dressed up like it's prom all over again. And they act so fake while trying to impress one another on who has the most money, but they can't come right out and say it, so they talk about all their newly acquired possessions and their exotic vacations. It's annoying."

"Okay, Grant. It's not high school anymore. You need to get over your hang-ups about stuff like that. These rich people are just like you and me. They just have nicer stuff, that's all."

"Easier for you to say seeing how you have a rich boyfriend to count on," he muttered.

Elaine stopped midstride and turned to face him. "Seriously? That's a low blow, Grant. Eric is a great guy. So what if he's ambitious and likes to spend his money on things? He's earned it." She paused. "Okay, maybe he hasn't *earned* it as much as *inherited* the business from his father, but still, he's an honest guy, and it's not his fault that he was born into wealth."

Grant shrugged. "You're right. I'm sorry. Let's drop it before this turns into a fight."

The two of them hadn't always seen eye to eye over the topic of wealthy people. Elaine had always wanted to be more like them in hopes of fitting in with the "it" crowd at school, many of whom came from the wealthier families in town. It was part of the reason she let Eric buy her so many things instead of asking for more romance and intimacy. She wasn't proud of that side of herself, especially since Daphne and Mildred had raised her to be not so materialistic and to be kind to others. They were adamant she learn the value of money at an early age and paid her an allowance for doing chores around the house and running errands for the antique store when she got her driver's license. Kindness, too, they explained was not a weakness but a strength. They demonstrated that to Elaine on a regular basis by treating customers fairly and helping others who were down on their luck.

Grant would never admit it, but a lot of the popular students grew up to be fairly down-to-earth people. They had never rubbed anyone's nose in the fact that their parents could buy them the latest trendy clothing and material goods, nor did they now that they could do the same for their children. Years of being in their homes and observing their family dynamics while he built customized shelving and repaired their appliances had taught him that. Still, he had difficulties acknowledging his peers' entitled lifestyles simply because, as teens, they appeared more carefree, whereas Grant had to struggle to help his mother keep food on the table and had to go without a lot of things. He even had to wear raggedy, used clothing his mother had purchased from secondhand stores or charity organizations. Even now, he struggled to afford her care at the nursing home. Money—or, in Grant's case, the lack thereof—always seemed to be the one barrier he used as his excuse to separate himself from them and view their lives in a better light than his own.

They walked a few more paces in silence before reaching the last door at the end of the hallway. A nameplate on the wall read "Prof. Edmund Wallace, PhD., Museum Director and Senior History Professor. Lincoln College Alum." Elaine knocked on the honey-colored door with the classic rectangular window so commonly seen in older buildings. They heard the professor's muffled voice, but they couldn't quite make out the words, which sounded gruff and strained.

"Sounds like he's on the phone," Grant whispered.

Elaine nodded. "You're right. And it doesn't seem like it's a pleasant conversation. Should we wait here or what? I saw a bench a little ways back."

"No, that would be weird to knock and walk away. Let's just wait." Grant crossed his arms and leaned his back against the wall across from the professor's door.

Elaine perused the bulletin board next to the office. Old pamphlets from past fundraisers and museum exhibitions littered one half of the board while the current fall syllabus and course description, torn and curling, hung haphazardly with multi-colored push pins on the other. The course was simply titled Early European History. The description was brief and mentioned some major events spanning from the Renaissance to the Enlightenment. Although Elaine's major from the state university two hours away was in English, she had a love for history and often wondered if she would have enjoyed taking more history courses when she was a student. Maybe she would have even continued her travels and toured more of Europe, studying at Trinity College in Dublin, touring old historical sites in southern France, or dancing with Roma in exotic places like Budapest. "It doesn't matter now," she sighed. "I'm stuck in this town as just the librarian. Surrounded by curmudgeons and an old lady with dementia."

"Hey now, don't talk about Mrs. A like that," Grant commented. He was standing behind Elaine, staring at the old pamphlets as well.

Startled, Elaine turned and whacked Grant on his upper arm with the back of her hand. "Don't sneak up on me like that!"

"Sorry." Grant chuckled. "And for the record, I'm not a curmudgeon."

Elaine sheepishly looked at him. "I didn't mean ... It's just I ... Well ...." She was at a loss for words. She realized she had inadvertently hurt his feelings, but she also didn't mean for him to hear her worries or complaints either.

"I know. But you're more than *just* a librarian, Elaine. You really need to go easier on yourself. People love you, and you're doing good things for this town. Who else would have arranged the monthly speaker's series of storytellers, authors, and activists or teach a course on technology to teenagers for college credit? Not many people I know."

"Well, those programs were needed. It seemed easy enough to get them started, but I doubt they're all that effective. Attendance at those things has been at an all-time low. I just feel I could be doing something more with my life, you know? I just feel like I haven't found my purpose yet." A lump caught in her throat, and she coughed to push down a sensation of shame and embarrassment.

"Hmm ... Well, if you're failing at life, then I'm screwed," he replied.

"You know what I mean," she said.

"Yeah, I do. You're supposed to be off galivanting around the world, making a difference, and being recognized for your many accomplishments while the rest of us walk blindly through life settling for mediocrity." He moved away from her toward the professor's door. Impulsively, he knocked.

"What are you doing?" she exclaimed. "I thought we were going to wait!"

The professor bluntly called out, "In a minute!" He uttered a few sharp words to whomever he was currently speaking, then there was silence. Clearly the phone conversation was over. Paper rustled, and the professor's shoes thudded across the room. They backed away from the door just as he opened it. His face transformed from a scowl to surprise before he worked it back to its pleasant and stately gentleman's posture.

The professor nodded his head in their direction. "Elaine, Grant, so good to see you," he said, clearing his throat. He turned and looked at the contents of his office, clearly searching for something before he turned back to face them. He raised one eyebrow, as if deciding what to do next.

"Sorry to disturb you, Professor Wallace. The receptionist told us to come right up. I know we had planned to meet, but is this a bad time?" Elaine hedged her words and immediately regretted it. He was the one who insisted on today's appointment in his office. She was doing him a favor trying to accommodate *his* schedule.

Grant stepped forward. "Good morning, Professor Wallace." He extended his hand, and the professor shook it without the same warmth and vivacity as when they had first met. The professor's hand trembled ever so slightly before he slid his fingers into his pocket.

"Yes, yes. Do come in, please," he said. His voice seemed constricted, and he cleared his throat again. He peered into the hallway, scanning from one end of the corridor to the other. Satisfied, he closed the door behind them.

The three of them crowded between two floor-to-ceiling bookcases on either side of the door. Trinkets and photos lined the shelves, and wrinkled papers with hand-scrawled notes were tucked between many of the spines of the old books. A tall window at the end of the office allowed in natural light that illuminated the shiny and dark wood floor. Two overstuffed leather chairs butted up against each other and faced a wide mahogany desk filled with more books and papers nearly ready to topple over; a small computer screen sat in the center of it all.

"Please, sit," the professor said as he walked behind his desk. He reached over and covered some type of brooch or necklace medallion before sliding it down by his side. As he took his seat, he stared at Elaine. "Just a little trinket I was trying to authenticate for the exhibit next month," he said. "Nothing of importance, really." He then slid open a drawer and placed whatever he had in his hand inside. He pushed the drawer shut and shuffled a stack of papers off to the side.

"Now then," the professor began, "I hope it wasn't too much trouble for you both this morning? This place is a bit hectic this time of year. Students cram every corner of campus, trying to find a place to study or distract themselves for as long as possible."

"No, it was fine," Grant said. "Listen, Professor, I don't mean to be rude, but I couldn't help but notice what you slid into your drawer. Was that an art nouveau piece? That's one of my favorite eras, along with arts and crafts followed by art deco, of course. I've been working on some small wood carvings to add to some handcrafted furniture in my spare time, and I'm trying to really capture those sinewy lines that are so elegant from the early 1900s. Would you mind showing me that piece? I'd love to take a quick look at it."

Professor Wallace waved his hand in a dismissive gesture. "I'm sure your carvings are lovely, Grant, but I'm afraid I can't let others handle it. It's far too, er, delicate." He turned and faced Elaine. "I've been doing some thinking about that key of yours."

Momentarily dejected, Grant bounced back at the mention of the key. "What have you found out? Is it worth anything?"

"That's what we're here to discuss, my good man." The professor turned his glance back toward Elaine.

"Oh, right. That's my cue," she said with an uncharacteristic attempt at humor. She picked up her purse and fished out the small case with the key inside. She hesitated before opening it. She glanced over at Grant, whose lips were pursed together and eyebrows raised in nervous anticipation. The only way to know if the key was glowing was to lift the lid. When she opened it, a sigh of relief escaped her, and Grant's face softened.

"Would you look at that?" Grant said as he smiled at Elaine. "It's normal."

Elaine shot Grant a look to stop him from going farther.

"It's far from normal, my dear young man," Professor Wallace said as he extended an open palm to Elaine. "May I?"

She looked at Grant, who nodded, before she passed the box into the professor's waiting hand. He took the box and set it down in front of him. He found a pair of wire-rimmed glasses near his computer screen and put them on to examine the key more closely.

"This is beautiful," he began. "And many would argue this is of no consequence, but they would be wrong. As I suspected, the key appears to be from the early to mid-1800s and comes from Europe, more than likely somewhere in Germany or France. Starting in the Middle Ages, craftsmen and artisans of a particular trade created guilds to teach and pass on their crafts, and to ensure employment and protect members in trade ventures. These guilds— these 'brotherhoods,' if you will—not only taught the mysteries and secrets of the trade, but also initiated their members in rites and rituals with secret handshakes, sworn oaths, and moral and ethical codes of conduct. The master craftsmen would present symbolic and ritualistic gifts to the initiates, such as embroidered sashes, hand-carved walking sticks, or stone-encrusted ceremonial necklaces after they passed a series of tests or rites."

The professor set the box down on his desk, stood up, and walked over to one of his bookcases. He scanned a few shelves before pulling out a weighty book and flipping the pages until he came across a specific page. "Ah, yes, here it is," he said, tapping his pointer finger on the page before placing the opened book on his desk. He turned it so it faced Grant and Elaine. "The Freemasons are the most well-known and talked about guild in modern society. Yet, there are many guilds that lasted past the Industrial Revolution, such as the Order of the Free Gardeners and the Odd Fellows.

Some guilds and journeyman groups, like the French Compagnons, supported other trades of carpenters, butchers, barbers, and even cooks. And there was a little-known guild that seems to have gone by the wayside—the Apothecary Guild." He nodded toward the book's open pages.

"Hey!" Grant exclaimed. "That photo looks a lot like your key, Elaine!"

Elaine leaned forward and looked at the photo. It was in black and white, but the object did have a lot of the same features with a gemstone in the middle and small etchings along one side. "Are you saying my key is one of those symbolic gifts you mentioned, Professor Wallace?" she asked.

He smiled and then sat down again behind his desk. "It is. This one in the book is from the Apothecary Guild's headquarters in southern Spain. It was an honorary key given to top members. I will need to do a bit more research, but it seems your key is worth quite a bit of money. I think you'll be pleased to know that the museum is going to be putting together a display about the Industrial Revolution in Europe and the European migration to the United States in the mid-1800s. I think a key like yours would make a nice little commentary on the various trades and services provided around that time frame."

"How would I go about selling it?" Elaine asked. Her cheeks blushed because she was all too aware of the blunt question.

Professor Wallace smiled and nodded. "I'm glad you broached the subject of money, Elaine. It's never easy to talk about financials when discussing the historical and sentimental value of a piece. I would need to get the board's approval and do a little more research to verify my claim, but I'm sure I could have the museum cut you a check by early next week."

"How much are we talking?" Elaine bit her lip and then inhaled deeply. She was hoping the sum would be enough to cover the costs Mr. Sadler brought to her attention yesterday.

The professor picked up his pen and scrawled a figure on a notepad. He slid it across the desk. "That's an approximation."

Elaine leaned forward to get a closer look.

Grant couldn't help himself and glanced at the figure as well before he let out a low whistle. "That's a lot of greenbacks," he said, touching Elaine's shoulder. "I know it was my idea to come here, but are you sure you should sell it just like that? It's not like you to be so rash." His gaze went to the plastic case containing the key and then back to her, almost like he was willing her to remember their bizarre, shared experiences with the key yesterday.

She suddenly felt uneasy about the whole idea. She looked at Grant, whose face reflected a look of concern as well, then back at the key. Although she knew this sum of money would save the antique store, Professor Wallace's eagerness to have the key in his possession as soon as possible didn't exactly help Elaine to trust him. Her own desire to be rid of it and take the money without knowing more about its powers was also concerning.

She peered over at Grant again, silently questioning him.

Grant's brow furrowed, and he bit his lip. "I'm not sure, Elaine. I thought we were coming here just to get it appraised. This seems to be happening awfully quick." He leaned in closer, his face inches in front of her, and whispered, "And what about what Adele told us the other day?"

Elaine looked at the professor, who gave no indication that he heard them. His face was stoic and his shoulders square. His clasped hands rested on the desk while his gaze focused on the key. Then his eyes seemed to darken, and his jawline and cheekbones became more pronounced—different somehow.

Must be the lighting. Elaine blinked and tried to compose her thoughts. Knowing Grant also had some doubts now confused her. Maybe, just maybe, there was something very important about the key. Otherwise, why would Mildred and Daphne have searched for it and researched it in that book a few years back? She also couldn't deny there was some physical connection every time she touched the key. What would happen to her, or someone else, if it suddenly activated while on display here at the museum?

"I believe not only that the museum will pay you handsomely but also that we would keep the key quite safe. I assure you." His smile widened.

Elaine peered at her hands in her lap and absently picked at a fingernail. She sighed. The sale *would* alleviate one of the biggest problems she was facing in her adult life. She could keep her aunts' legacy alive. Besides, she loved her childhood home, the land, and, if she were being honest, the antique store, whose contents held so many rich stories. That seemed to push her to her final decision.

"I'll do it, professor. I'll sell you the key." The words were out of her mouth before she had time to think about them too much and form regrets.

"Wonderful!" Professor Wallace clapped his hands together, scooped up the book in front of them, and closed it shut before he set it back down on his desk. "I will need to keep the key for a few days to do some more research, and the board members' meeting is next Monday. If given approval, I could have a check to you by Thursday." Elaine saw the faint quiver in his lips as he stared at the key in its case, a clear sign to her that he could barely contain his excitement over this new acquisition.

As if the transaction was complete, he picked up the case and removed the lid to admire the key. Elaine couldn't help but notice a gleam of greed flash across his gray-blue eyes and then instantly disappear.

"You're really going to sell it?" Grant interjected. "Even after what happened the other day?" He had a point, but she really couldn't think of any way out of the financial predicament Mr. Sadler spelled out for her.

Intrigued, Professor Wallace focused his attention on Grant. "What happened the other day? Did someone else try to buy it ... or steal it?" There was more than a hint of nervous energy behind his questions, and his voice seemed to rise an octave as he spit out the last two words.

"Nothing happened," Elaine said hastily. "He's just a worrier." She gave her friend a pleading look in hopes he would go along with her. "Seems like the museum might be the safest place for the key, right, Grant?"

Grant looked at her for a beat before he conceded. He cleared his throat. "So what kind of security system does the museum have anyway?"

Professor Wallace looked at them both for a short moment before speaking. "State of the art, my boy. State of the art. Besides, it's just a small key, and no one really would know the value of it besides collectors of locks and keys from the eighteenth century or those who are really into trade guilds. The key would be mixed in with other items on display as well. Most people will only glance at it before moving on."

"See, Grant?" Elaine said. "My aunts' treasure would be kept safe in a state-of-the-art museum and used as an educational display. What's the harm in that?" She let out a sigh and unconsciously rubbed her hand over the bandage on her palm. Although Elaine was curious about the key's seemingly unusual powers, she was relieved she wouldn't be tempted to activate it again or be in physical danger.

"I see your point, Elaine," Grant said contemplatively. "Professor Wallace, may I make a suggestion? How about I take pictures of the key and email them to you so you can do your research? That way, Elaine has some time to weigh her options." Grant's voice was even-keeled but firm. He looked Professor Wallace squarely in the eyes and let it be known these were the terms, not a request or a suggestion.

"Yes, yes," Professor Wallace said. "That would work too. Clever thinking, my boy." He clenched his jaw tightly and cleared his throat. "Go right ahead." He set the case down, and Grant took out his phone. He started snapping photos of the key at various angles both with the flash on and flash off. He used the edge of his blue shirt to flip the key over and take pictures of the other side as well.

Professor Wallace gave Elaine a questioning look. "He doesn't want to smudge it," Elaine said quickly.

"All done," Grant said. He put the lid on the box and handed it back to Elaine. "What's your email address, Professor?"

While Grant was busy typing into his phone, Elaine slid the small case back into her purse and did her best to disguise the unease and anger she was feeling. It was unlike Grant to be so insistent and make a snap decision, especially when the decision was *hers* to make. Saving the antique store and her home was in the forefront of Elaine's mind. Still, she *was* reluctant to hand over the key without an immediate exchange of money. She began to fidget. The tightness she felt in her stomach about letting the key go would just have to be ignored.

She looked at the professor, and his steel blue eyes met her gaze unwaveringly. "What's the next step in this process then?"

"Well, if my research comes back and validates my claims, we will finish the business of the key next week." The professor clearly saw the worried look on her face. "I see you're still reticent, my dear," he added as he stood up to usher them out of his office. "Why don't you have dinner with me and my companion next Thursday evening? That will give us a chance to get to know each other a little better, and I should have a check for you by then. Let's say seven o'clock at Barrington's on Main? My treat."

Elaine glanced at Grant and then back at the professor. She felt trapped by his persistence and Grant's skepticism. She sighed and reluctantly said, "That will be lovely. We'll see you there."

"Splendid! See you then." The professor closed the door behind them, and they began walking down the quiet hallway until they reached the wide set of stairs. They made their way down the first flight, the echo of their footsteps the only break in the silence.

Elaine gazed up at the large, stately windows that filled the third- and second-storied walls and sighed, wondering what Adele would say when she learned Elaine was selling the key. Not that it was any of Adele's business, Elaine rationalized, but she didn't want the headache of having to explain her decision to her aunts' best friend, especially after how adamant Adele was that the key had been special somehow to Daphne and Mildred.

They finally reached the first-floor landing, when Grant spoke aloud, startling her. "So Barrington's. Wow. That's a classy place. I don't know if I have anything nice to wear."

"You don't have to worry. Eric will be in town. He's been wanting to take me to Barrington's for a while now."

"Oh, Eric. Yeah. That makes sense. Sorry, I just assumed when you said 'we,' you were referring to me because I was standing right there." They were in the lobby now, and the young woman at the front desk was nowhere in sight. Grant walked quickly ahead of Elaine; this time, she was the one who had to jog to catch up to him.

"Sorry, Grant. I didn't mean to come across as rude." She touched his arm, but he pulled away from her. "You should come. You're right. You already know the professor and the key's history. It will be fun. I can get Eric to take me to Barrington's another night."

He looked straight ahead and shoved his hands in his pockets. A chilly autumn wind ruffled his hair. "No, it's okay. You should go with Eric. Besides, I have a lot of projects to finish up. I still have to go to the Overton's house and finish installing their bathroom cabinetry now that they finally decided on a design."

"I feel bad—"

"It's fine. Really. Go. You'll have a nice time."

She felt the curtness in his words even though they were polite. His ears were red, a telltale sign she recognized as embarrassment. "Well," she said, "the offer is still open if you'd like to come."

He nodded and kept walking toward the car. She followed quietly. It was going to be a long drive home.

CHAPTER 7

When they got in the car, Grant tuned the radio to the '80s station. As they backed out of the parking space, Elaine turned down the radio and cleared her voice. "Grant," she began, "I'm sorry if you misunderstood. It's nothing personal. I just thought you knew I was going to ask Eric to come along with me. He's my boyfriend, you know?"

Grant kept his eyes on the road as he turned right onto the main street leading them back toward Brightonville. "Yeah, I know," he said and nodded, then turned the radio up again. The theme song from *The Breakfast Club* blared from the scratchy speakers, the lead singer singing in his punk-style British accent.

Elaine slumped in her seat and looked out the window. Although the sun was now brightly shining and streaming through the gold-tipped leaves of the trees that lined the street, a palpable tension hung between them.

Three more songs and a strand of commercials passed before Grant broke the ice. "Do you want to grab a bite at The Greasy Spoon before I take you to your car?" They had reached downtown and were heading toward the library.

"Nah, that's okay. It's pumpkin pie day. It already looks packed," Elaine remarked as they passed the diner on their right. There was a small line already forming outside the door. Jilly's trademark pumpkin pie brought people from surrounding towns and was one of the signature seasonal desserts at The Greasy Spoon.

They reached the library in silence, and Grant pulled up near Elaine's car. "Thanks for driving, Grant," Elaine said as she unbuckled her seat belt and opened her car door.

"You're welcome." Grant scratched his dark hair and then pushed up his glasses. "Elaine? Wait," he said as she stepped out of the car.

"Yes?" She bent down and stuck her head inside to meet his intense stare.

"Are you really going to sell it? What about everything Adele told us the other day? What about what happened at the library afterward? And that weird glow at the diner? It seems like there's more to the key than even the professor knows about. Aren't you the least bit curious?"

She lied. "Not in the least."

She came close to telling him about how she might lose her aunts' store and the home she grew up in if she didn't come up with a large chunk of change soon. Professor Wallace's sum was far greater than anything she was expecting. If the key turned out to be as authentic as the professor believed, all her problems would be behind her, and the key's strange qualities would never be discovered. It would just sit behind glass next to other old objects that portrayed daily life or played an insignificant role among a brotherhood of craftsmen or tradesmen. She looked at Grant and the worry that spread across his face. "It's all right, Grant. I have my reasons for selling it. You'll see. It will all work out." She gave him a reassuring smile.

He nodded. "I just hope it's the right thing to do."

"It is. I know it is." She looked at the time on her phone. "I need to get home. I was hoping to drop off a few more of my aunts' boxes at the thrift store before it closes."

She stood up fully and took out her key fob and, leaving Grant's passenger door open so they could still talk, unlocked her gray Ford Escape.

"As long as you're sure, I guess I have to be too," he said.

"I am. I'll see you later," she said with a little more finality in her voice than she had intended.

Grant sounded defeated. "All right, I'll see you later. Be safe driving home."

Elaine closed his passenger door and got behind the wheel of her car. Before she put the SUV in reverse, she looked at her reflection in the rearview mirror. There were bags under her eyes, a sure sign she was stressed. "What would Daphne and Mildred do?" she asked herself. "No! It's not for them to say. This is *my* problem now." She drove out of the parking lot. The rest of the way home, she tried her best to convince herself that selling the key would put an end to all her troubles.

* * *

Several days passed, and Elaine and Grant saw very little of each other; when they did, there was an air of discomfort and embarrassment between them. Grant still came to the library every day to work on the finishing touches for the media room, but he tried to steer clear of the circulation desk where Elaine and Mrs. Armested worked and checked out library patrons. Elaine kept herself busy also. She prepared flyers for next month's speakers' series, returned phone calls, updated the library's website, and reshelved Mrs. Armested's stamped books from the prior day's returns. In the evenings, she went home and continued to clean out her aunts' office. Elaine had packed so much, her muscles tightened from bending over and carrying boxes from her house to the car to Sophie's thrift shop nearly every day before work. All this busy work helped Elaine not to fret so much about her strained friendship with Grant, her financial worries, or her untapped grief.

On Thursday afternoon, work was slow, and Elaine didn't have much to do. She rifled through her desk drawers so she could clean and organize them. When she pulled out the drawer that held office supplies, she came across the sticky note on which she'd scribbled the phrase etched on the key. She had written it down the day she showed the key to Teddy and Mrs. Armested. Curiosity got the best of her, and she typed *Dein Herz ist mein Herz* into a search bar. Once again she found random German websites with scanty translations or silly videos from a cheesy German talent show where people sang the song with this phrase. With her scholarly background and analytical mind, she knew the internet wasn't the best place to find the most in-depth research. The professor's assessment of the key as merely a decoration from a secret group, possibly an apothecary's guild, appealed to Elaine's imagination and romantic side, not to mention her love of antiques. These past few days, she had pushed away the more mystical aspects of the key and the fact that she and Grant had witnessed some "magic," for lack of a better word, while it was in their possession.

"It's better I let this thing go," she said to herself as she put down the sticky note. She exited the browser, then leaned down to grab her phone out of her purse. She read two texts from Eric, an email from one of her favorite online shops, and saw another missed call from Mr. Sadler. She had avoided his call from earlier this morning and let it go to voicemail instead. She listened as he reminded her about the looming deadline of the first installment she owed the IRS. A deep-rooted anxiety settled in her solar plexus just thinking about all the money she might owe. Elaine took a breath and reminded herself of the meeting with the professor later that evening. *Tonight, I will be one step closer to resolving my aunts' financial woes.*

She stood up and leaned against the circulation desk, staring at the rows of bookshelves in front of her and feeling as though she was in a trance. Minutes passed, and she shifted from one hip to another. Yet, her gaze remained fixed on the large wooden bookshelves that housed the nonfiction section. In these brief moments, Elaine's mind settled down, and she was able to sort through her problems and focus on possible solutions.

She didn't see Liz Herbert, the young high school German teacher, approach the desk until they were face-to-face. Elaine wrestled herself away from her thoughts and politely smiled at the petite woman who stood a little over five feet in heels.

"Hi, Liz, how are you?" Elaine asked.

"Oh, I could be better, Elaine, but to tell you the truth, I'm glad we're near fall break. These kids are driving me nuts." She hefted her books up on the counter, arranging them from largest to smallest, and then straightened them so their spines were all even with one another. Elaine scanned the inside of each cover, hiding her smile when she came across a smutty romance novel with a title that made the teacher blush. "I'm not proud of that choice, but a single lady in my profession needs to have a little excitement in her life, you know?" She smiled and lifted her eyebrows in a pleading gesture.

"Your secret is safe with me, Fraulein Herbert," Elaine said as she placed the books in one of the cloth recycling bags with the library's name and location stamped on it.

"Thank you." Liz reached for one of the free bookmarks resting on the circulation desk. "What's this? Are you learning German, Elaine?" She picked up the sticky note and read the quote aloud. "Quite a romantic line for German sensibility. Whatever made you choose this quote, may I ask?"

"Oh, I uh, um," Elaine stammered, searching for the right words. "I found it written on a scrap of paper while I was cleaning out my aunts' office. It was wedged between one of the old, dusty books they had in their collection."

"That's sweet. If I remember correctly, it's a phrase from an old folktale called, 'Das kalte Herz,' which, loosely translated, is 'Heart of Stone.' A young man, Peter, is granted three wishes by a fairy sprite, and the sprite tells him the third wish won't matter if the first two are foolish. So you can guess that Peter made foolish wishes, right?"

"Right. Otherwise, it wouldn't make for a good story. I love folktales and mythology," Elaine said. "How does the story end? Does it have an evil sorcerer in it?"

"Of course!" Liz replied. "Dutch-Mike is the evil sorcerer who roams the Black Forest. Peter escapes him and has fun with his two wishes ... for a while. But he's unsatisfied and winds up losing his popularity and all his money, which is what he wished for. So he strikes a bargain with Dutch-Mike, who said he could give him earthly possessions in exchange for his heart. Peter agrees, and Dutch-Mike replaces his heart with a heart of stone. Peter is rich, marries, and seemingly has it all. But in the end, Peter is a bitter and angry man and winds up killing his kind wife in a blind rage—"

Excited, Elaine interrupted her. "Let me guess. He finds the sprite and asks for his third wish, to bring his wife back to life."

"Yes!" Liz exclaimed. "You're good, Elaine. But the sprite can't grant his wish because the first two were foolish. Instead, he teaches Peter how to trick the devilish Dutch-Mike by conning him into believing the stone heart was a fake. To prove it wasn't, Dutch-Mike takes out the stone and replaces it with Peter's original heart. Then, Peter runs away. When he finds the sprite, he is reunited with his wife, whom the sprite brought back to life because of Peter's cleverness to trick Dutch-Mike, and they live happily ever after."

Elaine shook her head knowingly. "Ah, yes. The 'happily ever after' story. I do love a good German folktale, though. There's always an element of gore. So who said that phrase? And what does it mean?"

"Oh yeah, the phrase," Liz said, shaking her head as if to bring herself back to reality. "It means, 'Your heart is my heart.' I can't remember who said it in the story. But you could interpret it literally as Dutch-Mike taking Peter's heart from him or metaphorically speaking: when we do good for ourselves and others, we're connected. Anyway, a lot of people don't realize that the Black Forest area and other towns near the Rhine River were covered in wilderness and not very populated. That's where tales of werewolves, witches, and vampires came to life. To know that someone's heart was under your protection—and vice versa— from the evils of the world was quite comforting. When Germans immigrated to Pennsylvania and the Appalachians and later here in the Midwest, those old sayings and folklore got passed down in oral tradition. In fact, some people say there are still witch doctors and medicine folk who create charms and spells for a small sum or a trade of goods." She pushed away a strand of thin black hair and tucked it behind her small ear, revealing tiny freckles that danced across her snow-white cheek and made her blue eyes sparkle.

"My goodness, aren't you a wealth of information." Elaine could feel the excitement pulsating in her chest. Liz's words made more sense now in connection with the key. They also brought back fond memories of her youth when she had been in the woods in search of the old German widower's treasure. She never found it, of course, because it was an old urban legend that had been passed down through the years. But what if there was some truth to it? What if she had activated a spell or charm when she had uttered the key's phrase while holding it? She handed the teacher her bag of books.

"Thanks, Elaine. I believe Wilhelm Hauff is the author of that fairy tale, if you want to read it yourself." The young woman blushed again as she hefted the bag onto her shoulder. "And about the trashy romance novels in here …"

"Mum's the word. But if I were you, I'd return your books through the drop-off slot outside. If you bring them back in, Mrs. A is bound to ask you for a detailed book report." They both chuckled and glanced over at Mrs. Armested, who was dozing at her computer.

"Good idea. Thanks, Elaine. See you in a few weeks. I'm looking forward to the next speaker in the lecture series. Who would have ever thought we'd get a published author to come talk to us here in this small town?" They said their goodbyes, and Fraulein Herbert walked out into the brisk fall air.

***

It was nearly time for Teddy to pick up Mrs. Armested. Elaine planned on leaving right at closing time. She had to get home and get ready for her seven o'clock dinner with the professor. Eric's text said he would pick her up promptly at 6:30 p.m. He never liked being late for a social outing, especially at the town's finest restaurant where he could run into prospective clients.

At 4:45 p.m., Teddy walked in the door. He wore a red plaid, button-up shirt with a black bow tie underneath his white orderly jacket. His thick, black-framed glasses paired well with his bow tie, ankle-rolled black jeans, and black-and-gray Vans sneakers with red-and-white checkered accents. He had grown a goatee over the past week, and he looked like a real cool cat that had stepped out of the 1950s jazz scene.

"You look great, Teddy! Going out after work so early on a school night?" Elaine joked as she shut off her computer and locked the cash box.

"Me and a couple of guys are playing jazz at the Wine Bar this evening. You should come out tonight. Bring your guy." He gently nudged Mrs. Armested on the shoulder and waited for her to wake up.

"Teddy, dear, is it time to leave already?" Mrs. A asked as she shook her head and pushed her glasses up on her nose. "Did someone say 'Wine Bar'?"

"Playing with the boys tonight, Mrs. A. I'll dedicate a song to you."

"You're such a love, Teddy," she said and patted his hand as he wheeled her toward the door.

"Thanks for the invite, Teddy, but Eric's taking me to Barrington's tonight. Maybe another time?"

"Sounds great. Be sure to tell our boy Grant. Maybe he can riff with us again like he did a few weeks ago. What *can't* that guy do?" With a shake of his head and wave of his hand, Teddy pushed Mrs. Armested out the door to the nursing home's van waiting in the parking lot.

Elaine was a bit dazzled at hearing Grant could play music. Teddy was right—there wasn't much Grant couldn't do, but Elaine hadn't known music made that list. She made a mental note to ask him when he had taken up an instrument. She then remembered it had been several days since they had a full conversation after their car ride home from the museum.

She walked toward the back door and made sure it was locked, then completed her daily walk-through of the library. She glanced down every aisle and straightened up the magazines and books in the reading room. The entire place was empty. Grant had left around three to go across town to check in on his mother. Elaine looked at her watch. It was 4:57 p.m. She could lock up without feeling guilty that it wasn't on the hour. Tomorrow, she'd open a few minutes early to balance everything out … Not that anyone cared except her, but she took pride in her work and dedication to the job.

On her drive home, she began to think of the German folklore and spells Liz Herbert had mentioned to her earlier. Was it possible her key was some sort of charm or protection to ward off evil spirits? Elaine remembered a book she had once glanced through while she was shelving the nonfiction section. It was about early German and Scotch-Irish immigrants and their customs and influences in the Appalachian region. According to the author, an anthropologist who had gathered oral history from that region, many people believed in witches and curses and used talismans and other objects to ward off their evil. Some witches, however, were considered light witches and were able to fend off dark magic. Was it possible her key was somehow related to this folklore and more than just an item that symbolized an old trade from the 1800s? "Now I've really lost it," she muttered. She turned on the radio to drown out her thoughts.

However, something Liz had said, about needing and appreciating another person's protection in the wilderness, struck a chord in Elaine. Her parents had died in a car wreck, too, when she was a child. She lived with Mildred and Daphne the majority of her life. They were the ones who protected her and enriched her imagination with books along with their knowledge and anecdotes of the various treasures they sold in their antique store. A piece of her heart felt lost without them in her life.

She pulled into the driveway and parked her car. As she switched off the engine, she glanced at the front porch. One of the rocking chairs swayed despite the lack of a breeze. She made her way to the back door, where some wood had been scraped away from the doorframe. She ran her finger over it, and a chill went up her spine. "Did someone break in while I was gone?" she whispered to herself.

She peered through the door's small window. Nothing in the mudroom looked as if it had been disturbed. Taking her phone out of her purse, she turned the key in the lock and walked in.

"Hello? Is anyone here?" she yelled. She set her purse down but held on to her phone while she walked through the kitchen into the living room. Everything appeared normal, yet Elaine had a sneaking suspicion something was off. She backtracked through the kitchen and went down the hallway toward her aunts' office. All the boxes from the other day were where she had left them. "It's just my overactive imagination. A lot's been going on lately," she said to herself.

After glancing around the room one more time, she determined she was merely being paranoid. This whole business with the key this past week had her more on edge than normal. She checked her watch and noted she had a little over an hour before Eric arrived. It wouldn't take her long to get ready. She had taken her shower this morning, so her hair looked soft, and her natural wave added volume to her medium-length hair. Rarely did she wear makeup, but she thought she would throw on some mascara and lipstick and maybe a little bronzer to give her skin a glow. Her primping routine would take no more than fifteen minutes. What was she supposed to do with herself in the meantime?

Anxiety swirled inside her stomach, and she felt the need to do something useful to keep her restless mind occupied. She skittered upstairs and chose her outfit for tonight's date—a black A-line dress and an antique wrap from the mid-1940s or early 1950s. She owned one pair of vintage-style black high heels that she rarely wore for fear of being thought of as eccentric like her aunts. But she knew they would pair nicely with the dress, and it didn't hurt to channel her inner Hollywood glamour now and then.

After she selected her outfit, she went downstairs and made her way to her aunts' office. There was still more cleaning to do, so she made up her mind to jump into the task. "Might as well get to it," she said out loud. Cleaning helped her clear her thoughts anyway.

She turned her attention to the built-in bookshelves behind Daphne's desk. This evening, she decided she would focus on weeding out the old books on the dusty shelves. Fifteen minutes into her task, Elaine had only cleared off the shelf with Mildred's homemade scrapbooks. Her plan was to box them up and take them to the attic later, but curiosity got the best of her, and she opened one labeled "Elaine's Elementary School Days" on the spine in red glitter paint.

Tears welled up in her eyes when she ran her hand over the cardboard cover with a collage of birthday cards she received over the years. Nostalgia bubbled up, and a soft tenderness overcame her. It couldn't hurt to reminisce and see photos of Daphne and Mildred and the life they had built for her. She took the photo album and walked down the hallway into the living room. She sat on the overstuffed couch and opened it on her lap. Inside, Elaine looked at all the pictures of her childhood self with loving eyes. She laughed at her third-grade picture. Her hair was pinned up with a red ribbon, and she wore a rainbow turtleneck underneath a blue corduroy jumper. She remembered sneaking a tube of Aunt Mildred's red lipstick into the front pocket before walking to the bus stop that morning and smearing some on her lips while she waited in the photo line during lunch.

Elaine leafed through the scrapbook until she landed on the page that contained a big photo of her and her aunts. It was the fall of her tenth birthday. Daphne had set up her tripod and put the camera on a timer. Elaine had on rolled-up jeans and the old, yellow cotton muumuu Daphne wore around the house. She stood in the middle of her aunts, who were in their midsixties at that time. Mildred was dressed in a 1950s black cocktail dress and had her pearl choker around her neck. Her silver, frizzy hair stuck out at odd places, and she jutted out her chin in defiance. Pinned to her shoulder was a gold brooch in the shape of two crescent moons on either side of a circle.

"Wait a second," Elaine mumbled to herself and flipped to another picture a few pages back, to Daphne boarding a train to see her beloved Chicago Cubs at Wrigley Field. She had on a white-and-blue-striped, button-up jersey and knickers complete with socks rolled down to her ankles. Upon closer inspection, Elaine saw that Daphne wore a necklace of twine that also had two crescent moons in the center of a medallion. Elaine recalled that her aunts had only worn those on special occasions, like the day Elaine got her first period or when Mildred learned to drive at the age of eighty-three.

"Oh my goodness!" she exclaimed as she touched the photo and looked more closely at the brooch. "This symbol ... It's been right in front of me this entire time." She turned back to the photo of the three of them. "Adele was telling the truth! Daphne and Mildred really *were* part of some secret society. Oh, I'm such a fool." Her voice trailed off as she recollected the events in this photo that commemorated her tenth birthday.

As a special treat, her aunts had arranged a treasure hunt for Elaine. The treasure, they told her, was a special one. Elaine begged them to tell her what it was, but they insisted she had to find it on her own. In typical fashion, Daphne and Mildred had wild imaginations to go with the wild story they said was connected to the treasure. They loved to stir Elaine's imagination, too, especially since Elaine catered to their whims whenever they bribed her with ice cream and peanut butter fudge to pull her nose out of a book.

Elaine ran her fingers across the puffy glitter paint below the photo. Mildred had always loved crafting and took great pains to decorate the photo albums, bedazzle tissue boxes, and macramé plant holders and wall hangings. In red glitter, the caption read, "Elaine's great adventure, Fall 1994." Elaine sighed and recalled the day her aunts had told her a treasure containing the means to travel to worlds beyond this sleepy midwestern town hid inside the woods behind their house.

Daphne smoothed down Elaine's hair before tying a colorful scarf around her neck. "Why can't you just tell me what it is I'm looking for?" Elaine asked as she pulled at the knotted scarf. "Is it money or that video game I've been asking for?" She managed to loosen the scarf enough so she could take it off once she got outside.

"Those are all good gifts, Laney, but you'll just have to get out there and follow this map we made you," Mildred said. She patted Elaine on the head and then reached down and loosened the scarf some more to slide it over Elaine's head, only catching it on her ears once before pulling it all the way off.

"It's not a My Little Pony doll, is it? No girl at school plays with those anymore. I want a Tamagotchi. It's a digital pet, and you carry it around on your key chain." Elaine fussed as she buttoned the top of the muumuu she was wearing. She thought it made her look like an avant-garde artist.

Daphne grabbed the scarf and tossed it aside. She reached for a blue Cubs baseball cap and pushed it onto Elaine's head. "Legend has it that the one who finds this treasure will be able to unlock one of the five powers of the earth," Daphne added as she adjusted the hat and smiled at the sight of Elaine's ears popping out from under the brim.

Elaine perked up. "Am I getting jewelry? Can I wear it to the fifth- and sixth-grade dance this year?"

"No, dear," Mildred replied, handing Elaine her backpack. "You can't wear it to a dance. Only on very special occasions, which we will share with you once you've turned thirteen and begin to learn the importance and power of what you find today."

Daphne thrust the map into Elaine's hands. "You follow this map, and you'll be fine, dear. But be careful, Laney. There are people who want what you must find, and they will stop at nothing to get it."

"Daphne, don't be so cryptic and creepy," Aunt Mildred huffed. She turned and faced Elaine. "What you will find today is of great *importance to our family and what we do. But you are safe, and you know these woods like the back of your hand. Have fun out there, and use your imagination and your smarts, and have an adventure!"*

"Do you think we should tell her about the sacred rituals?" Daphne asked Mildred, forgetting Elaine was listening to their every word.

Mildred swatted Daphne's arm and reproached her. "Daphne, don't fill the poor child's mind with wild stories that will make her quake in her boots before she's even walked out the door."

Elaine busied herself with rearranging the book bag she had packed full with her notebook, her small camera, and a variety of pencils and markers for drawing. When Mildred thought Elaine wasn't looking, she mouthed to Daphne, "Not now!"

Daphne let out a grunt and put her hands on her hips as Elaine made her way to the door. "She's already ten," she whispered. "Laney's not as afraid as you think she is. She should know the story at least."

Mildred cleared her throat and fussed around the kitchen to throw in more provisions for Elaine. She tossed in string, a worn-out paring knife, a handful of mints, and a few packets of ketchup, mustard, and mayonnaise.

"Should we really be leading her to this without proper training, Mildred?" Daphne asked as she took off the baseball cap and tied a bandana around Elaine's forehead, placing her long braids on each shoulder.

"You worry too much, Daph. The girl will be fine in the woods today," Mildred replied as she finished packing Elaine's book bag with a sack lunch of bologna and grape jelly sandwiches and saltine crackers. "Just follow this little treasure map we drew up for you, Laney. You will like what you find. Then, we will all go out to eat at the pizza joint tonight. They have a deal on personal pans and the salad bar."

Elaine struggled to zip up her overpacked book bag. "What if I can't find the treasure?"

"Nonsense, child. You could walk through those woods with your eyes closed," Daphne said. She pulled out the wad of cut-up tissues Mildred had shoved into the book bag. "Mildred! How many times have I told you that cutting up the tissues doesn't save us money?" She threw them away and then walked over to the cabinet and pulled out a bunch of napkins from various fast-food restaurants. "What?" Daphne asked Mildred, who was giving her a disgusted look. "They're more practical."

"Yes, but tissue is far more civilized," Mildred retorted.

"I wonder what the jewelry will look like? Will it be made of gold and have lots of diamonds on it?" Elaine asked.

"You will just have to wait and see," both of her aunts said in unison.

"The mysteries in each of our lives are revealed to us when the time is right," Mildred said. She adjusted the crescent moon brooch on her shoulder and then patted Elaine's cheek.

Elaine smiled up at them and then gave them each a hug—a surprising gesture she rarely doled out to anyone. Flustered and blushing, Daphne and Mildred ushered her out the door. Elaine waved goodbye and then unzipped her jacket when her aunts weren't looking. She figured they were just trying to get her to have fun and use her imagination, but the idea of "a story" intrigued her nonetheless.

Elaine searched all morning and afternoon, ducking under thickets, climbing over downed trees, and even wading through a small creek. Right as she was about to give up, she walked inside a grove of beech, hickory, and oak trees. Tucked inside a small, hollowed-out section of a tree trunk was a rickety wooden box with an old-fashioned lock and a faint etched design of two crescent moons. She pulled and pried on the lid numerous times, yet she couldn't open the box. She threw it on the ground in hopes of smashing it open. Nothing happened, so she picked it up and stuffed it into her book bag. The entire walk home, she was dejected and thirsty. Her canteen was empty, and she only had half of the bologna and jelly sandwich left.

When she returned home, her aunts praised her for finding the treasure so quickly. Elaine asked them to open it for her. "Go grab the key, Daphne," Mildred said as she helped Elaine pull off her book bag.

"You have it, Mildred. It's in the lockbox in the storage room, remember?"

"No, no, I gave it to you this morning to put in a box and wrap it for Elaine to open when she got back. I put it right here in the buffet table. Top drawer on the left."

They walked over to it, and Mildred slid open the drawer. Nothing was inside.

"The key! It's gone!" Mildred shouted. "Daphne, hurry. Contact the others."

"No, no, not yet. It's around here somewhere. Quick, you go upstairs and look through the armoire, and I'll go into the back room here. We'll meet in the living room," Daphne instructed.

Both women began rushing around furiously, knocking into furniture and nearly upsetting a potted plant. They crossed paths again in the kitchen and started arguing. Daphne insisted again on contacting the others.

"The others? What's going on? I'll help you look for it," Elaine interjected. "Let's think this through. When was the last time you saw it?"

Daphne and Mildred began to speak at once. Their bickering words hurt Elaine's ears, so she stood on top of a chair and whistled to get their attention. Her shrill whistle caused them to stop in their tracks. Mildred spoke first. "Sorry, Laney. You won't be able to get into the treasure just yet. Something's come up. Come on, Daphne, let's go. He's back, and we've got to tell the others." She picked up her purse and grabbed the car keys from the porcelain fruit bowl on the dining room table.

"Who's back? What others?" Elaine's voice betrayed how frightened she was.

"No need to worry, dear. It's all a big misunderstanding. Stay here, and we'll be back in an hour, tops," Daphne reassured her.

"In the meantime, your birthday cake is on the cabinet, and the chocolate ice cream is in the freezer. Help yourself."

Her aunts left in a hurry, leaving Elaine with the "buried treasure" she had brought back. She wondered what was inside, but she just couldn't get into it. She spent the next hour trying to pry it open with a butter knife, a screwdriver, and even a bobby pin. But the lock would not budge. She shook the box, yet nothing shifted and she heard no noise. Exasperated, she finally gave up and helped herself to a slice of cake and a large scoop of ice cream. She sat in front of the TV, watching Mr. Wizard *and* You Can't Do That on Television.

When Daphne and Mildred finally returned home, they were exhausted yet determined to give Elaine a memorable birthday. Daphne held a large piñata in her hand, and Mildred carried a big bag of candy. They set both on the dining room table and told Elaine to put her shoes on. They were taking her out to dinner at the local pizza hub.

"I even have a roll of quarters so you can play your favorite songs on the jukebox," Daphne said.

Elaine didn't push them to tell her where they had gone. However, she did ask them about her treasure box. "Will I ever be able to open it?" she asked as she sat in the back seat of their rusted out 1956 Bel Air.

"Yes, one day. We promise," Daphne said from the front passenger seat.

When they returned home after a fun evening at the pizza place and a trip to the mall, no one mentioned anything more about the jewelry box or the treasure hunt. After gorging themselves on cake and ice cream, Daphne and Mildred fell asleep in their matching recliners. Elaine kissed both aunts on the cheek and covered them up with their afghans, placed the box in the TV cabinet, and tiptoed her way upstairs to bed.

Elaine closed the scrapbook and sat down on the couch. She placed her head between her hands. The weight of never talking to her aunts about the box or its contents all those years ago rested heavy on her chest; they had never brought the subject up again. She mourned the loss of that dusty, wooden box she carelessly donated to Sophie's thrift store.

A floodgate opened inside her, and the grief finally poured out in waves of heavy sighs and salty tears. Oh, how she missed those incredible and incorrigible women. She wished her ten-year-old self could go back in time and tell them it was a great adventure and a lifelong memory, regardless of never discovering the hidden treasure inside the box. They loved life so fully and encouraged her to dream and explore. But here she was, a thirty-five-year-old orphan who was struggling to pay her bills, dating a man who sometimes didn't seem like he was interested in her, and wishing she could ask for their advice as they bickered about the prices of inventory in their overstuffed antique store.

After a few minutes of deep crying, Elaine's breaths came in short spurts and then dwindled into long, low sighs. She blew her nose and tried to gather her composure. In her haste to push away her grief, she had dropped that silly jewelry box off at Sophie's along with other items of her aunts, thinking it was part of the healing process. The treasure hunt her aunts had created for her was far more memorable to her and had made a greater impression in her psyche than the box ever had, anyway. Now, however, she chastised herself for not holding on to the jewelry box as a remembrance of her aunts and all the love and joy they had infused in her life.

Why did I let that box go? Why didn't I try harder to open it or go to a locksmith and discover what was inside? Elaine felt another wave of grief snaking up her throat. She pushed it down and tried to think logically. Maybe she could go to the thrift store tomorrow and see if it was still there. A flutter of hope rippled through her. She stood up, determined to get up early and be at Sophie's a few minutes before it opened. She'd text Grant and ask if he could open the library and tell Teddy and Mrs. A she would be a few minutes late. She'd buy coffee for everyone and use that as her excuse for her tardiness.

"It will all be okay tomorrow," she told herself and smoothed her hair. She dried her eyes on her sleeves and looked around the living room. She admired the wall lined with crookedly framed family portraits, bird prints, and mandalas made from various items, such as semiprecious gemstones, antique hardware, old coins, and other miscellaneous items her aunts had collected over the years. They glued these repetitive designs of junk onto old wooden slats pieced together from milk crates, weathered barns, or shipping crates. If she softened her eyes and stared without thinking too much, these mandalas began to take on a life of their own. Their radiating patterns and designs pulled her in and soothed her in a way that was nearly meditative.

The cozy room and its shadows from the fading sunlight comforted her. This place and all its clutter and chaos had been "home" ever since she was five. It would remain her haven as long as she had the money to make it so. She could waste no more time thinking about bygone childhood days right now. If she was meant to have the box, she would find it at Sophie's tomorrow. For now, she had to get ready for her dinner date. The professor would be waiting, and a large sum of cash would be in her hands before the end of the night. She set the photo album on the coffee table and made her way upstairs. At least she still had all the photo albums Mildred had lovingly created so she could look through them and reminisce whenever she wanted.

She dressed quickly so she had a little extra time to play with her hair and makeup. "Why not go for the entire vintage look?" she said to herself as she gazed into the mirror. She began to comb, wrap, and then secure her hair with bobby pins until she had created a 1940s victory roll hairstyle. She dug through the bathroom cabinet until she found some hair spray. She rarely used hair spray, and after a few zigzag mists across her hair, she realized why. She couldn't stop coughing and had to step out of the bathroom to catch her breath. She grabbed her heels and sat down on her bed to put them on. Just as she buckled the last strap, a sound like the screen door slamming jolted her. Reflexively, she grabbed her phone and bolted upright. She slowly descended the staircase and stood in the stairwell for a few moments, holding her breath. The stillness unnerved her. She squared her shoulders and crept into the kitchen.

"Hello? Is anyone there?" she called.

Silence.

"Show yourself, or I'm calling the police."

The back door creaked open, and she heard footsteps descend the wooden porch stairs. The clacking noise sounded like someone who was wearing stylish boots or high heels. Elaine ran to the window to get a better look. It was now dusk, and there was no nearby streetlight to reveal the intruder. She rushed to turn on all the lights in the kitchen and then the living room before passing through the hallway and walking into her aunts' office.

Nothing seemed out of the ordinary, but Elaine could sense that the intruder had been in there. What could she—presuming the intruder *was* a she—possibly have wanted? There was no petty cash in the office, and all the antiques were in the store. Elaine felt confident the intruder wouldn't be able to get into the store itself. Mildred and Daphne had invested in a security system with an alarm that alerted the police when a code wasn't punched in. Besides, they hadn't stocked high-end items for a while now.

Elaine stepped farther into the office and turned on her aunt's desk lamp. She froze. Her pulse quickened as her brain resisted what her eyes were seeing: the jewelry box, resurrected from the thrift store and just as intact as her memory had left it, sat snugly on her aunt's desk.

CHAPTER 8

The idea of telling the police that someone had broken into her home and gifted her with an old box seemed ridiculous to Elaine. *Breaking and gifting, is that a thing?* she mused to herself. If the strange events of the past week had taught her anything, it was that her life was no longer a series of safe and predictable outcomes anchored by her librarian job, the antique store, and occasional date nights. She knew the answer to opening the old box, even if she didn't know who had broken in and brought it back to her.

Without hesitation, Elaine walked to her purse and unzipped the inside pouch. She picked up a rag on her aunts' desk and pulled out the key. As if on cue, the key glowed a bright green, and a soft hum reverberated as she approached the box. Making sure the key didn't make contact with her skin, she wrapped the rag tighter and then inserted the key into the lock. The low hum vibrated in her ears, causing her a bit of vertigo. The box was somewhat rusty, so she had to jiggle the key a few times before she felt it catch. She turned it, and the lid popped open. Using both hands, she gently lifted the lid and peered inside. There, resting on green velvet that had discolored slightly due to age and disuse, was a gold, double crescent moon brooch.

Elaine gently picked up the brooch and admired it. "Wow!" she said with a sigh. "So it really was jewelry my aunts were going to give me all those years ago." The piece was no more than two inches in length. She put the brooch under the desk lamp to get a better look. Inscribed on the disk was what appeared to be the same writing that was on the key. "How interesting. I guess it makes sense," Elaine murmured as she turned the brooch over to check if there were any markings on the back as well. There was only an old-fashioned clasp the wearer would use to pin the brooch to her dress or scarf or whatever piece of clothing she was trying to accent.

She drew the brooch closer to her. A small notch in the center of each crescent moon appeared to be part of the design. "Okay ... so obviously these two go together," she whispered. That would explain why the key radiated so much energy when it neared the box. The brooch activated the key on some level. But that didn't fully explain why the key activated when she first found it, or when she was at the diner with Grant, or when she was at the library talking to Teddy and Mrs. A.

Elaine realized there had to be something more to this mystery. Wasn't this the same type of brooch her aunts had worn on special occasions? She closed her eyes and brought up the image of the three of them in front of the camera on her tenth birthday. Yes, Mildred had been wearing hers, but Daphne's brooch was nowhere in sight. They must have intended to give it to Elaine that day, nearly twenty-five years ago. They had so many opportunities over the years to give it to her, though, like her sixteenth birthday or her twenty-first, for example.

Why hadn't they? Elaine pondered.

Her stomach clenched as she recalled how she had begun to distance herself from their eccentric ways in her teen years. She had pretty much rejected their love of curiosities, oddities, and mysteries when she refused to go to another women's circle after her sixteenth birthday.

"I pushed them away," she admitted out loud, "but they obviously wanted me to have this ...." With trembling lips and a few tears, she found the resolve to pin the brooch to her dress. Taking the key out of the lock, Elaine walked over to the mirror hanging by the front door and used her reflection to help her hook the key in the two notches on each crescent moon.

She recalled the phrase the petite German teacher had translated for her earlier in the day. "Could there be a connection?" she said out loud as she ran her fingers across the brooch. "Only one way to find out, I suppose." She stood up straight and looked at herself fully in the mirror. "*Dein Herz est mein Herz*," she said rapidly three times in a row.

Just then, the gemstone glowed a pale green, and the room began to blur. When she looked at her reflection, she saw as much as felt a rustling breeze toss her hair. She then felt a tug, causing her to teeter. It was as though she was being pulled forward by some unknown force. She pressed both hands against the side of the mirror for resistance.

A flash of bright golden light shot up around her, forming a tunnel where the mirror had been. A strong wind whipped around her, and the golden tunnel gave way to a billowy vision of a sky-blue horizon stretching out as far as the eye could see. She looked down, and the floorboards morphed into tall, dry grass reaching up to her knees. She was standing on a rolling hill in the middle of the prairie near thick woods. The leaves on the trees shimmered in the sun. The green leaves dipped in gold and orange hues reminded Elaine of the stained glass windows of the church she used to attend as a child. There was a low stone wall in the distance, and hay bales were lined neatly in rows. The wall surrounded a quaint cottage made of similar stone. Two windows with shabby white shutters flanked a wooden door that appeared slightly off its hinges. Scraggy rose bushes with their blooms nearly dropped, and showy goldenrod nestled up to the cottage, acting like miniature sentinels of the weatherworn home.

The wind eventually settled, and Elaine took in more of her surroundings. Wildflowers, more goldenrod, and a smattering of purple coneflowers surrounded her. "Am I dreaming?" she asked herself. She took in the grassy hills dotted with wide patches of wildflowers swaying to and fro. The rustic cottage butted up to woods filled with tulip poplars, oaks, and hickories all pressed against the vista of dense foliage with a smattering of blue sky above.

A kindly old man, probably in his late seventies, stood slightly off the path, one leg propped up on the stone wall. His large nose protruded from under a brown woolen cap that rested low on his brow. He wore baggy brown pants held up by suspenders and a white cotton shirt rolled up over his elbows. A walking stick in his left hand held his balance, and a light breeze rustled his shirt.

When the man turned and looked at Elaine, he raised his hand in recognition. His smile cracked into a toothless grin. An aura of mischievousness pervaded the very air surrounding him. He pointed at her and winked. Then, he turned back to look out at the flowers, taking Elaine's gaze with him. The wind picked up again and blew across the field. Elaine swore she saw the various groupings of yellow and purple flowers change to white, feathery yarrow and pink wild bergamot and then back again.

"What's happening? Where am I?" Elaine whispered. She shook her head to prove she was not dreaming. "Hello there!" she called out. "Can you help me?"

The man ignored her calls and stepped away from the wall. He put his walking stick to use and began the slow descent down the hill, toward the cottage and away from her.

"You there!" she called out again. "Where am I?" Oddly, she couldn't shake the feeling that this place felt familiar. Maybe all the time spent outdoors as a child in a landscape similar to this had imprinted itself deep into her subconscious. The cottage's stone foundation seemed anchored to a place she instinctively knew. It couldn't be the same ruins of the old man's cottage near her aunts' house. That place had been abandoned over a hundred years ago or more.

She waved again to the old man in hopes he could explain where she was and what had happened to her. He looked back at her and paused. He grinned again and pressed his fingers to a brooch similar to hers. It was pinned to his suspenders. A glow of bright green light enveloped him. Elaine shielded her eyes, unable to move any closer. She looked at the ground and noticed the bright flash had retreated. When she finally looked up, the elderly man was gone. The trodden grass and flowers where he had walked were the only indication he had been there.

A swell of anxiety arose in Elaine's throat. She stepped toward the cottage and tripped over a low mound of dirt. The key dropped from her brooch, and she scrambled to reach it. She found it tucked between a clump of dirt and blades of grass near her feet. She picked it up, then remembered the words she had uttered earlier. *"Dein Herz est mein Herz,"* she said as she hooked the key to the brooch. She uttered the phrase two more times. The wind shifted directions, changing the flowers' colors to yellow and red. The wind began to blow more forcefully, and this time, she felt as if she were being pulled backward. She watched the scene quickly fade back to the living room. The golden tunnel of light shrank in on itself, and she found herself staring into the mirror, her hair slightly askew and her cheeks flushed.

Elaine instinctively ran her hands over her face and body, checking for any cuts or scrapes before coming to rest on her pounding heart. It took a few minutes for her to catch her breath and calm down, but once she did, she grabbed her phone and thought of Grant. He would be so curious about what she had just experienced. He might even help her decide what her next step should be. He had a knack for creative solutions to difficult problems. Right at that moment, however, the doorbell rang. She checked the time. It was exactly 6:30 p.m. That would be Eric at the door, then. She didn't have time to decide what she was going to do or how the discovery of the brooch and this latest occurrence changed the sale of the key. Instead, she put the key back in its case, slid it into her purse, and straightened the brooch on her dress. The doorbell rang a second time. Eric never liked to be kept waiting.

She smoothed down her hair and checked her makeup in the small mirror, worried she may be pulled into some vortex again. She looked more glamorous than she was used to, and the brooch highlighted her vintage style. She worried her lips were a little too red, so she blotted her lipstick with a tissue and lightly ran her finger over her eyes to remove most of the eyeshadow that highlighted her brown eyes. Squaring her shoulders and putting on her most seductive smile, she opened the door.

Eric stood leaning against the doorframe, talking on his phone. The silver sheen of his dark and expensive suit glimmered under the porch light. He held up his finger in a request to give him a minute to finish the call.

"That's right," he said, "tell them we will settle for no more than 30 percent and the exclusive rights to be their proxy. That should appeal to them and still give us what we need."

Elaine moved out of the way as he brushed past her and stepped inside. Eric managed a nod and wink in her direction as he paced around the living room, enthusiastically engaged in his work conversation.

"Listen, Harry, I gotta go. I'm at my girlfriend's house, and we're getting ready to go out. Just send them an email tomorrow and give them a deadline for Monday, and we'll see what they say. Okay. Okay. Sure. Talk to ya later, man." He hung up the phone and walked over to Elaine and kissed her briskly on the lips. "Ready to go, babe?"

In her fantasies about tonight, she had imagined he would passionately kiss her after he told her how beautiful she was and then continue to seduce her, making them fashionably late for dinner, but that wasn't Eric's style. Elaine had to remind herself that men like Eric didn't fall under the category of "Hollywood romantic leads who emoted their every sentiment through poetry and boyish charm." No need to get her hopes up for a night of romance; Eric was just as pragmatic as she was.

He looked at his phone again and typed a short text before looking up. "Wow. You're wearing makeup," he remarked as he shoved his phone in his pocket.

Immediately, Elaine became self-conscious. "I, uh ... well, I thought it would be nice since we're going to Barrington's?" She ended her explanation like a question that punctuated the nervousness she exuded whenever Eric spoke so bluntly, which was often. "Should I change?"

"No, you look great. Sorry, Elaine. I'm a little stressed out from work. I just wasn't expecting you to be so dolled up, that's all. You usually take pride in your plain Jane persona." He gave her a peck on the cheek. "Who did you say we were meeting tonight?"

Elaine felt dejected and a bit embarrassed that he had forgotten everything she had told him the other day. She walked to the mirror to check and make sure she didn't have too much makeup on. She fought back the urge to tell Eric what had happened to her right in front of this exact mirror only moments before he arrived. She answered him instead.

"Professor Wallace from Lincoln College, remember? He's interested in the old key I found. I may sell it to him this evening. But let's not make this just a business deal, okay? Let's pretend it's our fancy date night." She tacked on the last part hastily as she walked toward the door. A nonchalant Eric followed. His attention was back to his phone and another important text while she locked the door behind them.

They made small talk on the drive to Barrington's. Eric's silver, two-door sports car hugged the two-lane county highway into town. Elaine clutched her purse tightly at each stoplight on Main Street. Eric was heavy-footed on both the gas and the brakes. When they turned into Barrington's busy parking lot, Elaine recognized the lime-green Volkswagen Beetle with eyelashes on the headlights.

"What could Adele possibly be doing here?" she murmured as she got out of the car and made her way to the front entrance.

Eric lagged behind her, texting on his phone again. He was standing in the spot next to his car, focused intently on relaying some other important message. Someone honked at him. Clearly the driver wanted the last available parking space, and after a second *beep*, Eric finally put his phone in his pocket and walked toward Elaine.

"Who is Adele, again?" Eric asked as they walked toward the maître d' station.

"She's my aunts' closest friend. She owns that eclectic homeopathic store downtown, remember?"

"Oh yeah ... vaguely," he said. His gaze was focused on the restaurant's clientele. Eric must've known a handful of them because he waved or nodded in various directions as the hostess walked them to their table.

Elaine spotted the professor. He was wearing a navy blazer, white button-up shirt, and gray trousers. He stood in anticipation and pulled her chair out for her. "Elaine, lovely to see you this evening. My, don't you look like a young Ava Gardner. And who is your escort this evening?"

"Thank you, Professor. This is Eric Havener, my boyfriend."

Eric and Professor Wallace shook hands. "Ah, Phillip and Silvia Havener are your parents, I presume?"

Eric perked up. "Yes, my parents are on the board of trustees at the university, as I'm sure you know, Professor. What a pleasure to meet you."

"Er ... yes, I know *of* them. I haven't actually had the pleasure of meeting them, but I am delighted to learn of their continued support of our museum. Won't you two have a seat, please? My date will be back in a moment. She's in the ladies' room, freshening up."

As if on cue, Adele floated toward the table. She wore a black linen tunic with long, wide sleeves and black leggings. A chunky turquoise necklace snaked around her neck, and her dangling silver-leafed earrings sounded like a rain stick as she glanced between the professor and Elaine. "This is the young lady you said we were going to meet?" Adele hooted with laughter. "Of course. The universe works in mysterious ways." She sat down in her seat and linked her arm around the professor's.

"You two know each other?" The professor appeared baffled. "Well, what a small world. It seems like I'm the only stranger in this group."

"Yes, what a small world. So tell me, Professor, how did you and Adele meet?" Elaine smiled and took a deep breath. The business card Elaine had found on Adele's counter now made more sense. If she was going to get through this night, she would have to "play nice," as Grant reminded her the other day. Besides, Elaine had to admit that the professor and Adele made a handsome couple.

"A curious encounter, one could say. I happened to be walking down Main Street after having my weekend breakfast at the diner and saw Adele's shop. I decided to go inside on a whim and found so many lovely items, I was taken aback. I daresay, I loved looking at her gemstone collection, and we struck up a conversation from there."

Professor Wallace winked at Adele, whose rosy cheeks indicated she was a bit embarrassed by the professor's mention of her small collection of stones and crystals. She had just begun studying their healing properties and even attended the weekly class taught by the Daoist and Chinese medicine expert Sarah Ylang, whose great-great-grandmother brought the teachings to this town from China over five generations ago.

"Adele's talk of the properties of rose quartz and the meaning behind the tiger's eye stone was really charming to hear and so different from my world. I was intrigued," Professor Wallace added, then ordered a bottle of red wine for the table.

"Oh yes, Adele can be quite the connoisseur of all things weird," Elaine said under her breath as she handed her drink menu to the waiter.

Adele laughed sheepishly. "Just some things I picked up on my travels over the years," she said as she sat her glass down. "Honestly, Edmund was the only customer to ever inquire about them. Then, funny enough, the very next day, a sweet, young girl—a college student probably—expressed interest in them as well." Adele laughed and turned to her date. "You two are the only ones who seem to be remotely curious about them."

"Well, they're lovely additions to such a quaint shop," Professor Wallace said as he leaned back and rested his arm on the back of Adele's chair.

Elaine braced herself for Adele's sharp response to his use of the words "quaint" and "lovely" to describe her shop and wares. If there was anything Elaine knew about Adele, it was that she was passionate about homeopathic remedies and fully believed in the healing and mystical properties of every single item she sold. Adele opened her mouth to speak but then stopped herself, let out a soft sigh, and then demurely batted her eyelashes at the professor.

Elaine glanced between the both of them in disbelief. This wasn't the feisty Adele she was used to. Apparently smitten, Adele touched her necklace while she placed her other hand on the professor's forearm, and then she laughed at one of his witty comments. The waiter came back around to take their orders. Elaine didn't have as big of an appetite as earlier. She chose a small dish of pan-seared scallops and a light salad. As everyone else placed their orders, Elaine noticed how charming Professor Wallace acted toward Adele and how Adele soaked up his every word and action.

They make a striking pair, she thought.

He was tall and debonair looking. Adele was graceful, and her bohemian style enhanced her beauty. Now, here was Adele looking ever like a young woman in love—twinkling eyes, vivacious giggles, and nervous energy. It was true Adele had annoyed Elaine lately and their relationship was strained, but even Elaine couldn't deny Adele her happiness. In an unexpected gesture, Elaine tapped her knife against her wine glass. Everyone at their table stopped talking, and Elaine raised her glass in a toast.

"What are we toasting, Elaine?" Adele asked as she and Professor Wallace lifted their glasses too.

Elaine nudged Eric, who then stopped texting long enough to pick up his glass. "Yes, what is the special occasion? Is it about the key?" he added as he slid his phone back into his pocket.

"No ... Well, yes, but not exactly. I-I just, um, I just wanted to say," Elaine stammered. She cleared her throat and tried again. "I just wanted to say congratulations to you, Adele, and you, Professor Wallace. I'm glad you found each other." She then took a small sip of the very expensive wine, and the others followed suit.

Adele set her glass down first. "This is so unexpected, Laney. Thank you," she said with a smile. She turned her gaze toward Eric. "What is it you said about a key, Aaron?"

"It's Eric," he responded. He cleared his throat, and a smug smile crossed his face. He became all business and looked directly at the professor. "Elaine told me she was going to sell an old key to the museum this evening. Professor Wallace, I'm sure you're aware my parents were a bit hesitant about the museum paying such a large sum for an old skeleton key from the early nineteenth century. I'm curious why you're so interested in it."

Before he could answer, Adele leaned forward and took Elaine's hand that was resting near her wine glass. "Oh, Elaine! Please, no. Tell me it isn't true," she said. The timber of her voice shook as she continued. "You have no idea what that key means."

"Yes, it was very special to my aunts, if that's what you're saying," Elaine replied cryptically. "And I know it opens a jewelry box I, um, recently came across," she added as she reached up and touched the brooch. "This was inside it."

"Ah, their brooch, or at least one of them anyway," Adele cooed. "Your aunts ... they loved their collections, that's for sure. I just know the brooch and the key were something they were planning on giving you ..." She hesitated and rubbed her hands together. "Oh, it's all so complicated. I do wish they were here to explain things to you." She dabbed the corner of her eyes with her cloth napkin and composed herself. "It's just that—"

"Adele, is this one of the brooches you were hoping I'd give to you as something to remember them by?" asked Elaine, who was now beginning to suspect her aunts and Adele were involved in some type of bizarre society or cult that involved some magic or strange energy she could not begin to comprehend. How else could she explain the glowing key, the return of the jewelry box, and the brooch inside? And she couldn't forget her bizarre "episode" only an hour or so ago. There were also the recurring moon symbols that had been popping up a lot this past week.

"The brooch is quite alluring. Might I see it for a moment?" Professor Wallace asked. His brow furrowed, and there was the dark look in his eyes again.

Elaine covered her hand over the brooch. "It's a family heirloom," she explained.

"Right you are," Professor Wallace said and pulled his handkerchief out of his pocket and blew his nose. He grinned sheepishly. "You'll have to excuse me. Hay fever."

Elaine shook her head, then turned her attention back to Adele. She needed answers, but she wasn't certain she should just blurt out her questions. "This brooch and the key ... I feel like ... maybe ... I remember them in your women's circle?"

Adele appeared startled. She took another sip of wine and waved her hand dismissively. "Oh, those silly meetings are part of our little eccentric ways, like you've always said."

Elaine couldn't help but notice how jittery Adele was suddenly.

"Ladies," Professor Wallace interceded, "let's have a little nosh of these delicious appetizers, shall we?" He served Adele a poached pear in a glaze and then put one on his small plate as well.

Eric reached for the charcuterie knife and served himself a large helping of the expensive cheeses and paired meats on the cutting board.

Elaine slid a pear onto her plate as well and began poking her fork at it. She took a small bite and then looked directly at Adele.

Both women stared at each other, daring the other one to speak first. Professor Wallace and Eric were mere spectators at this point.

Adele finally broke and said, "Oh, Elaine, your aunts and I were just old ladies having some fun at those monthly gatherings. However, they did want you to have that brooch. It looks stunning on you, by the way."

"Thank you," Elaine replied flatly. She narrowed her eyes and with a scoff and a measure of snark, she added, "But what *is* so special about this key and this brooch, Adele? Are they magical or something?" She hoped her sarcasm belied the truth in her question.

"Elaine, come on, you sound ridiculous." Eric couldn't hold back his laughter. "Let's not talk about magic. We're all grown-ups here, right, Professor?"

Professor Wallace seemed less amused than Eric. He arched his eyebrow and leaned forward on his elbows, placing his chin on his folded hands. "I'm not one to believe in magic, no," he began. "However, like I told Elaine when she came to see me at the museum, I do believe this key is very special and an excellent representation of a ceremonial marker many European tradesmen used as initiation into their guilds. I can assure you, Elaine, the museum will take great care of this piece."

"Thank you, Professor. But now that I know this key unlocks an old jewelry box that belonged to my aunts and also belongs with this brooch, I'm afraid it's much harder to sell it. What about putting the key on loan?" Elaine herself was surprised that she was willing to take little to no payment for the key. She felt torn between the love she had for her aunts and the necessity to save their legacies. She also couldn't ignore how intrigued she was by the key's powers.

"Oh, they'd be glad to know you're not going to sell it," Adele sighed, clearly relieved at what she believed was Elaine's final decision on the matter. "You don't know what it means to keep it in your possession."

"Means?" Elaine questioned. "To whom? To you? My dead aunts? I didn't say I wasn't going to sell it, Adele. I'm just thinking of options. If you only knew the financial pressure I'm under from Mr. Sadler regarding their estate, you'd understand." She tried to hide her anxiety around the disturbing realization she needed cash now to get the bank and the IRS off her back.

"What troubles? Oh, Elaine, please talk to me." Adele reached across the table and took one of Elaine's hands in hers. "Maybe there's something I can do to help."

"There's a lot of debt, Adele. A lot more than I can handle on my own. The professor here has been so generous and informative. Selling the key to the museum seems like such a good option and a way to keep their shop open—and keep the house too." Elaine sounded ashamed with each word she spoke.

Adele didn't let up, though. "Well, if it's money, Laney, I can lend you some. How much are we talking? I have some investments I made through Mr. Sadler's firm. I can call him and have him check on my money market account. We could consider it a gift, and you won't have to pay me back."

"That's very kind of you, Adele, but I'm not going to take any of your money. And you really should consider getting rid of Mr. Sadler. I just don't trust that man." She took a big gulp of wine as the waiter came back and served their meals.

The artistic presentation of the meal helped lift the heavy mood, and they ate in a mixture of silence and small talk about Eric's business, the speaker series at the library, and Adele's latest inventory from Thailand.

When they finished, the waiter approached and offered dessert. Everyone but Professor Wallace, who opted for decaf coffee, selected the chocolate mousse. The waiter cleared their plates, and Elaine thought it was a good time to bring up the subject of the key again.

"Professor, what are your plans with the key once it's in the museum's possession?" she asked.

"Well, I'm glad you asked, Elaine," the professor said as he wiped his mouth with his napkin. "I was thinking—"

"Hold up, Edmund," Adele interrupted. "Elaine, you absolutely must keep that key in your possession. Your aunts have instructed me to share with you ... the, uh, family history behind it. I've just been delaying it ever since their deaths. I thought it was grief, but now I know it's because of your pigheadedness." Her nostrils flared, and she sat her spoon down on her plate, leaving half her dessert uneaten.

Elaine steeled herself against Adele's admonishment. She had fairly made up her mind to sell it; she needed to get out of the looming debt. "The key's mine, okay? I finally was able to open the jewelry box my aunts had given me a long time ago, and the brooch was inside. It's a delayed birthday present. One I didn't expect. I guess I was feeling sentimental earlier, that's all. But I *am* selling it."

"It's a mistake to sell this key, Elaine. A big mistake indeed. This is not a good idea."

"Adele, sweetheart," chimed in Professor Wallace, "I can assure you that I will be the one directly handling this key. I will keep it safe. And to ensure Elaine and her aunts get recognized, I'll have a small plaque with their names on it next to the display."

"Adele, I swear—I know what I'm doing. Just trust me, okay?" Even Elaine had a hard time trusting her motives that went against her intuition and Adele's words. She averted her gaze from Adele and looked at Eric, who was texting again. "Eric, could you please put your phone away for one minute?"

Eric looked up at her. "Hmmm? What?" he asked distractedly.

"Your phone?" she reminded him.

"Oh, sorry. This is actually pretty important. Will you all excuse me for a moment? I'll just step outside and make a call and then be right back." He pushed his chair away from the table, stood up, and nodded at them all. Then he walked toward the front entrance without waiting for their replies.

"You'll have to excuse him," Elaine said with a hint of embarrassment. "He's been really stressed out lately with work. This is a busy time for him." She spooned a little chocolate mousse in her mouth and relished it. Its sweetness was the best part of the evening.

"Seems like he's always too busy," Adele snapped back. "If you'll both excuse me, I feel the need to powder my nose again." She, too, pushed back her chair, stood up, and walked away before Elaine or Professor Wallace could acknowledge her departure.

Professor Wallace broke in, "Well, this has been quite the eventful evening, hasn't it, my dear?" Professor Wallace said. He sipped the last remnants of his coffee and placed the mug back on its saucer. Elaine just sat there quietly and stared at her water glass. "To answer your question about the key," he continued, "it will be kept in the museum's small vault until we set up the displays for this year's gala and the opening show. We have an excellent security system. I assure you—your key will be under lock and key." He winked at her and chuckled at his wordplay.

She looked up and half-heartedly laughed with him. "Thank you, Professor. I believe you. I'm sorry for Adele's outburst. She's still really upset about losing my aunts. I sometimes forget that she's mourning as much I am. They really were exceptional ladies and good friends to her." She looked down at her empty plate.

The waiter approached and cleared away their dishes. Professor Wallace graciously asked him for the check. "I'm sure Adele will be fine," he said after the waiter walked away. "Shall we go ahead with the key exchange? I have your check right here." He pulled out an envelope from his inside jacket pocket and presented it to her. "Go ahead—open it. I'm sure you will be pleasantly surprised." He slid the envelope toward her and winked.

She opened the unsealed envelope and caught her breath. The sum was even more than they had discussed. "P-professor?" she stammered. "Are you sure? I mean, it is just a key."

"Please, Elaine, don't worry about it. This is the sum the board agreed upon, and I am happy to present it to you. Now, if you wouldn't mind, may I see it?"

"Oh yes, of course." She fumbled through her small bag and pulled out the case. She wasn't sure how it would react being so near her brooch.

Professor Wallace opened the case and peered inside. "Ah." He sighed. "This is such an intriguing little piece." He reached to pick it up right as Adele walked up to their table.

"Stop!" Adele said emphatically and placed her hand on his wrist.

Elaine stood up. "Adele, please! You're making a scene," she hissed.

"*I'm* making a scene? Ha! You're the one betraying your aunts and carelessly tossing away their, uh, dedication!" she snapped.

"Dedication? To what? They ran an antique shop, Adele. And mind you, it was turning into more of a junk shop these last few years because they became so hyperfocused on oddities and curiosities as opposed to real antiques and collectibles. They were sweet women, but they didn't operate the business very well, and now I'm left cleaning up their financial mess." Elaine slowly shook her head, knowing how callous her words sounded.

"And what will you be left with, Elaine, after selling off something they have been wanting to give you since you were ten? What will you have left to remember them by?" Adele questioned. "Don't you want to preserve one of the last, um, mementos they left for you?" Adele leaned closer to Elaine and lowered her voice, whispering, "Aren't you a bit curious as to why they, too, had brooches similar to the one you're wearing? Or why they were on this hunt for keys? Please, Elaine, you need to listen to me. They have been waiting to talk to you."

Elaine pulled away from her. "Not again! No! I'm not going to indulge your fantasies of being able to channel and communicate with the dead. You have no idea what's happened to me lately. None at all." Elaine's voice shook, and tears gathered at the corners of her eyes.

"Honey, is there something else you're not telling me?" Adele asked with genuine concern filling her voice. "Whatever it is, we can fix it. Together."

Elaine hesitated a moment before responding. "Please, not now, Adele. I already sold the key. It's done. Let's just put it behind us."

The waiter stepped up, and Professor Wallace, visibly rattled and embarrassed, gave him a few large bills and told him to keep the change. A few restaurant patrons who had been staring in their direction seemed to realize that the entertainment of the night was coming to an end and turned back to their personal conversations, sneaking glances as Eric approached the table.

"Ladies, ladies, you're embarrassing yourselves. Please, calm down. A handful of these customers are my clients. They're very important, and I can't have a scene right before one of the firm's biggest deals is confirmed." He put his hand on the back of Elaine's chair and gestured for her to sit.

Elaine's nostrils flared. She stood up straighter and squared her shoulders to face Eric. However, before she could say anything to him, Adele chimed in. "I wouldn't want to cause a scene in front of these oh-so-very-important people," she said in a raised voice and swept her hand to survey the onlookers. "I know how appearances and good impressions mean more to you than people or precious things." She directed her words at Eric but ended by looking at Elaine. "Come, Edmund," she added. "Clearly, we're no longer wanted here." She turned around and walked away.

"We're sorry, Professor," Eric said on his and Elaine's behalf. "And thank you so much for the delicious dinner. It was a kind gesture. We should do lunch together soon, perhaps with my parents? I'm sure they'd love to personally discuss next month's gala with you."

"Yes, thank you, Professor. I'm sorry for how the evening ended. It was a lovely dinner," Elaine responded meekly.

Professor Wallace shook Eric's hand and bowed ever so slightly to Elaine. "Thank you, my dear, for the key and the opportunity to meet your beau. You two make a dashing couple. And, no hard feelings. If I've learned one thing from my short time with Adele, it's that her passion is woven deeply in the fibers of her being. She'll be fine, and I'm sure you two will be back on friendly terms soon. Goodnight to you both."

Elaine watched him catch up to Adele, who she could see from the semiclosed blinds of the restaurant's windows. She didn't know who to be angrier at: Eric for his cavalier ways and need to be "on" in public or Adele for her persistent questioning and insistence on not selling the key. And underneath all the anger, if she was being truthful, was a sinking feeling that Adele was right and Elaine didn't know what she was doing. She was certainly having difficulty rationalizing the bizarre events she experienced with the key in her hands.

Eric's voice broke through her conflicting emotions and thoughts. "Elaine? Did you hear me? Let's go over and talk to Bruce and Elizabeth Carlton. They're important clients of mine." He started walking toward them, leaving Elaine alone with her frustration and confusion. She just let out a sigh and followed. He was her ride home, after all. She never got around to installing the ride app on her phone like Grant had suggested a while back, and she definitely didn't feel like calling Grant and asking for his help, especially since she had insulted him by not inviting him. He would have known what to do, though. He also knew how to connect with Adele on a level she just couldn't. And he would have at least offered to pay the tip or bought them all dessert as a polite gesture for the expensive meal Professor Wallace just bought.

Once again, Elaine was beginning to question what she saw in Eric. They were from such different worlds and had different priorities. Yet, she couldn't shake how Adele's eyes had landed on her when she made the comment of keeping up appearances. As much as Elaine didn't want to admit it, Adele's words rang true.

As she approached the Carlton's table, she shoved her shame down inside her and shook their hands and played the role of supportive girlfriend. All the while, her thoughts kept drifting back to Adele's words about the possible meanings of the brooch and key and the idea of talking to her aunts once again. She thought of the old man and the changing flowers and the golden tunnel of light too. Could he be connected to the stories of the apothecary in the woods? The one who had immigrated from Germany? Or was he a descendant of his? Was this the man her aunts had rushed off to see when they left her alone on her tenth birthday? Elaine wondered.

"Ridiculous," she said under her breath as Eric and Bruce laughed at an off-color joke Elizabeth just made. They sat there for an eternity, sipping an aperitif, but in reality, they had been there for no longer than twenty minutes when Eric finally stood up, shook their hands, and thanked them for the drinks. Elaine allowed both Bruce and Elizabeth to air-kiss her on both cheeks and make fake plans of getting together soon. When she and Eric stepped outside, the night's air revived her growing anger.

Tonight, she thought to herself. *Tonight, I am going to end it with Eric.*

They walked toward his car, Eric prattling on about something Bruce had said about investing more in the firm, when suddenly Elaine noticed a body lying in the parking lot underneath a streetlight.

"Elaine? Where are you going?" Eric shouted as she ran toward whoever was on the concrete.

Elaine reached the injured person. It was Adele! It seemed like she was coming to and struggling to open her eyes. The contents of her purse were splayed out around her, and Professor Wallace was nowhere in sight. "Quick, Eric, call 9-1-1!" Elaine yelled. Stunned, Eric simply stared at the formidable Adele lying helpless and frail on the ground. "*Now*, Eric! She needs help!"

He picked up his phone and dialed, pacing around Elaine and Adele as he did so. "The ambulance is on its way," he said, winded. "Should I go look for the professor?" he asked.

"No need. He's gone," Adele croaked.

Elaine helped her sit up and brushed small bits of litter and gravel out of her hair. "Adele, what happened?" she said behind tears she hadn't realized were now streaming down her face. "Who did this to you?"

"It was the strangest thing," Adele began. "Edmund was walking me to my car, and then out of nowhere, someone came from behind and put a handkerchief over my mouth. Right before I slumped over, I heard Edmund arguing with a man and woman about the key. Then, I saw them dragging him away into a cream-colored car. As they sped off, a woman walked out of the bushes over there." Adele pointed in the direction of the perfectly manicured landscaping between the restaurant's parking lot and another establishment.

Elaine looked in the direction Adele was pointing. "And then what happened?" she asked.

"Nothing. I passed out, and now here we are." Adele tried to stand up, but her legs nearly gave out from underneath her.

Elaine gently put a hand on Adele's arm and propped her up against her. "No, please, stay down, Adele. You're weak. No telling what was on that handkerchief."

"Thank you, Laney. You're right. I do feel a little lightheaded." She leaned her head back and rested it against Elaine's upper arm. Elaine peered at her and saw, for the first time, just how fragile Adele was in this moment. Her face was pale, and her skin felt cold and clammy. It saddened and frightened Elaine to see Adele in such a vulnerable state.

Elaine rubbed Adele's arms to try and warm her up. "Don't worry, Delly," she softly said, using the nickname she used to call her as a young girl. "The ambulance is on its way. By chance, did you get a good look at this mystery woman? Any notable physical description that could help police identify her?"

"I remember she had short-cropped red hair. And she was wearing a tight black turtleneck, black pants, and a green cape," Adele said.

Shivers went up Elaine's spine. Could it be the same woman she and Grant had seen the other day in the library? "Did she appear to be in her thirties, Adele?" Elaine asked.

"Oh yes. She was around your age," Adele responded. "You know, I could've sworn she asked me something before I fell unconscious."

"Try and remember what it was, Adele. It could be important."

At that moment, sirens blared and strobe lights flashed, and an ambulance came to a stop in Barrington's parking lot. Medics began to swarm around them, checking Adele's vital signs and asking her questions. A police car pulled up shortly afterward. The medics swiftly loaded Adele into the brightly lit ambulance.

Elaine looked over at Eric, who was talking on his phone again. "That's it," she said as the medics started to close the door. "Move over, gentleman. I'm coming with you." Before anyone could protest, Elaine climbed into the back of the ambulance and sat next to Adele, the last loyal friend to her great-aunts and the last person who could explain to her more of the key's significance in their lives.

CHAPTER 9

After receiving Elaine's text, Grant arrived at the hospital thirty minutes later. Elaine was in the waiting room, sipping a hot chocolate and trying to stay warm. She had goosebumps on her bare arms, having accidentally left her wrap in the restaurant's parking lot.

"Where is she? Can I see her yet?" Grant asked as he approached Elaine and gave her a hug.

"Not yet. Two police officers are in her room taking her statement. This is awful, Grant. I feel like it's all my fault. That stupid key has brought me nothing but bad luck lately." She set the hot chocolate down and wrapped her arms around herself. The warmth from holding the hot chocolate helped, and she deliberated whether or not she should tell Grant about her latest, and wildest, experience with the key. She held off, believing Adele's well-being was the most important thing they should focus on at the moment.

Grant took off his jacket and handed it to her. "It's not your fault, Laney. Do you have any idea what could have happened to the professor? Where they could have taken him?"

Elaine hesitated. She didn't want to tell him about the woman they had seen in the library and how she could have possibly been the professor's assailant. "No, you know about as much as I do at this point. I just hope he's okay, wherever he is." Right as she said this, the two police officers came out of Adele's room and approached them.

The female officer spoke first. "We finished taking your friend's statement, Miss Colemar. She's in stable condition. They are monitoring her for a concussion, and she has quite the cut on her head. Luckily, she gave us a detailed description of the woman she saw right before she blacked out. We'll contact you if we need anything else. In the meantime, if you hear or see anything strange or out of the ordinary regarding the professor's disappearance, please don't hesitate to contact us."

"Thank you, Officer Santos. Officer Mattox," Elaine said as she shook their hands before they parted ways. She and Grant walked toward Adele's room, but he stopped her before they entered.

"Woman?" Grant interrupted. "What woman, Elaine? You didn't mention anything about that. What were the officers talking about?"

Elaine let out a deep sigh. "I'm sorry, Grant. I didn't want to say anything because I saw how you looked at her and didn't want to crush you, but Adele described someone who looked a lot like that woman we saw in the library." She pushed his jacket away from her shoulder to reveal her brooch. "The one with the brooch similar to mine. I should've told you, I know, but, well ..." She paused. His look pierced her guard, and she felt unsettled. "I just didn't want you to get hurt. I'm so sorry."

"I want to be mad at you, Laney, but I'm more confused than anything. I thought I got a good vibe from her the other day. I just can't believe she would be involved in or do something so terrible. I know I don't know her, but I'd put money on it that she didn't hurt either of them. Call it a gut feeling."

"Geez, you're too trusting, Grant. And like you said, you don't even know her. Criminals can be charming yet ruthless, you know."

"Yeah, I know," he said as they walked into Adele's room, "but there's got to be a better explanation for her being at the scene than stealing that key. I just have this feeling ..." His voice trailed off when he saw Adele resting in the hospital bed. He walked up to her and grabbed her hand and kissed it.

"My sweetheart," Adele said as she patted his cheek with her other hand.

"How are you, Delly?" he asked.

"Well, I could be better given the circumstances. But they brought me Jell-O and keep coming in to check on me and fluff my pillows every fifteen minutes. I feel like I'm at a five-star resort, except for the IV, fluorescent lighting, and smell of bleach they use to cover up spilled bodily fluids in this godforsaken place."

Grant kissed her cheek. "Well, I hope you're not here for too long. Can we do anything for you?"

Adele glanced at both of them, hesitant to ask a favor. She looked back at Grant and smiled. "Actually, would you mind going to my house to get my robe and the large quartz crystal I keep on my windowsill in the kitchen? I'd feel much better having those two things around me. My aura could use a good cleansing, and this hospital gown is just so unflattering."

"Of course we can, Adele," Elaine replied. "Grant, would you mind? We could take your car and go to Adele's house, then you could swing me back home. It's late, and I'd like to change out of this dress and high heels too."

"Sure. We'll see you soon," Grant said as he gave Adele another peck on the cheek.

Elaine noticed the strange look on Adele's face. It was as if she was looking at someone and having a silent conversation. Elaine looked around the room, but she didn't see anything out of the ordinary. Adele held her gaze and simply nodded in some type of agreement. Grant seemed to witness the behavior as well and searched to find where Adele's gaze was pointed. Just then, like nothing happened, Adele looked over at Elaine and said matter-of-factly, "They're here, Elaine. Whenever you want to talk to them, they're here."

"Who? Who's here?" Grant asked nervously. He put his hand to the purple crystal he always wore around his neck and began to rub it between his thumb and pointer finger. "Adele? This crystal—it's warm, just like you said it would be, but I don't see …"

"Shhh," Elaine whispered. "Let's not get Adele too excited, Grant. She's had a rough evening. She has a mild concussion, remember?" Grant started to protest, but Elaine spoke louder, "We'll be back soon, Adele." Elaine took Grant's arm and ushered him toward the door.

Adele rubbed her temples and spoke to Grant as they backed out of the room. "I'm so tired. I don't always have the energy for these visits. You would think they'd know not to visit at a time like this."

Grant circled back to Adele's bedside. "I know, Delly, I know. You're doing great, though. We can talk later. Get some rest, and we'll see you soon." Grant blew her a kiss and then closed the door gently behind him as they left. "You know, I think she was talking to your aunts," he said as they made their way into the elevator. "She can see beyond the veil, whether you believe it or not. And I'm certain they'd want to talk to you when you're ready." He pressed the lobby button, and they watched the heavy elevator door slide closed before making their descent.

Elaine rolled her eyes. "I suppose she's tricked you into believing in magic too. Let me guess—she told you that everybody has the gifts of sight and intuition if only they let themselves believe and feel them?"

"It's not so much having 'the sight' as it is a feeling tone. It's like watching a dream while you're awake. And, yes, trusting your intuition is part of it," Grant replied.

"But don't you think a person's trauma or grief or wishful thinking, even, can make them think or see things that aren't really there?" she asked, more for herself. It was a vain attempt to explain away the all-too-real feeling of being transported to that cottage in the prairie this evening when she had hooked the key into her brooch.

"Why won't you believe Adele when she tells you what she sees or what she knows? For me, at least, I feel like magic surrounds us every day. We just have to stay open to it."

Elaine didn't know what to say to that. A side of her was starting to open up to what he meant, yet making room for magic felt way too chaotic for her. "So she really has roped you into her hocus-pocus?" she said in a weak attempt to defend her linear way of thinking.

"Hocus-pocus or not, I can't help but be drawn to what she has to say." He grinned playfully and raised his eyebrow. "I've always been a sucker for headstrong women who say what's on their minds."

Ruffled by his flirtatiousness, Elaine felt a flutter in her heart. *Is he including me in that category?* She couldn't help but be disarmed by his words. Grant had been giving her a lot of mixed signals lately. She couldn't get past how he had been disappointed she didn't invite him to dinner at Barrington's, yet the next thing she knew, he was crushing on a mystery woman who could have possibly abducted Professor Wallace and hurt Adele. True, Elaine and Grant had always squabbled like siblings since they were children, but lately, there seemed to be a more complicated set of emotions that pushed them together and pulled them apart. But she didn't have time for interpreting mixed signals. She was in a rocky relationship, for sure, but it was a relationship nonetheless, and she didn't want to do or say anything she would regret before speaking to Eric.

"Huh. I didn't realize you were that gullible to womanly charms, Grant." The look on Grant's face told Elaine she had pushed back harder than she had intended to. He immediately clenched his jaw and turned ever so slightly away from her. She wished she could take her words back, or that she'd at least had been a little more playful with them like Grant had been. But it was too late for that. His feelings were hurt, and she knew it.

The elevator came to a halt, and the door slid open to the lobby. Frustrated, Grant walked out ahead of Elaine. As they made their way to the sliding glass door into the dark night, Grant turned and looked at her, his purple crystal resting on top of the collar of his black T-shirt underneath his heavy flannel shirt. "When will you learn to stop being so cynical all the time and just let a little magic and mystery into your life, Elaine?"

"When science proves magic is real, I guess," she said as they made their way across the small parking lot to his beat-up old car. The experience of transporting to the wildflower meadow in the woods earlier sat in her stomach like a heavy stone. Now was definitely not the time to reveal to him what had happened to her. He wouldn't understand that she wasn't ready to fully lean in to admitting there wasn't a simple, logical explanation to it all. However, maybe it wasn't the best idea to keep it to herself. She definitely was risking her friendship by doing so, but her stubbornness to handle life's problems alone still overruled her desire to let people fully into her life.

Elaine was skeptical and standoffish by nature, but her fierce independence always flared whenever she felt out of control. And right now, her life felt more out of control than ever. Letting people into her inner world would make her vulnerable. It was better to keep the world at arm's length because at least then she couldn't be crushed when it was suddenly taken away too soon, like her parents or her aunts or the impending loss of the store and her home.

"What will it take to convince you? A glowing key with swirling light in its center gemstone, perhaps?" His tone was lighter but also a bit chiding.

More like being transported to another place.

"Perhaps," she said as she opened the passenger door and slid into the seat. "But now we may never know, seeing how the professor and my key are missing," she quipped.

"Touché," he replied as he ducked into his seat and closed the door. "Let's just hope for the professor's safety and, for science's sake, we get to find out." He started the ignition and backed out of the parking space before turning on to Main Street in the direction of Adele's house.

They were both quiet during the short ride. The yellow glow of streetlights illuminated the rows of old 1940s bungalows with well-manicured lawns in Adele's neighborhood. As they rumbled over the uneven brick-paved street, Grant broke the silence.

"When were you going to tell me about the woman we saw the other day, Elaine?" He glanced over at her.

Her shoulders scrunched up toward her ears as she wrapped his jacket tighter across her shoulders. "I'm sorry, Grant. Truly. I just don't know what's going on, and I guess I was trying to work things out in my mind first before saying anything to anyone."

"You analyze too much. Sometimes you just need to get out of your head, Laney. Other people deserve to be let into your world, too, you know."

"Yeah, I've been told that a lot in my life." Her voice trailed off as they pulled into Adele's driveway. The tires crunched over the gravel before Grant put the car in park. He turned toward her again, but she was already out of the car.

"Elaine, don't shut me out on this. I want to help," he said as he jogged toward her. "I just feel that this woman Adele saw has some of the answers to what's been happening. Maybe we should look for her. Ask for her help."

"Don't be ridiculous, Grant," Elaine commented. "This woman may be the cause of all these problems. She could be dangerous. Besides, let's just start with what we know and go from there, okay? We know she was at the library the other day and maybe heard some of my conversation with Teddy and Mrs. A, and we know she was in the parking lot and was the last person Adele saw before blacking out. It doesn't put her in too good of a light, if you ask me."

They approached the front porch, and Elaine started up the front steps. Grant tugged on her arm to stop her. "Shhhh," he hushed and then gently nudged her to move aside. He pointed toward the wooden front door and the scraped wood around the lock. "It looks as if someone shimmied the lock and broke in."

Elaine's breath caught in her throat. "Just like at my house earlier this evening," she whispered. She touched the brooch pinned to her dress, recalling the old jewelry box on her aunt's desk and the receding click of heels that still echoed in her mind. She stepped past him and opened the unlocked door.

Grant's eyebrows lifted, and his eyes widened. "Are you serious?" he hissed. "You had a break-in? Did you contact the police?"

"It was nothing. I ... Nothing happened," she muttered and twisted the doorknob. The heavy wood frame creaked and moaned when she pushed the door slightly ajar.

"Elaine!" Grant whisper-yelled. "Just a second ago, you were cautioning me not to do anything rash. What has gotten into you?"

"I don't know, Grant," she said, and she really didn't. It was just that a feeling of déjà vu had overcome her. Something told her that whatever they needed to know or whomever they were to meet was somewhere inside Adele's house. "Let's just say I've got a gut feeling about this."

She peered inside the dimly lit living room. Nothing seemed out of place, yet an overwhelming urge to step over the threshold and face whatever was on the other side pulled at her like a strong magnet. It was time to face her fears now, or she would never do it. Regret had shadowed her too much lately. The answers could be on the other side of this door if only she were brave enough to open it all the way.

She turned to look at Grant, took a deep breath, and threw her shoulders back in defiance. "You said you had a hunch about that woman, Grant, and maybe you're right. Besides, aren't you always up for an adventure?"

She pressed her shoulder against the door and pushed until she was able to step fully inside. Grant hastily followed. The layout of Adele's living room was exactly as Elaine remembered it—the soft velour couch with plush throw pillows faced the white painted-brick fireplace. Even with just the glow of streetlights flowing through the opaque curtains, Adele's tidiness and penchant for chic décor and coziness filled the room. All the knickknacks and books on the built-in bookcase were in their rightful spots. Without Adele's presence, there was an eeriness to the empty house, but nothing seemed out of the ordinary.

The sudden approach of footsteps startled them, however. Grant grabbed one of Adele's heavy candlesticks from the table behind the sofa. A figure stepped in front of the window, where the glow from the street lamp lit up her features. It was the redheaded woman.

"You," Grant whispered. "Who are you?" He lowered the candlestick back onto the table and continued to stare in amazement. Her bobbed hair curled up at her chin, offsetting her square jaw and ruby-red lips.

"It was you who left me the jewelry box this evening, wasn't it?" Elaine stepped forward. "What were you doing tonight at the restaurant? Where's the professor?" As an afterthought, Elaine reached into her purse and pulled out her cell phone. Maybe the intruder had a gun or planned on taking them hostage too.

"You're not going to call the police, Elaine." The woman, dressed all in black and wearing a sleek green cape just like Adele had described it, took a step forward. "There's too much to explain, and no one will believe your story about a glowing magical key. Besides, you want answers. That's why I'm here."

Grant shook his head in disbelief. "Can you help us?" he questioned. "The key—it's gone. And Elaine and I both saw it activated the other day. I also saw you disappear in a golden glow outside the library. What's going on? Who *are* you?"

"I realize you both have a lot of questions, but let's start with the formalities. My name is Florence Singleton, and I knew your aunts, Elaine. They were dear friends of mine. I'm sorry they're no longer with us, but they're the reason I'm here." She moved away from the window and stepped closer to the fireplace, centering herself near the small alcove that led toward the back rooms. "We don't have much time for more than that. They'll be looking for us soon." She opened a small bag she pulled from underneath the sash tied around her waist.

Both Elaine and Grant tensed. Grant reached for the candlestick again, but in his haste he dropped it, causing it to clank on the hardwood floor.

"Careful now," Florence said in a steady and calm voice. "I'm not going to hurt you. I just needed this." She held up a small brass key, similar to the one Elaine had only hours ago. But in the center of this key was a deep orange carnelian stone. "Quickly now, gather around me."

Elaine looked at Grant. He wore the same mesmerized look he had when he first encountered Florence in the library. Elaine worried that maybe Florence's presence and Grant's apparent attraction to her would only distract him from learning the truth. She had to get him away from Florence so she could face her one-on-one. She nudged him on the shoulder. "Grant," she said. "Let's get out of here. Come on!" She turned to leave, but Grant stood there, transfixed.

"Grant, come on. This woman is clearly trespassing. Let's go!" Elaine argued and walked back toward him.

He turned toward her, and she noticed his purple crystal was glowing. "No, Elaine. Florence is right. Your aunts brought her here. They want us to go with her," he replied. He touched his crystal and smiled.

"Are you okay? What's wrong with you?" Elaine asked, clearly shaken. "What have you done to him?" she asked Florence. "What kind of warped person are you to break into two homes and attack an old lady—and all in one evening?" This time, Elaine's anger and confusion spilled out, and she could barely keep her composure. "I need answers, and I need them *now*."

"I know this is all so confusing to you, Elaine," Florence began. "I can explain everything, just not here. We're short on time." She glanced nervously around the room and then located a clock on the wall and watched the second hand continue to tick.

Grant faced Elaine and added, "Elaine, I'm not in some kind of trance, if that's what you're thinking. I'm beginning to sense your aunts' presence. Adele's been teaching me. You have to trust

Florence. And if you can't trust her, at least trust me. We have to go with her. That's what Daphne and Mildred want."

Outnumbered, Elaine refrained from protesting anymore. She had two choices: go with Florence and Grant, or walk out of here and call the police. She wasn't sure how she could explain to herself, never mind the police, half of what had happened tonight, let alone this mystical talk of hearing voices and trusting your gut. So, she took a deep breath and sighed.

"Fine," Elaine said. "You win. I've got to be crazy for even thinking you two know what you're doing, but I'm in." She joined them near the fireplace, and Florence had them form a small triangle facing each other.

Florence held up the key, and the light caught the gemstone and gave it a glowing warmth. "*Dul leis an sruth*," Florence said and then latched the key onto the double crescent moon brooch pinned to her shoulder.

"Is that Gaelic?" Grant asked.

"Yes," Florence said. "It means 'Go with the flow' It's an old Irish saying." The gemstone glowed. It's light accentuated Florence's high cheekbones. "Come closer," she whispered. Grant and Elaine huddled closer. "Elaine, take my arm. Grant, grab ahold of Elaine. It's quite a rush the first time you travel by starlight."

"By *what*?" they both exclaimed.

Florence locked the key into the center of her brooch and repeated the phrase two more times.

The light was so bright, Elaine had to close her eyes. Wind blew from all directions, and suddenly, there was no hardwood floor underneath her feet. Nothing supported her, so she clung tighter to Florence and Grant. She felt as if she were either flying or being sucked up into a vacuum. And then, there was nothing but a warm, golden light flooding past her and enveloping her at the same time.

CHAPTER 10

When Elaine opened her eyes, she was on the floor. Adele's living room had transformed into a rustic room with a peat fire in the hearth. She stood and surveyed her surroundings. Next to the fire, a tattered leather chair and a woven footstool rested in tandem. An old-fashioned candlestick with fresh wax drippings stood on top of a wooden table. Grant was lying in the middle of the room, rubbing his eyes. Florence stood near the fire. Besides a few hairs out of place, the redhead appeared unaffected by their strange means of transportation.

Elaine cleared her voice. "Where are we?" she asked in between coughs. The fire was dying out, and the smoke tickled her throat.

"We're in the head guardian's home," Florence replied. "He should be here any moment. I didn't have time to tell him we were coming, though."

"'Head guardian'? Just where are we exactly?" Elaine walked over to Grant and extended her hand to help him up.

"Thanks, Laney," he said and dusted off his pants. "Man, what a rush! I've never experienced anything like that. How did you do that, Florence?"

"What? Travel by starlight? It's easy if you know how. What we're more curious about is why Elaine's key activated without her having been trained on how to use it."

"Who's 'we'?" asked Elaine. "And how did you know about the key?" She turned to face Florence, who had picked up a small carving from the mantel and was turning it around curiously in her hand.

"Those of us who are members of the guild, of course," she remarked, placing the wooden object back down and sauntering toward the small bookshelf on the other side of the room. "We were alerted that the emerald key—your great-aunts were its guardians—had been activated without prior authorization."

"What guild?" asked Elaine. The edge in her voice went up a notch. "As far as we know, you and this guild have something to do with the professor's disappearance. And now, maybe ours. By the way, you haven't answered my questions. Where *are* we?"

"Right, I know. Elaine, you must trust me," she urged. She slid a book back onto the shelf and turned to face Elaine. "We're in the Scottish Highlands, right outside of Inverness. You're here because I'm trying to protect you. Your aunts were senior members of the guild and my friends. I swore to them I'd protect you until you were ready to accept your place as a guardian. Unfortunately, they died before they could initiate you."

"Initiate me? What if I don't want to be 'initiated'?" Elaine asked, making air quotes with her fingers. "What if I want to live my own life and be free of the antique shop and their constant quest for finding and selling other people's junk?" Elaine knew what she'd said wasn't true. She *was* angry, however, that everyone always assumed they knew exactly what she needed or wanted instead of simply asking her.

"I understand your hesitation and anger, Elaine. I'm sure this is all a shock to you. I brought you two here to see if you can help us locate another key and return it to the guild."

Grant stepped forward. "Hear her out, Laney. How can this not have piqued your curiosity?"

Elaine looked Grant square in the eyes. The earnest look on his face tugged on her emotions. "Grant, I … I can't take much more of this. Magical keys. Traveling by starlight. Strange objects appearing out of nowhere. The professor's disappearance. Adele getting attacked. My aunts' deaths on top of it all … It's just too much."

"*Can't* take it or *won't*, Laney?" he challenged her. "You have to face the fact that you can't control every little outcome or compartmentalize and rationalize everything. Life is mysterious and scary and beautiful and so much more, all at once. You had a sense of wonder and imagination at one time. Where's that part of you?"

"Gone. It disappeared a long time ago," she said. She turned around and walked toward the desk that was tucked in a corner near the fireplace. A stack of papers was piled on top. She picked a page up but was unable to read the handwriting. The cursive was in long and flourished strokes, and the language looked different too. She held the paper up to the firelight. A watermark image of a full moon flanked by two crescent moons appeared in the middle of the parchment.

She turned the paper over again to study it more closely when a gruff man's voice boomed behind her. "I'd put that down if I were you." A rich Scottish brogue rolled forth and echoed throughout the room.

Elaine turned around abruptly. "I'm sorry, I …." She was unable to finish her sentence.

A tall, broad-shouldered man stepped fully into the room. He had an air of dignity about him with a note of fierceness right below the surface that reflected in his intense gaze and was magnified by his flared nostrils. For a man in his mid- to late fifties, he appeared athletic and strong. He leaned a slight amount of his weight on a wooden walking stick, the only hint of his vulnerability. He wore a green-and-navy plaid kilt, a tweed woolen jacket, and cream-colored socks up to his knees. His brown leather boots matched his jacket and the woolen brown cap on his head; tufts of white, thick hair peeked from underneath his hat. His white, close-shaved moustache and beard finished off his well-groomed appearance.

"Who are you?" Elaine asked. She pressed the paper closer to her chest.

"I could ask you the same thing, lass, seeing how you're the one standing in my study with one of my possessions in your hands." Elaine placed the paper back on his desk and eyed him suspiciously. He walked nearer to where she and Grant stood. "And who in the bloody hell are you?" he asked as he pressed his walking stick into Grant's chest.

"It's all right, Hugh. They're with me." Florence stepped out of the shadows and held up her key. "They know a little something about these."

"Christ!" Hugh blurted out and set his walking stick down by his side. "Why didn't you say so?" He slid the letter into the top drawer. "So you're not after this, are ya?"

"No, but, Hugh, who are you writing to?" Florence asked.

"Don't worry, lass," Hugh smiled. "It's from Vivienne. She wrote down another herbal remedy and incantation for the new project." He winked then cleared his voice. "Now, how about some proper introductions?"

"Right," Florence began. "Hugh McCauley, this is Elaine Colemar and her friend, Grant. Mildred and Daphne were Elaine's aunts."

"Ah, God rest their souls," he said quietly. "They were quite the women. I'm sorry, lass."

"Thank you," Elaine said. Just hearing their names struck sadness in her heart.

Hugh nodded and turned to Grant. "And who might be your clan, young lad?"

"My clan? I'm not sure I know what you mean, sir." Grant scratched his head and looked at Florence for clarification.

"Your ancestors, my boy," Hugh said quickly and pointed at Grant's flannel shirt. The sleeves were rolled up past his elbows, revealing a tribal tattoo of some sort. "You're wearing a tartan pattern I've never seen before," Hugh said and pointed at Grant's red-and-black checkered flannel shirt with thin white, blue, and gray lines running through the pattern. "Strange not to wear a kilt, lad, and stranger still is that tattoo on your arm. It's quite interesting."

Grant placed his hand on his right arm and pushed the rolled sleeve farther up, revealing a dark band of black in an intricate Celtic knot pattern. "A passing fad from my college days," Grant said. The tips of his ears flamed, and his cheeks flushed.

Hugh grunted and studied the tattoo before Florence intervened. "Hugh, I'm afraid we're in some trouble," she said tentatively.

Hugh faced her. "Trouble?" he began. "What sort of trouble? Is it about the rumor that Lazro has resurfaced? Because I will have you know, I'll bust that bloody mongrel's nose." His blue eyes blazed with intensity.

"It's not a rumor, I'm afraid to say," Florence began. "That's the reason we're here. I followed a hunch, and though it worked, I think Lazro and his gang have been alerted by it."

"Gang?" Grant and Elaine asked simultaneously.

"You mean, like mobsters and molls kinda stuff?" Grant asked. "I'm confused."

"That makes two of us," Elaine whispered.

"No," Florence said. "Not like those Hollywood gangster movies at all. Lazro and his followers are daring and clever and dangerous now that your key has been activated. It's possible all the keys are becoming unstable. Mine shocked me as I was making my way to you tonight, and Vivienne reported that hers melted the hinges off her jewelry box. If this continues, it's likely that Lazro can activate them by himself without any form of protection, such as the brooches, to ground their electric currents." Florence focused her gaze on Elaine. "Surely, you've heard the name Lazro before, Elaine."

At the mention of Lazro's name, the hairs on Elaine's arms stood up. "My aunts used to tell stories about him when I was a kid. I thought it was all nonsense, an elaborate scheme to keep me entertained," she said.

Florence smiled and touched Elaine's arm. "Your aunts were marvelous storytellers," she said. "I'm afraid they sometimes got carried away with their embellishments and the excitement of the moment, so they never fully prepared you for what the guild is and why Lazro wants to destroy it."

"So you're telling me that Edward Lazro is real? He's not some fictional villain my aunts created from their wild imaginations?" Elaine nearly laughed at the thought of her aunts' involvement in a clandestine society dogged by a man with a dark past and desire to destroy their group and steal all their secrets.

"And don't forget the part about magic," Grant chimed in. His face beamed, and a twinkle of excitement sparkled in his eyes. "I want to know more about that."

Hugh leaned slightly forward on his cane and looked at the floor. He cleared his voice. Everyone stood motionless, waiting for him to speak. "I think tea and a bite to eat is in order," he said before turning around and walking toward the kitchen.

The kitchen was a small space and even more crowded with the four of them. Florence made herself at home, opening cabinets, pulling out dishes, and arranging scones and other tasty morsels on a serving platter. Grant and Elaine stood closest to the small table, unsure of what to do.

"Is anyone going to elaborate on this Lazro guy or the secret guild?" Elaine asked indignantly. "How can either of you possibly think now is the best time for tea and crumpets?"

Hugh ignored her and busied himself with the kettle. He appeared to be deep in thought.

"Grant, why don't you stoke the fire in the other room?" Florence delegated. "Elaine, why don't you chop some of these fresh fruits and set them on the table?" Worry creased Florence's brow, and she kept her eyes on Hugh while she bustled around the kitchen. She smiled at Elaine as she handed her a knife and guided her to the chopping board. "I'll use the tea service in the sitting room if that's all right, Hugh?" she asked. He nodded in her direction then peered out the window above the kitchen sink. Florence squeezed past Hugh and Elaine and made her way to the sitting room to retrieve the tray.

With Grant and Florence momentarily out of the way, Elaine took the opportunity to speak to Hugh. "How did you know my aunts?" she asked as she set the last of the fruit on the platter.

Hugh didn't answer her right away. He continued to peer out the window, his eyes scanning the horizon. After a moment, he let out a deep sigh and turned toward her. "We met at my guild initiation when I was in my late twenties. Close to thirty years ago. That would've made them in their early fifties when we met, I suppose." He chuckled at this last bit of information. "The last time I saw them, they were old women, but they still had the same vivacious spirit and energy as when I first met them."

"It wasn't that long ago that you saw them, then?" Elaine sounded hopeful. Any information she could gather about the last part of their lives might help her feel more connected to them. Less alone in this world. She set the fruit platter on the table and faced Hugh.

"No, lass, it wasn't—maybe six months ago at the last guild meeting." Hugh walked toward her and took a seat at the table.

Just then, Grant and Florence walked in together. Grant was carrying the tea service, and Florence walked to the cabinet and retrieved four teacups and saucers. Once they had both set the table, they silently took their seats.

"These guild meetings," Elaine began, "do you all have to travel by, um, starlight, to meet? How does it work exactly?" She was reluctant to acknowledge all this magic, but she had a yearning to know more details. Of course, she had to coax her rational mind to catch up with this wild fantasy in which she found herself involved.

Florence and Hugh looked at each other. There was a long pause before Hugh nodded at Florence. She took a sip of tea, then set her cup on her saucer before speaking. "As you may have gathered, we guild members live in different parts of the world."

"Are you time travelers too?" Grant asked, a smile beaming across his face. "That would explain your style and some of your phrasing, Hugh. What time period are we in now?"

Florence smiled directly at Grant. "It's the same date and year as when we left Adele's house tonight. Sorry to let you down on that one."

"Oh," Grant replied. "I guess it was asking too much to be in the past as well as transporting to a different geographical location." He took a small bite of scone and mumbled between chews. "It sure would've been cool, though."

Clearly agitated, Elaine was in no mood for superficial conversation. "Is anyone going to tell me more of why we're here?" she asked. She sat on her hands and tapped her heels on the floor.

Hugh huffed and took a bite of his scone. Florence took that as a sign she was to continue. "You, Elaine. We're here because of you and who you are to the guild."

"Because of me?" Elaine exclaimed. "That's so cryptic! You're going to have to do better than that." She stared icily at Florence.

Florence took a deep breath. "Hugh," she said, "where shall we begin?"

"From the beginning, I suppose," Hugh replied. He slid a few pieces of fruit onto his plate and popped an apple slice into his mouth.

"Very well." Florence turned back to Elaine. "But don't get mad at me for what I'm about to ask." She waited until Elaine nodded to continue. "What made you decide to activate the key once I returned that brooch to you?" She pointed at the brooch still pinned to Elaine's dress. "And don't deny it, please," Florence continued. "Anton reported seeing you near his cottage in the woods this evening."

"Anton? Who's Anton?" Grant interjected before Elaine had a chance to respond. "And what woods? Where?" Grant's voice was mixed with worry and disbelief. "What are you talking about?"

Florence crossed her arms. "Elaine?" She sat back in her chair and waited.

"I was hoping that was just a hallucination," Elaine replied. She broke the rest of her scone into small pieces. When she realized they all were waiting for more, Elaine continued. "This evening, before going to the restaurant, I unlocked the brooch with my key." She saw Grant's eyes widen. "I know," she told him. "I didn't heed Adele's advice. Instead, I looked into the mirror to help me hook the key into the brooch. And then on a hunch, I decided to repeat the phrase on the key a few times." She explained to them all about her trip through the tunnel and seeing the old man.

"Why did you keep this from me?" Grant exclaimed. "That's amazing! Elaine, you have powers!"

Hugh clapped his hands together and let out a laugh. "Right you are, lad." He looked at Florence. "So you tested your theory and gave her the brooch before she was ready? A very impulsive thing to do, Florence, even for you."

Florence gave him a sheepish grin. "You're right, Hugh, but I'm not sorry. Time is of the essence, and we need Elaine to help us find Lazro before it's too late."

"You're brilliant!" Hugh commended her. "I wish I would've thought of that myself."

Florence blushed.

"Excuse me, but who's Anton?" Grant asked.

"Oh yes. I should explain," Florence replied. "Anton is the gatekeeper for the particular portal your key unlocks," she said to Elaine. "When you looked into the mirror and activated the key, you opened the portal. Anton was in his garden when you arrived. You startled him, Elaine, so he contacted Hugh and told him that someone who wasn't Daphne or Mildred had appeared out of nowhere. He was worried one of Lazro's recruits had activated the key. Obviously, I knew it was you. Your aunts always bragged about how brave and smart you are. I thought I'd put you to the test. Give you a little nudge. They would've been so proud of you, you know."

A wave of guilt swept over Elaine. "Yes, they were always so good to me. I wish I could say the same. I feel I've let them down a lot. And now that the fate of their shop is in the balance, I'm afraid I can't help you like you had hoped." With regret, she told them how she had sold the key to Professor Wallace that evening.

Upon hearing the whole story, Grant let out a low whistle. "Elaine, you never told me. That explains everything."

She put her hand on his shoulder. "I didn't want to worry you, Grant. But yes, there's a big financial mess going on, and Mr. Sadler has been harassing me a lot lately. That's why I sold the key. I'm not proud of it now that I know all this." Grant smiled at her. Nervous, Elaine looked down at the table. "Florence," she said after she had collected her thoughts, "why did they never tell me about this society and the key's power? I can understand why they wouldn't have told me everything when I was a kid, but I've been an adult for quite some time now."

"They knew the risk for you, I suppose," Florence conceded. "You'll have to forgive me, Elaine. I involved you before you were ready. But your ancestry, from both parents' lineage, is deeply rooted to the guild. And since it appears Lazro has been meddling and made the keys somewhat unstable, I knew we needed you to help us trap him, or at least confront him, before the guild and the secrets it protects are lost forever."

"Adele's mention of the guild and her warning of the key makes way more sense now," Grant added. "This is heavy stuff."

"Adele told you about the guild?" Hugh asked. "She was sworn to secrecy. It's just like her to go blabbin' her mouth. Who else did she tell?" He buttered another scone and stuffed a big bite in his mouth.

"Just us," Grant replied. "It was when we took Elaine's key into her shop after we saw it glowing. She mentioned how the key came from Europe and was connected to ancient medicine or something like that."

"Ach, aye. She was blabbin' all right, then," Hugh said with bits of scone dropping onto his plate.

Florence delicately wiped her mouth with her napkin. "Well, Adele is an honorary member, Hugh. Maybe she thought it was her duty to pick up where Daphne and Mildred left off. Elaine was going to have to find out sometime, anyway."

Elaine sat up straighter in her chair. "You're right, Florence. So tell me everything. What is this guild? Who are the guardians? Why does Lazro want these magic keys? What exactly is my part in all this? I have so many questions." Elaine rubbed her temples with her fingers. "Oh man, I'm starting to get a headache."

Florence put her hand over her heart in sympathy with Elaine. She cast a glance at Hugh, who rolled his eyes and then nodded in agreement as he took the last sip of his Earl Grey tea.

"When you were ten," Hugh began, "your aunts were going to introduce you to the Apothecary Guild, tell you about its history, and give you the brooch you're currently wearing. Your father was a direct descendent of Anton, who was from the Alsace-Lorraine region and immigrated to the Midwest in the mid-1800s. Your mother's ancestors came from central Europe. She was a distant relation of Isabella, a Romani woman who compiled the *Book of Secrets* from the spells of five apothecaries. These apothecaries each possessed an ancient key with a powerful gemstone. They learned and used the earth magic that had been passed down to them for generations. They were apothecaries by trade, healers to many. Some people in their villages labeled them as witches.

"Due to political and economic unrest, Anton fled with his family to your town, Brightonville. Florence's ancestor, Maureen O'Shea, left Ireland with her husband and three children due to the potato famine. William Peters left England and worked as an indentured servant off the coast of North Carolina. Bernard LeFleur, my ancestor and a descendant of the Jacobites, was more fortunate. He inherited a large plantation in Provence, France, where his family made wine and grew lavender. And then your other ancestor, Isabella Rueda, the Romani woman, fell in love with a man named Eduardo Lazro.

"She and her mother were in southern Spain at the time. It was his family who created the golden brooches as payment for her agreeing to cure Lazro of tuberculosis. No one knew why she wanted them as payment, but Lazro seemed to be getting well, so no one asked. Isabella and Lazro spent so much time together that she unwittingly began sharing the secrets she and the guild had been collaborating on in their numerous correspondences. What she didn't tell Lazro was she had figured out a way to harness starlight into the keys and make portals where the guild members could transport themselves to one another's homes to talk more in depth about their important work. Isabella gave each of them a brooch as a way to not only help activate their keys, but also to ground their wild energy.

"Unwittingly, one of the tinctures Isabella gave Lazro in one of her curative sessions caused an allergic reaction and nearly killed him. His lungs were scarred, and his face developed pockmarks. He was in a lot of pain and lashed out at her. One night, he saw her transport to a guild meeting. He didn't know she was going to seek answers. He believed she was a witch trying to kill him, and upon her return, he accused her of just that. He was in a feverish rage and began destroying her home. He smashed her potions and cracked her pestle and mortar.

"She and her mother, Magda, escaped their tiny home with only the clothes on their backs, the ruby key and brooch, and her *Book of Secrets*. They were forced to live in secrecy, but with no money, they could not leave Spain. They managed to escape Lazro, but, out of fear he would exact revenge, they lived a clandestine life. It was only later she realized the curative she had given him had immortal powers. Aided by Isabella and Magda, the guild members all decided to drink the tincture as well. Later, they gave strict instructions to their descendants to guard the keys and the brooches, and in return, each generation's guardians could access some of the earth magic each original member had curated. All of us guardians, including your aunts, swore to protect the guild and its magic from Lazro and anyone else seeking to use the herbs, gems, spells, and other secrets for ulterior, dark motives."

Elaine had to admit that Hugh's story was not only very compelling, but also solidified the fact that she really had activated a magical key and been transported to Anton's cabin tonight. The stories and legends that floated around her town and had sparked her imagination as a child *did* have an element of truth to them. She could see that now, and she felt an old excitement and pull to explore and dream like when she had been a little girl traipsing around the woods in search of "the treasure" her aunts used to tell her about. She sighed with relief. "Thank you, Hugh. I'm assuming after my parents' deaths, my father's aunts, Daphne and Mildred, could only activate the green key, right?"

Hugh nodded in agreement. "Yes, that's right," he admitted. "Your mother and her family were estranged. They didn't want anything to do with the guild or the secrecy that went along with it. And you, my dear, have the double duty of being the guardian of both keys. A heavy task your aunts were afraid to put upon you at such a young age."

For the first time in days, Elaine briefly felt the muscles in her chest and legs relax a little bit. "Oddly enough, I feel lighter just knowing all this. Yet, I'm also more worried knowing Lazro is still out there." She put her hands on the table and started rubbing them to comfort herself.

Florence reached across the table and touched Elaine's hand. "It's a lot to take in, I know."

"Yes, yes, it is." Hugh rapped the table with his knuckle. "Your aunts took over for your parents when they died. They were so worried about you and knew that one day, Lazro may find and harm you to get what he wants. Daphne and Mildred spent so much time hiding the red and green keys and keeping you safe. I know they had your best intentions at heart, but now I see they—no, *we*—should have done so much better. We should have prepared you long ago."

Grant swept the remaining crumbs of scone onto his plate. "What made Daphne and Mildred believe Lazro was back this time?" he asked.

"There was an anonymous buyer for a lot of their antiques about a month before they died," Florence said. "This buyer apparently got a little too curious about artifacts from the 1800s, so they stopped selling to him ... or they at least attempted to redirect his interests."

"And they believed it was Lazro?" Grant asked.

Hugh spoke up. "They did, yes. Daphne and Mildred saw it as an opportunity to draw him out of hiding. Just like your parents tried before them."

"Lazro killed my parents, didn't he?" Elaine asked matter-of-factly.

Hugh solemnly nodded his head. "We believe so. Lazro had discovered their secret society. Your mother dated a slightly older man in college, Elaine, before she ever knew your father. And like any young person in love, she trusted him with her secrets. Your aunts worried that he had some connection to Lazro, but they never could prove it. It caused a lot of friction between all three of them for a while."

"Did my mother end her relationship with this man because of my aunts' concerns?" Elaine asked. To learn something, anything, about her parents and their lives, no matter how difficult, mattered to her since she was robbed of the chance to get to know them.

Florence answered first. "She did. Your aunts were pleased when their nephew, your father, Elaine, got up the nerve to ask out your mother when he came to pick up Daphne and Mildred after one of the guild meetings."

"I'm assuming she said yes," Elaine said with a grin.

Florence smiled widely. "You'll be happy to know your aunts always said your parents were a happy couple."

"I only met your mother. We were both initiated into the guild at the same time. She was still in college when she became guardian of the red key. Lovely young gal," Hugh chimed in. "And to answer your other question, Elaine, no one really knows the full circumstances of your parents' death. They died protecting the keys. Even though your aunts never passed their guardianship on to your father, he was loyal to the guild. After that, we changed meeting locations. For decades, there was no sign of Lazro, and we foolishly believed we were safe."

"So you think Lazro is after the red key now?" Grant asked.

"Most definitely," Hugh responded. "At the last guild meeting, your aunts mentioned they had plans to speak to Elaine about how to use the keys. I thought it was too risky, so I asked them to return the ruby key to me for safekeeping because it's the master key, so to speak. I thought it best Elaine learned how to use the green one first."

At the mention of the red key, Grant perked up. "Elaine, I bet that's the key Adele mentioned your aunts showed her during their women's circle a few months ago," he remarked.

Elaine became excited by this connection as well. "Oh yeah!" she exclaimed. "I bet it was. And I bet it was the one Daphne gave Mrs. A as a Bingo prize—the one that Mildred subsequently reclaimed."

"Wait? What?" Florence said loudly. "Why would they have been so obvious with the keys like that? That's just begging Lazro to come after them."

"They were good at hiding things in plain sight," Hugh mumbled. "I never could figure out how they did it."

Florence gave him a strange look, but before she could ask what he meant, Grant spoke up. "Are the gemstones what make the keys important?"

"Yes," Hugh said. "These gemstones are infused with certain … earth energies, shall we say. They're activated by the brooches. They unlock the portals Florence mentioned. No guardian, except Vivienne, is skilled enough to practice some of their magic. In fact, even she doesn't know all the spells or incantations or the full powers these gemstones hold. We only know some of the mystery. Maybe your aunts were wrong in waiting so long, but they did want to pass down this heritage to you in their own way and in their own time, Elaine."

"Looking back," Elaine began, "I realize there were many moments they tried to talk to me about some of this. But I just blew them off. I was always too busy with college and my grades and trying to fit in. And then later, my job and my relationships. Maybe they got tired of trying to talk to me about it all ...” She stared at the table.

“Well, you’re here now,” Grant said reassuringly. “It’s not too late to learn.”

“Grant’s right,” Florence added. “Hugh, why don’t you show her the red key? It has so much history with it.”

At the mention of the key, Hugh’s face went ashen. “About that ...”

Florence inhaled sharply. “Hugh, please tell me you have the key.” Her words came out in a rush. “Daphne and Mildred risked their lives to get it back to you.”

Hugh pushed back his chair, stood up, and walked to the kitchen window. He peered outside, hands clasped behind his back. “No,” he whispered without facing them. “No, I don’t. They called and told me they had to retrieve it from its hiding place first, then they’d be on their way. That was the last I heard from them.” His voice caught, and he dipped his chin toward his chest.

Elaine’s voice trembled. “Their late-night drive out in the country. The car wreck. Their deaths. That key. They’re all connected, aren’t they?”

Hugh turned and faced them all. “I’m afraid so, yes.”

Florence admonished Hugh. “Why did you lead all of us to believe that you had the key, then? We could have gone out and searched for it!”

“And put all the other guardians at risk too?” he responded. “No, no, I couldn’t do that. If Lazro has the red gemstone key, he can’t do anything with it yet.”

Hugh turned to Elaine and Grant to further explain. “Lazro needs the other four keys to activate the red one. We guardians can use our key and brooch to travel by starlight to any location we’d like, as you two discovered tonight,” he said to Elaine and Grant. “However, the individual portals can only be opened by their respective keys and brooches when the guardian is in front of a mirror, locks the key into the brooch, and repeats the specific phrase three times."

"That's how I visited Anton," Elaine added. "I opened the portal without even meaning to when I looked in the mirror to pin the brooch to my dress."

"Quite right," Hugh responded. "We're afraid Lazro is close to figuring out how to get inside the portals on his own, which is troubling enough as it is. He could steal some ancient relic or one of the rare plants the original guardians keep or even kidnap the original guardians, like Anton, and hold them for ransom ... or do far worse. But as far as getting to Isabella, he needs all five keys to be activated at once to open the red portal. And only the true guardian of the red key can activate its magical properties."

"That true guardian being me," Elaine said with a heavy sigh, feeling the weight her aunts must have felt all those years caring for Elaine, giving her every chance of a happy childhood while at the same time trying their absolute best to keep her safe and protected.

Hugh ran his fingers through his hair. "I was going to search for that portal key myself. I'm the head guardian, after all. I should never have put Daphne and Mildred at risk like I did. I'll never be able to forgive myself."

"But now there's more urgency since you found out that Elaine activated the green gemstone key. You think Lazro has tampered with her key somehow, right?" Grant intoned anxiously.

"Right," Florence said. "But Elaine unwittingly sold it, and now the guild and our secrets are even more vulnerable."

Elaine's guilt and shame caused her voice to raise. "You make it sound like I've done something terribly wrong! How was I supposed to know any of this?"

Florence nodded and sighed. "You're right, Elaine. You're absolutely right. I'm sorry. We've gone and made a mess out of things by keeping you in the dark for so long. Can you ever forgive us?"

"They're dead," Elaine started. "They're dead, and for what? For some ancient herbal remedies and magical potions? For a long-ago lover's quarrel? I-I can't do this. I just want to go home." She put her head in her hands and cried right there in Hugh's kitchen.

Everyone became silent. A heaviness hung in the room. No one spoke or moved for several minutes. They just stared at their plates, unsure what to do. After a while, Elaine's breath stuttered until she was finally able to gain some composure. She looked up from where she was sitting and turned to her friend. "Grant? What am I supposed to do?"

Elaine felt a sense of calm and reassurance in the way he smiled at her before speaking. "I think your aunts were very intelligent women who lived their lives with courage and heart, despite what others said or thought about them. They were loyal and passionate about life. I never knew them to do anything they didn't want to do. I think you need to trust that they would want you to live your life in a way you could be proud of and feel good about. Only you can decide what you need and want to do, Laney. If they were given a mission, like retrieving this red key, they did it out of their own free will and choice. You're not responsible for their deaths, Elaine."

"But why not tell me what they were involved in? I could have helped or at least gone with them," she asked, bewildered.

"It takes a lot of patience and time to learn about the keys," Florence said delicately. "Maybe they were just concerned that you were a little too busy at the moment to take on an added responsibility? I'm sure they were just waiting for the right time."

Elaine nodded in agreement. "It's true. I'm not the most patient of people. I always found reasons to stay busy. I forgot they had needs as well."

Hugh interrupted Elaine's melancholy with a brash declaration. "If anyone is to blame, it's me. I'm the head guardian and should've insisted I be the one who looked after it." His bottom lip trembled ever so slightly. "But it's over and done with. Time is of the essence. We need to find that red key." With that, he walked out of the room and into the adjacent sitting room that acted as his study as well.

"Hugh's right," Florence conceded. "Elaine? Do you want to be a part of the guild? Do you think you can carry on your aunts' legacy and help us finish what they started?"

"Honestly, I feel like I don't have a choice. My aunts gave their lives for the guild and whatever secrets it possesses. I'm here now—might as well see if I can put some of the puzzle pieces together. Plus, their store may be history soon, so I want to do something for them in their honor."

"But you do have a choice, Elaine," Grant began. "Never forget that. Your aunts believed in you. You should believe in yourself now too. Don't do this out of obligation. Do this for yourself. You owe it to yourself to see what you're truly made of."

Elaine picked up her empty plate and saucer and walked them over to the sink. "That's nice of you to say, Grant, but I don't think I'll ever be anything more than just a boring librarian who can't get her rich boyfriend to commit to more than an occasional fancy dinner to impress his clients. But I would like to help you all out. It seems Lazro still holds a torch or grudge for Isabella, even after so many centuries have passed, then he will stop at nothing to get what he wants. I've got to at least try and honor my parents and my aunts."

Hugh cleared his throat from the next room, clearly impatient for them to join him.

"Let's go and sit by the fire, shall we?" Florence said.

"Great idea," Hugh barked from the living room.

"You guys go ahead. I'll finish up in here," Elaine said and set about cleaning the plates and saucers and tidying up the kitchen.

Knowing Elaine needed a minute to compose herself, Grant took Florence by the arm and nodded for her to follow him into the sitting room. Hugh was standing next to the fireplace, leafing through a leather-bound journal. He glanced at them as they walked in and then returned his focus to the book, obviously in search of something important within its pages.

Florence took a seat in one of the wingback leather chairs facing the glowing fire. Grant walked over and stood on the other side of the fireplace. All of them seemed lost in their own thoughts, and a heavy silence filled the room. A few minutes later, Elaine walked in. Florence motioned for her to take a seat in the other wingback chair. Elaine's nose was red, and her eyes looked a little puffy from crying, but she maintained her composure.

Grant knew from experience that Elaine liked to pretend she didn't feel as deeply as everyone around her. As an adult, he never once saw her cry or laugh uncontrollably like he had when they were children. He couldn't figure out why she tried so hard to close off her heart to everyone. Maybe she was afraid of getting too attached to someone and losing them like she had with her parents, and now her aunts, or perhaps she didn't like to show her vulnerability to people. In any case, it was very much like Elaine to hide her tender side like she attempted to do now.

"So are you and Hugh members of this guild because you are healers? Were Daphne and Mildred as well?" asked Grant. He stood behind Elaine's chair, elbows propped on its high back, his chin in his hands. He looked reminiscent of his geeky twelve-year-old self who enjoyed reading science fiction and watching oddball movies.

"No," Hugh said bluntly. "We are the guardians. The ones who keep the keys that protect the secrets that have been written down by the original healers. I told you about the five original healers of the Apothecary Guild, but there were more healers scattered all over central and western Europe."

"Why do you still gather if you don't learn about and practice this magic then?" Elaine asked.

"We're trying," Florence answered. "Vivienne seems to be the only one skilled in the healing arts, however. I'm assuming she's writing down what she's learning?" She looked to Hugh, who merely nodded. "Well, it seems now Isabella is inaccessible to us since we don't know where Daphne and Mildred have hidden that ruby key."

"Or if Lazro actually has it," Grant added.

"That's true," Hugh admitted.

"The good news is the red key cannot be activated unless all other keys are together and activated," Florence said. "Isabella and the *Book of Secrets* are safe for now."

"The bad news," Hugh conceded, "is that the emerald key is missing now, too, and we don't know if Lazro has it or what he's capable of doing if he does."

"How do you suggest we get these keys back, Hugh?" Elaine wrapped her arms around her chest, as if noticing the slight draft from the rear cottage door for the first time.

"It's safe to say he may try to get the rest of the keys when all of us are together at a guild meeting," he replied. He walked a few steps over to the back door and pushed it tight to keep any more cool, fall air from seeping in. He made his way back to them before continuing. "Your aunts were our top guardians. They were the ones who banded us all together last year after so much time apart. They arranged for our monthly meetings by hosting them at Adele's apothecary shop. They were the ones who suggested we store the red key in a different place every month. They sensed Lazro was back on the scent after years of foiled attempts. I'm sorry to say, no one has their ability to hide things in plain sight. We just don't know how it's done." He let out a sigh. "And now they're gone, and I feel like I failed them. I failed all of you, as head guardian. I could've helped them more or insisted the key stayed only with me."

"It's not your fault, Hugh," Florence said. She placed her hand on his upper arm before dropping it by her side. "We all knew the risk when we took on the task of becoming guardians."

Grant snapped his fingers. "So that's why Adele was so anxious about the key when we showed it to her," he said. "She knows more than she let on."

"Yes," Hugh said. "Adele is not an official member of the guild, but she has the perfect space and has also helped Vivienne with some of the remedies and curatives that are written in Spanish."

"Adele has been a great ally to the guild," Florence added.

"Is Adele in trouble then?" Elaine asked. "Does Lazro know she possesses some of the knowledge?"

"I honestly don't know," replied Hugh. "That's why it's important for us to not only find these two keys, but also stop Lazro once and for all."

"But we don't know where he is or what he looks like or even where to begin," Elaine complained. "And if by some crazy miracle we get to him, how will we get ahold of the keys? What if Lazro has them hidden?"

"All excellent questions, lass," Hugh said as he shifted his weight onto his cane. "I'm afraid I don't have all the answers for you." He walked to his desk and began rummaging through his stack of papers until he found what he was looking for. "Here it is," he said and pulled out a small piece of parchment with a sketch of five different shaded keys and strange writing around each one. He opened up his leather-bound journal and closed the parchment inside.

"Hugh? Are you sure you want to give her this? It's too much information for her to hang on to." Florence's voice carried a note of worry.

"That's why I'm giving it to you, dear Florence." He wrapped the journal and handed it to her.

"If Florence thinks it's too dangerous, maybe we shouldn't take it with us when we leave?" Elaine tried to sound reasonable, but her anxiety betrayed her.

"We're also going to need to get in touch with Vivienne. Alert her that Lazro is zeroing in on us," Hugh said. He turned away and walked toward his bookshelf. His limp was more pronounced after standing for a while, and he leaned more heavily on his cane than he did when they first met.

There was a slight noise, like silverware clinking on the tea service they had left on the kitchen table. Hugh placed a finger over his lip in a gesture of silence and grabbed the fire poker. Grant leaned forward and snatched the small soot shovel. Hugh motioned for Grant to follow behind him.

Florence and Elaine sat on the edge of their chairs, like cats listening for the faint scurrying of a mouse. Elaine stared into the fire, searching for the most practical and logical thing to do in a strange situation such as this. She was at a loss. Her aunts taught her how to hike and camp, how to appraise antiques, and how to use her imagination and make up games and invent intriguing stories, but they never taught her how to fend off anyone intent on stealing ancient knowledge. She looked at Florence, who was standing behind Grant and holding the bellows. Fear washed over Elaine. A broom and an ash bucket leaned near the fireplace.

She reached for the broom, lost her balance, and knocked into the ash bucket. The metal bucket tilted sideways into the brick and rattled before it rolled over on its side, spilling a handful of ash as it did. The intruder took advantage of the commotion and slipped into the room. She was a tall, slender, young woman dressed in a black leather bodysuit. Her jet-black hair hung to her shoulders, and her fringe bangs nearly covered her eyes. She held a dagger in her right gloved hand, blade facing upward, close to her forearm. Her blood-red lips matched the licking flames of the growing fire.

Grant rushed at her and blocked her strike by shielding himself with the shovel handle. She punched him in the gut with her left hand and roundhouse-kicked him in the side. He was on the ground before he realized he had dropped his weapon.

Hugh proved to be more of a challenge. He drew the poker like a sword. Elaine watched in awe as Hugh and this woman parlayed across the small living room. For someone with a bit of a limp, Hugh showcased his athleticism as he danced around the room, dodging her advances and knocking her off-balance as she flipped over his desk. Hugh balanced himself on top of the overturned desk as he defended her attack. He jumped in the air and landed gracefully on the floor. In one flourish of his poker, he knocked the dagger from her hand.

Without losing a beat, the mystery woman picked up a box on the table and flung it in Hugh's direction. Florence screamed for Hugh to duck. The jewelry box slammed against the wall. Its contents tumbled to the floor. The woman lunged at Florence, but Florence had catlike reflexes and used the bellows as her defense by trapping the woman's wrist with the handles and twisting it. Right before their attacker struck Florence with the other hand, Elaine picked up the ash bucket and threw it in her face. The woman choked on the ashes and began coughing furiously. By this time, Grant had recovered and picked up a large book and knocked the woman in the head. She fell to the ground, unconscious.

Elaine stood stupefied at the soot-covered chair and ottoman. Dust swirled around them. Picture frames hung haphazardly on the wall, and the candlestick rolled across the floor.

Grant's attention was on the unconscious attacker sprawled out on the floor. "Oh my god, what have I done?" he worried. He bent over the woman and checked her pulse. "She's alive. Thank goodness."

Hugh coughed as he waved away clouds of ash. He grabbed the woman's outstretched hand and pulled back the glove to reveal a tattoo of a black perfect circle the size of a quarter on her wrist. "The dark moon. Just as I feared. You all must leave. Quickly," he said. "I will handle her when she wakes up."

"But how?" Elaine asked. "You never told us your plan. How are we supposed to find Lazro? And who is this woman? Is she one of Lazro's gang?"

"Florence knows what to do," Hugh said as he righted the wooden chair. "Help me sit her in this chair. Take down the ties from those curtains, Grant." Hugh and Florence picked the woman up off the floor. She moaned, but her eyes remained closed, and her head rolled forward when they propped her up.

Grant handed Hugh the gold cords from the curtains. Together, they bound the woman's hands and feet. "Alert Vivienne, Florence. Let her know that the portals have to be closed," Hugh said as he stood up. "I have a contact at Scotland Yard who will help me with her." He surveyed the woman and double-checked the knots to make sure they were tied tight.

"Seal the portals? Are you sure, Hugh? What about the dangers?" Florence looked intently at Hugh and then over at

Grant and Elaine, who both felt as disheveled and weary as they probably looked.

"It's highly unusual, yes, but it seems the safest way to keep Lazro and his gang from accessing the *Book of Secrets* before we do. Now, please, go. We don't have much time. I fear there are more of her kind on the way." He made his way to the fireplace and picked up his cane. He screwed off the handle and pulled out a key. This one had a lapis lazuli stone in the center. "I'll seal off the portal on this end. Don't worry. Now go!"

Florence hugged Hugh and gave him a quick kiss on the cheek. "Be well, old friend. I promise I won't let you down." Florence led Grant and Elaine to the back door. She opened it cautiously and peered outside. "If we hurry, we can make it to the barn and leave from there," she whispered. She then darted across the yard and down the hill toward the pasture barn.

Elaine hesitated, too afraid to move. Grant gave her a little push. "One foot in front of the other, Laney. That's all we have to do."

He took Elaine's hand, and together, they walked to the stone fence. Grant turned to take one last look at Hugh's cottage. The morning sun highlighted the auburn hairs on his arm and his day-long beard. Elaine stared at the back of his head and took in his broad shoulders and squeezed his strong hand. He turned and looked at her. "What an adventure we're on," he said, then released her hand and made his way to the barn.

Elaine followed. The only sounds she could hear were the crunching of a few twigs underneath their feet, the baying of sheep, and the twittering of birds. Strangely, Elaine felt a sense of lightness and peace in her chest. "Yes, we're on an adventure," she said to herself.

CHAPTER 11

Once inside the barn, Elaine had to wait a minute for her eyes to adjust to the darkness. She jumped when she felt someone's hand on her shoulder.

"It's just me, Elaine," Florence said. "Now, link hands you two, and we'll be on our way." Florence hooked her key onto her brooch and took Grant's hand in hers. "Quick! Take my hand, Elaine." Elaine squeezed Florence's hand and closed her eyes as Florence said the Gaelic phrase three times. Even though her eyes were closed, Elaine could sense the flash of light, and the rush of wind nearly knocked her over.

Moments later, she and Grant tumbled onto a hardwood floor. The flash of light retreated from around them, and there was an eerie silence. They were back on solid ground, but there were no lights on or a fire burning in the hearth. Only a soft glow from a streetlight outside the window nearby gave any hint that they were somewhere familiar.

"Oh, that's a rough ride." Grant moaned as he clutched his side.

Florence stood over him and extended her hand and helped him to his feet. "You get used to it."

"How long did it take you?" Elaine asked as she stumbled to the nearby sofa and sat down. She saw the stuffed bookcases on each side of the stone fireplace and recognized her surroundings. "There must be a mistake," Elaine commented. "This looks like Adele's living room."

"It's not a mistake," Florence said as she turned on the lamp next to the sofa.

"Why did you bring us back here when Hugh said we needed to go alert Vivienne to seal the portals?" Grant asked. He made his way over to Florence. Elaine felt out of place, so she stood up too.

"Well, call it a hunch, but something tells me that the green key is nearby. With Elaine's ancestry and financial concerns, we may just be able to lure Lazro into buying what he thinks he needs." Florence turned the lamp switch to its lowest setting. "My word, why do people use halogens? They're so bright."

"So you're going to use me as bait?" Elaine huffed as she placed her hands on her hips.

"Not exactly," Florence replied. "We've all heard the story of Lazro, but none of us has ever seen him. Except maybe your aunts. It seems to me that he would need someone, or at least *something*, to open your key's portal. The anonymous buyer your aunts were dealing with ... maybe he's in the market for something only the guild could sell him?" She straightened her brooch and then clasped her hands in front of her.

"You mean, sell him the brooches?" Elaine asked. "That's ridiculous! It would be trading one important possession for another."

Florence tilted her head and put her finger to her chin in a contemplative gesture and paused, seemingly deep in thought. "That is a conundrum," she said, more to herself than Elaine. "Maybe he didn't realize you were going to sell the key until the last minute. So he contacted someone in his network to come after you at Hugh's cottage."

Grant stepped forward. "That makes sense," he said. "Kidnap the professor in an attempt to steal the key, and then come after you to get you to open the portal."

"You're both forgetting one thing," Elaine said. "We don't know where the red key is or who has it, remember? Maybe we should focus our attention on retrieving that first."

Florence suddenly grasped Elaine's upper arms. "Elaine, you're brilliant!" she exclaimed. "I have an idea! Or, at least, the start of one. Quick, let's get to the hospital and check on Adele first. She may be able to help us yet." Florence rushed to the front door.

She was about to unlock the dead bolt when Grant exclaimed, "Wait!"

Both Florence and Elaine startled at his urgency. "What?" they asked at the same time.

"Adele's robe and crystal. She asked for us to get it," he said as he made his way to her back bedroom. Elaine and Florence stared at each other, unsure of what to do next or what to say to each other. Elaine broke the tension by rolling her eyes in a mocking gesture. Florence laughed and opened the door as Grant walked back in the room, holding a plastic bag under his arm. "Let's go save the day, ladies," he said, breezing past them into the cool night air. Florence and Elaine laughed even harder as they followed behind him.

Elaine set the lock on the front door's handle before closing it. An air of anticipation hung over her as she walked past Grant and Florence, who were now lingering on the narrow porch stairs. Grant pressed the button on his key fob and unlocked his car doors. He rushed past Florence and opened the passenger door for her. She slid inside and smiled up at him and straightened her brooch. "Thank you for driving us, Grant, and for trusting me from the beginning. You've been such a big help tonight."

Grant blushed and shrugged. "It's no big deal." He leaned in closer. "I'm glad you came back and properly introduced yourself." He closed her door, then walked around and opened the driver's side door, sat down, and started the car.

All of Elaine's excitement deflated like a balloon. She opened the back door and shoved aside Grant's toolbox, oily rags, and a crumpled bag from some fast-food restaurant before taking a seat. She pushed down the disappointment—or was that sadness?—of being the third wheel. She couldn't push away the growing seed of jealousy when she saw how Grant responded to Florence. She didn't want to admit she had gotten used to him always being there for her over the years. It stung a bit to see that maybe she hadn't always been there for *him* as much. She didn't want to deny Grant his happiness, which made it harder to watch how easily he and Florence got along. She had to admit, though, it was nice to see Grant displaying the innate confidence he had been missing since his mother's sudden illness. She just wished she could have been the one who had brought it out in him.

Grant backed out of the driveway and drove through the narrow, brick-paved streets of Adele's neighborhood while he and Florence carried on about the night's events and mulled over Hugh's well-being and their next steps. Elaine set her head back in the seat and closed her eyes, feeling dejected and alone in what she earlier had considered a great adventure. They drove on in this way for two miles, navigating the darkened streets that led to the county hospital, oblivious to the headlights of the silver car that had been following them since leaving Adele's house.

***

At the hospital, Grant led the way through the lobby into the elevator and down the corridor to the nurse's station on the fifth floor. After they checked in, they headed toward Adele's room. They passed the waiting room, where Officers Santos and Mattox were talking to a tall, gray-haired man in a blue blazer and khaki pants.

Elaine was the first to recognize him. She watched as he reached into his pocket, retrieved a small bottle, and shook out a tiny pill. "Professor?" she said as she steered herself in his direction. He swallowed the pill before looking up. His brows were furrowed, and he had bags underneath his eyes. His white hair was disheveled, and he had grass stains on his knees. A small cut on the top of his forehead was covered with a butterfly bandage.

"Professor?" she said with more emphasis as she neared him. "We thought you were missing. Thank God you're all right." She couldn't help but notice how his face looked different somehow—pallid and swollen with a small, metallic-coated blotch on his cheek. Upon closer inspection, all that melted away, and he looked exactly like the man she had met last week.

Maybe it's the harsh overhead lighting, she thought.

"Elaine, my dear, so good to see you," he said. He grimaced and stood up straighter and patted her on the shoulder. "Yes, yes. Had a bit of a caper, I suppose, but I'm all right."

"Professor, it's so good to see you! We've been worried about you!" Grant exclaimed as he stepped forward and shook the professor's hand.

"Thank you, my boy," Professor Wallace replied, then dropped Grant's hand and coughed into his handkerchief. He turned to the same two police officers who had questioned Adele earlier. "I believe I've answered all your questions and recalled everything as best as I could. I'd like to see my friends now, if that's okay?"

"Sure, Professor," said Officer Mattox. "If we need anything else, we'll let you know."

Both officers nodded their goodbyes before Professor Wallace ushered Grant, Elaine, and Florence over to the vinyl couches in front of a medium-sized TV that was blaring a late-night infomercial. None of them took a seat, and the professor reached up to the mounted TV set and turned down the volume. "Now, Elaine, about the key," he said. "I'm afraid it's lost. You'll not be able to cash that check I gave you. I'm terribly sorry."

"We're just happy you're all right, aren't we, Elaine?" Grant asked.

Elaine nodded, afraid to say anything that would reveal she had been focused only on the key this entire time, especially now that she knew Lazro was out there looking for her and the red key. Tonight's skirmish at Hugh's house proved that she and the guardians were in danger.

"How did all this happen, anyway?" Elaine asked. "Eric and I weren't in the restaurant that long after you both left. I can't help but think that if Adele and I had never argued and we all left together, neither of you would've been harmed."

Professor Wallace shook his head. "No, no, Elaine. None of this was your fault. Just some hooligans out to make some trouble, that's all. The police believe it could've been a prank gone terribly wrong. Carried out by one of the campus fraternities. A hazing debacle. They kidnapped and blindfolded me, tied my hands in front of me, and dumped me in a field a few miles away. That's how I got this lesion." He lightly placed his fingers on his forehead.

"So they never took the key?" Elaine's voice sounded hopeful.

"No, they didn't. They didn't even take my wallet or anything. That's why the police suspect it may have been a hazing. Last year, they arrested some college students during pledge season for antics such as this." The professor paused and inhaled deeply before speaking again. "But it's true your key *is* missing. It must've fallen out of my pocket when I was out in that field. I did manage to roll to my knees and take off my blindfold. It was a bit of a struggle to stand. I was so distraught that anything but finding my way back home was the furthest from my mind."

Grant suggested going back to the field to look for the key. "I have a flashlight in my car. Where did they leave you, Professor? Do you remember?"

"No, I'm sorry to say I don't remember the location. I was fortunate enough to get a ride from a farmer and his wife, who were heading back from a night on the town. They called their babysitter to ask if she could stay longer and took me to the hospital, where the police were called."

"We could ask the couple who brought you here, then," Elaine said. "Surely they would know. Do you have their phone number?"

"Sadly, no, I don't. I'm sorry, Elaine." Professor Wallace moved closer to one of the small sofas and sat down.

"Well, the police might. Let's ask them and then go look." Elaine sat down next to the professor. She noticed the tip of a gold or brass bracket protruding from his pants pocket. Maybe it was his key chain, she rationalized.

"Yes, I guess we could," he replied as he moved his hand to his pocket and pushed the protruding item down and out of sight before Elaine could get a better look at it. "Truly, I have a headache, and I'm quite sure I told them about the key. No need to worry, my dear. It will turn up."

"But what if it doesn't? What then? My aunts' antique store will close, and I may have to sell the house and everything. Professor, are you sure you don't remember where you were dropped off? Any small amount of information you could give us that maybe you forgot to mention to the police? Like a landmark or house or barn or something that stood out? Anything?" The desperation in her voice embarrassed her, but she couldn't help it.

"Elaine, it will be okay," Grant interjected. "I'm sure the police are searching for it right now. Right, Professor?"

Professor Wallace grimaced and leaned forward. He placed both forearms on his legs and clasped his hands. "Yes, yes, that's right. I'm sure they're looking for it."

Elaine leaned forward, too, and looked up at Grant and Florence. "We could go look with the police. We all know what we're looking for, and maybe if I show up, the key will glow."

"Let's leave the search to the police and go see Adele, shall we?" Florence said quickly. She looked at Professor Wallace to see if he reacted to Elaine's mention of the key's properties. His head was still in his hands. "I'm sure the professor needs some rest."

"No," Elaine replied adamantly. "No, I need that key. My aunts' store is at stake. And you said yourself that the key is important to unlocking—"

"Elaine, drop the subject."

Elaine looked up at Florence. Her eyes were wide, and she looked extremely determined. Every ounce of her intense gaze was willing Elaine to be quiet. "Yes, yes, of course," she said as she realized her mistake. "I'm sorry you had such a horrible night, Professor." She stood up and crossed her arms over her chest. She really did wish tonight had never happened, but she also couldn't stop thinking about how to recover the key. All her determination to find the keys and her insecurity over the future of her aunts' store boiled up to the surface and made her body harden like she was preparing for battle. She became aware of her shallow breathing. It wasn't until she took a deep breath and anchored her hands to her hips that she made up her mind she'd search for the keys with or without her friends' help.

She then noticed Professor Wallace was staring at her, so she forced a polite smile. He heaved himself up from the sofa, and his tall athletic frame wobbled ever so slightly as he caught his breath. He pulled out a handkerchief from his back pocket and dabbed his forehead, avoiding his cut, and then placed it back in his pocket before speaking. "My dear, I am sorry about the key. I really hope it's found, but I need to go home and get some rest now. I'll be sure to call the police on my way out and let them know you will be joining the search. Your friends are right—you should go see Adele. She's been asking about you since I got here."

As they watched him go, Elaine noticed he moved quicker and with more ease than when they had approached him earlier or when he was talking to the police or even when he sat down on the sofa.

Grant touched Elaine's upper arm as an indication to follow him. "Elaine, let's go check on Adele and give her the robe and her crystal. I'll go look for the key with you after that."

Elaine inhaled and held her breath for a count before sighing it out. "Okay," she relented. "Just give me a moment." She glanced down the corridor in the direction the professor had walked only to see him pass through the double doors at the last second. Just then, a tall, bald man wearing a black leather jacket and dark pants came out of a room and walked through the double doors as well. He stood waiting for the elevator, blocking Elaine's view of Professor Wallace. "Did either of you notice the professor wasn't limping like he did earlier when he walked toward the sofa?" she asked Grant and Florence. But when she turned around, they had already passed the nurse's station and were knocking at Adele's door.

In a moment of haste, and rashness, she decided to confront Professor Wallace. Her high heels clacked across the hospital floor as she hurried down the corridor. The elevator doors opened, and both men stepped in before Elaine could reach the double doors.

Her feet ached, and the small blisters on her heels slowed her down even more. By the time she reached the double doors and pushed them open, the elevator door was closing. "Professor, wait!" she called out. She realized she couldn't catch up with them in time, so she kicked off her heels, abandoning them, and trodded down the hallway barefoot.

It was too late.

Inside the elevator, the bald man reached into the pocket of his leather jacket and pulled out a small, plastic case, the same size as the one Elaine had used to deliver the key to the professor. Her body felt cold when she saw him look up at her and taunt her with his dark eyes, sneering at her before the door closed in her face.

CHAPTER 12

Elaine stared at the elevator door, unsure what to do next. "Lazro," she whispered to herself. "That was him. I just know it." A surge of adrenaline rushed through her body, and she felt her heart beating faster. Without thinking, she ran to the stairwell door and pushed it open and began running down the cement stairs, grabbing the railing on each landing, propelling herself forward. As she rounded the corner and continued her descent, she hiked up her dress around her thighs so she could move more freely.

She was out of breath by the time she reached the first floor. She wasn't used to running down five flights of stairs barefoot. The few people in the lobby, most of them patients waiting to be admitted to the ER, stared at her in confusion. She probably looked like a mess. Her hair was in disarray, and she felt a bead of sweat forming on her upper lip. She suddenly realized that her bare thighs were revealed to everyone. She felt gross, but for once, she didn't care how she looked. She scanned the lobby and the elevator area to see if she could catch Lazro before he left. Or at the very least find Professor Wallace and ask him about the man who shared the elevator with him.

No one fitting their descriptions was in sight, so she ran out the sliding glass door and into the cold night air. The contrast between the bright yellow outdoor lights of the overhang and the indoor fluorescent lights caused her eyes to water. She rubbed her eyes and blinked hard a few times. Cars were scattered in the parking lot, but she didn't see a single soul. She must've missed her chance to confront Lazro. "What would I have said or done if I did catch up to him?" she wondered aloud as she made her way back to the entrance.

The truth of the matter was, she didn't know. She couldn't even be sure it was really him. Florence and Hugh had never seen Lazro. Even her aunts, who secretly were training her to become a guardian, only ever told her the story of him being a "bad man" on the day of her tenth birthday. Yet, the menacing look in the bald man's eyes disconcerted her. Her intuition told her that Lazro was on that elevator ... and the box he was holding in his hand contained her key.

Elaine suddenly became very aware that she was standing outside a hospital lobby in her bare feet. Her shoulders slumped, and she heaved a sigh of disappointment. She shivered as the automatic doors hissed open. The hairs on her arms stood up, and her teeth chattered. She wrapped her arms around herself and made her way to the elevators. As she approached, a handsome man who looked a lot like Eric exited the elevator farthest away from her. Without thinking, she dashed behind a potted palm tree and watched him pass. It was Eric all right. He was still wearing the silver shark-skinned suit and expensive wingtip shoes from their dinner that evening. He appeared deep in thought and was holding a bouquet of flowers wrapped in plastic.

She scooted around the palm and pressed herself into the corner so he couldn't see her and jumped when she saw a little toddler siting in a chair next to her, staring at her curiously. She put her finger to her lips, signaling to him not to say anything. "I'm playing hide-and-seek," she whispered to him. He giggled and waved at her, but he didn't say anything when his mother called him over to sit on her lap and read a book.

She watched as Eric approached the lobby attendant at the front desk and presented her with the bouquet of flowers. "Turns out my friend's allergic to these," he said to her. "They're for you now." He leaned up against the desk and put on his most charming smile. Elaine leaned closer so she could hear what he said next, but all she could discern was that whatever he said made the young attendant laugh. The woman typed something into the computer and then wrote on a sticky note before handing it to Eric.

"Snake," Elaine hissed under her breath. Eric must've decided it wasn't worth the effort to check on Adele to avoid Elaine confronting him about how he treated his supposed girlfriend this evening. She clenched her hands into fists as she watched him leave. When the coast was clear, she moved away from the palm tree and walked up to the desk attendant.

"Hi," Elaine began. "Um, this is going to seem like an odd request, but could you tell me what that gentleman just asked you?"

"I'm sorry, who are you?" the young woman asked. "I can't give out that information. Are you here to see a patient?" She stared hard at Elaine and then looked down at her feet. Her eyes widened when she noticed Elaine wasn't wearing any shoes.

"I must seem like a crazy lady," Elaine said to her. "But, that man, Eric, he's my boyfriend, and, um, well ..." She really didn't know what else to say. It wasn't like he had done anything bad or illegal. Why was she acting so insane? She could easily call Eric later and say she saw him when she went down to the lobby to find the vending machines. She just stood in front of the desk, thinking of numerous excuses she could use for why she hadn't tried to catch up to him. She also tried to think of good questions that would get him to open up to her as to why he was at the hospital.

The front desk woman's voice cut through Elaine's calculating thoughts. "Ma'am, are you all right? Do you need to see a doctor?"

"Huh? Oh, no, no. Sorry," Elaine replied hastily. "Never mind. I'm here visiting a friend. I just stepped outside for some fresh air.

That's all. Have a good night." Elaine backed away from the desk and power walked to the elevators. Her face and ears felt flushed, and she realized she must have looked like such an idiot. Goodness knows she felt like one. After what felt like forever, the bell dinged, and the elevator door slid open. She moved inside and hit the button excessively in hopes that it would shut before anyone else got on the elevator with her. The door closed, and she leaned back on the dark wood paneling. She readjusted her brooch and smoothed down her hair.

"Why didn't I confront Eric?" she questioned herself as the elevator began its ascent. She didn't have to search too hard for the answer. "Because I don't trust him anyway," she finally said out loud. Just admitting the truth to herself gave her a sense of relief. She turned her attention to the fact she wasn't wearing shoes and felt a bit grossed out by that fact. The thought of what was on the floors of a hospital made her mind spin with worry.

When she exited the elevator, she found her high heels where she had kicked them and pushed them onto her feet. "I'm definitely in need of a shower right about now," she mumbled to herself as she hobbled her way back down the hallway toward Adele's room past the nurse's station.

Adele's door was ajar, and she could see Grant's profile nearest the bed. She made sure her dress was in place before walking into the room.

Grant turned and looked at her. "Elaine, where did you go? Adele's been asking for you," he said as he walked over and hugged her.

Elaine's reaction to Grant's hugs had always been the same. She would stand limp with her arms by her sides while he wrapped his arms tightly around her. When she realized he wasn't going to stop hugging her until she hugged back, she would pat him on the shoulders with both hands and then gently push him away. She was worried that hugging another guy while she was dating Eric would send the wrong signal. This time, however, she held on a little longer and pressed her cheek into his chest before moving away from him to avoid his gaze. She didn't care that Florence and Adele were looking at them. She needed her friend right now.

"I think I just saw Lazro," she whispered as she stared at the floor. "He was in the elevator with the professor. He has my key." She glanced up at Adele, who looked less frail than she had earlier. The color had returned to Adele's cheeks, and her breathing was deep and even.

"Lazro?" Florence stepped forward from where she was sitting in the chair near the foot of the hospital bed. "How can you be sure?"

"I can't exactly," Elaine said. "But I just know it was him. He had these intense eyes, and when we made eye contact, it was like they were taunting me. And then, there was a plastic case in his hand. It looked exactly like the one Adele put the key in at her store. I know because I used it to transport the key to the restaurant." She looked over her shoulder at Adele and then went to her. "Adele, you believe me, don't you?"

Adele stared up at her. Her liquid brown eyes teemed with tenderness. Her hair, always so chic, was ruffled and matted from the fluffy pillow propping her up. She raised her hand and held it out to Elaine, who took it. Adele placed her other hand on top of Elaine's and patted it. "I believe you, Laney. I do."

"Have you seen Lazro before, Adele?"

"No, I haven't seen him, but I know your aunts have. That night, after the circle I told you about, remember? When the red key glowed and we saw someone running away down the alley? Well, they told me they had to leave because they had to return the key back to Hugh immediately. They had a sneaking suspicion the person spying on us was Lazro, or at least one of his followers." Adele began to tear up, and Florence handed her a tissue. "I offered to drive them back home to get their brooches and the other key so they could pass through the portal, but they refused. They said it was urgent and that everything would be fine. That's the last time I saw them. They died some time that night or early morning on that old country road."

Elaine took Adele's hand. She remembered that night all too well. Now she knew why they had been driving on that dark road so late at night. After they were found, Elaine had mentioned to the police that they had called her about a half hour before the wreck and left her a voice message. She had been deep asleep and didn't hear the phone ring. She only noticed the flashing message when she awoke that morning, feeling groggy and disoriented. She couldn't comprehend the urgency in their voices and their cell service was spotty. All she could make out were random words like "box" and "office." She heard Mildred tell Daphne to go faster and that Elaine would be able to help. Then the line went dead.

She had changed quickly and was out the door before six. She drove around to her aunts' favorite places to scour for antiques—John Bay's abandoned barn on the edge of town, Stu's junk lot, and even the local dump. They were nowhere to be found. Panicked, Elaine called the police. A small unit was dispatched, and the search began. By the time the paramedics found her aunts, it was eight-thirty in the morning. They had been dead for several hours. Their car, a brown Dodge Plymouth station wagon with wood-paneled doors, had rammed head-on into a large oak tree on an overgrown lane a few miles away from their house. Oddly enough, both Mildred and Daphne were farther up the lane, lying on their backs and without a scratch on them. No one had reported seeing the accident, but several neighbors mentioned to police that right before dawn, they saw a strange flash of lightning that streaked across the sky.

"Your aunts visited my mom the evening before their death," Grant said as Elaine recalled that fateful day. "Remember how Jilly told us there were rumors people in her neighborhood saw a weird streak of light at my mother's house the night she ... you know ... lost it?"

Florence cleared her throat when Grant mentioned this. Adele pulled her hand away from Elaine's, a startled look across her face. She rubbed her fingers in small circles around her temples as she closed her eyes in an attempt to gather her thoughts.

"Shall I tell them?" Florence asked.

"It's better they hear it from me," Adele said as she pushed herself up in bed and sat up straighter.

"Hear what?" Elaine asked. "Why does it seem like there are secrets upon secrets at every turn when we talk about my aunts and this key?"

"Yeah, now I'm even more curious than I was before," Grant chimed in. "What? Was my mother involved in this secret society too?"

"Hugh and I did tell you the basics about the key and the secret society," Florence replied. "But lately, our members have been searching for a possible link to the red key. A quest, so to speak, to find a new guardian. And Grant, we thought maybe your mother had ancestral ties to the guild too. We invited her to attend one of the meetings about six months ago. She seemed interested, but then a few days leading up to the last women's circle, she began to complain of a persistent migraine. Daphne and Mildred became worried about your mother and asked Adele to make a tincture for her using some of the herbs and essential oils from the portal that leads to Anton's cottage."

"It was a bending of the rules, but we never broke them," Adele interjected. "I want to make that clear. But we were so worried about Gladys, and I wanted to help. And those woods, a secret and magical place for sure, house some of the most potent botanicals I've ever come across. We decided we would only forage for the ones closest to the portal and never go any farther than that. But we didn't expect Lazro to uncover the whereabouts of our central location: my shop. We think he placed a mole in our circle to spy on us and gather information." Adele paused, reached over to her nightstand, and grabbed a tissue to dry her eyes and blow her nose before continuing. "And so, this last full moon, right after the women's circle ended and all the women left, we activated the portal, and Daphne and I stepped inside with my basket and a pair of shears."

Adele shifted to readjust her pillow, clearly uncomfortable—
with her bed or this conversation, Elaine couldn't tell—and then
continued. "When we got back, Mildred looked disheveled, and
your mother, Grant, was frail and slumped against the wall.
Mildred told us that the other key, the red one, had begun to glow
right after we stepped inside, and Gladys's headache worsened. We
all decided it wasn't worth putting your mother through such a
risk. Then we all saw glimpses of the intruder, like I mentioned.
You know the rest of the story and how it ended from there." Adele
began to softly cry. Florence handed her more tissues.

Adele's full revelation of what had happened at that last women's
circle sparked Elaine's analytical brain. Pieces of this strange puzzle
started to slowly reveal themselves to her. "Adele, the newcomer to
your group—was she tall and athletic with long black hair?"

Adele pulled the covers up to her chest. "My God, yes, Laney.
How did you know? Her name's Giselle, and she's new to the area.
She's a foreign exchange student at the university. She said she was
studying psychology, but she always had an interest in metaphysics.
Makes the best braided bread I've ever tasted too. She uses the right
amount of butter and egg mixture to give it that golden tone."

"That's great, Adele, but can you remember anything else?"
Elaine asked. "Like, did she have a tattoo on her wrist?" Grant and
Florence looked at each other. They must've realized where Elaine
was going with her line of questioning.

"Why, yes, and it was a strange tattoo. Just a black circle about
the size of a quarter. She always covered it up at our meetings, but
I noticed it once or twice when she came into my shop to buy our
goat's milk lotion and soap. Why do you ask?" Adele appeared to
be growing anxious and looked at all three of them for an answer.

"She's with Lazro," Florence confirmed. "We saw her tonight
at Hugh's home. She must have either been in Europe and Lazro
contacted her, or Lazro and his followers have figured out some
way to travel the same way we do."

"My bet is on the latter," Elaine replied. "It could explain the
instability you've noticed in your key lately. And mine too. We're

missing something, though. Grant, when did your mother start suffering from migraines? She never had them when we were growing up."

"No, she didn't. She didn't start getting them until about four or five months ago. She always complained about how they felt like knives slicing through the front of her brain. There were times she wouldn't eat barely anything because she felt so nauseous. The only thing she said soothed her was Adele's headache tonics."

"Ah, yes, my feverfew tea. I get the dried flowers from this lovely village right outside of Budapest. I was there a few years ago on a tour, and I came across this lovely shop—"

"I'd love to hear your adventures, Adele, but another time, please," Elaine interrupted. "Did Giselle ever buy feverfew from you?"

"No. A few times, she bought ashwagandha and ginseng root, great antiaging properties when made into a paste or tincture. She doesn't need it, though. She has such lovely skin," Adele replied. "But now that you mention it, I did do a trade with her. She had brought a small packet to the shop with her, said it was from her small town in Hungary. I gave her a small brooch in return that she had been eyeing for weeks." Adele paused and then suddenly she gasped. "Oh! It was a crescent moon brooch that looked similar to the ones the guild members wear. I bought them years ago in a small boutique in Paris. They reminded me of the ones Daphne and Mildred used to wear on occasion. They aren't antiques, though. Just some factory-bought, gold-plated fakes."

"Thanks, Adele. You're a huge help," Elaine said and then unexpectedly kissed her on the cheek.

"Do you still have any of those brooches?" Florence asked. "I have a better idea than the one I had earlier."

"Yes, I do. An entire box full in my shop," Adele answered. "Do you think Lazro and his 'followers' believe my brooches are the ones used for the keys?"

"It's a strong possibility," Florence replied.

"I have a question, Delly," Grant began. "That feverfew Giselle gave you—did you ever sell any of that?"

"No, it was such a small packet that I simply gave it to your mother, Grant." As soon as she finished her sentence, Adele gasped. "What if the feverfew was poisoned? What if Giselle was trying to take your mother out of the picture so she could somehow get a hold of the red key?"

"It does sound like something Lazro would coordinate," Florence conceded.

Grant stared in disbelief at the wall in front of him. "My mother? Poisoned? How could anyone do such a thing?" He ran his fingers through his hair and then along the back of his neck. The dark stubble on his face was more noticeable in the soft glow from the reading lamp above Adele's bed. His eyes were watery, as though he was fighting back tears.

"This has gone too far," Elaine said. She had positioned herself near the door. "It's one thing to come after me, but to harm Grant's mother in an elaborate ruse is crossing the line. I need to make direct contact with Lazro. If I'm a true guardian of both the green and red keys, then it's up to me to finish this once and for all. I say we lead him right to where he wants to go. He needs someone to lead him to the *Book of Secrets*. To Isabella. Why not let it be me?"

Excitement was building in Elaine's voice. A stirring of emotion stemming from her aunts' dedication and ultimate sacrifice overcame her. She bit her lip slightly and looked at them all with newfound conviction. "Florence, what happens if he can get me to unlock the portals and steal Isabella's *Book of Secrets*?"

Florence was shocked at Elaine's abrupt change of thought. "Unlock it? That's exactly what we're trying to prevent him from doing, Elaine! My intention of using you as bait, as you said earlier, was to corner him and get the key back. Not lure him closer to the inner circles of the guild and destroy everything the guardians have been protecting for centuries."

"I know," Elaine responded with calculating certainty, "but what if I was trained and fully initiated? Wouldn't I be able to at least get him to meet me and maybe convince him I want what he wants?"

"You mean, act like a double agent of sorts?" Grant asked.

"Well, yes," Elaine answered. "I could play it off that I felt my aunts were being deceitful to me and keeping me from my rightful place in the guild. Let him think that I want revenge."

"It's too risky," Florence added quickly. "Lazro is already powerful as it is. Look what happened to Grant's mother and to your aunts and your parents. He may have a web of spies all over the world. Elaine, this is not a good idea."

"Which is exactly why it just might work," Adele added confidently.

CHAPTER 13

"Adele, you can't be serious!" Florence exclaimed. "This goes against everything the guild is about. We're meant to *guard* the secrets. Preserve them for generations. Not lure in the one person who could destroy them all and use them for personal gain!"

"Who said he would get to use them?" Adele countered. "I think what Elaine is saying is that we need to let him believe she's malleable, that she can be persuaded to join his cause. Get close to the source and take away his power when he's least expecting it."

"Florence has a point," Grant said. "Maybe I should be the one who makes contact with Lazro. I mean, my mother is still alive, and it would make sense that I would want to take him down for what he has done to her. He would be expecting me to come after him, and I'm sure his ego wouldn't want to back down from a good old-fashioned fight."

"That's exactly the point, Grant," Elaine said, going over to him and putting her hand on his shoulder. "He would be expecting you. Who knows? He may already have a plan in place on how to deal with you if you ever did come after him. In fact, I bet he already expects all of us to come directly after him. If I prepare myself and learn the ways of the guild, then I can seek him out and convince him to let me be the one to reach my ancestor, Isabella, through the portal. Let him think I have a grudge against the guild too. My aunts did die protecting the keys, the very things he wants and the very things they were keeping away from me." She looked at Florence, who was biting her thumbnail and tapping her foot on the gray-tiled floor.

Florence looked at her. A mask of doubt clouded her face momentarily. "I see your point, Elaine," she began slowly. "However, it's just too risky. I suggest we all turn in for the night and meet again tomorrow morning when we're refreshed and have a clear head. Our emotions are all high right now. A lot has happened."

"I agree with Florence," Grant replied. "Adele, what do you think?"

"I suppose you're both right," Adele conceded. "I was just assaulted, and I'm lying here in a hospital bed. Elaine, let's put your idea on hold." She held her hand upright as Elaine opened her mouth to protest. "For now, I think a little rest would do us all some good."

They all stared at Elaine, who folded her arms across her chest. "Fine. I'll try to think of something else, if that's what you want." She swung around and made her way toward the door, whispering under her breath, "but I can't guarantee anything," as she walked out of the room.

Grant caught up with Elaine in front of the elevator. "I'll drive you home," he offered.

"Thanks."

They stepped into the elevator and stared ahead as the doors closed in front of them. After a second, Elaine rested her head on the back of the elevator, closed her eyes, and let out a sigh.

"Heavy stuff we learned tonight, huh?" Grant asked. She kept her eyes closed but nodded in consent. "It makes a little more sense now. About my mom, you know? I mean, she and your aunts were very close, and I always knew they went to the women's circle together each month. Heck, I even drove them there numerous times and waited at the diner until they finished. But to learn my mother was partially involved too? And possibly poisoned? It's a lot to take in."

Elaine opened her eyes as the elevator reached the lobby. Grant was visibly upset: his nostrils flared, and he had a wild look in his eyes. Elaine only saw him like that a few times over the course of their friendship. It was the same look he'd had when a few bullies in middle school pushed him to the edge. One time, he dumped milk on their heads after they taunted him about his secondhand clothes. And a few years ago, a library patron had made a vulgar remark to Elaine in front of Grant. He followed the guy to his car, let loose a barrage of insults, and postured himself in such a way that one year later, the man had racked up a significant overdue fine because he was too afraid to even go near the library.

"Grant, promise me you're not going to do anything rash," Elaine said as they walked outside.

Grant didn't respond until they got in his car and he started the ignition. "I can't promise anything right now. You're not the only one with money problems. It's complicated."

"Then enlighten me," she said as he put the car in reverse and backed out of the parking space.

"It has to do with Mr. Sadler too." Grant turned right on Main Street and passed the courthouse. "He advised my mom to withdraw early from her teacher's pension and roll it over into some type of annuity when she retired. He made it sound like she would get a large sum of money. He failed to tell her the taxes on it would be heavy and that he would be getting a nice chunk of change as well since he brokered the deal."

"Mr. Sadler? That rat!" Elaine exclaimed in disbelief. She huffed as she looked out the window and watched the streetlights stretch out in front of them as they cruised down the two-lane country highway. "Is that why she's in the assisted-living home? Grant, did your mother lose her home because of Mr. Sadler?"

A wave of sadness passed over Grant's face. "Yes," he responded quietly.

"I'm so sorry. I didn't realize it was that bad." Elaine became quiet and pressed her head up against the cold window and closed her eyes. Grant drove on in silence, his hands gripping the steering wheel so tight his knuckles were turning white. Neither spoke the rest of the drive home, both swimming in their own sadness at everything and everyone they had lost within the past month.

"Do you want to come in?" Elaine asked as Grant pulled up the driveway. "I can make you some coffee or tea. It's late, and I'd hate for you to drive home tired."

Grant tried his best to suppress a yawn, but it overcame him. "Yeah, I guess that would be the smart thing to do."

They made their way to the back door. Elaine noted the chipped wood around the frame. The scene of the ironic break-in returned a long-forgotten link to her past. She had Florence to thank for that. Florence with the jewelry box and the brooch and the key and the wild night of magic and mystery centering around a secret guild that members of Elaine's family were a part of for generations, apparently. It was hard for Elaine to wrap her mind around all that had transpired in the past twenty-four hours. If it wasn't for the fact that Grant had experienced this night with her, she would have believed she was dreaming or having delusions brought on by a nervous breakdown.

In the kitchen, Elaine scooped out the coffee, poured the cold water into the coffee maker, and hit the power button. She set out two mugs while Grant paced around the room. His hands fidgeted, and he bit his lower lip.

"Do you think Mr. Sadler is a part of this?" he finally asked as Elaine opened a package of her favorite oatmeal chocolate chip cookies.

She stopped what she was doing and looked at him. "You think he's working for Lazro?"

"Maybe." Grant opened the cabinet door and took out two plates and set a cookie on each one. "Mr. Sadler probably knew your aunts handled a lot of valuable antiques over the years. If Lazro or one of his gang found out that Daphne and Mildred were members of the guild, maybe they used Sadler to get to them."

"Huh ... But how does he fit in to all of this ... except for the fact that he gave some really bad financial advice to your mom and my aunts?"

"Well, let's think it through," he said as he poured them each a cup of coffee. "If he knew about the keys and their worth and importance to Lazro, maybe he thought they would be more willing to sell them to the right bidder if they went into financial ruin."

"That's a pretty intricate plan, don't you think? Why not just get someone to steal the keys? Which seems like the case based on what Adele told us tonight," Elaine said as she sipped her black coffee. Grant poured in creamer and a heaping teaspoon of sugar and stirred before taking a sip. "Good grief! How can you drink that? It's like hot pudding," she observed as he slurped his coffee and sighed happily. It reminded her of how they used to drink hot chocolate after playing in the snow when they were kids. She grinned and raised her mug to her lips and savored the warm, robust coffee with earthy hints of dark chocolate.

"What? It's good like this. You should add more sweetness to your life, too, Elaine," he replied and gave her a cheeky wink.

A sudden shyness overcame her, and she felt her cheeks grow warm. Was Grant flirting with her? She pushed a strand of hair behind her ear as she took another sip. Before she could think of something clever to say, a ding came from Grant's phone, indicating he had a message. He picked it up and read through the text and smiled.

"Florence," he said, and then shot off a quick text to her. "She says Adele is finally sleeping, and she's made herself cozy on the small sofa." He looked back at his phone and laughed. "She just sent a funny gif. Hold on, let me find a good one to send back," he said more to himself than for Elaine's benefit.

"When did you two exchange numbers?" She tried to act nonchalant, but her question came out more interrogative than she had intended.

"This evening, when you went on your wild goose chase," he said, looking up from his phone briefly to reply. His phone dinged again, and whatever it said had him cracking up. "Oh man, that's funny!" He sent off another text, and an awkward silence fell between them.

"That reminds me," she said, finally breaking the silence. "I should probably text Eric. We didn't really part ways on the best of terms this evening." She didn't mention she had seen him in the hospital lobby. She stood and walked over to her purse to grab her phone. She looked over at Grant to see if he was paying attention, but he was now engrossed in some conversation with Florence that obviously excluded her.

When she looked at her screen, she noticed she had two missed texts. One was from Eric that simply said he hoped Adele was all right and to call him when she got the chance. The other was from a number she didn't recognize. She was afraid to look at it in case it had some kind of virus attached, but curiosity got the best of her. When she tapped on the number, the phrase "YOU'RE BEING FOLLOWED" jumped at her off the screen.

She had to get her breathing under control before she could ask, "Grant, what's Florence's number?"

"Her number? Why do you ask?" He set his phone down and looked up at her.

She walked over to him and handed him her phone. "Read this text."

"This was sent about a half hour ago when we were leaving the hospital. It's not Florence's number, though."

"Then, whose is it?" Worry crept into her voice as her chest tightened.

"It looks like Teddy's. Let me double-check." He scrolled through his contact list and matched Teddy's number to the one on Elaine's phone. He looked at her with concern. "I don't think it's wise that you stay here alone tonight. I'll sleep on the couch. Where are the blankets?" he said as he made his way into the living room.

Elaine started to protest, but then thought better of it. It would be nice to have her best friend around on a night like this. He was directly involved now, so they needed to stick together and figure out their next move. "In the hall closet. I'll get things set up for you in just a sec."

"Wait. Do you think we should call Teddy?" The coffee's effect on Grant was evident. He sprang from his chair and tapped his fingers on the counter.

"Yeah, I guess that would make sense." Elaine shot off a text asking, "What makes you say that?"

In less than a minute, Teddy responded. "He says he will explain more tomorrow at the library," Elaine told Grant. "Okay, I'll grab you some sheets and a pillow."

Once they had set up a cozy spot for him on the couch, Grant peeked out the front window to check if anyone was lurking around or watching them from the street. "I don't see anyone, but that doesn't mean anything. Should we call the police?"

"And tell them what? That I received a weird text from our friend with a cryptic message on it? There's not much they can do at this point, I don't think."

"You're probably right. Still, it's kind of creepy."

She plopped down on the couch. "I'm exhausted, but I can't sleep because of the coffee."

"Yeah, me neither. Wanna have a pillow fight and watch scary movies?" he joked.

She giggled and rolled her eyes. "Weirdo." Leave it to Grant to make her laugh when she really felt like crying and freaking out about all that was happening.

"What's this?" Grant asked as he picked up the scrapbook Elaine had flipped through earlier, before the brooch was returned and her life went from strange to chaotic.

"Aunt Daphne and Aunt Mildred used to make scrapbooks of my life when I was a little girl. There are a lot more than just this one. I'm sure I can find some that have embarrassing photos of you when you were growing a rattail braid back in the day." She got up and went into the office and came back with three or four more scrapbooks as gaudy and filled with as many memories as the first one.

She sat next to Grant and they opened it up. "Oh wow, it's a picture of us in band!" She laughed. "Look how awkward we were. All limbs and big noses and big teeth."

"Not to mention big hair," Grant said as he pointed out a picture of Elaine with big bangs and braces. "Why did girls think that looked good?"

"Shut up! I was in style," Elaine said, and she jokingly jabbed him in the ribs. They laughed their way through a few more scrapbooks. Elaine couldn't help but realize how much Grant had physically changed since they were kids. Where he once had bad hair and pimples, he now had dark hair with a sprinkling of silver at the temples. And his square jaw and scruffy whiskers gave off a wild look tamed by large, liquid brown eyes that twinkled as he laughed and told her stories about how he pranked his chemistry teacher or how he couldn't believe Elaine threw their school bus bully into a headlock and made him eat a clump of grass. In all those years, Grant was the only one she could count on to help her navigate those confusing school days when no one seemed to understand her or include her in their sleepovers or tell her about their crushes.

Elaine started to tell him how grateful she was having him as her friend, but another text message interrupted her memories and desires. She jumped at the beep and grabbed her phone off the coffee table. Grant sat on the edge of the sofa, tapping his fingers on the cushions while he waited for her to relay the message. "Teddy says he'll meet us at the library tomorrow right after it opens. He has some information he can't share over text. Do you think he knows about Lazro or the guild?"

"With everything that happened tonight, I think anything's possible. I'll make sure to come in and work in the media center so I can stay in the loop."

"You've been a big help tonight, Grant." She stopped speaking when she noticed he was giving her a very intense look. His dark eyes bore holes into her and made her feel exposed yet safe at the same time. She caught her breath and dropped her gaze to the coffee table in front of them. "Well, it's getting late. I'm going to bed now. Do you need anything else?"

"No, I'm good. 'Night, Laney." Grant kicked off his shoes and stretched out on the sofa, throwing a blanket over his legs. "I'll be here for you in the morning."

"Grant? I-it was, um … it was nice reminiscing with you tonight."

"Yeah, you too," he said between yawns. He closed his eyes, and Elaine waited a beat before slowly making her way upstairs. Though she doubted she would be able to sleep with her heart flipping around in her chest and the nervous lump catching in her throat.

Chapter 14

The next morning, Elaine came downstairs and found Grant in the kitchen making a large breakfast. "Morning, Laney," he said as he whipped a few eggs and cream in a small mixing bowl and poured it into the skillet to make one of his fancy omelets. "Hope you don't mind that I helped myself to your food. I'll make you some eggs, too, if you'd like. There's also toast over there. Couldn't find the jelly, though." He took another sip of his coffee, set it down, then lightly sprinkled some salt and pepper onto the bubbling omelet.

Groggy from a restless night's sleep, Elaine poured herself a cup of coffee. "Scrambled eggs would be nice. Thanks." She shuffled around the mess Grant had made and set out plates and silverware. As an afterthought, she opened the refrigerator and found a half jar of raspberry preserves with crusted remnants around the lid.

Grant watched Elaine butter some toast before he spoke. "I talked to Florence this morning. She wants to meet up with us at the library too. She said Teddy's mother is a member of the guild and is curious if his involvement means he's ready to be initiated." Grant flipped the omelet, laden with cheese and tidbits of vegetables, then began cracking a few more eggs in the mixing bowl. "I'm assuming his mother is Vivienne, the woman Hugh mentioned?"

"Must be," Elaine said distractedly. She sat at the table and took a bite of toast. She had pulled out Mr. Sadler's letters from the cluttered catchall box on the table and spread them out in front of her. She examined the papers in hopes of finding something that keyed her in on Mr. Sadler and his connection to Lazro.

"Did I do something wrong?" Grant asked after a few moments of awkward silence between them. He set their eggs on the table and took a seat across from Elaine.

"What? Oh, no. Sorry. I was just thinking about Mr. Sadler and his timing on selling my aunts' estate so soon after their deaths. Do you think the estate sale is a ruse to get to the keys? Liquidate all their assets and repossess the contents of the store?" She took a bite of her scrambled eggs. "These are good, by the way. I was starving."

"Thanks. Yeah, Sadler's timing is definitely suspect," Grant said between bites. "I'm curious about what Teddy knows. Florence said he's always been reluctant to get involved with guild activity."

At the mention of Florence's name, Elaine felt a pang in her heart. "You like her, don't you?" she asked. She'd tried to keep her tone light and playful, but her throat felt a little constricted as she tamped down some emotions she wasn't willing to allow to the surface.

Grant had to think before he answered Elaine's question. "I don't know where you're going with this, Laney. I think she's nice, if that's what you're asking." He quickly finished the last bite of his omelet and buttered another slice of toast. "I'm more interested in learning about our roles in this key business and secret society. I mean, we just found out yesterday that your aunts and parents, and my mother by association, have been a part of something secretive and ancient. That's where I want to focus my energy. Don't you?"

"Yeah, of course. You're right," she said as she shook her head. "Sorry. I was being nosy. It's been a while since you dated, and I couldn't help but notice how you two act around each other."

Flustered, Grant got up from the table and rinsed his plate and coffee mug. He placed them in the dishwasher and began to clean up the mess around the stove. "I'm surprised you notice anything about me," he mumbled as he put the carton of eggs back in the refrigerator.

"What's that?" Elaine asked. She folded and stacked the letters, then wrapped a rubber band around them.

"Nothing. I'm going to wash up and then pick up Florence at the hospital. Adele gets discharged today. I'll take her back home, and then we'll meet you at the library around ten."

"What about Teddy's text saying I'm being followed? I should go with you." Elaine tried to hide her anxiety about being left alone, but he could hear it in her tone. "Besides, it's James's turn to open the library this morning. I have a little time before I have to be there."

"Okay. Fine." Grant sounded defeated, but he smiled at Elaine and nodded. "I want to leave in ten minutes, though. I told Florence I'd be there soon."

Elaine cleared her plate and put everything in the dishwasher before heading upstairs. She couldn't shake her annoyance at the mention of Florence's name, but she tried to hide it as best she could.

Ten minutes later, Elaine walked back downstairs wearing a fresh pair of leggings, tennis shoes, and a midlength, teal-blue fleece pullover. She had wrapped a cream-colored scarf around her neck and completed her sporty ensemble with matching fingerless gloves and a hat Mildred had knitted for her a few years ago. Her long hair was tied at the nape of her neck, and she wore the turquoise earrings Daphne had given her from her aunts' trip to Santa Fe last year. She had pinned the brooch to her tank top underneath, too afraid to let it out of her sight.

"Wow. You look nice," Grant said as they made their way to his car.

"Thanks. I feel bad that we don't have time for you to go home and shower and change. I hope you get a chance to relax at some point today," Elaine said as she strapped on her seat belt.

"Yeah, me too." Grant's response was distant. His focus seemed to be more on their surroundings. He looked in his driver-side mirror and then in the rearview mirror before starting the car. "Sorry, just checking if I can see anything out of the ordinary that might indicate we're being followed. That text really does worry me."

"I know what you mean. I'll help keep a lookout."

When they were closer to the hospital, Elaine checked her passenger-side mirror. A familiar maroon-colored four-door sedan was behind them. Elaine felt a flutter in her stomach and her thighs clenched, sure signs that her intuition was telling her something important. "Grant, have you ever seen Mr. Sadler's car?" she asked.

"No, why?" he asked.

"Check your rearview. He drove to my house last week, and I'm pretty sure that's his car behind us."

Grant peered in the mirror and then focused back on the road in front of him. He decided to take a side street downtown and work his way to the hospital using that route. Thankfully, the sedan didn't follow. Elaine tried to get a look at who was driving but couldn't distinguish who it was because a large, blue post office drop box on the corner of the sidewalk obstructed her view.

When they made it to the hospital, they found Adele and Florence in the lobby. The doctor determined Adele didn't have a concussion. With the exception of the bags under her eyes and her matted hair, Adele appeared her usual composed and effervescent self. Elaine rushed to Adele's side and hugged her tightly.

"What's all this about?" Adele chuckled as she hugged Elaine back. "One would think you were worried about this old broad."

"I'm just glad you're okay," Elaine responded. "Let me carry that." She picked up the plastic bag containing Adele's robe and crystal.

Adele swept her hand in the air. "Thank you, dear," she replied and linked arms with Grant, who guided her out the lobby door.

Florence and Elaine followed behind them. "I'm assuming Grant told you about Teddy's cryptic text I received last night?" Elaine asked Florence once they were out in the parking lot.

"Yes, and it's a good thing he did too," Florence said. "We all have to stick close together now and be on the alert. Lazro has a lot of influence and resources at his disposal. Who knows whom he has recruited to help him track down the missing keys."

On their way to the car, Elaine began to think about Mr. Sadler. The fact that her aunts and Grant's mother had been his clients and something drastic happened to all of them bothered her. She decided to take a gamble and lay out a theory she had been puzzling out last night. "How much value are these keys if they were to be sold on the black market? Is it possible that someone like Mr. Sadler would want to get a hold of the entire set of keys for himself? I know from my aunts' years of antique dealings that sets of anything collectible are way more valuable than just one or two items. Maybe that's what all this boils down to."

They stopped in front of Grant's car, and Florence took a breath and faced Elaine. "Grant told me about his mother's money problems and about Mr. Sadler. You make a good point, Elaine. Lazro is clever, and he may have recruited Mr. Sadler to help him retrieve the keys. But, please, make no mistake: Lazro knows the power the keys would give him if he possesses all of them. You've only witnessed using one at a time. Imagine if he gets someone to help him unlock all the portals and gets to Isabella's *Book of Secrets*. Everything the guild has protected for centuries would be wiped away. Lazro could unleash chaos and use the magic and its properties for selfish means and hoard precious resources meant to heal others and the earth. This Mr. Sadler is one we should definitely watch out for, but we have to root out who Lazro really is."

"And where he is," added Grant after unlocking his car doors.

Florence smiled and nodded. "You're right, Grant. We need to figure out where he is."

"Tally ho!" Adele chuckled as she sat down in the passenger seat. "Before we begin our quest, please take me home so I can shower. I smell like disinfectant and stale cheese puffs."

When they arrived at her house, Adele insisted she was fine and wanted to check on her shop once she had a chance to relax and freshen up a bit. They made plans to meet her at the diner for a late lunch and then headed downtown.

The library was in sight when a strange figure caught Elaine's eye. A bald-headed man wearing a black leather jacket had one foot propped up on a bus-stop bench and was checking his phone. "That's the man I saw in the elevator last night with the professor!" Elaine exclaimed.

Florence turned around in her seat and strained to get a good look at him. By then, he was talking on his phone and walking away from them, so she only saw his back. "I couldn't get a good look at him. Are you sure, Elaine?"

"It's Lazro. I just know it," Elaine stated as Grant turned into the library's parking lot.

Grant whipped the car around, but the man had disappeared.

"Where is he? Do you see him?" Grant asked.

"He couldn't have gone far," Elaine responded. "Turn here and drive down to the hardware store. Maybe he ran down the alley?"

Grant took her advice. He drove down the alley and then around the block. The man was nowhere to be found.

Disappointed, Grant turned the car around and drove back to the library. He pulled into an empty parking space closest to the back entrance.

The three of them dejectedly walked up the small set of stairs and passed through the lobby entrance, murmuring quiet hellos and good mornings to the library's familiar faces: James was shelving books in the children's section, and Syd and Tom were sitting at the table in the reading room setting up another chess game. Mrs. A chatted for a minute with Elaine before wheeling over to get some coffee. She had convinced Elaine to set up a donation-based coffee station to offset the purchase of new beanbags in the children's section.

Elaine walked behind the circulation desk, logged on to the computer, and then checked to see if Teddy had texted her. "Nothing," she said as she glanced up at Grant and Florence, who were both anxiously looking around.

"What should we do now?" Grant drummed his fingers on the countertop.

Florence picked up and put down one of the staff's recommended reading books. "Wait, I guess. Elaine? Any suggestions?"

"Let's stick fairly close together," Elaine said as she locked her purse in her drawer. "I'll get some work done here at the desk. Why don't you two go and hang out in the reading room? We can see each other and the entrance from there. If Teddy or Lazro walk in, we'll know."

"Good idea, Laney," said Grant. He ushered Florence past him, and they walked over to the reading area.

Elaine couldn't help but notice how close they were standing as they scanned the magazine racks together. Grant whispered something to Florence. In turn, Florence touched his arm and laughed. Elaine fought the temptation to go over there and break up their conversation, so she checked her phone again for any messages—one voicemail and a text.

Call me. I came looking for you at the hospital. Let me make it up to you.

Eric's text was followed by a wink and a heart emoji.

She deleted it.

Maybe Eric was trying to be a better boyfriend, but she really didn't know what to say or do about their relationship right now. Maybe she would agree to see him once the key business was resolved. She reasoned that time apart might help her gain a little more perspective on why she was with him in the first place.

How she had missed the voicemail notification earlier was beyond her. It was from Mr. Sadler. Elaine held her breath and decided to bite the bullet and listen to it. It was in the same fashion as all the other ones he had left except in this one, he mentioned they needed to set a date for the auction of the contents of the store.

Anger washed over her. How dare he assume the role to make plans to sell her aunts' antiques! She was their next of kin, not him. She had half a mind to call him back and read him the riot act when Teddy walked through the lobby doors.

"Teddy, hi," Elaine said to him as he approached her. "Mrs. A was wondering why Gus brought her in instead of you this morning. I'm sure she'd love to see you." Elaine felt very on edge. She was delaying Teddy so she could gain her composure before learning whatever it was he had come to tell her. She stood on tiptoe, looking past Teddy and scanning the room for the old lady librarian. She saw her at the coffee table, asleep in her wheelchair with a foam cup hanging precariously from her limp hand.

"She's fine, Elaine. She probably forgot I took the day off to study," Teddy said calmly. "Let's not wake her." He surveyed the front desk area before turning his attention back to her. "I just came here to look for a book. Can you help me, please?" He gave her a look telling her to play along in case anyone might be eavesdropping.

"Sure, yeah," she said. She looked toward the reading room, where Grant and Florence were talking quietly. They didn't see her, even though she signaled with a wave in their direction. "Let me tell Grant and Florence you're here."

"This will only take a minute, Elaine. Besides, it's something only you can help me with." He walked toward the biography section near the back. He picked up the pace, and she knew she had no other choice but to follow him. After making certain they had privacy, he chose a random book from the shelf. It was a selection about the history of shipbuilding in early America. "Act casual," he said quietly, "and just listen and nod a few times to make it look like we're discussing this book."

"Teddy, you're scaring me. Are you okay? How do you know I'm being followed?" Elaine clenched her hands behind her back and forced herself to pretend the book was the focus of their conversation.

"I'm fine. Elaine, you need to know ... I worked for your aunts on occasion. Little errands here and there, mostly delivering heavy antiques or picking up something they had purchased online."

"They never mentioned that," Elaine said.

"Well, it was never anything official. They paid me in cash. Just a little bit of money to help me cover the cost of my textbooks. Anyway, on the day before they died, I was to pick up a package from this professor on campus, a Professor Wallace in the History Department. But I never went because I got called in to work. There was a shortage of staff, and I needed the overtime pay. Your aunts told me it wasn't a big deal and that they would get it themselves. The next morning, I got the news that they ..." He shifted his weight to his other leg and put the book back on the shelf and pulled out another one.

"Right ... died in the car crash ... So, how did my aunts know Professor Wallace, Teddy? What did they have to pick up from him?" Her cheeks flushed, and she felt the tips of her ears grow hot. Professor Wallace knew about her aunts and their business. Did he know more about the keys and their roles in the guild? And why had he never said anything about them? Her suspicions grew as she stood together with Teddy in the narrow aisle.

"Well, I was on campus a few days later, and I decided to follow up with the professor about the package and to inform him of their untimely deaths. I don't know if you're aware, but he is also the head curator of the history museum there."

Elaine nodded. "Oh, I'm aware, all right."

"Well, he wasn't in his office, so I left. As I walked by the reception desk, I saw this tall, bald-headed guy in the lobby. He stood around and just eyed the place like he was scouting it out. I approached him, and when he saw me walking his way, he made some kind of lame remark that he was looking for the registrar's office and then quickly made his way out of the building. Then, last week, I saw him lurking around town and again outside the library yesterday as Mrs. A and I were driving away. That's why I texted you. Elaine, I think he's after something your aunts had or the professor has—"

"Or wants," Elaine said.

"Elaine!" Grant huffed as he and Florence walked up to them. "Why didn't you come get us? Hey, Teddy." He and Teddy shook hands.

"Hello, Theodore," Florence said flirtatiously.

"Hey, Florence." Teddy raised one of his eyebrows and grinned. "I shoulda known you would be caught up in all this. Did Hugh send you to fix this mess?"

She smiled back before nudging him with her elbow. "Hey! I've been fully initiated. It's not my fault your mother keeps badgering you to join the guild after you've completed your studies."

"Hey now, you better leave my mother out of this," Teddy said.

They would've continued their playful banter, but Elaine could no longer take being left out of the conversation. "Okay, okay," she chastised. "Just stop." She took the book out of Teddy's hand and replaced it on the shelf. "Teddy, why didn't you say anything about the key when I showed it to you and Mrs. Armested last week?"

"I don't believe in magic keys, healing stones, or mysticism," Teddy said. He lifted an eyebrow and shook his head back and forth. "But I do believe in my mother, and when she told me that two of the keys were missing and that Daphne and Mildred were attempting to get the source key back, I knew I had to step in and help."

Florence spoke first. "Teddy's mother is Vivienne. You heard Hugh mention her. She's a skilled herbalist, powerful guardian, and one of the most amazing women I've ever met. I just wish you would have a little more faith in what we do, Teddy."

"Listen," Teddy started, "I may never fully understand what it is y'all do, but I do know my mother has a lot of knowledge and skill when it comes to healing, and she believes deeply in the guild and what it stands for. Part of me definitely wants to believe she hasn't been wasting her time or energy all these years protecting something that is beyond explanation to my academic mind." He looked at his watch. "I should go soon, but I thought you needed to know, Elaine, that I think this professor friend of yours has gotten you involved in some shady business. It sounds like you already knew that, though, so maybe your plan of attack should be to go on the offense? Try throwing whoever is following you off the scent."

Grant scratched his chin and shifted his weight, anxious to start some plan in motion. He was about to suggest they all sit and hash it out when the younger man started talking again.

"Before I forget," Teddy said, "I'm putting you down as my special guests for the museum's gala at the end of this month. My band and I will be playing, and my mom and Aunt CiCi are coming to watch me. October twenty-ninth—put it on your calendars!"

"Hmmm ... that's giving me an idea," Elaine said, smiling for the first time. "Perhaps a little cat-and-mouse game ... Maybe I tell the professor I've found both keys and that I'd like to present them as a gift to the museum the night of the gala. I could suggest he advertise it to create more buzz."

"Very clever, Elaine," Florence broke in. "Make Lazro believe that the keys are within his reach that night and set a trap to catch him in the act of stealing them."

"If anything, we can draw Lazro into a public setting and confront him that way," Elaine said. She turned and gave Teddy a big hug. "You've been a huge help. Thank you!"

"What about the guy who supposedly is following you, Elaine?" Grant chimed in. "What if he is Lazro, or at least one of his gang members? He would know that you don't have the green key since you said he had it last night in the hospital."

"True." Elaine paused for a moment. "But remember how weird Professor Wallace was acting when we saw him with some sort of brooch in his office that day we were there?" Grant nodded. "We should use that information to our advantage. Professor Wallace obviously knew my aunts before we met him, and he started dating Adele right around the time of their deaths. He is either connected to Lazro somehow or has motives all his own for certain antiquities. We should invite him to the auction."

"What auction?" all three asked in unison.

"The one we will be holding to sell off my aunts' estate," Elaine declared and turned around to confront the pudgy bystander lurking behind the shelf of books next to them. "Don't you think, Mr. Sadler?"

CHAPTER 15

Elaine moved the books aside on the metal shelf and glared at Mr. Sadler, who was standing there wiping his glasses with his handkerchief. Elaine could tell his actions were an attempt to cover up his unease at her discovering him. His glasses shook ever so slightly in his hands, and his eyes twitched uncontrollably. Florence and Grant walked around to where he was standing, with Teddy following close behind.

"Elaine," Mrs. Sadler said as he placed his glasses back on his nose, "I'm glad I caught you. I, uh, I've been trying to get ahold of you ever since our last meeting. Whatever caused your change of heart, I'm glad to hear you are coming to your senses about this matter of your aunts' estate." Beads of sweat glistened on his brow, and his brown suit jacket was ruffled at the collar.

Elaine narrowed her eyes into a piercing gaze. "Don't pretend you don't know about Lazro and the keys, Mr. Sadler. I know you're working for him. He sent you here to spy on me, didn't he?"

Mr. Sadler tilted his head. "Lazro? Keys? I have no idea what you're talking about. I'm here because you didn't return my calls." He stood up straighter and stuck his chest out. "It's imperative we begin liquidating your aunts' assets to appease the bank and the

IRS. Not a moment to spare in the financial world. Time is money, as they say."

Grant stepped closer. "Is this the type of pressure you used on my mother to get her to sell her home and turn over her investments to you?" His fists were in a tight ball at his sides, as though he were ready to throw a punch any moment, and his jaw was clenched.

Mr. Sadler backed up and knocked into the bookshelf behind him. A few books toppled over and fell to the floor. "Now, listen here—I didn't coerce your mother into anything, young man. She needed my assistance and I merely, um ... uh ..." He swallowed hard and pushed up his glasses. "I spelled out the risks for her, but she chose to go along with the deal. All my clients know there is a possibility of high loss in return for high gains. You have to spend money to make money, as they say."

Grant grabbed him by his necktie. "I've had enough of your clichés, you bastard. My mother never would have given her money to some low-life, seedy character like you had she not been coerced."

"Grant, stop," Elaine interjected. "Now's not the time. We need to stay focused on what we're really trying to figure out, remember?" She stepped alongside both of them and stared intently at Grant.

Grant's shoulders relaxed as he looked into Elaine's eyes. She felt his passion and his sadness and wished she could take away his pain. He had a strong need to protect his mother—or anyone he believed was being bullied, really—but Elaine had to help him see they needed some type of strategy to go after Lazro and the missing keys before they could get to the bottom of his mother's sudden mental decline and financial straits.

Florence reached out and touched Grant's arm. "She's right, Grant. Let him go."

Grant paused in deliberation. With a sigh, he released Mr. Sadler and took a step back, shooting a death glare at him. "This isn't over," he said between gritted teeth before stomping away.

"I'll go talk to him," Teddy said, following Grant.

So that left Florence and Elaine to handle Mr. Sadler. "I'm not going to apologize for Grant, Mr. Sadler," Elaine said. "It does seem you take advantage of elderly people and single women. However, I've thought about your recommendation, and it seems like there's no other option than to auction off the contents of my aunts' store."

"I'm glad you've come around to this reasonable solution," Mr. Sadler hissed as he straightened his tie. "I have the paperwork here in my briefcase, if you'd like to take a look at it." He rifled through his leather bag and produced a manila folder.

"How convenient," Elaine muttered as she took the folder from him.

Mr. Sadler wiped the beads of sweat off his forehead with his handkerchief. "Well, then. I guess my work here is done. Be sure to sign and date it where I've highlighted, then call my office, no later than tomorrow, and my secretary will make all the necessary arrangements." He picked up his bag and held it to his chest as he spun around and walked to the side door. It was clear he desired no more encounters with Grant, who was standing at the circulation desk and watching his every move.

"Well, that's done," Elaine whispered. She opened the folder and read the first few sentences of the document outlining the sale. "It's too bad it's come to this."

Florence shook her head. "I'm so sorry, Elaine. I can only imagine how difficult this is for you."

Elaine's heart felt heavy, and she realized a part of her life—an era really—had come to an end. She had to remind herself it wasn't her fault her aunts weren't savvy business owners. She needed to come to terms with viewing herself as a victim in all this. She'd made choices to look the other way or get wrapped up in her life and ignore all the warning signs that they were having money problems. As a young adult, she disregarded her aunts' requests for her to learn more about the business, her heritage, and their life stories. Now, she found herself wanting to place blame on Florence, Hugh, Adele, and the guild for getting her involved. Yet,

Florence had been nothing but helpful and encouraging from the moment they met. So had Adele in her own way. And Teddy and Grant too. It was time she stepped up and took ownership of what was happening, even if she didn't fully understand the magic or the mystery of it all. "Thanks, Florence," she said. "That means a lot. Now, let's get Grant and meet Adele at the diner. I think she deserves to know about the professor and his prior business dealings with my aunts."

They walked toward the circulation desk together and caught up with Teddy and Grant, who were discussing their dislike of Mr. Sadler. Elaine went behind the desk, unlocked the drawer, and took out her purse.

Grant leaned over the counter. "Why did you agree to the auction, Elaine? That seems so unlike you. And why give that jerk and his firm any money for setting it all up?" he asked.

"You're right," Elaine said with a sigh. "It is unlike me, and he is a jerk. But my intuition told me the auction seems like a good place to draw Lazro into the open. Teddy said so himself that Daphne and Mildred were already dealing with Professor Wallace, and we know he might have had some type of brooch that day at his office. So, if we have an auction, Professor Wallace's interest will probably be piqued as well. We can figure out his connection to the guild and his true interest in these quaint items from a bygone era."

Grant pushed off the counter as Elaine made her way around. "He did act weird about that piece of jewelry, and he seemed to have just the right book at his disposal to show us about these trade guilds. I understand a little more of where you're going with this, but won't you be sad to close the shop?"

"Of course, I'll be sad," Elaine responded. "But look at it this way: if I'm in control of going through their inventory and getting it ready for the auction, it will buy us some time to look for anything else related to the guild and keep it out of Lazro's, or anyone else's, hands."

"That's true ... but Daphne and Mildred were experts at hiding things in plain sight, remember?" Florence said. "How will we know what to look for and where?"

"In all the obvious places." Elaine smiled, recalling the scavenger hunt from her tenth birthday. She had found their gift in a hollowed-out trunk of an old hickory tree that rested by the stepping stones at the creek. It had been her favorite reading spot as a child.

The three of them said their goodbyes to Teddy, who was late for his jazz band rehearsal. He agreed to try to keep tabs on the bald-headed man who had been following Elaine. "Leave it to me to run interference with that guy. My mom's an expert with spices. I'm thinking he needs to become acquainted with her ghost pepper spray recipe," he said with a wink.

Elaine couldn't help but laugh at his random comment. "What's that supposed to mean?"

"Let's just say there's more than one way to 'ghost' a person," Teddy remarked.

"Teddy! It's so unlike you to be so ..." Elaine searched for the right word.

"Devilish?" He grinned. "Like I said, I don't really believe in all this hocus-pocus stuff, but I do believe in my mom. I've seen what she's been able to do with a little bit of ground pepper, and it would surprise you." He waved and headed out the door, still grinning.

Elaine made arrangements with James, who agreed to stay and close the library so she could take the rest of the day off—something she rarely did—and then she, Florence, and Grant walked out the door as well.

Florence stared in the direction of the bank's parking lot across the street, then slid in to the back seat of Grant's car. "Is that him?" she whispered. "The bald man Teddy was talking about?"

They all caught a glimpse of the man sitting behind the wheel of a silver Lincoln Town Car.

"Do you think Teddy saw him when he left?" Grant asked.

"I'll text him and let him know," Elaine said as they pulled out of the parking lot. "You focus on driving to the diner, Grant.

Florence and I can watch and see if he follows us." Sure enough, a few seconds later, the silver car followed them. However, it only lasted for about a block before the driver turned right at a stop sign.

"I wonder where he's off to ..." Grant remarked as he glanced in the rearview mirror. They all watched the car drive down the side street and blend into the lunch-hour traffic.

"As long as he doesn't show up at the diner, I don't care right now," Elaine replied, feeling mentally exhausted.

Grant parallel parked the car a block away, and the three of them walked in silence. As they entered the diner, the smell of grease seeped into their clothing and hair. Grant inhaled dramatically as they made their way to the booth where Adele was already sitting. "Ah, nothing like fried food to take your troubles away."

"Hello, darlings," Adele cooed and took Elaine's and Grant's hands. She looked so much better and was even wearing an ocean-blue headscarf decorated with magenta and yellow flowers. Her dangling earrings were yellow, which seemed to be part of a set with her chunky yellow bracelet and beaded necklace. A large, yellow plastic belt cinched around the waist of her ocean-blue knit sweaterdress completed her look. Her magenta lipstick highlighted her beautiful skin. On anyone else, this '80s-style outfit would look like a costume, but Adele had a way of embodying a bold look and making it appear natural and fresh.

"You look well rested, Adele," Florence said as she slid into the circular booth next to Grant.

Adele smiled. "It's a wonder what a good nap and some cold cream will do. Shall we order?" she asked just as Jilly approached with pen and paper in hand.

"I've never been here, so I'll need to look at a menu," Florence stated.

"Oh, honey, try the special," Jilly said. "It's about the freshest thing on the menu today. Country-fried steak with gravy, mashed taters, and green beans with almonds. Pecan pie is the special dessert of the day."

Adele clapped her hands. "Say no more, dear! That's what I'll have. And a cup of coffee too, please."

Elaine ordered a chef salad and whispered to Florence she'd be better off with something light because the gravy stuck to your ribs, and its aftertaste lingered for hours afterward. Florence chose to play it safe and ordered the same as Elaine while Grant risked the daily special and a soda. Jilly left to give the chef their order, so Adele caught them up on her day and how the new inventory she just received in her store, a hemp lotion infused with CBD oil, was good for the joints and daily aches and pains. Elaine was afraid to broach the subject of Professor Wallace as she recalled how he and Adele had seemed so happy together last night at the restaurant.

Jilly brought them their food, and they spent a few minutes eating in silence. Elaine wished she would have gone for the special. Mashed potatoes were a comfort food, and she could've asked for the gravy on the side. Florence regretted her choice as well, but then Grant graciously gave Florence a few bites of his meal, and she relished it with delight.

"That's it," she said. "Next time, I'm going for fried food. Sorry, Elaine, but this is good. Is it too much to ask for a bite of your pecan pie, Grant?"

"Not at all," he said and divided it in two.

Elaine couldn't watch them sharing food, so she asked Adele if she had heard from the professor.

"It's strange," Adele began. "I've called him twice this morning, but I got his voicemail each time. I left a message asking him to lunch, but I haven't heard from him. I hope he's okay. I know he was very shaken by last night's ordeal."

Grant scraped the last bits of pie onto his fork. "I'm sure he's all right, Delly. Maybe he's busy teaching his classes and preparing for the museum gala?"

"Yes, yes, you're probably right," Adele said as she patted his hand. "The man is dedicated to his work. Why, he told me that he traveled as far as Spain once to track down an item he believed would be a great addition to the museum's personal collection."

"What was the item?" Florence asked. The mention of Spain made her put her fork down on her plate. Southern Spain was the red key's country of origin. It was where Isabella had written the *Book of Secrets* and created the keys' portals using the brooches for all the original apothecary healers. The portals allowed them to not only protect the book and its contents of healing magic but also gave the original members places to gather and deliver their findings of new plants and medicinal properties from their regions to Isabella.

Florence knew Isabella's source portal in Spain was vulnerable if Lazro was able to access it by finding the red key and its corresponding brooch. With Elaine as its rightful guardian, she was the missing link the guild needed to enter Isabella's realm. What harm could Lazro bring to the guild and Isabella? He blamed her for his illness. More importantly, it was Isabella alone who could provide him with the immortal elixir, which he would no doubt use for dubious means. He could easily replace Anton— or any of the other original guild members and gatekeepers—with people he could manipulate to do his bidding. Together, they could hoard the cures and earth magic, along with other antiquities, that would help Lazro acquire wealth and power.

"I'm not sure," Adele replied. "I believe he said it was part of a larger set. It was during one of our first dates together. He said that Spain—the city of Granada, to be specific—was the last place the item had been seen, but he didn't have any luck finding it."

"Florence," Elaine said, "didn't two of the original guild members, the mother and daughter, live in Spain?"

Florence nodded in confirmation. "Yes, Magda and Isabella. Magda was of central European descent and moved to Spain with her parents when she was a teenager. Isabella and Magda were Romani and traveled across Europe. They were living in the Sacromonte caves of Granada, Spain, when Isabella formed the guild."

"Oh dear," Adele said. "Could Edmund be looking for the same thing we are?"

"It's awfully suspicious," Elaine answered. "And now the green key is missing after it was in his possession for only a short time."

Adele stared at Elaine in disbelief. "Do you really think my sweet Edmund could be so deceitful?"

"Well, Adele, what does your intuition tell you?" Elaine asked. "I'm being serious here," she added when Adele gave her a skeptical look. "You truly have a gift of knowing things by trusting your feelings. I see that now."

Adele sat up straighter in the booth and placed her hands over her solar plexus. She closed her eyes and began to breathe deeper and exhaled through parted lips. After a few rounds of slow breathing, she opened her eyes, and a tear streamed down her cheek. "He's involved. I don't know how exactly, but he's involved. We can't trust him. Oh, how could I be such a fool?" She placed her head in her hands and her elbows on the table. "I led Professor Wallace right to you *and* the keys. Maybe he was never interested in me or my store or my travel stories. I'm such a fool."

"No, Adele, you're not," Grant said as he hugged her.

Elaine, who was also sitting next to Adele, put her arms around the older woman, and her hand brushed up against Grant's arm. She leaned her head against Adele's and whispered, "Grant's right. You're not a fool, Adele. I should have trusted you a long time ago. Can you ever forgive me?"

Adele sat up, and Grant and Elaine removed their arms from around her. "Forgive you? I'm the one who allowed myself to be duped by a handsome stranger and led him right to what my best friends had been trying to keep hidden for all these years. I regret ever selling him that piece of jewelry the first time he walked into my store. I swear, Elaine, all I ever wanted was to be a good friend to your aunts and to help you learn about your heritage after they died. I was too pushy with you, I suppose."

"It's all right," Elaine assured her. "I was thinking—"

"What's that about a piece of jewelry?" Florence interrupted. She took the last bite of the pecan pie Grant had given her and set her fork down on her plate.

"Oh, it's how we first met," Adele replied. "He walked in the store, we flirted a bit, I showed him some of my latest inventory, and then he bought a bauble of sorts. A moon-and-star pin, like the one I told you I sold to Giselle. He said it was for his sister, who lives in Iowa." A curious look passed over Adele's face. "I guess I have always coveted those brooches … I couldn't help purchasing look-alikes." She chuckled a bit at her own envy and then brushed it away with a wave of her hand. "Those gals. I sure do miss them."

"Where did you say you kept those baubles?" Florence asked. She dabbed a napkin at the corners of her mouth to ensure she didn't have any pie crumbs lingering there.

"In my shop. They were very popular with the young college women when fall semester started. Why?"

Florence took a sip of water. "No reason," she said. "You were saying something, Elaine?"

Clearly annoyed for being interrupted, Elaine pressed forward. "I was going to say, I think it's time I do something I thought I would never hear myself say I would do."

"What's that, dear?" Adele questioned.

"I'm coming to the next women's circle, Adele. We're going to contact Hugh and Vivienne to meet afterward, and then you're all going to initiate me into the guild. Lazro won't succeed in finding that red key, and I'll get the green one back as well."

"Oh, darling, that makes my heart so happy!" Adele exclaimed. She pinched Elaine on the cheek, then she wrapped her hands around her coffee mug and stared at it for a minute. "But … why does my intuition tell me that's not the shocking part?"

"You're right, again," Elaine said. She smiled and took a deep breath before continuing. "The shocking part is that I need you to channel Daphne and Mildred that night so they can tell us exactly where it is they hid the red key."

CHAPTER 16

"Oh my," declared Adele. "This is a lot to take in." Jilly came back to their table and reached over to remove their plates and drop off the check. "You're not the first to say that about our daily specials," she quipped. "Would you like a to-go box, Adele?"

"Huh?" Adele asked. She had been so lost in thought, she probably hadn't realized Jilly was there until that very second. "Oh no, dear. I'm fine. Thank you."

"Okay. Just holler if you guys need anything. Hope you liked the pecan pie, sweetheart," Jilly commented to Florence as she picked up her plate. She turned and walked away with an armload of dishes and teetering knives and forks.

Grant picked up the check and insisted on paying the bill. "Elaine, are you sure?" he asked. "Just the other day, you mocked all this. It's a lot to process."

"I'm positive, Grant. I can't deny anymore what I've witnessed. Besides, once you've traveled by starlight, you can't ever go back to thinking your life is normal and humdrum, now can you?" Elaine took out her wallet and pulled out some bills to leave as a tip.

Florence threw in a couple more dollars and giggled. "It definitely lights you up."

Grant smiled at Florence. "That's true," he said as she slid out of her seat so he could make his way to the counter. "I will say, it's a relief to know that you're on board with everything now, Elaine."

"Yes, darling. Your aunts will be so proud." Adele patted Elaine's hand and extended her other hand, palm up, to Florence, who took it and squeezed it before letting go.

"There's lots to do before the next full moon, which is in two days if my calendar is correct," Florence said. "I'll notify the other guardians that you'll be joining us, Elaine. In the meantime, I think it's best that you and Adele and I meet tomorrow at her apothecary shop so I can begin your training."

"Oh, you're sticking around here, then?" Elaine asked, inwardly wincing at how strained her voice sounded. "What about your life back in Chicago? Won't your friends miss you? Your work?"

"I'm, um, an independent contractor, so to speak," Florence replied as she threw on her jacket and slipped her purse over her shoulder. "I can easily work from anywhere as long as there's a connection."

Adele and Elaine slid out of the booth and put on their coats as well. "I guess Wi-Fi connections are easy to come across these days," Elaine said as she took Adele's arm and walked her toward the exit.

"Starlight is more like it," Florence whispered as she followed behind them.

They all packed into Grant's car and rode in near silence, each one commenting on the weather and other mundane details of the day. Now that Elaine had agreed to take her part in the guild and their mission to locate the red key was decided, no one seemed to know what else to say. There was an underlying agreement that Florence was to train Elaine, and Adele and Grant would contact Daphne and Mildred to find out as much information as they could about their hiding spot. It all seemed too easy, which was why everyone seemed a bit on edge.

Elaine wondered how much training she needed to do to become a full-fledged guild member and guardian. She also worried about the fact they may never find the red key. How much more of a threat would Lazro become each passing day the key remained undiscovered? These thoughts, and more, swirled in Elaine's head after Grant dropped her off at home. As Grant, Florence, and Adele pulled away, Elaine faced the two-story house she called home. How much longer would she be able to call it that if the auction didn't generate enough money to pay off her aunts' debts?

She had to maintain her sanity, and the best way to do that, she realized, was to do her best to forget all this for now. She went upstairs and changed into a raggedy pair of jeans and a long-sleeve T-shirt, making sure to pin her brooch onto it, then pulled her favorite turquoise fleece back over her head. Always economical like her aunts, Elaine kept the thermostat at a low temperature and simply chose to layer up instead. "Midwestern practicality at its finest," her aunts used to say.

Elaine made her way down the stairs and pushed away her sadness of losing them and what they could have taught her if only she would have listened. If she couldn't answer all these questions that had been building inside her, she could at least spend some time in the shop clearing out display cases, tagging and categorizing items for the impending auction, and searching for the missing key all at once.

She walked down the hallway past her aunts' office and unlocked the door to the shop. The store had been closed since the day of her aunts' death. She found it hard to believe it had been close to a month since they'd been gone. The store smelled musty and was dank and dark. Elaine fumbled to find the light switch and scanned the 750-square-foot open space. Everything was just like she remembered. The cash register and the glass counter display cases for small trinkets sat in the middle of the store. The exposed wooden rafters glowed a golden, honey brown, with artificial light from the wrought iron chandeliers and natural light from the large windows that faced the small parking lot.

A layer of dust rested across every surface. Elaine sneezed as she picked up a rag from a small bin by the cash register and ran it across the counter. Fortunately, the day after their funeral, she had draped sheets and tarps across big pieces of furniture, bookcases, mirrors, and other large items. But the shelves, the end tables, and the knickknacks that rested on them had been exposed to the settling of time.

Unsure of where to begin, Elaine looked at her phone's calendar and chose a few dates for the auction before calling Mr. Sadler's office and setting something up with Judy, his secretary. The auction would be in two-weeks' time—right before the new moon in November.

"There, it's settled," she said to herself and then let out a sigh mixed with both grief and reassurance. It was hard, but she knew she was doing the right thing.

Next, she decided she should respond to the numerous messages Eric had left and try to clear the air after last night's tiff. She hadn't really given him a chance to explain himself, and she knew he had been under a lot of pressure the entire evening. Weren't romantic relationships complicated? No need to add more stress to their lives since they'd both been so busy lately. Besides, Elaine decided, she might need Eric's help with the financial and legal aspects of the sale. This was all new territory for her. She also considered the perk of being connected to him. His parents had a lot of friends who might be interested in purchasing some of her aunts' inventory.

Sounding distracted, Eric picked up after the second ring.

"Eric? It's me. Elaine?" She hated the fact that she ended her statement like a question. As if she didn't know her own name. "Do you have a minute?"

"Uh-huh. What's up?" His tone was casual, but she detected a bit of annoyance in his voice as well.

"I, um, I'm sorry for how last night ended," she said. As soon as the last word was out of her mouth, she regretted it. What did she have to be sorry about? It was too late to take it back, though, so she pressed on. "I was wondering if you had some free time today? I'm at my aunts' store ... I've decided to go ahead with the auction."

"And you need my help," he stated matter-of-factly. "Well, you're in luck, Elaine. I just left work for the day. I was planning on going to the gym for a bit, but I guess I could come there instead. There's something I've been wanting to talk to you about."

Instantly, she feared he was going to break up with her. Maybe that had been his plan when he went to the hospital. "You don't have to come over." She rushed her words. "I understand you already have plans." A breakup was the last thing she wanted to deal with right now.

"I'm only about ten or fifteen minutes away. I can go to the gym later. I'll see you in a bit."

"Okay," she replied and then waited for him to say something more, but silence met her on the other end. "Bye," she said awkwardly, but when she pulled the phone away from her ear, she saw he had already hung up.

She needed to keep herself distracted, so she set her phone down on the counter and picked up another box. She walked over to a coffee table filled with wooden and brass candlesticks and wrapped each one in old newspaper before folding the box lid into itself and labeling it with a black marker. Small activities like this one helped calm her nerves. She moved the box off to the side and was scanning the area for the next set of items she could box and tag when she heard her phone's message alert. She walked back over to the counter and picked up her phone.

I'm coming over. Florence asked me to pick up something. It was from Teddy.

I'm in the shop, she texted back.

Keep the doors locked in case you were followed there. I'm on my way.

"Shit!" In her busyness, she had dropped her guard and forgotten about the bald-headed guy they had seen earlier. She ran to the front of the store and double-checked the door. It was locked. Thank goodness. She then ran to the other side of the store, dodging furniture, bookshelves, floor lamps, cedar chests, and other random antiques, and threw the dead bolt connecting the store to her aunts' office.

She was grateful Teddy was on his way. So was Eric. Until they arrived, she was safe in the store as long as she didn't open the doors. As a precaution, she turned off the lights but left the blinds open so she could at least see what was happening. She shoved her cell phone into her back pocket and made her way over to the far corner of the store, where Mildred and Daphne had set up a small reading nook for customers. From this inconspicuous spot, she could peer out the window while staying close enough to the emergency exit in case she needed to escape.

She squatted down next to an oversize sofa and peered through the side of the curtain. A silver Lincoln Town Car sat in the parking lot. "Lazro," she whispered as the bald man in his midthirties and dressed in the same dark jeans and black leather jacket from the night before stepped out of the driver's side and scanned the area before walking up to the front door. Elaine ducked and situated herself between the sofa and the bookcase. She pulled out her cell phone and dialed Teddy's number. "Where are you?" she whispered when he answered.

"I'm here. Stay where you're at." Then he hung up.

A car door slammed and then a man shouted, but she couldn't quite make out what he was saying. She risked looking out the window again and saw Teddy approaching the bald-headed man. In his hand, Teddy held what looked like mace or pepper spray. "Who are you?" Teddy shouted as he approached the door. "What do you want with Elaine?"

Right then, Eric's car pulled in. His tires crunched across the gravel as the car came to a stop right behind Teddy's. Eric jumped out of his car. He had on black running pants that were way too tight, a form-fitting long-sleeve blue running shirt, and an electric orange-and-blue hat that matched his tennis shoes. "Hey, what's going on?"

Surprised, Teddy turned to look at Eric. "What the hell are you doing here, man?"

The bald guy used Teddy's distraction and ran toward his car. Teddy took off after him but quickly realized he couldn't chase him because Eric had blocked his car. Baldy threw his car in reverse, spun his wheels, and spit gravel before pulling out of the parking lot and racing away.

"Move your car!" Teddy shouted as he got into his car.

Elaine ran to the front door and flung it open. "Eric, move your car!" She ran toward Teddy, who was honking his horn.

"Will someone please tell me what's going on?" Eric yelled as he stood in the middle of the parking lot. His black tights really stood out against the white gravel. "I can't believe I'm missing the gym for *this*," he muttered as he dramatically waved his arms up and down in frustration.

Teddy got out of his car and slammed his door. "It's too late now, man. You ruined everything."

"I don't appreciate being talked to like that. What exactly did I ruin?" Eric asked as he walked toward Teddy, his chest puffed out like he was looking for a fight.

Elaine stepped up. "Eric, do you remember my friend, Teddy? He's been looking out for me. That guy who was just here? We think he may have had something to do with the professor's disappearance and Adele's hospital stay last night. We were hoping to get some information out of him."

Eric looked from Elaine to Teddy and back again. "Oh, that's rich. Now you think you're a detective too? Come on, Elaine. What were you guys going to do? Play good cop, bad cop and get a confession out of him? This is beneath even you, Elaine. Have some class."

Teddy jumped to Elaine's defense. "Who do you think you are? Elaine is one of the classiest ladies I've ever met, and if you bothered to spend more time getting to know her instead of using her as arm candy for your stupid business meetings and conferences, you would know that too. And what the hell are you wearing, man?"

"Excuse me, *man?*" Eric said. "You don't know anything about our relationship. And I don't need some two-bit hipster who works at a *nursing home*, by the way, telling me what I do and don't know." Eric pointed his finger in Teddy's face to emphasize his point.

"Back off," Teddy said as he stood up straighter and adjusted his glasses.

"Or what? You'll spray me with that can of pepper spray in your hand?" Eric taunted.

"You're so glib," Teddy said.

"*Oh,* big guy knows a cool word," Eric sneered. "Next thing you know, you'll be throwing double-entendre insults at me."

Teddy's hand squeezed the pepper spray, and he flipped the cover back with his thumb. "You know what?" Teddy said, his nostrils flaring. He stood there momentarily, probably wrestling with the idea of punching Eric's lights out. After a few short breaths, he said, "You're not worth my time or energy." He turned to Elaine. "What do you need me to do next?"

"Leave," Eric answered for her.

"I was talking to Elaine," Teddy said through clenched teeth. He looked back at Elaine, waiting for her to respond.

"I think you should go, Eric," she said.

"Come on, Elaine. I drove out of my way for you," Eric whined. He took Elaine's elbow and pulled her toward him. "Let's go inside, and you can fix me something to eat before I help you load up some of those boxes."

Disgusted, Elaine pulled herself away from Eric. A fire of emotions flared up inside her. She tried to fight back tears and found her voice to speak, despite the fact it was trembling. "I-I'm tired of you," she said through watery eyes. "I'm s-so tired of you. We're over. Take your fancy car and your clown clothes and shoes and get out of here!"

"Right on," Teddy whispered, smiling and shaking his head. "Right on."

Eric looked confused. "You don't mean that," he said and reached for her arm again.

She slapped him away and grabbed Teddy's pepper spray, aiming it at Eric's face. "I said *leave*! Go away and don't bother to text or call me because it's over. I should've ended it a while ago, and I definitely should've ended it last night. You're nothing but a pompous, narcissistic asshole, Eric. Find yourself another date to the museum gala, someone who doesn't mind being made to feel worthless and unappreciated, because that person is not going to be me anymore."

Eric held his hands up in surrender. "You're crazy, you know that? The only reason I ever dated you was because I felt sorry for you. You looked like someone who could use a little bit of excitement and adventure in your life. Guess I was wrong. I can't believe I've wasted my time with such a loser."

On a moment of impulse, Elaine sprayed the pepper spray directly into his face. "You saw him physically and verbally assault me, right, Teddy?" she asked as Eric bent over screaming obscenities.

"Oh, most definitely," Teddy replied.

"You bitch!" Eric shrieked as he ran in circles, stopping to spit on the ground. He wiped his eyes with his long sleeves and gagged numerous times as tears and snot poured down his face. He stumbled to his car and opened the glove compartment, pulling out a rag and sticking it over his face and coughing hard.

"Will he be all right?" Elaine asked Teddy, worried she had gone too far. "Do you think he'll call the cops on me?"

"He'll be all right," Teddy said. "He just needs to puke a few times and clean his eyes out with some water. Knowing him, he'll be too vain and embarrassed to call the cops."

"True." She then yelled out to Eric, "There's a hose on the side of the house if you need it!" She gestured for Teddy to follow her back into the store. Once they were inside, she locked the door again. "My compliments to your mom and her pepper recipe," she said with a grin as she handed the spray back over to him.

"It's a secret family recipe," Teddy said as he pushed it back into his pocket. "I think she uses a dash of the Carolina reaper, the hottest pepper on record."

Elaine collapsed onto an overstuffed chair and began to laugh like a maniac. She couldn't control herself. She doubled over and laughed until her stomach hurt. It felt so good to be free from others' expectations and always doing what they wanted her to do. What did she ever see in Eric, anyway? Of course, she knew the answer to that. He was predictable and stable. He seemed to have it all—money, good looks, a good family, a good job. Those were things Elaine craved to hold on to for fear of standing out as an eccentric and imaginative dreamer who fit in as well as a square peg in a round hole.

She realized now that she was the one who had been holding herself back. Her aunts had tried to help her embrace who she really was for so long, and she spent so much time and energy fighting against that. How sad. She wished she had been brave enough to embrace her wildness and creativity with an unbridled fierceness when she was younger. Instead, she chose to keep herself small and hidden from the world. Her laughter turned to tears, and she found herself doubled over again, head and arms in her lap, crying.

"Hey," Teddy said softly as he walked up to her and put his arms around her. "What's wrong, Elaine?"

She looked up at him. His handsome face and big brown eyes held so much empathy and concern. It somehow made her feel comforted. "Teddy, I'm so stupid," she said between tears. "I wish I would've been better to my aunts when they were alive. I wish I would've listened more to them. Hell, I wish I was more *like* them!" Grief poured out of her like rain from a heavy cloud.

"Ah, it's okay, girl. You're not stupid," he said and then hugged her again. "Your aunts loved you, I promise. They were so proud of you. You should've heard the way they bragged about you every time I saw them."

"Really?" Elaine asked as Teddy took her by the hand and helped her stand. "They were proud of me?"

"Of course they were," he said and walked behind the counter, searching for something. "They were always telling me the latest thing you did to improve the library and how you really made it a safe and happy community spot. And they loved that you kept Mrs. Armested on as assistant librarian. That worked wonders for her self-confidence, you know."

"I didn't know that," Elaine said under her breath. "I always thought my aunts were disappointed in me because I didn't go into the family business."

"Nah," he said as he reached inside one of cubbyholes. "They knew the antiques biz wasn't that lucrative, anyway. Not unless you were a top-notch dealer who had exclusive deals for exclusive clients, at least. No, they liked the antiques business because they liked junk, and because it was a good front for hiding things for the guild. Like this." He set a familiar-looking wooden jewelry box on the table.

"Did this belong to one of them?" she inquired. Her heart began to flutter. "How did you know where to look for this?"

"This isn't your aunts' box, Elaine. They told me this one belonged to your mother. Come here. I'll show you where it was."

Elaine stepped around the counter and stood next to Teddy. "If you bend down and look in the back of this shelf," he said kneeling down, "you'll see that it looks like a normal cabinet. But if you just trace your fingers along the back board here, you'll feel a tiny groove. Go ahead." He moved out of the way, and Elaine took his place.

"It feels like a backward C," she said as she looked up at him.

"Guess again." Teddy smiled.

"Oh, it's the crescent moon!" Elaine said, feeling excited. "And here's the full moon and the other crescent moon. It's the symbol of the guild. This is so cool!"

"Right? Now, press on the full moon and slide your hand to the right ever so gently."

As she did, the board shifted and then slid to reveal a false back. "So this is how they hid things in plain sight. Those beautiful, sly devils." Elaine giggled.

"This was the system we used whenever they needed me to run things for the guild," Teddy explained. "They swore me to secrecy. Not even my wonderful mother knew I was helping them out like this. If she had, I think she would've worried because she knows of the dangers not just from Lazro but from people who like investigating myths, secret societies, and the unknown."

"So where's the red key then?" Elaine asked as she searched the cabinet with her fingers. "You thought it was here, didn't you?"

"I did, and I was going to take it and give it to my mother or Florence or you even. But I guess it truly is missing. If Lazro has it, then all he needs are the brooches to unlock each portal and steal all the secrets and healing powers within."

"Hmm," Elaine said as she stood up. "That bald guy, who is quite possibly Lazro, was probably coming here to ransack the store and look for the key. In any case, I think the guild members and guardians may be in danger, don't you?"

"For sure," Teddy answered. Something outside must've gotten his attention because he suddenly looked out the window and grinned. "Hey, looks like your guy got enough of the pepper spray out of his eyes to drive."

Elaine glanced over and saw that Eric was backing out of the parking lot. Like the asshole he was, he scraped Teddy's car with his side mirror before turning on to the road. "Oh my gosh, I'm so sorry, Teddy! I'll pay for any damages."

"Nah, it's all right. I think insurance will want to see this," he said as he pressed the button on his phone to stop recording. Elaine laughed as they gave each other a high five. "Your aunts always taught me to look for the simplest of solutions and go from there," Teddy said as he slid his phone back into his pocket.

"Wow, I haven't heard that phrase in a long time. They used to tell me that all the time. When I was stuck on a word problem in math, or having problems with making friends, or even deciding on what to major in at college. They always said, 'The simplest solution to any problem is always what our minds and our hearts overlook every single time.'" Elaine thought of their advice and actions throughout the years. Simplicity was part of her aunts' creative, outside-the-box way of thinking and living, whether that was cooking, doing business, or storing keys in cardboard boxes or false backs of cabinets, or hiding jewelry boxes for her tenth birthday in a hollowed-out tree.

Suddenly, an idea popped into Elaine's head. "Teddy, that's it! You're brilliant! C'mon! I know where the red key is."

She grabbed the box and took off running. When she reached the office door, she unlocked it and raced down the hallway into the house. Teddy followed not too far behind. She passed through the living room and went to the shelf where all the scrapbooks resided. She slid the box into her fleece pocket, then pulled out the scrapbook she had been looking at the other night. Elaine flipped to the page that contained the large photo of the three of them on her tenth birthday. "There!" she said as she sat it down on the coffee table. "See?"

"What am I looking at?" Teddy asked her as he scanned the photo. "Aw!" he gushed. "You were such a little cutie, Elaine."

"Thanks," she said, blushing, "but look closer. Out the window, behind my aunts and me. Do you see it?"

Teddy squinted his eyes. "Yeah ... isn't that the big maple tree right outside in your front yard?"

"Yes! And do you know what's carved on it?" Elaine asked him. Her face was beaming. She couldn't contain her excitement.

"The symbol of the guild?" he asked, then shook his head. "Of course ..."

"'Look for the simplest of solutions and go from there,'" they said in unison.

Together, they went outside and walked up to the maple tree. Elaine remembered how she had leaned her head on it after Mr. Sadler left last week and her hair had gotten tangled. She walked to the side of the tree and recreated the scene. She turned and saw the small etching of the guild. "Here it is." She pushed on the center of the full moon, but nothing happened. Frustrated, she tried again. "Surely some secret cabinet or hidey-hole is supposed to reveal itself, right?"

"Not necessarily, but look here." He bent down at the base of the tree and ran his hand over its roots and pulled back a pile of leaves.

A few millipedes scattered across the dirt and leaves, searching for new cover. A black beetle scurried away and went inside a hole the size of Teddy's fist at the base of the tree. "I think we found it." He tried to reach inside, but he couldn't get his hand through it.

"Here, let me try," Elaine said, bending down next to him. "Oh, this is so gross. I hope nothing reaches out to get me." She stuck her hand in and pulled back, screeching.

"What is it?" Teddy exclaimed.

"My hand just touched a big spider web!" she wailed. "Teddy, I can't do this. Go get a spoon or something from the kitchen. This is just way too creepy."

"You can do this, Elaine."

"Okay, okay, here I go." She took a deep breath and slowly moved her hand toward the dark hole. "Maybe take off your shoe in case you have to swat or stomp something really quickly?" she asked him, stalling.

He couldn't hold back his laughter. "Go on! It's just dirt and insects and moss. All natural stuff," he said as he brushed away a locust shell.

"Ugh, okay." She took another deep breath and plunged her hand inside again. The earth was damp and cool. She moved her fingers around and turned her head so she could stick her arm farther inside. Her fingers circled around what felt like a long, wooden stick. "Wait, I feel something!" She pulled the object out, but it was just a piece of rotted wood. Disappointed, she tossed it down between them. The wood flipped over, exposing its back side. Tied there was the red key!

The gemstone at the center of the key glowed a brilliant red. Elaine knew exactly what was making the key glow this time. She reached into her pocket and pulled out the jewelry box and unlocked it with the key. Inside gleamed a double crescent moon brooch. She picked it up and held it close to her heart. Had she believed in signs from the beyond, she would have sworn she saw Daphne and Mildred smiling at her that very moment.

CHAPTER 17

Teddy reached out his hand and helped Elaine stand.

"Teddy, what should I do?" Elaine asked as she brushed some dirt off her jeans.

"I'm not sure. We should definitely get inside, though. No telling who's lurking around here."

She followed Teddy back to the antique store and into the house, making sure to lock up before joining him in the kitchen, where he was already pulling the blinds shut. She set the key on the dining room table and studied it. The key head was shaped like a hexagon, and in the center was a small red gemstone.

Teddy peered over Elaine's shoulder and said, "It's a ruby if you were wondering. My mother told me each key's gemstone when she first talked to me about the guild. It comes from somewhere in central Europe. Budapest most likely. Pretty, isn't it?"

"Yes, it is," Elaine said. She picked up the key and searched for an inscription similar to that on the green one. Nothing was written on it, but there was a symbol on the key face, below the ruby. It was a small engraving of a tree. "Teddy, why does this key have a tree on it, but the green one had an inscription?"

Elaine passed the key over to Teddy, and he held it up to the light. He set it back down and shrugged his shoulders.

"I honestly don't know. My mom could tell you, though. Y'all are getting together for some kind of video chat soon, right? You can ask her then."

Elaine didn't want to tell Teddy the guardians were going to teleport or star travel or whatever it was into Adele's shop on the evening of the full moon on Sunday. There was no way he'd believe something like that, so she simply nodded her head. She reached into her pocket and opened the box with the brooch inside.

"These two definitely go together," she said as she sat the brooch down beside the key. She wondered why the red key wasn't glowing or acting strangely like the green one had. And, if she touched it directly, would it have some effect on her and cause her to get dizzy like the green one had?

She had already touched it once when she used it to unlock the brooch, and nothing happened to her then. But with her luck lately, she didn't want to risk it, so she walked over to the counter, pulled out a worn dish towel, and wrapped the key in it.

"My mother was this key's guardian before she died. I'm assuming this brooch used to be hers too." Elaine figured it would be best to keep the key and brooch separate. She placed the wrapped key into her purse and slid the brooch, which was still in its small box, into her fleece pocket. Then, she set about making them coffee. Moving around the familiar kitchen helped her think of what to do next.

Teddy opened up a box of chocolate donuts that was sitting on the countertop and placed two on some napkins. "It makes sense. The guild loves passing guardianship through family bloodlines. That's why my mom has been on me for years to come to meetings with her and go through initiation." Teddy shrugged in disinterest and took a bite of the chocolate donut.

"I've got double the pressure since both my parents inherited a key," Elaine said. "Do you take cream in your coffee?"

Teddy nodded, so Elaine reached into the refrigerator and set it out. She poured them each a cup, and they sat down at the table. Teddy stirred in the cream and took a sip. Elaine bit into her donut.

"You know," she said, crumbs dribbling down her chin as she spoke with her mouth full, "my aunts were always talking about how my parents were a special couple and did everything together, but I didn't really know them. I was only five when they died."

"I'm sorry to hear that. I bet Adele could tell you more about your parents. She was close to your aunts. Aren't she and Grant's mom about the same age? I wonder if they both knew your parents."

"Adele did. I just never really bothered to take the time to talk to her about personal things. I'm starting to regret that ... I'm starting to regret a lot of things." After she spoke, they both sat in silence for a few minutes, each one sipping their coffee and devouring their donuts.

When she was finished, Elaine dabbed the napkin with her finger and licked off the last of the donut crumbs. "What should we do now? Do you think we should put the key and brooch back in their respective places?"

"Nah, it's too dangerous. Another thing I learned from your aunts was to keep moving. I think we should go to Adele's house. She or Florence could contact Hugh. That old curmudgeon would know what to do."

Elaine stood, picked up their napkins, and threw them away. "The first and last time I saw him, we were attacked by some karate-chopping lady in black leather. I never did ask Florence if he was all right."

"Wow!" Teddy laughed. "You've had quite the adventure lately, haven't you?" He finished his coffee and stood to rinse his mug in the sink.

"You can say that again," Elaine said. "Would you mind following me in your car? I know you've got things to do after this, but I'd feel a lot safer knowing you were nearby."

"True. I have a big test coming up, and I really need to study," Teddy said while he texted someone. He received a responding chirp a moment later. "Okay, your boy Grant is gonna head over to Adele's house after he finishes installing some countertops at the Bracken's house. I'll make sure you get there safely, and then I have to get to the library. I have a study date with a lovely lady I met in my economics class." He winked, and they both laughed.

Elaine picked up her purse and wrapped it around her shoulder. As a reassurance, she stuck her fingers in her pocket and touched the box containing the newly discovered brooch. She also double-checked that the other brooch was still pinned to her shirt underneath her fleece. Satisfied, she grabbed her phone and headed out the back door with Teddy close behind her. She turned and hugged him before getting into her car. "Thanks again for looking out for me, Teddy."

He hugged her back and then shut her car door behind her. She rolled down her window as he bent down to face her. "It seems like you've had my back longer than I realized."

"It's no problem, Laney. I'll always have your back. Now, let's get you to Adele's. My study date won't wait around forever," he said with a grin. He tapped the roof of her car and walked across the parking lot.

Thankfully, the drive to Adele's house was uneventful. Elaine kept checking her rearview mirror every minute or so to make sure Teddy was behind her and no silver Lincoln—or any other car for that matter—was following them. When they arrived, Elaine pulled into Adele's gravel drive, and Teddy pulled in behind her. Elaine walked up to him, and he rolled down his window.

"I can take it from here," Elaine said. "Enjoy the rest of your afternoon, and text me later just to let me know you're all right."

"Will do, Laney. I'll just wait here to make sure everything's copacetic, you know?" He winked, and she once again found herself comforted by his casual tone and cool demeanor.

Before heading inside, she peered through Adele's garage door window to make sure her car was there. Satisfied to see Adele's quirky lime-green VW Beetle in its usual space, she walked up to the front door and rang the doorbell. She heard some rustling and assumed Adele was making her way to the door. She waved at Teddy, letting him know all was well. He waved and backed out of the driveway.

When the door opened, Elaine gasped and took a step back. The bald-headed man was standing in front of her, one hand on Adele's shoulder and the other holding a gun to her head. "Get in here *now*," he growled.

"Elaine, do what he says!" Adele pleaded, looking terrified, which caused Elaine to hesitate.

The man took advantage of the distraction, and in one swift move, he released Adele, grabbed Elaine by the arm, and pulled her inside. He slammed the door shut, locking it in the process, and turned to face them both. "Drop your purse and move over to those chairs," he said as he pointed his gun at them.

"You better do as he says, Laney," Adele said as she backed up to the kitchen chairs he had apparently moved into the center of the living room before Elaine knocked on the door.

Elaine put her purse down and made her way to one of the chairs. Elaine and Adele sat back-to-back, unable to see each other. The man kicked Elaine's purse out of the way and pulled a thin cord from his jacket pocket. He looped the cord through Adele's chair with one hand and knotted it before walking around and wrapping the cord tightly around them and securing it with another knot. He set his gun down on the fireplace and removed two large, plastic zip ties from his other pocket. Using them like handcuffs, he fastened them around Elaine's wrists and then Adele's before picking up his gun and pointing it in Elaine's face again.

"The key. Where is it?" he demanded.

"You'll never find it, you bastard!" Adele piped up. "Elaine will never tell you, even if she did know."

"It's in my purse," Elaine replied calmly.

Adele stomped her feet and turned her torso, trying to get free. The cord pressed into her arms, and she winced in pain. "Elaine! Why are you telling him?"

"Just take it and leave us alone," Elaine said coolly. "That's why you're here, isn't it, Lazro? You want the source key. Well, go ahead and take it. But you'll never be able to unlock its powers." She silently prayed he wouldn't discover the brooch she had in her fleece pocket. As long as Lazro possessed the keys but not their brooches, she had time to get Hugh, Vivienne, and Florence to help her figure out the next step.

"Lazro?" The bald-headed man snorted. "I'm not Lazro, lady. I just work for him, and he's going to be quite pleased that I brought him the source key." He fished the key out of Elaine's purse and slipped it into his inside jacket pocket. "I'll be getting a nice little bonus when he sees this." He patted his jacket and then slid his gun in the back of his jeans.

"You're not going to kill us?" Adele asked.

"If it was up to me, I'd cap you right now. But I have my orders." With that, he made his way across the living room, passed through the kitchen, and snuck out the back door.

"Grant," Elaine whispered. Her heart was racing, and she could feel the sweat pooling under her armpits and beading on her forehead.

"Is he here?" Adele asked. She continued to twist and turn, but the bungee cord didn't give way and only dug more deeply into her skin.

"No, but Teddy had texted him earlier, telling him to meet me here when he finished his job. We just have to sit here patiently until he gets here." Elaine breathed out a deep sigh. *Thank goodness for Grant*, she thought.

"Well then, why don't you tell me why you gave away the key?" Adele asked bitingly.

"Because Lazro needs the brooches to activate the keys," Elaine reminded Adele. "I didn't want him to hurt us or find the other brooch that's inside my pocket. Give me some credit, Adele."

Adele was silent for a moment, probably thinking over what Elaine had just said. "Yes, you're right. I would've done the same thing. But, honey, where did you find the other brooch? I didn't even know where your aunts kept it, let alone the keys."

Elaine filled her in on her and Teddy's discoveries from that afternoon. "I figured if Lazro believed he had the source key, then he would focus his energy and attention on unlocking the secrets, and in the meantime, we could get the guild together and develop a plan to take Lazro down." She tried to sound confident, but there was a quiver in her throat. "But now, maybe I've gone and screwed it all up."

Adele found Elaine's fingers with her own and squeezed them. "Oh, Laney, my darling, no. You were right to give up the key. I see that now. Let's just focus our energy on getting free from these cords. I don't want to wait on Grant. We've got to call all the guild members and assemble at my store. Tonight."

"Grant will be here soon, Delly. Just hang in there," Elaine said. She swallowed and felt a catch in her throat. She didn't like the idea of being tied up and feeling so vulnerable.

"The letter opener!" Adele suddenly said. "There's a letter opener on my desk over there. If we hopped over there and knocked it into one of our hands, we could cut through these cords and free ourselves."

"Adele," Elaine laughed, "that's impossible. And even if we did manage to catch the opener, I don't think it's sharp enough to cut through these cords. They're pretty thick. Just hold tight. Grant will be on his way."

"I can't sit by and do nothing," Adele remarked stubbornly and then began rocking back and forth with her weight.

"Adele, what are you doing?" Elaine shouted.

Adele had built up enough momentum that both chairs were wobbling now. "Come on, Elaine, put your weight into it! We can scoot ourselves to the table over there."

The chairs teetered over to one side, and Elaine planted her feet on the floor and used her leg strength to stop them. But she misjudged Adele's strength, and the chairs teetered to the opposite side before setting back down on the floor. Adele picked up her pace and tried scooting to the table again. Elaine moved the opposite way to counterbalance Adele's momentum. In her urgency to make Adele stop, the chairs teetered to one side before toppling over and taking Adele and Elaine down with them. The thud from their fall rattled the knickknacks on the shelves. Elaine's shoulder throbbed from the impact.

"Adele, are you all right?" Elaine asked, her voice rising to a near panic.

"I'm fine, darling. I'm fine," Adele replied. They lay there on the floor for a brief moment, neither saying a word. Then, Adele began to laugh.

Elaine grinned. "It's not funny, Adele. We could've been seriously hurt. What are we going to do now?"

Adele snorted and laughed some more. "We're in a real pickle—that's for sure." She swung her feet in the air, but the cords limited the movement of her legs. "Oh dear! I've never been tied up like this before." She hooted and burst out into a fit of giggles.

Elaine groaned. "Please stop. I don't want to hear anything more about you being tied up. Seriously, though. What are we going to do?" She looked at a dust bunny that was balled up on the hardwood floor. The white floorboards and white walls in the foyer reflected light from the oval lead glass window on the front door. She stared ahead of her, waiting for Adele to compose herself.

"Maybe I should've invested in that device you see old people wearing around their necks when they've fallen and can't get up. You know? One of those button jobbies that you see advertised on late-night TV," Adele said. Her giggling subsided, and she regained composure. "Oh, I'm sorry, darling. I didn't mean to get us into this. I just hate not being able to act in a moment of crisis."

"It's okay, Adele. I know what you mean. I don't like feeling out of control either. Grant should be here soon. He'll help us. Do you still have that spare key under the landscape rock out front?"

"No." Adele sighed. "When I got home from the hospital, I decided to take precautions and secure my home a little more. I brought the key inside and put it in my junk drawer in the kitchen. A lot of good that did, though."

"Don't beat yourself up, Delly. I would've done the same thing," Elaine reassured her. "And besides, a guy holding a gun at your front door trumps a break-in any time. We'll just wait for Grant and figure out what to do from there."

"Daphne and Mildred would have a good laugh if they saw us like this ... Remember that time Daphne convinced Mildred to get a perm?" Adele giggled again as she reminisced.

Elaine couldn't help but laugh as she recalled the event. "Oh yeah! Daphne purposefully added too much chemical, and the curling rods were small. Two hours later, Mildred looked like a poodle. She drove around town wearing headscarves and hats for an entire month."

The two of them lay on the floor and shared Daphne and Mildred stories for the next twenty minutes or so. Adele was in the middle of telling Elaine how Daphne had gotten trapped in a department store dressing room when a shadowy figure approached the front door. The doorbell rang, and Adele jerked forward, trying to sit up to see who it was. The cord pressed into her chest, and she caught her breath.

"Grant?" Elaine yelled. "Grant, can you hear me?"

"Laney?" the voice on the other side called out. It was definitely Grant. "Is that you? What's the matter?"

"Grant, listen! We're in a bit of a jam. We can't get to the door, so you're going to have to break in."

"Are you all right? What's going on?" Grant called back, sounding concerned.

"We're okay. Just get inside and help us out. We're tied up!"

"Oh geez, hang on, Laney! I'm going to get my toolbox." Grant rapped reassuringly on the door before presumably heading toward his car.

Elaine relaxed her shoulders for the first time since arriving. "Everything is going to be all right, Adele."

"I never doubted it." Adele chuckled. "Adventure and danger seem to be at my doorstep once again, and I'm glad for it. It's like Daphne and Mildred never left. Ever since you and Grant brought that key into my shop, I knew they were asking me to help you. To finish what they couldn't. I just didn't know how to help you. I'm glad this has all happened. I feel useful again."

"I'll always need you in my life, Adele," Elaine said. "I hope you know that. The three of you were always trying to get me to see that life holds so much magic, mystery, and intrigue. But I strayed from that and boxed myself in. I tried to keep myself small so I wouldn't have to deal with the wild, out-of-control side of me that feels the magic they tried to initiate me into. I've been stupid and selfish, and I'm sorry it's taken me so long to admit it. Can you ever forgive me, Adele?"

"Oh, honey, there's nothing to forgive. You're a smart, beautiful, and strong-willed woman. No matter what's happened in the past, we're here now, and we're facing this together. That's all that really matters."

"You're too kind, Delly. And just so you know, I think the same of you."

They fell silent and waited for Grant's return. They heard him muttering and the clanking of tools on the porch and scratches on the door. He called out a few times to reassure them he was doing the best he could. After a few solid minutes of trying different techniques to break open the door, he finally gave up. "I just don't have the right tools," he called out. "Hang in there. I have another idea."

They heard him rustling outside in the leaf-scattered garden on the side of the house, where Adele's small writing table rested next to the large double windows. "Hold on, ladies! I'm coming!" he yelled, followed by an echo of shattering glass. A large rock thudded on the hardwood floor next to Elaine's feet, and shards of broken windowpane littered the floor. Grant punched out a sharp hanging edge and then unlatched the window from the inside and pushed it open. "Sorry about that, Adele," he said sheepishly as he crawled through the window. "Sometimes you have to do things the old-fashioned way."

CHAPTER 18

Grant brushed himself off and then walked over to Elaine and Adele. He grabbed the back of Elaine's chair and heaved them both upright.

"What the hell happened to you two?" he asked as he fished out his pocketknife and began to cut the blue cord holding them together.

"It's a long story," Elaine replied. He cut her legs free, so she stood up and felt a dull pain in her shoulder where she had hit the floor.

Adele rubbed her wrists where the plastic tie had pressed into her skin. "Thank you for saving us, darling," she said to Grant as she wrapped her arms around his neck and hugged him.

He hugged her back and kissed her cheek. "I'm just glad you're safe. Here, Elaine, let me help." He walked over to her and cut off her plastic handcuffs as well. "From the state that you were both in, I'm assuming Lazro had something to do with it?"

Elaine shook her head. "Not Lazro, but one of his lackeys. And he has one of the keys too."

"A key? How? When?" Grant questioned.

Elaine raised her eyebrow and rubbed her wrist. "Just now. Teddy and I found it outside my aunts' house, hidden in the trunk of the maple tree out front." Elaine detailed the events that led to her and Teddy finding the red key and the other brooch.

"Okay, so what should we do now?" Grant asked when she finished. "Any suggestions, Adele?"

Adele looked up from her phone. "Hmm? Sorry, I was reading a text from Edmund. He wants to go to dinner this evening to make up for the strange events and see how I'm doing." She read the text a second time.

"You're not seriously thinking of going, are you, Adele?" Elaine questioned her. "We know he's somehow caught up in all this. I find it pretty suspicious that he started dating you right before he saw us at the diner and then, like a week later, purchased my key."

Grant nodded. "Yeah, I didn't want to say anything, but Florence feels the same way. She went to the university to talk to Professor Wallace after lunch."

"So she went there, did she?" Adele pondered and placed her phone on the table. Her brow furrowed as she rubbed her hands together. "Well, if he's been using me, we need to keep him thinking I still don't know anything. I just want to do right by Daphne and Mildred. They counted on me, and I can't let them down again." She sat down and rested her head in her hands.

Elaine placed a comforting hand on Adele's back. "I'm sorry, Adele. I should've said something earlier, but when we went to your shop to show you the green key, I noticed Professor Wallace's business card on your counter ...." Elaine walked over to her purse and retrieved his card from her wallet. "Look." She held it up to show Adele the faint watermark of the moon symbols in the upper left corner. "Now that I know more, I believe that's the symbol of the Apothecary Guild."

"What?" Adele asked, clearly shocked. She took the card and looked at it, then handed it over to Grant. "Surely I would've noticed something like that. It just can't be."

Grant gave the card back to Elaine. "No need to blame yourself, Delly. How would you know to examine Wallace's business card for an ancient guild's symbol when you first met him?" He patted Adele's shoulder, and she gave him a wan smile.

Elaine walked over to the table and picked up the writing pad and pen and began to jot down a list of familiar locations she and her aunts had frequented when she was younger. When she finished, she tore off the paper and handed it to Grant.

"Here," she said. "When Teddy is done studying, can the two of you go to these places and look for any clues that my aunts would've left about hiding spots for the brooches and keys? Teddy should know most of these places, but there are some on the list you and I used to go to as kids."

"Okay," Grant began, "but what are we looking for exactly?" He folded the paper and slid it into his pocket.

"Honestly, I'm not sure. But the maple tree in their front yard had a faint carving of the moon symbol on it, and so did the sliding cabinet in their shop. I'm sure they found some way to mark all their hiding spots. Teddy used to work for them, so I'm certain he knows some of their old tricks." She reached up under her fleece and unpinned her brooch. Then, she reached into her pocket and took out the box to reveal the second brooch. She held them out to Grant. "I need you to hide these somewhere only we can find them. I don't think they're safe with me anymore."

Elaine could feel the warmth and strength of Grant's hands as she placed the brooches in his palms. She folded her fingers over his. "I trust you completely," she said. Her breath caught in her throat, and her face felt warm.

He swallowed loudly and stared at her before looking at the brooches.

"I-it's just that, um, they're no longer s-safe out in the open like this," she stammered as she pulled back and tucked her hair behind her ear.

"Yeah, you're right," Grant said and set both brooches in the box before closing the lid. He sheepishly looked down at the floor and then back up at her. "Okay, I can do that. I'll text Teddy. What are you two going to do, then?"

"Adele's going to go on that date with Professor Wallace," Elaine replied.

Adele shot Elaine a concerned look. "I am?"

"Yes, and you're going to look fabulous and seduce him and get him to tell you all about his connection to the guild. Or whatever it is you do to get information out of a tall, handsome, ascot-wearing, tweed-jacketed professor." Elaine smiled and rolled her eyes.

Adele laughed. "Now that's a challenge worth accepting," she hooted. She shot off a text to Professor Wallace and set up a time to meet at Barrington's again that evening. "I'm going to need my low-cut red blouse and some fabulous earrings." She clapped her hands together and walked away toward her bedroom, preparing for battle.

"I guess I should run to the hardware store to get some plywood to board up the window before meeting Teddy. What are you going to do, Elaine?" Grant asked as he opened the front door.

Elaine ran her fingers through her hair and sighed. "I'm going to Mr. Sadler's to discuss the auction and fill out the rest of the paperwork." She slung her purse over her shoulder and dug around for her car keys. "Have Florence call me when she gets back. She and I need to get the guardians together sooner rather than later."

They called out their goodbyes to Adele, who came out to give them each a hug. "I heard you're going to get the guild together, Elaine. Here's the key to my shop. It opens the back door. Be sure to tell Hugh I said hello."

Elaine and Grant hugged Adele one more time before making their way outside. Grant tucked the jewelry box under his arm and got into his car. He put it in reverse and pulled into the street so Elaine could back her car out of the driveway. Elaine rolled down the window and called out, "Be careful, Grant! Call me later."

Grant rolled his window down further and leaned out to speak. "I have a better idea. Let's go out for coffee later. How does Ginger's Tea House at seven sound? My treat."

"It's a date!" Elaine said and then stammered. "I-I mean … Well, you know what I mean. Seven's good. I'll just meet you there." She felt her face heat up as she quickly rolled up the window.

As she neared the traffic circle on Main Street, she began thinking about her aunts. Their women's circle had been so important to them. There hadn't been one since Grant's mother had her episode and Lazro's spy, Giselle, had infiltrated their meetings. Clearly, Adele's shop seemed to be at the center of so much activity. Maybe there was something she needed to see there before she and the guardians were to meet. Maybe she could feel a connection to her aunts once again. Her heart warmed, and she realized there was a part of her hoping they would appear to her, like they had to Adele, to help her figure everything out.

At the intersection, she impulsively turned right instead of left. She drove the block and a half past the diner to Adele's storefront. She turned into the alley, passed a few street-side dumpsters, and parked in a gravel lot meant for local business owners.

"What am I doing?" she said to herself as she shut off the car. She grabbed her purse, then she got out of the car and locked it.

At the back entrance of Maiden, Mother, Crone, she took out Adele's key and unlocked the dead bolt. She pushed open the heavy door, and the scent of lavender filled her lungs. The old wooden floor creaked as she made her way inside. The storage room and Adele's desk were as neatly organized as the store itself. Labeled boxes lined the wooden shelves, and below them, woven baskets holding small throw pillows, plush handmade blankets, and other home items for sale were tucked neatly into the cubbyholes. Elaine set her purse on the desk, switched on the desk lamp, and sat in the wooden swivel chair. She turned herself around a few times and leaned back, realizing how comfy and cozy the office space was. "I could get used to working in a space like this."

The bulletin board hanging on the wall in front of her was meticulously arranged with a shipment's list, current inventory, and Adele's weekly to-do list. Elaine leaned forward and took a closer look at the alphabetized inventory list. The word "brooches" and "D7" were written under the letter *B*.

Curious, she read through the list and saw that next to each item was a letter and number. She assumed each letter and number corresponded with the boxes on the shelves, so she made her way over to them and scanned each box's label. There, on the third tier of the bookshelf, she found the box she was looking for. She slid the box from the shelf set it on the desk, and opened it. She uncovered a set of crescent moon brooches wrapped in plastic and similar in shape and size to the ones that had recently come into her possession.

"I see why young women came here to buy these," she said as she picked one up and held it near the lamp. On each side of the centerpiece were small, cut rhinestones set in what looked like copper prongs. "Why use copper on inexpensive costume jewelry?"

Before she could investigate further, the front door's bell chimed and a pair of muffled voices—a man and woman—discussing something. She scooped up her phone and walked toward the beaded curtain that divided the storage room from the sales floor. She gently pushed open two strands of beads and peered into the store.

"Let me get it from the back," the woman said.

Elaine's jaw dropped when she realized who was speaking. Without thinking, she stepped through the curtains. "Professor Wallace? Florence? What are you two doing here?"

CHAPTER 19

Florence whipped around, startled. "Elaine! How did you get in here?"

"Adele gave me a key," Elaine replied, her voice shaking with barely contained anger. "You didn't answer my question. What are *you* two doing here?"

"Good evening, Elaine," Professor Wallace said as he adjusted his tie. He was leaning his weight on a table display and looked a bit peaked.

"Hello, Professor," Elaine replied curtly. She couldn't help but notice his cheeks had a few visible pockmarks on them, and his hand trembled. "Are you all right?" she asked, despite her anger.

"Yes, just a bit under the weather, I believe." He stood straighter, as if trying to regain a bit of the gravitas he had displayed the last time he and Elaine were face-to-face. "I know this is a strange way to meet again—"

"You'll have to excuse us for a minute, Professor," Florence cut in as she walked up to Elaine, took her arm, and led her to the back room. "Elaine," she whispered, "you're going to have to trust me. Adele gave me a key when we were leaving the diner. I don't have much time, so just stay here, and I promise I'll explain everything."

She put her hands on Elaine's shoulders and guided her to sit at the desk.

"What? This is insane!" Elaine said. "Are you running some sort of scam, or are you working for Lazro?"

"Shhh!" Florence hissed. "Just stay here. Professor Wallace wants to purchase one of these." She held up one of Adele's generic moon brooches. Without another word, she turned and walked through the beaded curtains. Elaine could hear the clacking of heels on the wooden floor and Florence calling out Professor Wallace's name. The small bell rang, and when Elaine stepped out, she saw the door closing and Professor Wallace rushing out of the store.

"Great." Florence sighed. She leaned up against the counter and crossed her arms over her chest and glared at Elaine. "Now we've spooked him. What were you thinking, Elaine? I was so close to selling him another brooch and getting closer to Lazro." She pushed off the counter, marched to the front door, and locked it before facing Elaine again.

"When did you sell the first brooch to the professor?" Elaine asked. She stood in front of Florence to stop her from pacing.

"I didn't. Adele did when they first met, remember?" Florence replied. "I'm sorry. I wanted to tell you everything right away, but Adele didn't even know I was going to try to sell it to him. She just trusted I knew what I was doing when I mentioned finding Giselle, the young woman who had traded feverfew for a brooch."

"And the one who attacked us at Hugh's place." Elaine nodded in understanding. "Still, how do I know you're not working for Lazro? Or that Professor Wallace or Hugh isn't Lazro himself? You could be lying to my face, and I have nothing to prove otherwise." Elaine's chest tightened in anger, and the vein in the middle of her forehead pulsed ever so slightly.

Florence calmly walked up to her and put her hands on Elaine's upper arms. "You just have to trust me. I promise—I'm on your side." Elaine continued to glare at her, so Florence withdrew her hands and placed them on her hips. "In fact," she continued, "I was planning on telling all of you tonight when we got together. I don't know if Professor Wallace is connected to Giselle or Lazro, but I do believe he is searching for the keys for a different reason than displaying them at the museum gala in a few weeks."

Elaine hesitated before responding. "I'm worried about Adele. She's having dinner with the professor tonight. I should tell her to cancel. She could be in danger." She picked up her phone in an attempt to text Adele.

"No, don't," Florence urged, snatching the phone out of Elaine's hand and placing it on the desk. "If Adele is going to be with the professor, that will at least keep him preoccupied and keep him away in case he really is involved with Lazro. It's the perfect time for the guild to get together."

"But what if something happens to Adele again? What if Professor Wallace hurts her, or they get kidnapped, or worse? I couldn't bear it if anything bad happened to her. I just couldn't." Her aunts' accident suddenly flashed in her mind. Her voice caught, and she covered her mouth with her hand to force back her worry. "I should warn her or at least go to the restaurant with her or take Grant with me, and we can spy on them."

At the mention of Grant's name, Florence twitched. "I understand your concern, Elaine. I do. But I don't think you want to get Grant any more involved than he is. Besides, Adele can take care of herself. It seems to me that Professor Wallace is smitten with her. Let's just let them have a good night together. It's possible Professor Wallace could reveal something of importance to her. Either that or he turns out to be just an avid collector with an interest in mysterious, ancient guilds, and we've not harmed their budding romance."

Elaine bit her lip in contemplation. If Professor Wallace was connected to Lazro and searching for more keys and brooches, then keeping him distracted for the evening and clueless to any guild activity was the right thing to do. On the other hand, if Lazro believed the professor had another key or brooch in his possession, then Adele and Professor Wallace were at risk. "You're right." She sighed after weighing out the options. "But Grant needs to be here tonight. He knows as much as I do and could be a big help in retrieving the keys."

Florence nodded. "Fine. I'll contact everyone." She headed toward the exit then twirled around to face Elaine. "Be here by seven. Park a block over and use the back entrance."

Once she left, Elaine called Grant to reschedule their coffee date. She asked him to cancel plans with Teddy and bring the brooches to the shop instead for the guild meeting this evening. After they hung up, she reminded herself she needed to go to Mr. Sadler's office and discuss the details of the upcoming auction. Ironing out the details helped her feel more secure that she was doing the right thing. She also needed to run an ad in the newspaper and the local radio station announcing the sale. After that, she would go to the library and do some work and order takeout before coming back to the store.

She turned off the desk lamp and locked the back door behind her. The late afternoon air chilled her, so she pulled her fleece closer to her chest as she walked to her car. The drive to Mr. Sadler's office wouldn't take very long, but Elaine hated being cold. She turned on her seat warmer and waited for it to kick in before heading across town.

Fifteen minutes later, she pulled into the gravel parking lot next to a gray house with brown trim and a bowed porch. Overgrown bushes and weeds poked through the once-rock landscaping. The sign out front read, "Sadler Financial" and included a phone number and website address. Years of sun and rain had caused the wood to warp and the paint to chip and flake off. Elaine started to open her car door when Teddy walked out the front door and descended the stairs.

Elaine fought the urge to confront him. She ducked down in her seat. Teddy hadn't seen her. He just got into his car and drove away.

Could Teddy be working for Mr. Sadler? she asked herself. The connection didn't make sense to her. Teddy was so kind to her and showed unwavering loyalty to her aunts. She looked at her reflection in the rearview mirror. "Not everyone is against you," she reaffirmed.

Mr. Sadler had taken advantage of her aunts and Grant's mother. It was possible he had done the same to Teddy. Maybe Teddy had decided to end any business with Mr. Sadler after the eavesdropping incident. Mr. Sadler seemed to be tied to the guild members or those connected to them.

"Only one way to find out," Elaine declared. Emboldened, she flung open her door and marched across the parking lot, the gravel crunching and rolling underneath her quick steps.

She rushed up the stairs and pushed through the door, slamming it shut and causing the small table with business cards to rattle and shake. The dusty, plastic floral arrangement to the left of the cards tipped over and rolled onto the dingy linoleum floor.

"May I help you, young lady?" shouted Judy, Mr. Sadler's assistant. She stood up from her desk and placed her glasses on the bridge of her bulbous nose. Her beady eyes squinted at Elaine from behind dirty lenses.

"Where is that snake of a boss of yours?" Elaine demanded. "I know he's here. You tell him I know what he's up to, and he's not going to get away with it!"

"Now listen here, young lady," Judy said, her hands clenched at her side. "I'll not have you come in here and interrupt our place of business and accuse Mr. Sadler of anything. Go home and call and make an appointment when you've calmed down, or I'm calling the cops."

Before Elaine could respond, Mr. Sadler came out of his office. The hallway lights reflected off the wood paneling and highlighted the sweat on his brow and cheeks. He walked toward her, wiping his forehead with a handkerchief before speaking. "What's this? Why are you here, Elaine?" he asked. He shoved the handkerchief in his back pocket and put his hands on his hips. Sweat stains under his armpits made his tangerine shirt and brown tie look even more atrocious.

"I don't know what you're up to, exactly, but I'll be damned if I let you near my aunts' property ever again. The auction's off!"

He threw his hands up in the air in defeat. "Well, you're in luck. There's not going to be an auction, thanks to your friend and the large check he just cut me."

It took Elaine a moment to find her voice again, she was so baffled. "Large check?" She felt all her built-up anger deflate inside her. Her assumptions that Mr. Sadler had been working under Lazro's directives made no sense now. "What do you mean?"

Mr. Sadler grinned. "You didn't know?" He seemed to take pleasure in having something else to hang over Elaine. "He wrote a big check and paid off the double mortgage and all the back taxes. You're off the hook, Elaine. It must be nice having someone swoop in after you and clean up all your messes."

CHAPTER 20

Elaine fought the urge to throw something. How dare he insult her like that! If it hadn't been for him and his bad advice, her aunts never would have been so in debt. If anyone knew about cleaning up messes, it was Elaine.

She hiked her purse onto her shoulders, spun around on her heels, and walked toward the door. "At least I don't cheat old ladies or sickly widows out of their money!" She turned back around to face him, giving him a steely glare. "If I hear of you getting within ten feet of Grant's mother or Adele, someone will need to sweep you off the floor after I'm done with you."

With that, Elaine slammed the door behind her and marched to her car. Her nostrils flared, and her face flushed to the point she felt the heat in the tips of her ears. Elaine pressed her key fob and opened the car doors. As soon as she turned on the ignition, Elaine began to laugh so hard, tears trickled out of the corners of her eyes. She had really surprised herself lately. First, she told off Eric and sprayed him with homemade pepper spray, and then she threatened a middle-aged man, albeit a despicable one who preyed on vulnerable people in financial trouble.

Relief surged through her body. She was grateful Teddy had paid off the debts, but she couldn't understand why he did it and in secret, nonetheless. As hard as she tried to analyze Teddy's motives, she couldn't think clearly with a throbbing headache. She needed to eat something. Thankfully, her favorite Chinese restaurant wasn't too far from Mr. Sadler's office. "I'll tell Grant about it tonight," she muttered as she turned on to the busy highway lined with shopping centers and fast-food restaurants.

Elaine was the only customer at New Asian Cuisine. She placed her order and played a puzzle game on her cell phone as she waited. Fifteen minutes later, her sweet-and-sour chicken released a heavenly aroma as she drove down Main Street. Dusk was settling in, and the string lights that stretched across the street created a quaint postcard scene of the town she knew and loved. She was somewhat tempted to shove an egg roll in her mouth as she passed the familiar shops, but the last time she ate on the run, half of her meal had ended up in her lap.

There were only three cars in the library's lot when she arrived. The setting sun backlit the maple trees that lined the walkway, causing their colored leaves to shimmer like gems. Elaine threaded her right arm through the handles of her take-out bag and pulled open the heavy front door. Syd and Tom were packing up their chess game and arguing about the rook-to-king technique. James was playing video games on the desktop computer, and Mrs. Armested was asleep in her chair.

She set the food out on a long table near the fiction section. Her phone started buzzing just as she shoved a forkful of rice into her mouth. She finally picked up on the third ring. Before Grant could get a word out edgewise, she launched into detail about seeing Florence and Teddy earlier.

"Wow! That's a lot to take in," Grant said when Elaine finished her story. "That's amazing about Teddy. Who knew he could afford to be so generous? And I'm sure Florence has a perfectly good explanation for everything. Let's not jump to conclusions."

"That's what I like about you, Grant," Elaine said. "You're always trying to see the good in people." She sighed, feeling a bit calmer. "Anyway, I'm eating dinner at the library. I'll see you at Adele's shop at seven, right?"

"Roger that," Grant teased. "Elaine? I've been meaning to ask you something." His voice took on a nervous edge.

"What's that?" Elaine sat down, then dipped her egg roll into the sweet-and-sour sauce before biting off a huge chunk. Her mouth watered as she chewed and the sauce blended in with the steaming cabbage and carrots wrapped in the fried roll.

"It's about the museum gala next week. I was wondering ..." Grant hesitated. "Well, I mean, we could go together, as friends, you know? Check up on the professor and see who else shows up?"

"Sure, that'd be nice," Elaine mumbled as cabbage and sauce dripped onto her chin. She swiped at them with her finger and licked off the remaining sauce as she shoved the food back into her mouth.

Grant sounded confused. "So you want to go? It doesn't have to be a date. I just thought it would be a good idea. Keep an eye out for Lazro. Florence and Adele will be there, too, you know—"

"I think it sounds great," Elaine interrupted. She surprised herself at how nervous and self-conscious she felt. *What will Grant think when he finds out I broke up with Eric?* she wondered.

"You do?" Grant's voice conveyed his excitement. "Well, I guess that means I have to rent a tux or something, huh? Would you like me to pick you up, or do you want to just meet there?"

Elaine felt her stomach flip. Was it nerves or hunger she was feeling? She hadn't stopped moving since this morning, and that second egg roll looked so inviting. Food was what she needed before she could even begin to unpack her feelings about Grant. "Listen, I gotta go. I'm eating, and then I have a few tasks to do here at work before I lock up and head on over to the store. I'll see you soon, and we can talk about the gala later, okay?"

"Oh, yeah, sure. See you, Elaine."

She set her phone down and practically inhaled the last of her meal. She threw away the to-go box, dripping with leftover sauce, and told James he could leave.

There wasn't much for her to do once the place was empty, so she went through her normal routine of closing the library. It was ten minutes before seven when she flipped the sign in the window to "Closed" and locked the front door. Guilt consumed her for closing ten minutes early, but she knew once her life returned to normal, she'd get back into her old routine and keep her regular work schedule. Even though her regimented routine lent itself to a somewhat boring and static life, she could at least count on not having her world upended or her chest filled with anxiety every day. But wasn't she always anxious? And did her routine really protect her from life's unpredictable events?

If she was being honest with herself, this past week—what with finding and losing two keys—had been the most interesting and exciting time in her adult life. It had also felt good to dump Eric and tell off Mr. Sadler. It was exciting to think that her aunts and parents were a part of a secret society that went back generations and that she was a link in that chain. Traveling by starlight was exhilarating. Once upon a time, chasing after criminals and guarding magical keys had only existed in the books she checked out to people. Now, she was heading to a secret-society meeting in the back room of a small apothecary shop in her own hometown. A jolt of excitement shot through Elaine's stomach as she started up her car and made her way to Maiden, Mother, Crone and the unforeseen future.

Elaine arrived at the shop a few minutes before seven. She didn't see Grant's car in the back parking lot, but she hoped he was there. She wanted to apologize for how she handled talking to him on the phone earlier, especially when he brought up the museum gala. Of course she would go with him. He was her best friend, and it wouldn't be awkward at all, but she couldn't explain why she felt so nervous thinking about it. Could he possibly be interested in her romantically? She still believed there was chemistry between Grant and Florence. Yet, when he was at her house the other night, she had felt jittery and excited around him when it seemed like he was flirting with her.

"Enough of that," she told herself. She needed to focus on tonight's meeting. The streetlights and a scattering of stars illuminated her path. It was so cold, she could see her breath as she fumbled for the key and unlocked the back door to the storage room. Once inside, she waited until her eyes adjusted to the dim lighting.

"Hello, Elaine," a female voice said near the storage shelves, causing Elaine to gasp. Florence stepped into the light emanating from the desk lamp. "Sorry! I didn't mean to scare you."

"It's all right," Elaine replied, but then she realized she was clutching her purse to her chest. She exhaled and loosened her grip. The leather strap settled across her left shoulder and chest, and the bulky purse came to rest at her hip. "Is everyone here? Where's Grant?" she asked tentatively.

"Yes, they're all here. Grant too. Come. I'll introduce you to Teddy's mother." Florence walked over to one of the storage shelves and pulled on it. The boxes of inventory shifted forward slightly as the shelf opened like a door, but none of them fell over. Florence swung the shelf open wider. "Down here," she said. "Follow me."

Elaine marveled at the secret passageway. A warm glow of orange light filled the opening, and a set of wooden stairs led the way. The walls were stucco white and tinged with dirt that showed their age. A cobweb hung between the hinges and the top of the stair rail. Elaine couldn't believe her eyes. "Is this for real?" she asked as she descended the stairs. The storage shelf shut behind her. The boards squeaked under her weight. She smelled a subtle scent of lavender and sage as she neared the bottom of the stairs.

Florence took Elaine by the wrist and guided her to the center of the room, which was lit by candles. "You know Hugh, Elaine," Florence said as she dropped Elaine's wrist and took her place next to him.

"Hello, lass," Hugh said in his thick brogue.

"Hello, Hugh," Elaine said. At first, she felt relieved to see him there, safe and unharmed, but then she noticed the large cut on his forehead. She recalled the fight with Giselle, who flung a heavy object in Hugh's direction. "Did she hurt you?"

"No, lass. I'm all right. The only thing hurt is my pride," Hugh remarked as he touched the stitches above his right brow. "There was a spark of light from Giselle's chair that shot out like a firecracker, and some debris hit me in the head. When I looked up, I realized she must have used some form of interstellar travel that we're unaware of. Somehow that sneaky woman pulled a disappearing act right in front of my eyes."

"Beautiful and elusive women have that effect on a man," a deep voice said. Elaine felt a hand on her shoulder. She looked to her right and saw Grant standing beside her. "Hi," Grant said. The warm candlelight showed a sheepish grin on his face, and the tips of his ears appeared red.

"I'm so glad to see you," Elaine replied. "I wanted to tell you—"

Florence jumped in. "Elaine, this is Vivienne, Teddy's mother. She's the guardian of the yellow key."

Elaine followed Florence's gaze and saw a tall, elegant woman dressed in a light purple satin blouse and tight red pants. Her hair was wrapped in a purple, lime green, and red headscarf. She wore matching red-framed glasses and red high heels. Large, red hoop earrings with small seashells dangling from the center completed her colorful look. The candlelight flickered and gave her skin a glowing cinnamon color. Vivienne walked over to Elaine and held out her hand. "You can call me Viv," she said in a silky voice that sounded like jazz and oozed like honey. "Your aunts spoke so highly of you."

"Nice to meet you." Elaine's voice was barely audible as she shook Vivienne's hand. She couldn't believe she was standing in the room with all the guardians. She wished Daphne and Mildred were here to support her and give the proper introductions. She also felt like a fraud in front of them. She wasn't as great of a niece as her aunts had probably wanted the others to believe. If she had listened to them when she was younger and really believed in the magic from an early age, maybe she would have been as adventurous, loyal, and dedicated to a cause like they were.

"Sorry to be so abrupt," Florence interrupted, "but we don't have a lot of time. Grant, do you have the brooches?"

"I do." Grant pulled out the two brooches Elaine had given him earlier. "You said I was to keep the one for the red key, right?" He handed over the brooch Elaine had been wearing earlier today. She gave him a strange look.

"But ... that other brooch belonged to my mother," Elaine said tightly. "My aunts were going to give it to me—"

"Trust me, Elaine," Florence held up her hand, "everything will be explained tonight."

"Seems like there are always explanations upon explanations," Elaine retorted. "And speaking of explanations ... can someone please tell me how Teddy, a *college* student, was able to pay off all my aunts' debt? Where'd he come up with the money to do that?"

"Oh dear," Viv began. "We really must tell her, Florence. The poor girl can't be kept in the dark any longer."

Hugh stepped forward. "You're right, Viv." He faced Elaine, his face somber, but there was a twinkling in his eyes. "Your aunts, lass, were great women. They were the ones who suspected Lazro was back on the trail after all these years. Theodore had mentioned to his mother that there was an anonymous buyer with the handle @moonbeamdreams who was active on your aunts' online auction site this summer. The person had bought thousands upon thousands of dollars' worth of antique jewelry, all their midcentury modern furniture from Europe, and two or three pieces of high-end porcelain they had left in stock. They paid for it all by check under a company named Moon Beam Dreams. Teddy found the uncashed check written over to him in Daphne's handwriting. It was stashed in the plastic sleeve of his economics book that he finally cracked open today."

Elaine's eyes grew big, and she blinked back tears. Why would Teddy cash out a check and pay off her debt when he had more than enough debt as a college student? She couldn't get over how big of a heart Teddy had or how loyal he was to her aunts.

Florence stepped forward. "When I heard of the popular brooches Adele was selling, I recruited Theodore's help to try and reach out to the company's unnamed owner ...."

The proverbial light bulb went off, and Elaine started to piece together what they were trying to tell her. "You were hoping the anonymous buyer was Lazro or would lead you to him," she said excitedly.

Hugh nodded. "Yes, we hoped to draw Lazro out of hiding. And it worked. Except he was clever and had gathered a following since the time we all last saw him. We think they've learned how to activate these new brooches. It would explain how Giselle broke into my home and got away. Those generic brooches have some energetic property to them we're unaware of. My only guess is that Giselle somehow had it on her person and finagled a way to activate it. Maybe it was up her sleeve? I dunno."

"Copper!" Elaine started. "I remember looking at one of those brooches this evening and seeing some stones set in copper."

"Copper is a powerful conductor of electricity," Grant chimed in. "With the right amount of frequency from an electromagnetic current, you can generate power in a short amount of time."

"Maybe Giselle's tattoo is some type of electromagnetic current? Maybe these generic brooches Lazro and Giselle are interested in are why our original brooches and the green key are becoming unstable?" Elaine asked. "But it seems awfully risky to tempt either of them to buy more when we don't know if they can activate the keys with them, right?"

"Yes, it's risky," Florence said. "But we are certain that all the keys need to be together to access Isabella's source portal. Selling Adele's knockoff brooches seemed like a risk we were willing to take to lure Lazro out into the open. Just like Daphne and Mildred had tried to do."

"Professor Wallace!" Elaine exclaimed. "You suspect he's not who he says he is, don't you?" She looked around the room, directing her question to not just Florence but Hugh and Vivienne as well.

"That's right," Vivienne said. "Teddy let it slip during one of our weekly phone conversations last month that he was to drop something off to him as a favor for Daphne and Mildred. I called Hugh afterward, and he suspected that Professor Wallace was the man your mother had an affair with when she was a graduate student at the university. Before she met your father, of course."

Florence stepped forward and picked up where Vivienne left off. "I became suspicious of Wallace when Adele mentioned he had been to Granada, Spain, to look for artifacts. That's where the red key's portal that houses Isabella and her mother is located. It didn't take long for me to do a little bit more research on Professor Wallace's job history to learn he had recruited your mother and a few other graduate students to research the historical importance of guilds from the Renaissance to the Industrial Revolution. His publications in academic journals revealed hints of his obsession with the rituals of the guilds and the mysticism surrounding ones like the Apothecary Guild and the tales of the German herbalist who had disappeared from the woods surrounding Brightonville. The same woods located on Daphne and Mildred's property. I believe he manipulated your mother, Elaine, into revealing more of the details of the secret guild he suspected she was a part of."

"You think he's Lazro, don't you?" Elaine asked.

"We do," Florence confirmed. "I wanted to tell you—truly I did. But I needed to be certain. When you showed up at the store and he ran off, I didn't know exactly what to say." She walked over to her purse, pulled out a document, and handed it to Elaine. "Hugh found this in his research in an old library in Inverness. My research at your library confirms this information."

Elaine looked at the document, which appeared to be some sort of official document with a family tree stapled to the back.

"It's Professor Wallace's forged birth certificate. My friend at Scotland Yard obtained it for me. It's proof Wallace is Lazro in disguise," Hugh commented. "And attached is the family tree I ripped out of my sketchbook from my study. I have been trying for days now to find out who Professor Wallace really is and why he was so intent on buying your key for the museum's collection."

Elaine flipped to the rudimentary notations of the family tree Hugh had laid out. She saw that Isabella and Lazro had a child that was stillborn. Years later, Isabella had a son with a carpenter from Rota, Spain. The son grew up and married and had children of his own. One of them, who was Elaine's great-great-grandfather on her mother's side, immigrated to Pennsylvania and later to Ohio in the mid-1800s. "Lazro won't stop until he gets his revenge, will he?" Elaine asked as she folded the document and handed it back to Florence.

"No. He was in love with Isabella but felt she betrayed him for so many reasons," Florence said. "More importantly, we really need you to know we never meant to harm you or deceive you, Elaine. Truly. We hope that you can understand that the four of us felt it was right to pay off Daphne and Mildred's debts with the money as a way to honor them and help you out. We know we're asking a lot of you to help us, Elaine."

Elaine relaxed and smiled for the first time since she had arrived. "It's very kind of you all, and I'm grateful, but I don't know what else I can do to help. I don't know how to be a guardian. I definitely don't know the first thing about using the keys. And knowing I'm connected to both the green and the red key through my lineage seems like a heavy weight to carry."

"That's why I'm here," Grant said. He stepped forward and put his arm around Elaine's shoulders. "I've agreed to become a guardian too. I'll take on the red key. Even though I'm not a direct descendant, Florence has been teaching me some things these past few days. I'm ready, and I want to help. Lazro hurt my mother when she tried to help the guild."

Elaine hesitated for a moment and considered everything. She felt a ping of excitement in her stomach, and her heart began to beat quickly. "It makes sense now," Elaine said. She looked up at

Florence. "Does Adele know this? Stupid question ... Of course she does. You told her already, didn't you?"

Florence nodded sheepishly. "I called her right as she was leaving for her date with him. She said she'd keep him distracted as long as she could."

"That clever minx ..." Elaine's voice trailed off as she began thinking of how Adele and the rest of them had been one step ahead of her this whole time. "I want to say I'm mad at you all, but I can't. I've been a stubborn fool for too long now. I didn't take the time to really listen to my aunts as a child, but I'm listening now. Count me in. I'm ready to help. Let's make me a guardian!"

Before Hugh or Florence could chime in, Vivienne clapped her hands and replied, "Well, let's get to it! There's no time to waste." She pulled out a chain from around her neck and revealed her key looped through it. The key's face was circular with a triangular gemstone centered toward the bottom. Elaine couldn't help but admire how it shimmered in the glow of the candles. "It's citrine," Vivienne said. "Beautiful, isn't it?"

Elaine nodded, too much in awe to say anything else.

"This is the fire key," Vivienne explained. "It's associated with the sun and unlocks wealth and abundance, giving the bearer abilities to manifest things in the physical world."

Vivienne took the key and placed it into the brooch pinned to her blouse. She looked into the mirror on the wall and uttered, "Inlustris et luna trabem." Next, she turned the key in the lock situated in the center of the brooch's full moon shape. A bright beam of light shot out of the brooch and sparked upon the wall in front of her. The wall took on a watery visage, and then Elaine blinked and saw swaying palmetto and pine trees and a sandy, white beach and ocean waves stretching out far into the distance. Vivienne grinned and walked toward the trees. She reached inside the scene and drew out a small glass vial.

"This is a special ginger turmeric tea," Vivienne began. "I'm an herbalist by trade, and I give my clients this when they have upset stomachs. But they don't know that it comes from the yellow key's portal. I make my own remedies, but every now and then, in special cases, I go to the portal and pull out some of the more ancient remedies put together by the first guild members." She smiled and handed Elaine the bottle with the crushed roots. "For you, dear," Vivienne said. "Drink this once a day for the next few days, and you'll find it not only eases your anxieties but also gives you courage." Elaine took the bottle and hugged Vivienne. "That was magical. Thank you, Viv." She was overjoyed to see the keys in action. "I see now why Teddy says he believes in you and your remedies."

"You're welcome, dear." Vivienne laughed. She stepped back and unlatched the key from the brooch, and the portal disappeared. Vivienne slipped the key and chain back around her neck while Florence walked up to Elaine.

"My turn," Florence said as she pulled her orange key from around her neck and placed it in the lock on her brooch. The orange key was in the shape of a clover and had three carnelian stones in each clover leaf. "This is the water key. It cleanses the other gemstones and brings emotional balance, gives one confidence, and enlightens one's creativity." She, too, glanced into the mirror, uttered the same phrase three times, and turned the key. The scene on the wall morphed into what appeared to be a garden with a small pool of clear water surrounded by white tiles with painted blue and yellow flowers on them. A small fountain spurted from the center, and on each side of the pool were gorgeous red rose bushes, twining honeysuckle, hawthorn and serviceberry trees, and numerous flowers clustered together. Florence stepped up to the portal and stuck her hand in, drawing out another small bottle.

"This is rosewater infused with orange oil," she said, handing the small bottle to Elaine. "Put this on your wrists and right behind your ears every day, and you will find it gives you confidence and the ability to stay present in the moment."

Elaine took this bottle as well and slid it into her purse next to the other one. "That's very sweet of you, Florence. Thank you." Elaine felt overwhelmed by their generosity. She also felt confused.

Wasn't she supposed to learn the secrets of how to guard the keys? Maybe that would come next after this strange ceremony of gifts. She stayed quiet, knowing Hugh was next.

The face of his key was rectangular with a gemstone to match. "Lapis lazuli," he said when he noticed Elaine staring at it. He repeated the same ritual as Vivienne and Florence, and a beautiful French countryside appeared. Rows of planted lavender swayed in the wind, and Elaine could hear the cooing of turtle doves. A small, white stucco barn sat upon a hill, and someone far away was playing a lute that blended in with the doves' song. Hugh's vial was the same size as the other two. It had a cork on top, and when he popped it open, the smell of lavender filled the air and seemed to clear Elaine's sinuses and soothe her.

"My key is known as the 'ether key.' The lavender you're smelling comes straight from a distant farm in Provence. It's made from the ancient lavender of the first guild members. Open this vial only when you need it. It brings truth and self-awareness and also induces dreams. It's very powerful to counteract darkness of any sorts." He corked the bottle and handed it to her.

Elaine was stunned. "I don't know what to say. Thank you for these gifts. I'll use them wisely. But I have to be honest: I don't know exactly how these will help me become a guild member or a guardian. Shouldn't I be learning jiujitsu or some funky martial arts? Weapons training? Studying and practicing magic?" She didn't want to sound ungrateful, but surely there was more to guardianship than unlocking a portal and taking out some herbal remedies.

Hugh chuckled. "I know none of this seems important, but these are special herbs. Like we said, they come from the original healers. They're quite powerful, and these things and more are what Lazro is after. If he possesses all these along with the red source key's secret remedies, there will be no stopping him from using them to harm others or give himself the ability to travel by starlight to any place in the world. He could get inside museums and banks and steal anything he wanted."

"Then why did you risk opening the portals when I heard you tell Florence to shut them the other night at your house?" Elaine questioned.

"We decided you were worth the risk, Elaine. We want you to have a better understanding of what we really do." Florence smiled brightly, and Elaine felt a wave of guilt move inside her for even doubting Florence or her loyalty.

Grant cleared his throat. "Shouldn't we know a little bit more about the red and green keys, then?"

"Yes, you're right, lad. As you know, the red key is the source key. You'd be guarding the ancient secrets that Isabella, the original head guardian, wrote down. The other healers infused their keys with mantras and hid away the ingredients and other properties for the herbal remedies in these portals you saw tonight. The cures and spells she curated in that book are more potent when paired with the actual physical properties. We aren't one hundred percent sure where she hid the documents, but we do know they are more than likely hidden underneath a church that is connected to a series of caves in Granada, Spain."

"So if Lazro gets his hands on the documents, he could technically make himself head guardian?" Elaine asked.

Florence nodded in confirmation. "Yes, and your green key is a portal to a sweet cabin in the woodlands near your house, Elaine. It is in what you Midwesterners call the 'heartland,' which is why we sometimes call it the heart key. It contains the element of air and brings harmony and balance with nature and the self. It also possesses an antidote to any bitter poison that could kill anyone who drinks it. Lazro would probably destroy those plants or keep the antidote only for himself."

Elaine sighed heavily. "But you didn't bank on me selling the green key or finding the red one and losing that one too."

"It's all right, Elaine," Vivienne said in a soothing voice. "You couldn't have known what it was all about. We didn't know your situation until Teddy admitted to us a few hours ago he'd been working with Daphne and Mildred for over a year now. We all should've been more up-front with you. Your aunts just made us promise to not involve you until you were ready. They loved you so much and just wanted you to stay out of harm's way."

"Well, I'm ready now," Elaine stated. "What's our next move?"

Before anyone could answer her, footsteps and voices echoed above them. Grant put his finger to his mouth and crept up the stairs. Vivienne blew out the candles, and Hugh pulled out a penlight from his waistcoat. Florence and Elaine huddled closer together, unsure of what to do next. The voices were louder now, and the five of them heard a man's voice ask, "What's this? It looks like it's been moved away from the wall. You could get hurt, my sweet."

"Oh no, it's always like that," a woman's voice replied. "Please, don't touch it. I'm afraid to mess up my inventory."

"It's Adele and the professor," Grant whispered as he made his way back to them. "I think he noticed the bookshelf." Always the handyman, Grant held a small flashlight at the ready and switched on the power. The muffled voices became louder until Elaine and the rest of them could hear Adele's voice from above. "Oh no, no, you don't want to go down there. It's just a musty old basement, that's all."

"He found the secret doorway," Grant whispered. "Quick, we need to find a way out." He waved his flashlight around until it shined upon a crawl space window and some wooden crates lined up against the wall. "I have a plan. Follow me."

They crept toward the window, and Grant quickly stacked the boxes on top of each other. "Hurry!" He was already standing at the top of the last box and had unlatched the window. After crawling through, he stuck his head and arms back through the window and lifted Florence out onto the street. Vivienne followed, leaving Hugh and Elaine together.

Professor Wallace had bullied his way past Adele and was at the top of the stairs. "My, my, Adele." His voice took on a sardonic tone. "What have you been keeping from me down here?"

"Edmund, please don't go down there," Adele pleaded. "It's just an old basement, like I said. You could get hurt."

"Quick, lass," Hugh whispered to Elaine. "Get outta here. I'll handle him." He postured himself in a fighting stance.

"No, Hugh, don't," Elaine replied. "We both need to leave. Don't be foolish. Now's not the time to take on Lazro." She stared hard into Hugh's eyes. The wooden stairs creaked. Professor Wallace ... Lazro was at the top two steps, fumbling with the worn-out light switch.

Elaine was nearly in a panic, so Hugh took pity on her. "Fine," he said. "We'll take on Lazro when you know more about using the keys and brooches. Up you go!" He helped Elaine step onto the crate, and she scurried up as Grant pulled her out. She felt a sharp pain in her knee as it scraped against the concrete. She stood up and made way for Hugh, whose burly shoulders barely fit through the opening.

"Pull!" Grant commanded Elaine. She grabbed Hugh's other arm, and she and Grant pulled as hard as they could and hoisted Hugh out the window. His pants caught on the top latch and ripped, exposing his red boxer shorts with large white polka dots. Grant lowered the window gently and motioned for them all to step away. They pressed themselves up against the window just as Lazro stepped into the guardians' secret meeting space.

CHAPTER 21

Grant bent down and peered through the window. Elaine stood next to the window, too, and risked taking a look. Lazro's back was to her when she made eye contact with Adele, whose grimace mimed, "Get away from here." Elaine looked around to see if there was an escape. She spied a large green dumpster in the alley between Adele's shop and the building next to it. Elaine looked at Grant and nodded in the direction of the dumpster.

He took notice and signaled to Hugh, Vivienne, and Florence that they were going to make a quick run behind the dumpster. They gave him a thumbs-up, and on his silent count of three, they all tiptoed past the window toward the dumpster, their shadows cast in front of them by the streetlight marking the edge of the parking lot. The broken gravel from the numerous potholes in the alley rolled underneath their feet. Vivienne's high heel caught in a small pothole, and she twisted her ankle, causing her to cry out. When she ripped off her shoes, a pebble dislodged from the heel and knocked into the window. Without hesitation, Elaine turned back, took Vivienne's hand, and helped her to the dumpster, joining the others. If the professor had heard the ricochet, Elaine hoped Adele could explain it as one of the stray cats that snuck around the shops at night looking for mice and scouring the dumpsters for food.

"Vivienne? Are you all right?" whispered Elaine when they were safely out of view.

"I'll be fine once I can get home and elevate my ankle, then soak it in some mint-infused bath salts." Vivienne winced and edged her way down into a seated position to take the weight off her legs.

The others leaned against the wall, trying their best to hold their breath to lock out the sour stench of rotting trash. The height of the dumpster and the darkness between the buildings sheltered them. The only thing to do now was wait.

Elaine shivered. Her thin fleece wasn't enough to keep her warm from the frosty air. Vivienne whispered she had left her coat inside, and Florence said she had too. They huddled around Vivienne and squatted down. Hugh was the first one to hear Adele's back door open. He signaled for them to all stay quiet and flatten up against the wall to prepare for a possible escape.

"And you're sure that's all the brooches?" Lazro asked.

"Yes, I'm sure," Adele replied. "Now, if you wouldn't mind leaving, Edmund, I'm quite tired and need my rest."

"I do appreciate you giving these to me, Adele, truly," Lazro said. "I promise you—I will put them on display at the museum, and we'll be sure to write up a sizable check to compensate you. I hope you'll still consider being my date for the gala next week? We should have the display up by then."

Elaine was closest to the parking lot, so she leaned over and peered out from the side of the dumpster. Lazro held the box of brooches under his arm. Adele was rubbing her hands together, biting her bottom lip. She spotted a glimpse of Elaine's face in the streetlight and took Lazro's hand in hers. "I'd be honored, Edmund." She stood on her tiptoes and gave him a peck on the cheek and then spun him around in the direction of his car. Elaine ducked back behind the dumpster and exhaled in relief.

Lazro walked across the alley to his car. After a moment, Elaine heard his door close. She clenched her teeth and didn't realize she was holding her breath until she let it out after he drove away. "That was a close one." She sighed as she stood up to check if the coast was clear. She watched Lazro's taillights move away from them until they were only specks of floating red lights in the distance. "He's gone," she said and made her way over to where Adele was standing.

Florence and Grant helped Vivienne to the store. Hugh pulled an oily, smashed box of take-out noodles off his elbow and tossed it to the ground, muttering some Scottish curse word.

"Goodness!" Adele exclaimed as Elaine reached out and hugged her. "You guys had me worried. Come out of the cold," she said while she shepherded them through the open door.

Grant pulled out Adele's chair from behind her desk and helped Vivienne take a seat.

"Adele, why did you give the professor all the knockoff brooches?" Elaine asked.

Adele was taking down mugs from the cabinet in the storage room's kitchenette and pulling out tea bags from the jar on the counter. "Hold on, let me fix you all a cup of tea." She filled each mug with water, placed one in the microwave, and hit Start before facing Elaine.

"So you saw that Edmund got curious about the basement. Well, when we went back upstairs, the box must have tumbled over because a few brooches had dropped out. He saw them and began asking questions. I reminded him he had bought one of these for his sister in Iowa earlier this month, but he acted like he had forgotten. He began this long diatribe about their origin and design being a direct connection to the historical trade guilds of Europe. He insisted they needed to be displayed at the gala. I felt if I resisted, I might jeopardize your safety, so I simply played along."

The microwave beeped, and Adele took out the steaming hot mug and dropped a tea bag inside it before heating up another mug. "Here, dear, you must be cold," she said as she handed the mug to Elaine. "I'm really sorry for having sent that man off with all those fake brooches. I presume once he finds out they're fakes, he'll come after the keys more aggressively."

Adele walked over to the utility closet and completely missed the worried glances flying around the room. She started pulling out folding chairs and began setting them up around Vivienne.

"I hate to leave you before you fill Adele in," Vivienne said, "but I really must get home. My ankle is killing me." She hobbled over to the coat rack and wrapped a royal purple shawl around her shoulders. Before she set her key in her brooch, she set her big brown eyes on Elaine. "Be sure to drink that ginger turmeric tea every day, Elaine." She winked and then pressed the key into the hooks underneath the crescent moons.

There was a surge of energy, and all the lights in the office dimmed and then came back. A flash of starlight radiated from the brooch and closed around Vivienne. Elaine shielded her eyes, and when she opened them, Vivienne was gone.

"I'll admit, the dimming lights are new. But in general, you get used to it," Florence said when she noticed Elaine standing there with her mouth wide open and a bewildered look on her face.

"I don't know if anyone can ever get used to that," Elaine responded.

Adele passed around a tin of cookies and everyone sat, nibbling and drinking their tea.

Grant finally broke the silence. "Adele, you should know that Lazro has figured out how to use these fake brooches to travel via starlight."

"Oh goodness!" Adele said. "How in the hell did he figure that out?" Her bottom lip trembled as she used the counter to steady herself. "I really know how to pick men, don't I?"

"The professor is a charming man, Delly. He had us all fooled," Grant said and looked at everyone else who nodded in silent agreement. "Let's face the facts, though. Lazro knows he needs all the keys in one place at one time to activate the source key and get to Isabella. If what he told you is true, Adele, and he's going to display those brooches at the gala, he's probably trying to lure us into a trap. What if he's planning a heist at the gala ... Maybe he's planning to replace our brooches with the fakes?"

"Hmm, good point," Florence said. "But he still needs us, the guardians, the ancestral links that open the corresponding keys' portals, and there's no way Hugh, Vivienne, or I are going to give them to him."

"Me either," Elaine declared. "Remember, I'm the one he needs the most. Florence may have taught you how to travel with the key and brooch, Grant, but you can't unlock their portals."

"That's right, Elaine," Florence added. "You need ancestral lineage not just a mirror and the repetition of a special phrase to do that."

"True," Grant said, "but there was a reason Daphne and Mildred felt it important to hide the red and green keys and their corresponding brooches. Maybe we should do the same?"

"That's logical, lad," Hugh broke in. "And any other time, I would agree with you, but we've been running from Lazro for far too long. He will always scheme and come after us, whether we have the key sets or not. I say it's time we confront him and stop him in his tracks. He's already taken two of our finest guardians, not to mention Elaine lost her parents all those years ago for the same exact reason. No ... hiding from Lazro isn't an option anymore. I'm sorry, my boy, but it's just not."

"Elaine, what are your thoughts?" Grant asked.

Elaine felt an electric current move through her body the second they made eye contact. She clasped the warm mug tightly in her hands to help ground her. "Let's go after him," she stated.

"Well, there's our answer, then," Hugh said as he slapped his hands on his thighs and stood. "We're going to confront Lazro on his own turf at next week's gala. Now, I need to get back home. I'm sure the sheep are itching to get out in the field this morning. It's going to be a bugger staying up all day. I can get used to the starlight travel but never the time difference. Florence, be sure to take care of our Elaine. We're all counting on her."

"Right. We're going to need a new place for the guardians to meet if we're to train Elaine," Florence said. "Your shop has been compromised, Adele."

Elaine jumped in. "There's a storage room in the basement of the library. We could meet there after-hours."

Florence nodded and gave a weak smile. Elaine wasn't sure if it was because she was tired or if Florence dreaded having to teach Elaine anything about the guild and the secrets.

"Goodbye, Hugh," Elaine said as he latched his key to the brooch. "Be well, and we'll see you next week at the gala."

"Yes, see you all next week. Until then." He pressed his key, and a spark shot out from the brooch before starlight engulfed him.

Florence stared at the spot where Hugh had been a moment ago. She noticed another tiny spark jump out of a nearby wall socket a second after Hugh had disappeared. Just as quickly, *it* disappeared. Her eyebrows scrunched as she pursed her lips together.

"Penny for your thoughts?" Grant joked.

"Hmm? Oh, nothing," Florence said. She waved her hand at Grant's question, as if it were a translucent spider web. "Speaking of starlight, we really need to teach you how to do that among other things, Elaine. Can we meet at the library storage room tomorrow?"

"Oh wow!" Elaine's spine tingled with the thrill of it all. "Sure, tomorrow works. The library closes at seven o'clock."

"Great," Florence said. "I'll be there at seven thirty then. Grant, you should join us. You still need a little practice with your landing." She winked, pulling the chain from around her neck as she prepared to leave. "Have a good night, everyone. It's going to take all our effort to take down Lazro once and for all." She set the key in the hooks, and a glimmer of orange glowed and shimmered around her. Suddenly, sparks shot out from the brooch. A crackling sound like a small firecracker filled the room, and Florence fell to the ground.

CHAPTER 22

"Florence!" Grant shouted as he ran over and dropped beside her. "Florence?"

Smoke rose from the brooch, and the key spun to the floor. Florence was unconscious but still breathing. Grant checked her pulse. It felt slower than normal but strong. Her skin was cold to his touch, though. As he bent over her, he felt a draft from the back door. "Quick, Elaine, help me move her. Adele, can we use the sofa in the store?"

"By all means," Adele said. She had already grabbed a throw blanket from the supply shelf and unwrapped it from its packaging. "This is a wool pashmina from Nepal. Top quality and very warm." She tucked it under her arm and led the way into the store, turning on the large salt lamp in the seating area.

Grant gently slid his arms under Florence's torso, Elaine picked up her legs, and they moved her to the blue velour sofa. Adele placed the blanket over Florence and tucked in the edges. She smoothed Florence's bangs away from her eyes and patted her cheek softly.

"Oh dear. What should we do?" Adele asked. "Should we call for an ambulance?"

"I think she's going to be okay. Look." Elaine pointed to Florence, whose eyes fluttered open.

Florence groaned as she rubbed her head. "What happened?" she croaked.

Grant sat next to her on the sofa. "It seems the key malfunctioned. It sparked and then shocked you. You're lucky it only knocked you unconscious."

"But that's impossible," Florence said. "I've never had that happen to me before. Ever. I need to talk to Hugh." She sat up and must have felt dizzy because she swayed a bit. Grant helped her lean back onto the sofa.

"Florence, when Vivienne left, you said the dimmed lights weren't normal," Elaine stated. "What if all the keys are malfunctioning now?"

"But what could be causing it?" Adele chimed in. "And why is it happening to all your keys now?"

"Remember how the green key activated as soon as I picked it up and read the inscription?" Elaine asked, suddenly feeling a heavy weight of responsibility crash down on her. "Well ... what if my actions, combined with Giselle's bizarre tattoo and Lazro's tampering with the knockoff brooches, began a chain reaction in the keys?" She bit the edge of her thumbnail and tapped her heels on the floor, trying to think of a way out of this mess.

"I don't think you should activate that key again, Florence," Grant warned. "It's better we don't give Lazro any help in obtaining the remaining keys or brooches. We'll ask Teddy to contact his mother, and you can use my cell phone to call Hugh."

"You're right, Grant," Florence conceded as she smiled and batted her eyelashes at him. "Where will I stay tonight, though?"

Elaine forced herself to look away. Adele must've caught sight of Elaine's reaction to Florence's implied request because she firmly said, "You will stay with me, dear. I could use the company. I have a spare bedroom right off the living room that is nice and cozy and has all the comforts of home."

Obviously taken aback, Florence tried to protest. "Oh, I couldn't impose, Adele."

"Nonsense," Adele said, her smile implying there was no point in arguing with her. "I have a pashmina just like this one that you can use and a large coffee and tea selection. Oh, this will be fun! Just like a slumber party. Come now. Let's get you home and in bed." She winked at Elaine as she helped Florence stand. "Elaine, dear, can you lock up?"

"U-um, of course," Elaine stammered. She felt embarrassed that Adele had guessed her feelings about Grant, yet she was also relieved that Florence would be out of the way. "Let's all still meet at the library storage room tomorrow after closing. I think it's important we start coming up with a plan on how to confront Lazro."

"Great idea, Elaine," Grant said. He helped Florence into her coat. "I'll walk you to Adele's car, Florence. See you all tomorrow."

Elaine waited until she heard the door close before speaking to Adele. "Um ... thank you, Adele." Elaine was unsure how to voice her thoughts and feelings. "It's not that I don't like Florence, I just ... you know ..."

"No need to explain, Laney," Adele said as she patted her on the back and kissed her cheek. "We've all been rooting for you and Grant to get together all these years. Don't waste too much time telling him how you feel, though. That man is sharp as a tack when it comes to life, but he's daft as can be about love."

Elaine bit her thumbnail again as Adele straightened up the pillows and folded the pashmina. Love? Did she *love* Grant? She knew she loved him as a friend and that he'd always been right by her side in almost every major life change thus far, but he was more like a brother to her than anything. Yet, she couldn't deny the jealousy she felt *every time* she saw him interact with Florence.

"Come on, dear, let's go home," Adele called from her office.

Elaine sighed and turned off the salt lamp, her eyes adjusting to the sudden darkness. The streetlights beamed through the shop's windows, and Elaine had to carefully navigate her way to where Adele was standing. "You go on ahead, Adele. I promise to lock up. I just need some time alone to think. I don't want to drive just yet." She wanted to take one more look down in the basement before heading home. Her intuition told her there was something down there she needed to see.

"All right," Adele said, a note of concern in her voice. "Do you need anything before I leave?"

"I'm fine. I won't stay here long—I promise. I'll see you tomorrow." Elaine clasped Adele's hand, and Adele squeezed back.

"Check the incense burner in the basement when you're down there. Double-check Vivienne blew it out before you fled." Adele nodded knowingly and turned and walked out the door.

Elaine blushed. How did Adele always know what she was thinking? "It doesn't matter." She peered out the back door and saw Adele get into her car. She waited until both Grant's and Adele's cars backed out of their parking spaces before she closed the door and locked it. She walked over to the storage shelves and felt her hands along their edges until she found the lever and pulled open the hidden door. She flipped on the light and carefully made her way down to where they all had stood earlier that very evening. She looked at her reflection in the mirror and brushed away a wisp of hair before checking the incense burner. It was cool to the touch. She inhaled the earthy scents of lavender and sage before she began her search. She didn't know what she was looking for, but she trusted that whatever it was would reveal itself.

For a while, all she found were wooden crates, cobwebs on the rafters, a straw broom, a vinyl bench with a ripped cushion and rusted chrome accents, and some miscellaneous items. She jumped when she heard a sudden *thud* near the basement window.

"Just one of the cats," she reassured herself. Feeling a little silly, she was ready to give up her search when she caught a glimpse of a shape on the floor in front of her. "What's this?"

As she bent down, she saw a small tile inserted into the gray concrete floor held a decorated yellow star in the middle. "Starlight," she whispered to no one in particular. She stood up and walked out of the circle. There on the floor, in the shape of a pentagram, were five tiles with different colored stars. "One for each key." At the top of the design, she noticed the red star. "The source ..."

Then, everything went black.

CHAPTER 23

Elaine awoke and found herself tied to a chair in Adele's basement. Someone had dimmed the lights and lit the candles. "Hello?" she croaked. Her throat was dry, and her head throbbed. "Who's here? What have you done?"

A tall figure stepped out of the shadows. It was Lazro.

"Bring them here," he commanded before turning his attention to Elaine. "Hello, Elaine. I'm sorry our reunion turned out this way, but you and your friends really gave me no choice."

The bald-headed man led Grant to a chair next to her. Giselle finished tying up Florence next to Hugh and Vivienne, who were bound to chairs that had been placed in the circle. Their sluggish appearances indicated they'd been drugged, yet they were still semiconscious.

"Lazro," Elaine snarled. "How did you get in here? Where's Adele?" She scanned the room searching for her. Her vision adjusted to the dim lighting, and she squinted to block out the glowing candles around the circle. Across the room, sitting on a wooden crate, she caught sight of Adele tied to a beam. Her mouth was gagged. "Adele, are you all right?"

Adele's eyes widened, urging Elaine to do something. She nodded and signaled with her head and eyes to turn her attention to the circle.

"Careful, Adele," Lazro cautioned. "You wouldn't want me to think you were trying to get Elaine to do something rash now, would you?"

"Let us go, you bastard!" It was Grant. He no longer was in a stupor. His eyes blazed with anger as he struggled to break loose from the ropes.

The bald man walked over to Grant and backhanded him across the face. The ring split open on Grant's cheek, and Elaine gasped at the blood.

"Stop!" Elaine shrieked. "Just stop. What do you want from us?"

"I thought you'd never ask," Lazro replied. "That'll do, Buzz." He waved away the bald man, who stepped next to Giselle. They loyally awaited their next command.

A smirk flashed across Lazro's lips as he unbuttoned his trench coat and hung it up on a nail hook in the wall. He slid a prescription container from his pocket and popped the top. He tapped the edge of the bottle, and a round white pill slid out into his hand. He tossed the pill into his mouth and swallowed hard.

"That afternoon I met you and Grant at the diner, I recognized your key," he said between raspy coughs. "I saw it glow ever so slightly, and the look on your face let me know I had found it. Daphne and Mildred were sly old gals and hid it from me for so long. They hid *you* from me, too, by the way. Your mother was a star pupil of mine and only a few years younger than me. She was truly in love, but your aunts always hated me. They believed they had traced my lineage to Lazro's family, but it was your mother who came the closest to discovering my true identity. I needed her skills and the red key to help me procure the herbs for me to remain looking like Professor Wallace."

"That's why you need to take those pills? They're not heart medication or migraine reducers like you've claimed, are they?" Elaine interrogated. She clenched her jaw and looked Lazro directly in the eyes. "They somehow keep your looks from changing back to Lazro, am I right? Who made them for you? Giselle?"

"Clever girl, just like your mother." Lazro put his hand up to stop Giselle's advance, then he turned and glared at Elaine. "Yes, Giselle figured out some of your mother's formula. But it was your mother, naïve and blinded by love, who noticed my headaches early on. It was she who convinced the others to open the red key's portal during a guild meeting to later bring me a balm mixed with saffron and feverfew. I never let on that I was Lazro or knew of the guild or that she protected that backstabbing witch Isabella. All I had to do to get your mother to reveal secrets to me was profess my undying love for her and feign interest in her skills in herbalism. I was *so* close to convincing her to let me step inside the portal. I even proposed marriage, hoping that would secure my trust in her inner circle."

He stepped closer to Elaine with a menacing look on his face. "But then your aunts became suspicious and turned her against me. Convinced her to put the guild over her love for me. She broke up with me right after midterms and started dating the man who later became your father. She even went so far as to drop out of grad school to avoid me. Then not long after, you were born."

Elaine matched his glare with her own. "I'm not an idiot. I know you're not my father. You can't gaslight me or my friends. Florence found the records in the library. My father was an ancestor of the green key. It doesn't belong to you. None of the keys do. You're not part of this guild, and you never will be."

Lazro sucked in his breath, then bent over so his eyes were level with hers. "No, I'm not your father. I am, however, heavily invested in this guild. It was my family's gold that went into making the brooches in exchange for Isabella's curatives for my tuberculosis. And after I made Adele's acquaintance, it was all too easy to use her to lead me to the rest of you." He snapped his finger, and Giselle walked up to Adele and removed her gag.

"Elaine, I didn't deliberately tell him anything," she said. Her throat was hoarse, and she coughed a few times to clear it. "You have to believe me!"

"Don't worry, Adele. I do." Elaine turned her attention back to Lazro. "So you're here to reclaim the brooches, I suppose?"

"It's not that simple," Lazro said. "Once I learned that the keys were activated by the brooches, I began to do some research and discovered more information about the guild. I know my father paid Isabella in gold. She nearly poisoned me with her cures, yet they *still* gave her money. She used me to practice her witchcraft and build her power! She took my love and my money and gave me nothing in exchange except for scars ... and immortality, which is more of a curse than a blessing. She has to pay for what she's done to me!" His voice rose the more he talked.

Elaine had to take slow breaths to calm her racing heart. "But Isabella wasn't trying to curse you. She never intended to make you immortal or harm you. Her magic was just that powerful because she loved you. Just like my mother loved you."

Lazro winced when she mentioned love. "She was heartless. She forced me out of her world and left me to face a lifetime— no, life*times*—without her ..." His voice trailed off, and his brow pulled together.

Elaine could sense his emotional pain. He was talking about Isabella, she knew, but underneath his tragic story, she recognized her own pain as well. She also understood what it was like to lose people you loved with no explanation or a real goodbye. That's why he was so angry. He wanted revenge. He needed to make sense out of his senseless fate. He needed someone to blame. "You think my mother and my aunts betrayed you, too, don't you?"

Lazro looked up, his eyes gleaming with anger. "Yes. They all did. I deserve to know what's in that *Book of Secrets*. Isabella has been hiding it from me for centuries now. I need a lasting cure. She owes me at least that. Your mother and wily aunts did everything in their power to keep it from me!" He burst into a coughing fit and could barely regain his composure.

The pill's effects must be wearing off, Elaine deduced.

Vivienne, now much more awake, cut in. "Here's the thing you're forgetting, Lazro. You stabbed Isabella the night she returned from starlight travel to bring you another remedy for your disease. Your sickness blinded you to her goodwill!"

The drugs must've worn off for Hugh as well because he strained against the ropes and cursed under his breath. He barely could contain his seething anger. "You're using that story to get the riches and secrets from the guild. That's all you've ever been after, Lazro! It's not about personal vengeance to clear your name. Daphne and Mildred saw right through you from the very beginning!"

Lazro laughed. "Then, tell me why those old bats chose to sell me old antiques? They were more than happy to learn of an esteemed professor interested in antiquities who paid top dollar for rare items." He laughed at the irony of it all. "They were so intent on keeping me, Lazro, away from the guild and all its secrets that they forgot your mother's troubled love affair with a professor of a similar background, albeit my new curriculum vitae has more panache now that I'm the director of the museum. They also trusted the goodwill of an online buyer, with a ridiculous name 'moonbeamdreams' I might add, and sold me whatever I requested in order to keep their precious little store." He smiled, but it was more like a wolf baring his teeth. "They were too trusting for their own good and even caved to the advice of a sleazy financial adviser like Mr. Sadler."

"But they did figure it out eventually, didn't they?" Elaine couldn't resist goading Lazro. "That's why you killed them."

"Clever girl." Lazro chuckled and began to pace around the group.

Elaine shot Florence a glance that pleaded for support or validation. Florence shook her head slightly in response. *Not now.*

It was then that Elaine realized Lazro had brought them together tonight to activate the keys. She didn't want to say anything that would reveal to him that he might succeed, especially now that all the keys and brooches were in that very room. *Why didn't I keep that brooch safe and have Grant hide it instead?* She was so angry for her lack of foresight. She was more calculating than that. She should've known Lazro would eventually track them down.

In a flash, it dawned on Elaine that Lazro didn't know she had located the last brooch hours ago with Teddy. She drew in her breath and found her courage to protect her friends. "I know where the source brooch is," Elaine announced. "Let everyone go, Lazro, and I'll take you to it. You already have the red key. Let's end this once and for all."

"Elaine, no!" Grant shouted. "I won't let you do that." His voice was pleading, and he had a stricken look etched across his face. "I have the brooch, Lazro. It's in my pocket. If you want it, come and get it."

"Bloody hell!" Hugh yelled and lunged toward Lazro, who jumped back in fear, knocking into a stack of boxes and sending their contents scattering across the floor. Hugh took advantage of the moment and stretched out his leg in an attempt to trip Giselle, who at the last moment, flipped over him, landing directly to the side of Vivienne, who then lunged and headbutted Giselle in the thigh.

Giselle was slightly knocked off balance, but she regained her composure and pushed Vivienne over sideways in her chair.

"Elaine!" Grant shouted. "Look out!"

Out of the corner of her eye, Elaine saw Buzz nearing her. He knocked over a stack of cardboard boxes with his shoulder, giving Elaine enough time to scoot herself forward in her chair to stop him. As she stuck out her leg to try and trip him, Buzz recovered his balance and jumped over her leg and began weaving his way toward Florence and Grant.

This time, Hugh had gained enough momentum to rock his chair toward the center of the circle, tripping Buzz. With catlike reflexes, Giselle took the butt of her gun and hit Hugh in the back of the head. Hugh slumped over in his chair, his chin coming to rest near his right shoulder.

"Hugh!" Elaine screamed.

Buzz clamored to his feet and pulled Lazro up from underneath the spilled boxes. He then walked over to Grant to retrieve the brooch. As he leaned over to go through Grant's pockets, Grant headbutted him, causing Buzz to fall backward and knock into a stack of crates.

Relief momentarily flooded Elaine's body, but her hopes were quickly dashed when, amid the settling chaos, Giselle aimed her gun at Grant and fired.

CHAPTER 24

The shot hit Grant in the left side of his chest, right below his collarbone. Blood seeped from the wound, darkening his navy shirt.

"No!" Elaine screamed, straining against her ropes. "Grant, look at me! Grant!"

His eyes were glossy, and sweat was beading on his forehead and upper lip. His breathing was labored. His face was ashen, and he could barely open his eyes. "Elaine," he muttered. "The brooches ... jacket pocket." His eyes closed, and he swallowed hard.

"Don't talk. Just stay with me, Grant," she pleaded.

Lazro walked over to him. "This wasn't how we planned it, Giselle!" he hissed. "Lucky for you, I'm good at improvising." He cut Elaine's ropes, grabbed her arm, and pulled her up to standing. "If you're to save your friend, Elaine, we need to activate the keys." He pushed her aside, rifled through Grant's jacket pocket, and pulled out the brooches.

"You bastard!" Elaine shrieked. "Give those back!" She lunged toward Lazro and tried to grab them, but Buzz and Giselle grasped her arms and held them behind her back. Elaine looked at Vivienne, who was trying to unknot the cord around her wrists. Elaine broke down and began to sob.

"Untie us, Lazro. We'll help you activate the keys," Vivienne said calmly. Even though Elaine was desperate to save Grant, she hadn't been expecting Vivienne to comply with Lazro's wishes. She began to protest when Vivienne cut her off. "It's the only way, Elaine. One of us needs to get to Isabella and convince her to give us her *Book of Secrets* and some special herbs to heal Grant's wound."

Grant looked up at Elaine and nodded. Elaine knew Vivienne was right, but Grant's permission was what gave her strength. "Okay, let's do this." Elaine turned and looked at Lazro directly. "You can give me the source key. Give Adele the green one. And you can take Hugh's." She was in command now, and it felt good to be taking action. "Untie everyone, Lazro. Let's not waste any more time."

Lazro grinned at Elaine. "My, my, but aren't you the eager one," he said as he reached into his pocket and handed over the brooch. She snatched it out of his hand and quickly pinned it to her fleece.

When Lazro nodded at Buzz and Giselle, they began to cut everyone's ropes. Adele walked over and joined the circle, rubbing her wrists in pain.

"But I thought only the portals could be opened by guardians with direct ancestral connection?" Adele asked as she stood next to Elaine.

"Nonsense," Lazro replied. "Giselle can stay on this side and use one of our modified brooches to conduct enough energy toward the portal gates to press them open, if only for a brief moment." He nodded at his assistant, who came to stand next to him. She pulled a loose twine that was wrapped around her neck from out of her blouse and revealed the fake brooch that appeared secured like a locket. She then slid up her sleeve to reveal her wrist tattoo.

"Hurry up," Lazro commanded Elaine.

Elaine squinted her eyes at him and felt her nostrils flare. She whipped around and faced Adele, whose bottom lip was quivering ever so slightly.

Elaine relaxed her face and pinned the green key's brooch to her blouse, then squeezed Adele's hand. "You can do this, Delly. I believe in you."

Adele smiled up at her and squeezed back. "I believe in you too, Laney. Your aunts—they're so proud of you. I feel them here with us."

Elaine squared off her shoulders and walked confidently toward the circle.

Florence stood up and hovered over Hugh, stroking his hair from his forehead. "I'll get them back safely, boss," she whispered as she bent down and kissed him lightly on the forehead. He was coming around, but his eyes were still closed, and his brow was furrowed.

Florence unpinned his brooch and slid the key from around his neck. Before she took her place with the others, she caught sight of Hugh's slight hand gesture. He balled his fist and then released all of his fingers at once. She squeezed his shoulder to indicate her understanding. The portals were unstable ever since Lazro figured out how to travel with the new brooches. There was a possibility the starlight could cause an explosion. Hugh's and Vivienne's earlier departures, as well as Florence's attempted one, had made that quite clear. Florence's job was to make sure Elaine could not only get to the source but also get back in one piece.

Lazro walked up to Florence and took the brooch from her hand. "Quit delaying this," he demanded. "Get everyone into formation and hand me the key." He removed his tie and pinned the brooch to his shirt. Florence reluctantly handed over the blue key to him. "We do this on my command," he added. "Buzz, Giselle, grab the old man and Grant. Make sure they don't try to escape while we're gone."

Giselle grabbed hold of Hugh's chair, pulled him away from the circle, and positioned him near the beam, where Adele had been standing. She walked back over and helped Buzz move Grant, who had lost consciousness at some point and had sweat trickling down his forehead while blood still seeped out of his wound.

"He needs medical attention!" shouted Elaine. "You can't just leave him like that. He'll die!"

"I guess you'll just have to do your best to get the *Book of Secrets*, then, won't you?" Lazro taunted, standing on the blue-patterned star tile in the ceremonial circle.

"It's okay, Elaine. You can do this," reassured Florence. "I'll walk you through the activation. The guardian should be at the portal when you get there, just like when you saw Anton the other night."

Elaine nodded and then took her place on the red-tiled square.

Elaine held the red key in her hands and noticed they were trembling slightly. She willed herself to be brave. It would take all her focus and determination to do this right. Grant's life depended on them and her ability to find her way through the unknown world.

Adele stepped on her tile and took the green key from Giselle, who sneered at her. As an act of defiance, Adele straightened her brooch, stared past Giselle, and smiled into the empty space in front of her. Elaine couldn't help but notice that Adele seemed to radiate a golden aura. She also appeared to be channeling something of great importance.

Could it be Daphne and Mildred?

At once, Elaine felt her great-aunts' presence, but then all thoughts of them vanished as she watched Vivienne take her place on the yellow tile. She looked regal and was in full command of herself. Elaine locked eyes with her and drew from her strength. She took one last look at Grant. Of course she would realize she loved him deeply in such a dire moment. That was just her luck. She could feel his pain and the pain of unspoken love building in her throat. "I love you," she mouthed in his direction, even though he appeared to be losing consciousness.

She dried her eyes as a fierceness began to fill up inside her. She had a mission, and she was determined not to fail. Turning back to Florence, she asked, "How do we begin?"

"We lock our keys into place beginning with Elaine's—the red one. Then we follow in this order: me, Vivienne, Adele, and Lazro." Florence was all business now. "Once Lazro's key is locked, we must turn and look into the mirror and press the gemstones at the same exact time. On my count of three. It will feel as if the ground is trying to suck you down and tornado-like winds are trying to blow you away. But keep your fingers on your key's gemstone no matter what. After that, I will begin to recite each mantra to open the portals. Elaine, when I get to yours, you will see the red gate. Walk directly toward it and make sure you don't release your fingers from the center of the key. Once inside the gate, I can't help you. None of us can. We'll all be in our own portals, holding them open with our gatekeepers until you have reached the source."

"It sounds too easy," Adele remarked. "I'm assuming this is all very dangerous if something, anything, goes wrong?"

"Correct," Florence replied. "Elaine, no matter what you do, make sure you don't deviate from the plan. The red guardian's role is to protect the *Book of Secrets*. Isabella won't necessarily want to just hand it over to you. You'll need to persuade her somehow to give you the book. I'm sorry, I wish it was easier than this."

"It's all right," Elaine said. What else could she say? They were all committed to this. There was no turning back. The longer they waited, the more Grant's life was in danger. "Let's begin. I don't want to waste any more time."

"You're right," Florence said. Vivienne nodded, and Adele winked at Elaine. "Okay, Elaine, go ahead and lock your key in the brooch." Elaine hooked the key into the brooch. Everyone followed in the order Florence had instructed. "On my count, push your gemstones. Good luck, everyone."

On Florence's count of three, they all activated the gemstones. Nothing happened for a split second, and then a bright white light radiated from the mirror and filled the room, siphoning out the air and noise. It was like they were being sucked underwater. Time seemed to slow down. Then, a deep rumbling sounded, like a train moving quickly over its tracks. A huge gust of wind shot through the center of where she believed they were standing, and she caught her breath after it passed. The white light had now given way to a dark-blue sky, where swirls of stars were gyrating so quickly, they blurred together and then broke apart in succession. She felt some gravitational force pulling her down, and then a loud crack echoed as the ground around her broke away. The only thing keeping her from falling was the tiled space she was standing on. She looked up to see if the others were safe, but no one was visible. There was only dark sky and swirling stars. She was alone in a vast emptiness of space.

Suddenly, she saw something flying toward her. At first, she thought it was a meteor. Then, it came into full view: Lazro was hurtling toward her. He had released his finger from the key and had apparently been launched out of the circle into the void they were traveling through. As he neared her, she grabbed his arm with her free hand and pulled him toward her with all her might. The wind had picked up, and more ground was giving way around them.

"Hold on!" she yelled above the howling gusts of wind. He clung to her, and she nearly toppled off the red tile. With a sudden jerk, the tile gave way, and they began a quick descent into the dark space below.

There was no more wind, and Elaine smelled hints of rosemary and sage in the dry air. When she opened her eyes, she saw that the earth beneath them was made of red clay and clumps of wild grass. She sat up and took in more of her surroundings. Lazro was lying on his side in the dirt. A smoldering campfire next to him sent the last of its smoke into the early morning sky.

"Where are we?" Elaine asked as she stood and dusted herself off.

There was no sign of a red gate like Florence had mentioned. She looked at her brooch. The key was still in its hooks. She took in the panoramic view of mountains in the distance and the white stucco and red clay buildings clumped together in the valley below her. High on a distant hill was a brownish-red fortress spotlighted by the rising sun. Its shape and surrounding landscape looked familiar to her, like something she had seen in books and on television perhaps. A memory of a summer study abroad session during college materialized in her mind. She had climbed the winding stone-paved road numerous times with her classmates to that iconic fortress with a beautiful palace, trickling fountains, ornate tiled porticos, and lush gardens hidden inside the burnt orange walls.

"The Alhambra," she whispered as she stared at it in amazement and wonder. She touched her hands to her heart and took in the ancient site. The dream of once again returning to Spain had just come true.

Lazro coughed and startled her back to reality. He pushed himself off the ground and glanced around him. His hair was disheveled, and he had dirt on his elbows and knees. The brooch had come unclasped and was dangling at his chest, attached to the key around his neck.

A white-hot rage boiled through Elaine's blood. Without thinking, she rushed at him and pushed him hard. "What were you thinking?" she shouted. "You could've gotten us both killed!"

Lazro stared down at her. "Calm down. We're alive, aren't we?"

His apathetic response only enraged her more. "We may be alive, but we're also nowhere closer to finding the *Book of Secrets*. I don't even know if this is the portal!" Her voice echoed off the hill and the clustered white stucco caves with small, winding staircases leading inside.

Lazro scanned the area again and nodded. "This is it. We're in the neighborhood of Sacromonte. These are the cave houses of the Roma people who live in Granada."

Elaine watched as he took in his surroundings. It seemed that, for a brief moment, he was not a villain whose greed resulted in the loss of her loved ones. He just seemed like a wayward man. It then dawned on her that this was Lazro's homeland. This was where he had grown up and contracted a life-threatening illness, where he had fallen in love with Isabella and believed she had tricked him for wealth and power, never realizing she had only tried to save his life.

The curse of living for centuries like Lazro, Elaine realized, was that seeds of doubt, anger, and resentment caused a person to harden and feel alone and disconnected from the world. Hadn't that been the path she was on less than a month ago until she discovered the green key? She had shut so many people out of her life, especially after her aunts' deaths, and tried to control everything around her. She worked hard to fit her life inside a box she could manage and organize with precision. While she had functioned like this for most of her adult life, she eventually stopped learning to be open to all the other possibilities life could bring her. If she would allow life to flow through her instead of damming up her grief, joy, wonder, and creativity, Elaine may discover her desire for a perfect life had only kept her from fully experiencing this messy, magical, beautiful world.

Seeing Lazro and her life in this light dissolved some of the anger she had been carrying with her. She couldn't help but feel the buzz of excitement tingling in her nerves. She was here, in southern Spain, on a hillside overlooking a palace once built for kings. Maybe one of her ancestors had walked these very hills? She turned to Lazro, who had recovered his composure. His brows were furrowed, and his stone-cold eyes peered past her. Whatever moment of vulnerability she had glimpsed in him was gone.

"So now what?" she asked. "Should we wait or go up to one of these houses?" She began to walk toward the closest house when she saw an old woman with a floral kerchief tied around her head. She was wearing a button-down tan-and-blue-striped blouse and a black skirt. Old sandals showed her calloused feet. She motioned to Elaine, and instinctively, Elaine walked toward her. Lazro followed close behind.

The woman walked inside one of the homes and left the door wide open for them, so Elaine stepped indoors. Her eyes had difficulty adjusting to the darkness. For all his bravado, she could feel Lazro's nervous breathing on the back of her neck.

Once her eyes focused, Elaine made out the outline of furniture in the kitchen area, where copper pots hung on the wall. The woman shuffled toward the back of the house and lifted a latch on the floor. She pointed and then motioned for them to follow her down the rickety stairs.

Elaine went first, but she sensed Lazro's hesitation. "Why are you scared? Isn't this what you've been after all these years?" she asked him as she watched him descend the ladder and land on the dirt floor next to her.

He didn't respond.

Instead, he walked toward the old woman, who then lit a lantern and said something to him in Spanish. Elaine closed the trapdoor and folded up the ladder. This space reminded her of the attic stairs in the upstairs hallway at her aunts' home. The lantern cast its light on old wooden wine barrels lined up against the wall. Elaine noticed there was a passage up ahead. The old woman gestured again and turned and walked toward it. They followed her in silence, twisting and turning down the tunnel. Elaine was reminded of the old Greek myth of the labyrinth and minotaur. Goosebumps formed at the nape of her neck, and her calf muscles twitched. Looming ahead of them was a heavy wooden door. The old lady pulled out a key from around her neck and unlocked it, pushing the squeaky door open with her thick arms.

Elaine jumped and knocked into Lazro when the door slammed shut behind them. He didn't budge. She looked up at him, but his eyes were focused on the second wooden door in front of them. This door had a square window about the size of a book with black iron bars running through it. The natural light that passed through the window and the lantern's glow both cast a shine and shadows on Lazro's face. She saw the deep crevices of wrinkles she hadn't noticed before. A thick vein on his neck corded up like a snake. His nostrils flared, and the shadows made his eyelashes look long and thick. His brows angled upward and came to a point at the bridge of his nose. The only part of Professor Wallace she recognized in his features was his expensive button-up shirt and his brushed wool jacket with its silk pocket handkerchief.

They walked through the second door and entered what looked like a kitchen. Elaine noticed the soft, grayish tint of the stucco walls. A tall wooden table was in the center, and low whitewashed cabinets lined the wall. Dried herbs and copper pots hung above the table. There was a small room off to the side. Natural light flooded through the alcove, and Elaine caught sight of a small, wooden desk and chair. They hadn't climbed any stairs, so she wondered where the light was coming from. Then she saw iron grates on a small opening on the wall. Brown cobblestones lined themselves outside the grates, and Elaine watched pushcarts and people's feet passing by. "We're underneath the city," she remarked.

She peered at the alcove again and noticed the profile of a young woman sitting at the desk. She wore a long-sleeve, dark-red dress with a high collar of black lace. Her black hair was pulled back into a fashionable bun, and teardrop pearl earrings dangled from her delicate ears. She was writing with a fountain pen and dipping it into an inkwell. She pushed back the black lace cuff at her wrist, and when she finished writing, she folded the paper and sealed it with wax, then stood up and walked into the kitchen area. Elaine was surprised at how short the young woman was, only a few inches taller than the old woman. Yet, she had a regal air and commanded the room.

The young woman took down a bundle of herbs and tied them around the letter. "Take these and this spell to use for your friend," she said in a heavy Spanish accent as she handed them over to Elaine. "Vivienne will know what to do."

"Gracias," Elaine said and pressed the letter and herbs to her heart. "You're Isabella, am I right? How did you know what I needed?"

"Yes, I'm Isabella, and this is my mother, Magda. We are the gatekeepers of the red source key. But, of course, you know this. And you are Elaine. We knew your aunts. They were fierce guardians. You have our sympathy for your loss." She turned and pointed to a mirror on the wall. "I've been watching you for a while now. You have a natural talent for magic."

Isabella smiled slyly and then turned her attention to Lazro. "As for you, it's been a long time. I should've known you would use a disguise to get what you want, you wicked man. Well, here I am. Aren't you going to kiss me? It's been centuries since we've seen each other." Isabella turned so Lazro could kiss her cheek, but he just stood and stared down at her. Elaine noticed how his lips curled in disgust. "Very well, then. Have it your way," Isabella replied to his silence. "Now, Elaine, we don't have much time. You need to get back through the portal at once. You have what you need for now. Follow me."

Isabella tried to walk past them to the wooden door, but Lazro reached out his hand and grabbed her wrist, pulling her toward him. "I want the *Book of Secrets*," he hissed in her ear.

Isabella stared up at him. Her black eyes glittered with defiance, but then she glanced at her writing desk. He saw her slight mistake and tossed her to the floor, running to the alcove. Elaine sprinted after him and reached the book before he did. Lazro's face darkened, and he grabbed Elaine's forearm, his fingernails cutting into her flesh. Elaine screamed and dropped the book on the floor. When Lazro bent down to pick it up, Elaine kicked him in the face. He fell over and landed on top of the book.

Isabella rushed to Elaine's side just as Lazro pushed himself to a seated position. Isabella grabbed his hand. "Mother, show him to me," she commanded.

Magda, who had been quietly grinding herbs with a pestle and mortar at the large table this whole time, sprinkled the powder in her hand and rushed over to them. She uttered a phrase in a guttural tone and blew the dust in Lazro's face. He coughed violently and released Isabella's hand. He fell to the floor, trying to catch his breath. Elaine watched as the professor morphed into his true self, the Lazro who believed Isabella had deceived him hundreds of years earlier when, as a young woman blinded by love, she had tried to save his life.

Elaine looked at the man on the ground in front of her. His thick black hair was slicked back from his forehead. His aquiline nose and high cheekbones completed the look of his chiseled, weatherworn face. His skin was olive in complexion but tinged with a dull pallor of yellow. He opened his eyes. Mixed with the tears were the jaundiced eyes of a sickly man. Blood trickled out of his mouth, and he wheezed and coughed before pushing himself up to his knees.

Isabella took the *Book of Secrets* from him and pressed it into Elaine's arms. "The *Book of Secrets* is safer with you now. The others know what must be done." She pushed Elaine toward the entrance.

Elaine was mystified. Isabella had given the book to her without hesitation, but Vivienne had said it wouldn't be easy to get it from her. *I didn't even have to ask for it,* Elaine thought as she clutched the book to her chest.

Just then, a loud popping noise sounded above her head, and a bit of rubble and dust tumbled onto her shoulder. She looked up but saw nothing out of the ordinary. Lazro was still on the floor, moaning in agony. It appeared to Elaine that his illness had returned. Isabella walked back to him and knelt beside him, soothing him with her touch.

"I know it's painful, *querido,*" she said to him. "You're with me now. I cannot send both of you back through the portals without killing one of you. My magic is strong, but it is not all powerful ...."

Elaine couldn't help but ask, "What do you mean by that?" Another cracking sound scared her, and she covered her head with the book for fear the ceiling would cave in on them. "Isn't Lazro a threat to the guild? All these years, my aunts and the other guardians have been trying to protect you ... protect the guild. But all they needed to do was send him back to you?" She swallowed hard and got up the courage to ask the hardest question. "Did my aunts really die in vain?"

The boards holding up the ceiling cracked and popped under the weight of the building above them. Isabella gently lowered Lazro's head back onto her lap and glanced up at Elaine. "They died protecting what they believed in," Isabella began. "I saved my dear Lazro hundreds of years ago with the blood and stone elixir I wrote down in that book you hold. It possesses some of my essence in it. In order to save him, I had to relinquish some of my own powers. One of those being that I could never walk through this portal again. They were right to fear that he could get to me ..." She looked over at her mother, Magda, who had finished grinding the rest of the herbs and was now pouring the powder into a small bag. "But since the elixir holds a part of me and Lazro drank it, he now will never be able to leave either." The tears that had formed at the corner of Isabella's eyes now spilled over and trickled down her face. She brushed them gently away. Lazro's eyes flickered open, and he tried to sit up.

"Shh, rest, *mi querido*," Isabella said. His hand trembled as he reached up to her. She took his hand in hers but spoke to Elaine. "You see, by returning, Lazro's illness has returned. There's an imbalance now not just in him but in the earth energy I guard. Your aunts knew this might happen and that I may lose my powers. So they swore to protect him from me … and from himself."

Elaine finally understood her aunts and their loyalty to the guild. Her chest swelled with pride and love for them. What courage it must have taken Daphne and Mildred to protect Lazro from the guild and vice versa. For the first time ever, Elaine felt she owed it to these strong women who made such an impression in her life to carry on their legacy. They lived life with such gusto and passion. They were loyal to their friends and true to their word. And most importantly, they saw life as an ever-evolving adventure of mystery and magic. A world in which they participated without hesitation. Could she do the same? *Of course.* She was made of the same stuff. They knew that when she was only ten years old, and it was now up to Elaine to choose how she would move forward with all this knowledge and power. She hugged the *Book of Secrets* closer to her chest.

She was pulled out of her reverie by the sound of a beam crashing to the floor behind her. Magda rushed to Isabella and Lazro and began sprinkling the ground-up powder around them in a circle.

"Quickly now, go through the door. Use your key," Isabella urged Elaine. "We've held the portal open as long as we can, but it'll close soon, and you'll be caught with us."

"But … what about you? And how will I get this book back to you?" Elaine asked as cracks formed in the ceiling and dust showered down on them. The portal was closing, and soon, they would all be trapped. The large stone floor began to split open, and the iron rack holding up the pots and herbs crashed onto the table and pitched it over on its side. The ground beneath their feet trembled like an earthquake.

Magda tried to steer Elaine to the door while Isabella bent down to Lazro. She held a vial to his lips that she had pulled from a pocket in her dress. Elaine stood, dumbfounded, as Isabella poured the liquid into his mouth. Isabella cried and whispered in his ear, rocking him back and forth.

"What's happening to him?" Elaine asked. She felt paralyzed. She didn't know if she should rush to help him or if she should leave.

"He's dying," Isabella sobbed. "This is my last attempt to save him." She held the vial to his mouth one more time and allowed a drop of the golden liquid to fall onto his parted lips. "Lazro, *mi amor, mi querido*, come back to me," she begged.

He coughed, and by the sound of it, he wasn't long for this world.

Isabella gently took off the brooch and the key Lazro had around his neck and motioned for Elaine's hand. "Get these safely back to Hugh!" She pointed at the red key and brooch still connected to Elaine's blouse. "You'll be the new guardian and gatekeeper. You're the rightful heir!" she shouted over the crumbling walls and falling shelves. "Now go! You haven't much time."

Lazro mumbled, and Isabella turned her attention back to him. Magda pushed Elaine to the door, both of them stumbling over jagged chunks of the fallen ceiling. By the time they reached the large door, Magda had her key in hand and swiftly unlocked it. She signaled for Elaine to enter the chamber. Reluctantly, Elaine stepped inside.

Before she could say anything, Magda slammed the door shut. Elaine heard a loud click and knew she was locked inside between the two ancient, wooden doors. Darkness enveloped her. Except for a little bit of light that crept through the gap at the floor and the iron-clad window above, Elaine felt utterly alone and disoriented. She listened as she heard the walls cracking and the clatter of copper pots and shelves crashing and tumbling to the ground. She pinned Hugh's brooch and key on the other side of her blouse and shifted the *Book of Secrets* into the crease of her right underarm. The rolled-up scroll Isabella had given her to cure Grant was scrunched in her left hand.

As she stood in the still darkness, she peered through the iron bars, hoping Isabella would change her mind and come with her. She saw the three of them huddled in the doorframe of the tiny alcove. Magda held the bag of powdered herbs to her lips, chanting, while Isabella held Lazro in an embrace, shielding him from the falling debris. A large piece of stucco fell from the ceiling and landed near them. A wooden rafter broke free and fell at their feet, sending more debris and causing the ceiling to cave in. Elaine caught sight of them before a cloud of dust and light covered their forms. The last thing she saw was Isabella and Lazro embracing and looking tenderly at each other. A flash of light shot from the three of them and blazed across the room, knocking Elaine to the ground. The herbs and letter tumbled from her hand, and the *Book of Secrets* fell to her feet.

Her head pounded, and she ached all over, but she knew the portal was still open. The red key had fallen off the hooks of the brooch. She needed to get her key in the brooch before she lost her chance. The chain holding the key had broken, and the key now dangled precariously from it. More of the ceiling had caved in around her, and the key dangled above a crevice of stone and stucco. It took all her concentration to not make any sudden movements and lose the key in the debris. With her finger and thumb, she swiftly pinched the key as the chain slid from her neck and spiraled down into the rubble.

Wooden beams from the ceiling began to crack, and a few pieces fell next to her. "I can't waste any more time."

She found the brooch with her hand and hooked the key on the crescent moons. She pressed the gemstone without thinking and realized the book and the healing spell and herbs for Grant were no longer in her hands. "No!" she shouted as the starlight began to fill the chamber. She could feel the vacuum already beginning to take her away. She was on her knees, so she lunged forward to crawl toward the book, grabbing it and holding it tightly in her arm. With her other arm, she attempted to crawl toward the healing remedy Isabella had given her. She brushed the letter with her fingertips and rolled it toward her as best she could. The herbs had come untied and were scattered all over the floor. The floor disappeared, and she was falling through the portal. She clasped Isabella's letter so tightly that it crumpled in her fist.

Then, she landed hard on the concrete floor, and everything went silent and dark once again.

Moments later, Elaine heard a commotion above her. It was Adele tapping her cheeks with her fingers. She opened her eyes and saw Florence, Vivienne, and Teddy looking down at her. She was so confused and disoriented. "Teddy?" she croaked. "How did you get here?" She sat up and unrolled Isabella's letter. It was ruined. The sweat from her palm had caused the ink to bleed, and the mangled paper was torn in a few places. "I don't have the secret spell or the right herbs to save Grant!" she cried. "Where is he? Is he alive? Where's Hugh?"

"They're all right, Laney," Adele reassured her as she picked up the *Book of Secrets* and handed it to Florence. "They're both at the hospital and in stable condition. Teddy got here just in time."

Florence reached out her other hand and helped Elaine to stand. "It's all right, Elaine. Grant and Hugh are fine. Teddy apparently came in right after we all activated the keys. He had some of Vivienne's pepper spray with him and was able to sneak up on Buzz and Giselle before they knew what hit 'em."

Vivienne beamed. "He tied them up, called the police, and got an ambulance all in one fell swoop. I'm so proud of you, son," she said as she wrapped him in her arms and squeezed him. "We'll make a guardian out of you yet."

Elaine hugged Teddy, too, and then looked up at him. "How did you know we were all here?"

Teddy smiled as he put his other arm around Elaine and drew her in next to him. "Aw, it was nothing. Like I said before, I don't know about all of this magic stuff, but I know my mom. When she didn't answer my texts or calls I knew something was up, so I started looking for her. Thankfully, this was the first place I thought of. It's the harvest season, which means it's a mystical time, according to the guild's calendar. Mom always told me deep autumn is when the veil between the seen and unseen worlds is the thinnest and when the portals are most in alignment and can be opened all at the same exact time. I decided to come check it out and see if she was at the meeting place. That's when I saw Professor Wallace's car and realized he and Adele had probably come here after the restaurant, and I just went from there."

Vivienne hugged Teddy again, and he dropped his arm around Elaine and pulled his mother into a big bear hug.

Florence stepped forward and asked Elaine, "So, where's Lazro? What happened?"

"It's a long story. I'll tell you all the details soon. Right now, let's just say he's right where he should be." She smiled as she recalled how he'd been in the embrace of the one he had always loved. She knew he came after her and her family due to his need for revenge and desire to possess the *Book of Secrets*, but in the end, she knew it was only Isabella who could really save him. There had been a peace between them. A lightness of spirit. All that searching over centuries, the deceptions, lies, and manipulation to gain power, crumbled with one look and an act of her selfless love and tenderness.

Maybe it was too late for Lazro and Isabella to begin again after all the hurt and pain over the centuries, but it wasn't too late for Elaine. Grant had been by her side through this entire journey. He even risked his life to save hers. She knew he had tried to tell her over the years how he felt through his loyalty, kindness, and friendship, but she had discarded him in hopes of being somebody with prestigious credentials and a list of accolades and an influential boyfriend. How was she any different from Lazro? She stopped herself from spiraling and from convincing herself she wasn't good enough for him.

It doesn't have to be that way.

She turned toward Florence, Vivienne, Adele, and Teddy. Her heart felt like it could burst. They all had stuck by her, too, and believed in her when she didn't believe in herself.

"What are you thinking, Laney, dear?" Adele asked.

Elaine hadn't even noticed Adele had taken her hand. She smiled and squeezed Adele's hand. "I'm thinking that you're all my family now, and I couldn't ask for a better group of people to be with me on this journey."

Adele giggled. "That makes me so happy, dear." Her buoyant spirit glowed, and she pointed to the circle.

There, in glowing violet and white flames, stood the spirits of Daphne and Mildred. Their hands were over their hearts, and pride and love beamed from their eyes as they smiled.

Elaine was not shocked that she could see them. Some part of her knew she always had that ability. Now, however, instead of trying to rationalize away the vision of them, she smiled back. She lifted her arm and waved ever so slightly. Elaine hoped they could tell she was not only happy but also very grateful. Daphne and Mildred's unwavering devotion to help a young girl find her true self allowed Elaine to realize what true magic was. It wasn't glittering gemstones inside antique keys that unlocked ancient portals in accordance with the phases of the moon. True magic was that tenderness of the heart brought out by the love, nurturance, and kindness of those who believed in you. It had taken most of her adult life, but Elaine believed wholeheartedly in *this* kind of magic.

EPILOGUE

Fresh sunflowers, witch hazel, asters, and chrysanthemums decorated the museum's main gallery. Cocktail tables covered in cream-colored linens held delicious catered hors d'oeuvres. Waiters walked around offering champagne to guests. Teddy's jazz band played "Moonlight Serenade" while Adele, wearing a form-fitting, floor-length red dress, and Hugh, in a black tuxedo jacket and red-and-green kilt, danced with other couples in front of the stage.

Florence wore a vintage 1930s green chiffon gown that highlighted her freshly bobbed red hair and made her look even more like the spirited flapper-girl she had always embodied. She was standing next to Grant, who was dressed in a trim-fitting tuxedo and was clean-shaven for once. He looked quite dashing despite having his arm in a sling.

Vivienne walked into the museum gallery and presented her ticket to the volunteer. She cut a striking figure in her low-cut, sparkly yellow gown. Her yellow head wrap was tied in the front in a traditional African *dhuku* style. She waved at Teddy on stage and then grabbed a glass of champagne before joining Florence and Grant. "Where's Elaine?" she asked as she took a sip of bubbly.

"She's around here somewhere," Grant said. "I know she's been busy ever since she agreed to take Professor Wallace's place and organize the gala."

"Oh, has she decided to take the adjunct teaching position in the spring?" Florence asked.

"You can ask her," Grant said as Elaine appeared.

She glided up to them in her black velour, 1940s vintage gown. Her brown, wavy hair was swept to the side and framed her face. Her makeup was minimal, except for the red lipstick she had indulged herself in lately. Her crescent moons brooch rested on her shoulder, and she wore a gold chain that dropped down into her cleavage, disguising the red key she now kept close to her heart. She hugged Florence and Vivienne before turning to Grant, who took her in his arms and kissed her full on the lips. They had made their relationship official a few days after Grant had been discharged from the hospital. The gala was their first real date, and they both couldn't stop acting like giddy teenagers. "Stop, you're embarrassing me." She giggled as she pulled away but still clung to his embrace.

Adele and Hugh joined the four of them as Teddy's band finished their set.

"So good to see you all," Vivienne said. "I'm glad the both of you are doing better, gentleman." They nodded and thanked her.

Teddy weaved his way through the crowd and patted Grant on the back, making him wince a little in pain. They all waved at Syd and Tom as they wheeled Mrs. Armested to the buffet table.

"Do you have the emerald key, Grant?" Hugh whispered as all seven of them huddled together in the middle of the gallery.

"I do, yes," he said as he patted his breast pocket.

"Good because there's not a minute to lose," Vivienne stated. "Anton just reported there's been a sighting of Giselle, or someone like her, near his cottage. We knew something like this might happen when the police said she'd made bail."

"Everything's in place for travel this evening, then?" Elaine asked.

Hugh and Vivienne nodded.

"Elaine," Grant began, "I can't let you go with me. You've got the library and the museum to worry about, and you need to prepare for the class you'll be teaching. I promise, I won't be gone long."

Elaine put her hand on Grant's chest and looked him deeply in his eyes. "We're partners in this. In all things. It's nonnegotiable. Besides, aren't you the one who told me I should keep myself open to adventure?"